Vicky Pattison won the nation's hearts after appearing in *I'm a Celebrity Get Me Out of Here* in 2015, which made her a household name. Her autobiography, *Nothing but the Truth*, was a Number One *Sunday Times* bestseller in hardback and remained in the Top Ten for seven weeks. Vicky's novels, *All that Glitters* and *A Christmas Kiss*, have received rave reviews from her fans who fell in love with the witty one-liners and snappy comebacks Vicky is renowned for. Vicky has her own weekly column in *New* magazine and she is one of the original *Geordie Shore* cast. She is now the star of her own MTV show, *Judge Geordie*. Vicky is a genuine Geordie Girl, born and bred in Newcastle.

Also by Vicky Pattison

Nothing But The Truth: My Story
A Christmas Kiss

All That Glitters

Vicky Pattison

sphere

SPHERE

First published in Great Britain in 2015 by Sphere

3 5 7 9 10 8 6 4

Copyright © Vicky Pattison 2015

Edited by Faith Bleasdale

The moral right of the author has been asserted.

All characters and events in this publication, other than those
clearly in the public domain, are fictitious and any resemblance
to real persons, living or dead, is purely coincidental.

A CIP catalogue record for this book
is available from the British Library.

ISBN 978-0-7515-6133-3

Typeset in Baskerville by M Rules
Printed and bound in Great Britain by
Clays Ltd, St Ives plc

Papers used by Sphere are from well-managed forests
and other responsible sources.

MIX
Paper from
responsible sources
FSC
www.fsc.org FSC® C104740

Sphere
An imprint of
Little, Brown Book Group
Carmelite House
50 Victoria Embankment
London EC4Y 0DY

An Hachette UK Company
www.hachette.co.uk

www.littlebrown.co.uk

For everyone that believed I could

♡

Prologue

Issy Jones felt fat warm tears sliding down her cheeks. She grasped her dad's hand tightly; it felt cold and unfamiliar. She barely recognised the man lying in front of her on the hospital bed, multiple tubes and wires attached to him. He had the same familiar dark hair and even features she knew so well, but his face was pale and so, so still. She squeezed his hand tighter as the machines continued to bleep around them.

'I promise I will do anything, absolutely anything if you get better, Dad,' Issy whispered, unsure if he could hear her. 'And I'll never leave you again. Just be all right. Please, Dad. *Please.*'

Still holding her dad's hand, she slumped down in the hard, uncomfortable hospital chair next to him and rested her head on his arm, remembering how safe she used to feel when he hugged her as a child. She didn't want to let go, afraid if she did she would lose him forever, and she wouldn't be able to bear that. Even the thought of it brought tears to her eyes and Issy breathed deeply, trying not to despair.

It had all happened so suddenly. Only the day before she'd been working on an assignment at her hairdressing college in London, when she got a call from her brother, Zach, shakily telling her that their dad had suffered a heart attack. She'd dropped everything, rushed to the station and caught the first train she could home. A tear-filled three hours later, Zach had met her at Manchester station and had warned her that their dad was in a bad way. But nothing could have prepared her for seeing him look so frail.

The man in the hospital bed, wired up to machines, wasn't the gentle giant who had cared for her growing up. Issy's dad was a tall, handsome, muscular man, the years working in his garage had seen to that, but the figure in front of her seemed smaller and older than the man she knew.

The change in him had been so shocking her legs had almost given way when she'd first seen him. Zach had grabbed her to stop her from falling, and then held her while she cried. Her mum, Debs, who always had something to say, was silent as they stood together watching his chest rise and fall.

The three of them stayed by his bedside all night. At some point Zach had dropped off to sleep, and while he softly snored Issy and her mum had talked for hours, trying to keep each other's spirits up. But it hadn't worked. The fear was visible on their faces and in their trembling voices. Neither of them had wanted to think about what life would be like without the man who made them feel safe.

Issy took another deep breath, reminding herself to stay positive.

'Issy?' a husky voice said. She lifted her head off her dad's arm and tried to blink the tears away.

'Dad?' She wondered if she had imagined it. She felt a rush of hope as she saw his eyes flicker towards her.

'Isabelle, are you crying?' His voice was croaky and full of concern.

'Of course not,' Issy replied, brushing her cheeks. 'What's with the Isabelle? You only call me Isabelle when I've done something wrong.'

'I don't want you crying, kiddo. Help me out and find someone who can tell me what's really going on here, will you . . . ?'

'I'll call someone and get some help,' she said, getting up and reluctantly letting go of his hand.

She walked out into the corridor and took several long, deep breaths. A few hours after he'd been admitted the doctors had declared her dad 'stable', but she hadn't believed them. Not until now. This was what she'd been praying for, yet she still couldn't quite believe it.

After steadying herself, Issy grabbed the first nurse she saw, a young woman about her own age who looked perky enough to be early in her shift, so when Issy explained that her dad was awake she followed right after. She was the only member of the family left at the hospital and felt like a child, hopelessly out of her depth. Her brother had gone to check on the garage their dad owned and ran, while her mum had gone home for some rest. She wished they were both here.

When Issy followed the nurse back into the room, her dad had barely moved but his eyes were wide open and there was a sense of awareness about him. Relief flooded through her. He really was going to be all right.

'You gave us quite a fright, Mr Jones,' the nurse said sternly but with a smile.

'Yes you bloody well did,' Issy added, flashing him a beaming smile.

'Hey, love, sorry about the fright, but please, call me Kev.' He winked at the nurse.

'Really, Dad? One minute you're at death's door the next you're putting a shift in with a nurse!' Issy shook her head but she was still grinning.

Before he could reply the door to the ward burst open and her mum ran into the room clutching her yapping little dog, Princess Tiger-Lily, followed closely by Zach. She immediately launched herself on her husband, showering him with kisses.

'Debs!' Kev spluttered.

'You can't have dogs in here,' said the nurse sounding shocked and angry. 'We don't allow animals in the hospital and your husband is still *very* ill.'

'You shouldn't have brought her in here, love,' Kev said quietly. It was an effort to lift his hand but he gently stroked the side of Debs's face.

'I did try to stop her,' Zach said, turning his attention to the flustered nurse. He mouthed a silent 'sorry' at her and she visibly melted. Issy rolled her eyes. Her brother could charm his way into a nun's pants.

'Oh for God's sake, he's alive, that's all that matters. And surely you know how important pets are for patient rehabilitation?' Debs said, wagging a finger at the nurse.

'Just be careful. There are a lot of wires,' she simpered, eyes still fixed upon Zach. 'I'll go and see where the doctor's got to.'

'You do that, love,' Debs replied with a smile before carefully placing Princess at the foot of the bed and launching herself onto Kev again.

'Mum, you'll give him another heart attack carrying on like that,' Zach half-joked.

The nurse backed out of the room, her gaze firmly fixed on Zach, who had been pretending not to notice.

Issy stood in the small, grey hospital room surveying her family. She couldn't believe all their happiness had nearly been taken away from them. A rush of pure love filled her as she looked around at them all; her dad, her mum, Zach, even Princess Tiger-Lily, right now she'd even forgive all those times her barking interrupted a much-needed Saturday morning hangover lie-in.

It wasn't normal, it was quite far from normal, but they were hers and she loved everything about them. She meant what she had said before her dad had woken up; she would never leave them again.

Chapter One

THREE YEARS LATER

'So, what are we doing today, Vi?' Issy asked, wielding a pair of scissors and standing behind Violet, one of her regulars. They were in A Cut Above, her mum's hairdressing salon in Salford, on the outskirts of Manchester. It was the most popular salon in the area but that was because most of the clients belonged to the blue rinse brigade. Although there were a few younger customers, it wasn't exactly what you'd call edgy, and Issy longed to get her creative hands on people who wanted more than a trim and tint. Issy had asked what Vi wanted, already knowing the answer. She'd known Vi and many of her mum's other clients since she was a little girl.

'I just want a little bit off, duck. Not too short, mind. I don't want to look like a poodle,' Vi replied. Issy nodded. With her tightly permed white hair, no matter what she did Vi *always* ended up looking like a poodle.

'Of course not, Vi, God forbid,' Issy said, smiling warmly at Violet in the mirror.

Issy got to work on Vi's hair when suddenly a wave of nostalgia hit and she was catapulted back to her days at The Hair Academy. It felt like a lifetime ago that she'd walked away from her course.

The Hair Academy was the most illustrious hairdressing college in the UK, and Issy had worked her arse off to get a place on one of their courses. They only took a handful of students each year so competition was fierce, but back then Issy was full of confidence – and had the talent to back it up. Prior to her dad's heart attack, she'd been so driven and ambitious. Whether she ended up styling hair for magazine shoots or working backstage at fashion shows – one way or another she had been determined to make a name for herself.

It was a far cry from where she was now.

Issy looked around the salon. She'd practically grown up here – hairdressing was in her blood. Her mum had started teaching her how to style hair when she was barely a teenager. She'd practised on dummy heads, swept up hair, made notes – whatever it took to learn the trade. As a young girl, it had amazed Issy that people could come into the salon looking pretty ordinary and leave feeling amazing. Hair was powerful, she truly believed that. Hairdressing was about more than just the physical, there was a psychology to it too. People poured their hearts out when they sat in the hairdresser's chair and Issy understood that she was much more than a pair of scissors to them, they put their trust into her when they sat down in her chair.

Issy shook her head to dispel her nostalgia and tuned back into Vi's chatter about her latest ailments. Issy missed the glamour and the creative challenges of The Hair Academy, but her mum's salon had heart and the clients were important to her. They needed her and so did her family. Readjusting to living at home again had been hard but Issy had never once doubted that leaving her course and coming back to Salford had been the right decision.

A melodic hum of chatter filled the air. A Cut Above was a medium-sized salon and as well as Issy and her mother, Karen and Brenda, two other stylists, also worked there. Alice, their trainee, completed their small team and though at the moment she was shampooing, sweeping up hair and making tea, she was bright and good with the clients so Issy knew it wouldn't be long before she had the skills and confidence to start tackling cuts on her own. It was how they'd all got their start.

'Thanks, Alice,' Issy said as Alice delivered a cup of milky tea to Violet. Alice smiled back at Issy and said hello to Vi, before going off with her broom.

There was a commotion as the door opened and Issy turned to see Zach walking through the salon. He'd clearly come from the garage – it was just around the corner so they were always popping in and out – as he was wearing his oil-covered overalls, and his cuffs were rolled up to reveal his full-sleeve tattoo. Since their dad's heart attack, Zach had taken charge of all the manual labour at the garage and Issy's dad had taken a step back and focused on the office work. Kev insisted that he didn't mind the change but Issy secretly thought that he did miss getting his hands dirty.

'Ooo,' Vi said, turning her head suddenly and almost losing an ear in the process. Issy pulled her scissors quickly out of harm's way, she knew how Vi could get around Zach, or any young man, in fact. 'Zach, hi!' Vi waved flirtatiously as Zach made his way over to them.

'Hey, gorgeous,' he said to Vi. She blushed like a girl a quarter of her age and Issy shook her head.

At six foot two, Zach shared the same dark hair as Issy and their dad. He was definitely a good-looking lad, and had been for as long as Issy could remember. She'd been one of the most popular girls in school simply because girls thought they could get close to Zach through Issy. And he was still one of the fittest lads in Salford – not that Issy would ever tell him that. Zach definitely didn't have confidence issues.

'What are you doing here?' Issy asked.

'I had a few minutes so I thought I'd pop in for a sunbed.'

'Are you going to be naked?' Vi asked hopefully.

Issy's eyes sparkled with amusement. 'Vi, you're old enough to be his nan,' she rebuked.

'I am not,' Vi replied indignantly.

'No, Vi, I wear boxers in there,' Zach said conspiratorially, lifting his T-shirt to snap at the waistband of his Calvin Kleins and exposing a strip of muscular stomach as he did so. 'Got to protect little Zach!'

Issy looked around the salon. Alice was almost the same colour as Issy's crimson nails, Vi was grinning from ear-to-ear and Karen couldn't keep her eyes off Zach's groin.

'Right, that's enough.' Debs shouted, coming out from the back fresh from cleaning the sunbeds. 'Zachary Jones, get into that sunbed and leave everyone else to cut hair.' Zach threw Vi a final cheeky wink and then disappeared.

Vi chatted non-stop about Zach for the rest of her haircut. Issy shared a smile with her mum who was sorting out accounts and manning reception. Zach had taken on the lion's share of the work at the garage for the last three years and she was proud of him – despite the fact that he flirted with old ladies. Although in fairness he flirted with everyone and everything – dogs, pot plants, a packet of chocolate digestives. Nothing and no one was immune to Zachary Jones's charms.

Issy was just finishing up with Vi when the salon door banged open again and her father appeared.

'Hello, gorgeous,' Debs said coming round from the reception desk to kiss her husband, wrapping her arms around him in a display of affection that made Issy feel like an awkward teenager.

'Hi, love.' Kev looked around the salon and smiled. 'Hi, ladies.'

'Two handsome men in one day,' Vi said. 'I shall never recover.' Issy thought, not for the first time, that despite her age, Vi was still a saucy old flirt.

'What other handsome man?' Kev asked, sounding perplexed.

'Your son, love. He's having a sunbed.'

'*That's* where the bugger got to. He said he had to pop out for teabags half an hour ago. I should have known where he'd be.' Kev looked annoyed but deep down he was

11

more amused by Zach than angry. Father and son were like peas in a pod, but Zach was the new generation, for sure. He took care of himself in a way that Kev could never understand. Zach was a man's man, but a well-groomed one.

At that moment Zach reappeared, a few shades darker than when he'd come in.

'Bollocks!' he said on seeing his dad. He ducked down behind Vi's chair. 'Protect me, Vi.'

'Any time, love,' Vi said, a wicked glint in her eye.

Zach laughed. 'What are you doing here, Dad?' he asked, standing up but still keeping a good distance.

'Well, I was hoping for a word in private with our Issy,' he said, shuffling awkwardly from foot to foot.

'What about?' Debs asked.

'Yes, what about?' Vi repeated. Vi loved coming to the salon – it was better than an episode of *Coronation Street*.

Issy jumped in. Just because it was a family business didn't mean that everyone got to hear all their business. 'Give me five minutes and I'll come and see you – Vi's my last cut of the day.'

'Meet me at the café, I could murder a cuppa.' He shot his son a look. 'And Zach, get back to work.'

'Come on, Dad. At least I'm a lovely colour now,' Zach laughed.

'A lovely colour? You're starting to resemble a bloody tea bag, you big girl – now get back to the garage, will you?' Kev said, exasperated.

'Oh you really are a lovely colour,' Vi agreed. 'If only you'd show me your tan lines.'

'Bloody hell, Vi!' Debs shouted, but with a laugh. 'Boys –
out, any more of this and Alice'll be sweeping up fainting
pensioners instead of hair.'

Issy pulled her black cardigan around her as she walked
toward the café. It was cold, but she didn't have far to go.
She pushed open the door and saw her dad, sitting at a
corner table, reading a newspaper, with two mugs of tea in
front of him. She smiled at the woman behind the counter
and made her way over.

'Hiya,' she said, sitting down and pointing at his mug.
'There better not be any sugar in that tea?'

'Course not,' Kev replied, looking guilty. Since his heart
attack, Issy had been on a one-woman mission to make sure
her dad stayed healthy. She resisted the urge to take a sip to
check. He was pretty patient about her bossing him around
but she didn't want to push her luck.

'So, what's going on?' Issy had a sudden thought. 'Is
everything OK? Is it your heart?' However many years
passed, Issy didn't think she'd ever stop worrying about her
dad having another heart attack.

'No, it's nothing like that. I'm fit as a fiddle, promise.'

Issy relaxed back into her chair. 'Am I in trouble then?'
She smiled at her dad the way she always did when she
needed to get round him.

'No, you're not in trouble. I just ... well ... OK ... Look,
there's something I wanted to talk to you about.' Kev looked
awkward as he shuffled in his seat. 'The thing is, well, you've
been back at home for three years now.'

Issy frowned. *What was this all about?*

Kev took a deep breath before continuing. 'Here's the thing. Three years ago you were in London, following your dream, full of ideas and ambition. We both know why you came home but I'm not sure I know why you're *still* here.'

'Dad, what are you getting at?' Sometimes her dad took for ever getting to the point. Cars, rather than conversation, were Kev's strong point.

'I just want to make sure that you're happy, you know, living at home and working at the salon. Is cutting old ladies hair really what you want?'

'There are worse jobs,' Issy said defensively.

'I know that, and your mum's salon is grand. But you've always wanted more. You've got your mum's talent but we always wanted more for you as well. Once me and your mum met it was all marriage, babies and bloody dogs. Wish I'd put me foot down and insisted we got a cat.'

'Dad. I have no idea what you're talking about. Is this about me or Princess?' Issy looked her father straight in the eye.

'Bloody hell, Issy. Can't I have a proper conversation with my daughter?'

'Sure.' Issy smiled sweetly. 'And if I knew what this was about then I could join in with that proper conversation.'

Kev looked cross at first and then started laughing. He should've known better – Issy always cut to the chase.

'Here's the thing. It's time for you to put yourself first,' Kev said gruffly. 'You kept this family together when I was ill. Now it's time I did something for you, and I have a plan.'

'A plan?'

'I saw an advert for a new reality TV show. It's a

14

hairdressing competition and the production company is looking for contestants. The best thing is that it will be filmed in Manchester.'

'A TV show? Are you mad?' Issy loved watching reality TV, she was a hopeless addict, but that didn't mean she wanted to be on it. Of course the 'what if' had crossed her mind, but she couldn't see it. She'd never wanted to be famous.

'You're perfect for it,' Kev said. 'You have the talent for it and you'd still be nearby so you wouldn't even be leaving us really.'

'This show – what is it exactly?' Issy fiddled with a salt shaker as she tried to make sense of what her dad was saying. The idea of it had filled her with an uncharacteristic dread.

'All I know is that it's a competition for hairdressers, it's going to be on TV, and there's some big prize.'

'Well, that's not a lot to go on. It sounds all right but, Dad, a TV show? Come on. They probably wouldn't want me anyway.'

'The thing is ... that ... I sort of filled out the application form for you and it turns out they *do* want to speak to you.' Kev stared at the table as intently as if they were showing an episode of *Match of the Day* on there.

'You did *what*?!' Issy shrieked. 'Dad, have you gone mad?' Issy couldn't believe what she was hearing.

'Someone had to do something!' Kev looked annoyed until he saw the panicked look on Issy's face. He picked up his mug and then put it back down again. 'I only did it because I love you,' he said talking to the table again, a blush slowly creeping up his neck.

Issy was silent for a moment. *How am I meant to respond to that?* she thought.

'I love you too, Dad,' Issy said finally. 'But what's that got to do with some daft TV show?'

'The London thing . . . it was a big deal and you gave it up. For us, for me. I know you felt that you had to prop all of us up and we let you, but only because we thought you'd go back once everything was back to normal.' He smiled, back on more comfortable territory. 'It's time for you to get back to your life and stop living ours.'

'I'm not sure I have it in me anymore, it's been too long.' Issy felt confused. Of all the things she could have imagined her dad was going to say, this didn't come close. She didn't know how to react and it was bringing all her unacknowledged fears to the surface.

'Don't be so bloody dramatic, of course you have. You're only twenty-five. You've got your whole life ahead of you.'

'But Dad—'

'This show could open doors for you. Look, you're wasting your talents here and it's not on.' He looked stern and Issy wondered if she was still expected to do as she was told at her age.

'I'm scared, Dad,' she admitted, looking at the table herself now.

'There was a time when nothing scared you.' Kev reached for Issy's hand. 'Where's my brave daughter gone? The daughter who had bigger balls than most of the lads in my garage? Is she still in there?'

Issy laughed, despite herself. 'I don't know, Dad. I need to think about this properly. I'm a little bit blindsided.'

16

'OK, love, but don't take too long. They won't wait forever.' Her dad looked her square in the eye for the first time since she'd come in. 'The only thing that matters to me is that you're happy. And I don't think you've been truly happy since you moved back home.'

Issy stood up and walked round the table so she could sit next to her dad. She enveloped him in a hug. Kev gave her a squeeze back.

The two mugs of tea were left undrunk.

Chapter Two

Issy stared at the rain thumping against the bus window. Her mind had been racing ever since she left her dad a few hours ago. She'd needed to chill out and the best way she knew how was a bit of retail therapy. She'd treated herself to a pair of black Kurt Geiger peep-toes, and, although they probably weren't going to be the most comfortable, she'd felt some of her old confidence returning when she'd tried them on in the shop. *What harm could come from meeting the producers?* she'd managed to convince herself. *They might not even like me so the decision is out of my hands, really.* As she'd looked at herself in the full-length mirror, she'd felt a small spark of excitement – the first real excitement for a long time. She was always amazed at how a beautiful pair of shoes could make her feel more confident, even powerful. As the bus jerked around the corner on the way back home, Issy smiled to herself. At the very least, she'd wear her new shoes on her next night out with the girls. Maybe she'd even meet a nice lad wearing them.

Since moving back to Salford Issy had had a couple of short relationships but nothing meaningful. She was a romantic through and through, and wanted to meet someone kind and lovely and who she could spend the rest of her life with – she wanted the kind of relationship her parents had. They'd met at fourteen and had been together ever since. Because of them, Issy wasn't going to settle for just anyone, and she was sure the perfect lad for her was out there somewhere. It was just that lately most of the lads she met thought that buying her a drink would also buy their way into her knickers. It would take more than a G & T and a bit of banter to get Issy's attention.

Mind, she was in Salford, not a Jennifer Aniston film. Maybe she was aiming too high with that level of romance.

Issy's thoughts snapped back to the TV show. Shopping had made her feel excited about the prospect for a while but now on the bus, with the shoes in her bag and another charge on her credit card, the confidence she'd felt in the shop had disappeared and she was left with a gnawing anxiety in the pit of her stomach. Her mum and Zach thought the show was a good idea so Issy had then called Molly, her best mate, for support. Molly had been on the same side as the rest of the Joneses, but Issy remained unconvinced. Was she cut out for reality TV? Did she even *want* to be on a show that could make her a household name?

After the chat with her dad, it had all been a bit of a blur. They'd headed over to the garage office and he'd shown her the email from the TV company, presenting it to her as if it was a golden ticket. Issy had read the email over and over, unsure what to do, calling her mum again to talk it through and getting endless texts from Molly, along with Zach shouting through from the workshop every few minutes that she should 'just bloody get on with it' until eventually her dad had handed her the phone and *made* her call the producers.

And it had been fine. Good, in fact. They had talked about Issy's hairdressing background and her interests, and then they'd invited her in for a face-to-face meeting. Her dad had been standing right next to her, listening to every word, so she'd had no choice but to agree. That still didn't mean she was actually going to go though. Speaking to the researcher, whose name she now couldn't even remember she'd been so nervous, Issy had been full of excitement at the prospect of something new – the TV company sounded a million miles away from the blue rinse set – but she still couldn't shake her nervous feelings about the whole idea. She didn't know if she could put herself through it.

And she had so many questions. All the researcher had told her was that the show would be a competition and the contestants would have to live together somewhere in Manchester. They wouldn't even tell her what the prize was. Issy felt conflicted and having so little information wasn't helping. Mostly she wanted to run a mile in her new shoes but there was a small part of her that thought, *screw it*. Maybe she should go for it. Plus, she could barely walk in her new shoes, let alone run.

Issy thought back to how she'd felt when she'd first arrived at The Hair Academy – confident and full of excitement about the future. She was a talented stylist and she'd stood out from the beginning. She hadn't wanted to give up her life in London but nearly losing her dad had changed everything. It had been a wake-up call and now all she wanted was to keep her dad in sight and make sure he didn't eat too many Mars Bars or drink too much beer. Had her ambition simply gone away?

'Get a grip, Issy,' she hissed to herself as she got off the bus. Her emotions were all over the shop, and that was far from a good thing. She had a decision to make.

Issy was still rolling thoughts around her head when she arrived home. She walked into the lounge ready to collapse on the sofa and watch some mind-numbing TV to calm her nerves. Fat chance. Her dad stood in the middle of the room, arms behind his back. Her mum was on her reclining chair, Princess on her lap. Zach was on the sofa and next to him was Molly.

They were all clearly waiting for her – it was an ambush. Issy resisted the urge to flee back into the rain and sat down next to Molly instead, stunned that they'd called her in for reinforcements. No one spoke. It was weird. Issy's family wasn't the silent type. As she looked around, Issy realised they were all staring expectantly at her.

'OK . . . What's going on?' Issy asked eventually.

'We thought we should have a family meeting,' her dad said, sounding serious.

'A family meeting?' Issy raised her eyebrows. *Who are we, the Kardashians? Bit dramatic, isn't it?* The last time they'd had a family meeting, she'd been fifteen. Zach had thrown a party, emptied their parents' spirits cabinet and refilled all the bottles with water and cold tea. *That had been fun*, she remembered, *as her brother had tried to blame it all on her.*

'Here, have a Hobnob.' Zach shoved a plate toward her.

'Now I know something's wrong. Zach, you never share the Hobnobs,' Issy tried to laugh but her throat was too dry.

'We want to talk to you about the show,' Zach said.

'Right . . . ' Issy said warily.

'You keep saying you don't know if you want to do it,' Molly's voice was firm. 'But we think, no, we *know*, that really, deep down, you do know. You want to go for it but something's holding you back.'

Issy looked at Molly. She was petite, blonde and had gorgeous blue eyes. She and Issy couldn't have looked less alike if they tried, but in personality they weren't that different. They'd been joined at the hip since primary school, ever since Issy had chased away the playground bullies who'd made fun of Molly's stammer. The stammer had made Molly a quiet child but once she became friends with Issy, she'd come out of her shell. Now she barely stammered at all, only when she was upset or angry, and never when she was with Issy or the rest of the Jones family. She'd also become pretty good at standing up for herself and making herself heard. As she was proving right now. Molly looked determined, Zach steely, her parents concerned.

'Why are you all so keen that I should do it anyway?'

'Because it's perfect for you,' Kev said.

'Your dad's right, Issy,' Debs said. 'I love my salon – I wouldn't change a thing about it, but you're far too talented to be stuck doing shampoo and sets for the rest of your life.'

'It's good enough for you,' Issy protested.

'Issy, you're not me. All I've ever wanted is your dad, my small business, and you two. I'm lucky that my life turned out exactly as I hoped, but you used to have all these big dreams so it's time you started chasing them again.'

'Maybe I want what you have too,' Issy said quietly.

'Issy.' Molly put her arm around her friend. 'Before you came back from London you were unstoppable. But that's not the case anymore.' Issy should've been offended but she knew Molly was right. Molly was always right.

'And anyway, you're single, so you can't have what Mum and Dad have,' Zach pointed out.

Issy knew he didn't mean to be cruel but Zach didn't do subtle. She punched him on the arm. 'So what you're saying is that I'm twenty-five, have no lad and no career?'

'Yeah, kind of,' Zach agreed, rubbing his arm. Issy was stronger than she looked. 'Listen, this show could change your life. You might even end up on the cover of one of those magazines you're always reading.'

'No daughter of mine is taking her clothes off,' Kev growled.

'He said the magazines *I* read, Dad, not the ones he does,' Issy protested. Princess yapped.

'Bloody hell Issy, why are you making this so hard?' Debs said, looking at Kev. 'Kev, can you talk some sense into her?' she asked seriously.

'It's not about sense. I'm scared,' Issy admitted.

'Oh, love,' Debs sighed.

I'm only twenty-five, Issy thought. *That doesn't make me old with no future, does it?* As soon as the thought crossed her mind, it became suddenly clear that she was the only person holding herself back. Her parents had confidence in her, so did Zach and Molly. Why didn't she feel it anymore? Her parents were happy with their lives, and Zach was more than content working for their dad. But then she wasn't her brother, or her parents. Or even Molly, who loved her job as a teaching assistant at a local primary school. Issy had lost her way a bit, she had to admit that.

'Look, love, we just want you to start living your life again. And we think you may have forgotten how to do that.' Kev crouched down in front of Issy, like he used to when she was a child.

'Issy, what happened to your dad changed things for all of us. You gave up a lot to look after us, but we're OK now. You don't need to do that anymore,' Debs added.

'I know I have to make a decision but it's hard,' Issy said. She knew their hearts were in the right place but she was feeling pressured and that was making it harder.

'The last thing we want to do is make you feel ganged up on. It's just that the show is perfect for you, and we all care about you, Is,' Molly said. 'Of course it's your decision, but we all think you'll really regret it if you don't go for this now.'

Issy took a mental photo of them all. Her mum: Princess in her lap, all Dolly Parton hair and pink fluffy high-heeled slippers who always wore her heart on her sleeve. Zach: a softie underneath all the style and tattoos. Molly: with her core of steel, looking like butter wouldn't melt in her mouth – although Issy knew different. And her dad: striding around the living room like a general of this dysfunctional army. They might be bloody interfering but they were also annoyingly right.

'Argh, I feel so pressured!' Issy buried her head in Molly's shoulder.

'Calm down, Gwynnie. Stop being so dramatic. It's only an interview, they might not even bloody want you,' Kev said, patting her knee, but surreptitiously checking his watch. The United match was about to kick off.

Debs smacked Kev on the arm. 'Of course they'll want her! Is, we've got faith in you and we think you should do this. You have to *want* to do it too, though,' Debs added gently. 'Remember, if I was being selfish I'd want to keep you here. Good hairdressers are hard to find – and it doesn't hurt that you're quite handy to have round the house.' Debs stroked Princess and smiled.

'And I don't want you to move away either,' Molly added. 'I come over here all the time to get away from my mum and Pete rowing.' Molly's stepdad was always rowing with her mum, and Issy was always having to pick up the pieces when they upset Molly with one of their fights. It always made Issy even more grateful for her own parents. Zach looked at Molly in concern and handed her a Hobnob – this was as close to sympathy as Zach got.

'I'd probably be deep frying Mars Bars and sneak Guinness into my IV drip without you here,' Kev said.

'And who'd wax my eyebrows?' Zach said. Kev turned sharply to look at him and shook his head. Zach had the decency to blush – but only slightly.

'So do you want me to do it or not?' Issy laughed.

'Not!' they all answered in unison. Zach rolled his eyes.

'And what if I *do* want to go to the audition?' Issy said, with a mischievous glint in her eye.

'So you'll go? Great! I've put a bottle of Prosecco in the fridge to celebrate. I'll go and get it,' Debs said, kissing Issy's head as she walked past. 'Zach, share out those Hobnobs, love, before you eat them all.'

'Hang on,' Issy said. 'You already had a bottle in the fridge? So you knew I'd say yes?'

'Of course not, love,' Kev said, with a wry smile as he reached for the remote. 'We had no idea.'

Chapter Three

Issy's heart was hammering in her chest. She was standing in the centre of town outside the Malmaison hotel, about to go in for her meeting with the show's casting producer, Harry, and Laura, the producer and director. She checked her reflection in the window, and smoothed down her red dress for the hundredth time. It had taken her, her mum and Molly hours to choose the knee-length, fitted dress from Zara and in the mirror in her bedroom it had seemed perfect, but now she wondered if it was too much. Her new hair extensions looked good though, and the hours spent applying and reapplying her make-up, fake tan and eyelashes had been worth it. It was strange to think that a few days ago she hadn't been sure about the show, but she'd been kidding herself. The minute she'd said it out loud, she knew for certain that she wanted this. Badly.

A small spark of adventure had been reignited by her family pushing her into going through with meeting the producers – at first Issy had told herself it was purely curiosity but she couldn't deny it any longer. She was excited. It had only been a couple of days, but now she'd got over some of her reservations, her old drive and determination was coming back. And she was terrified. She was about to jump into the unknown. She tried to push the thought away, but in her head she kept repeating: *am I really ready for this?*

She had been summoned to the hotel for an 'informal' chat, but she knew that in reality this was an audition. She'd already had several long phone conversations with researchers, producers, and who-knew-who-else and Issy got the impression that the process was gaining pace and they were in a hurry to get the contestants signed up. They still wouldn't give much away about the actual format though. They hadn't even told her if she'd be cutting hair today, so just in case she'd packed her kit into her biggest Michael Kors handbag. The weight of it was making her totter on her nude platforms. She tugged down the hem of her dress. They'd told her to think of it as *The X Factor* of hairdressing. Brilliant. No pressure, then. Issy hoped they weren't going to ask her to sing on top of everything else. It took at least a bottle of rosé to warm up to that.

Her mum and Molly had offered to come with her, but Issy had insisted on doing this by herself. If the audition was going to go how she thought it was, and she was going to make a tit of herself, she didn't want anyone else there to witness it. Now that the doubts were creeping in again though, Issy realised the thing she needed most was a reassuring word, a comforting hug, and she wished she hadn't told them not to come along. Even one of Zach's stupid jokes would do. Why had she decided to do this on her own? It wasn't like they hadn't all seen her make a tit out of herself before.

Issy took a deep breath and put her hand on the big glass door. It was now or never.

She pushed open the door and walked up to the reception desk. She gave Harry's name to the receptionist and was told to wait. She sat nervously on the edge of one of the big plush seats in the lobby, plonking her huge bag down beside her. Issy looked around to see if there was anyone else waiting, but she seemed like the only person there. After a while, a short lad with messy dark hair and round glasses came up and greeted her. Issy couldn't help but think that he looked really young.

'You must be Issy?' he asked timidly.

'Yes. Are you Harry?' Harry had sounded like a grown-up on the phone.

'Oh God, no, I'm Danny, the runner. Follow me, I'll take you through.'

'OK, great.' Issy plastered a smile to her face and said a silent prayer. Danny's nerves weren't helping hers.

She followed Danny into a private room where three chairs were arranged around a coffee table and a camera was pointed at the empty chair. The two people occupying the other chairs, who must have been Harry and Laura, stood up to greet Issy as she walked towards them. Harry was tall, had thick, swept back hair and was dressed smartly in jeans, a shirt and suit jacket. If she hadn't been sure before, Issy could tell simply by his presence that this guy was important. Laura by contrast had a light brown bobbed haircut, and was dressed simply in jeans, a T-shirt and a pair of battered Converse. Despite how different she looked from Harry, she had her own sense of steely importance and even without a scrap of make-up she was still attractive, but miles away from how Issy was presenting herself. Instantly Issy felt ridiculous, overdone. The only way she could have looked more overdressed is if she'd turned up in a prom dress.

'Issy Jones, twenty-five, from Salford,' Danny announced seriously. Issy smiled and hoped it didn't look like a grimace.

'Hi,' she said as Danny slipped out the door and Issy wished she could follow him.

'Hi, Issy. Please have a seat,' Harry said after she'd shaken both their hands, desperately hoping her palms didn't feel sweaty. Harry sounded even camper than he had on the phone. He and Laura both had their pens poised over clip-boards as the camera's red recording light blinked at Issy. 'Try to ignore the camera,' Harry advised.

No problem, thought Issy, sarcastically.

'Relax and be yourself.' Laura smiled reassuringly. 'So you're working at your mum's salon at the moment, right?'

'Yes, A Cut Above. It's in Salford.'

'And do you like it?' Harry asked, smiling warmly.

'Well, yes, most of the time. I mean, it's mainly old ladies, lots of perms, blue rinses and that, but it's great because I know loads about hip replacements now. And I can tell you everything that's going on in *Coronation Street*.' Harry laughed so loudly that Issy jumped.

'But before that you were at The Hair Academy in London?' Laura's voice was soft and Issy felt herself relax slightly. She'd practised how she was going to talk about this bit.

'Yes, I went there but I wasn't able to finish the course.'

'Because your dad died?' Harry said, sounding sympathetic.

'Um, no, he didn't die. He had a heart attack. He was the one who applied . . . for me.' Issy was confused.

'Oh for God's sake, I can't read this writing. Does that look like died to you?' Harry leant over to Laura who nodded. 'Anyway,' he turned back and offered Issy a broad smile. 'I'm very happy he's still alive.'

'Thank you. Er . . . so am I?' Issy couldn't think of how else to respond.

Laura laughed and said, 'And you're single?'

'Yup, totally single.'

'And do you like men or women?'

'Men.' Issy put a hand on her thigh to still her shaking leg. 'I'm a bit of a romantic to be honest. Mr. Right is definitely out there but I haven't managed to find him yet.' When she said it out loud she knew it made her sound like a lovesick idiot but it was the truth and she'd promised herself she'd be honest. Harry and Laura were both smiling at her, but Issy had no idea if it was because they were pleased with her answer or because they thought she was a pillock.

'That's sweet. An old-fashioned romantic, not many of those around these days.' Harry laughed yet again and Issy nodded. 'You're very attractive, and you obviously like to take care of yourself. Would you say you're high maintenance?'

'I like to spend time on my appearance, it's important to me. Most women my age do, don't they?' She directed the question to Laura but noticing again her shabby Converse,

31

she regretted the decision instantly and instead quickly turned to Harry and his designer brogues. 'I have hair extensions.' Without really thinking about it, Issy flicked her hair and almost gave herself whiplash. *Oh my God, calm down*, she thought to herself. *This isn't a bloody L'Oreal advert.* She cleared her throat. 'I wear false eyelashes, I like to be tanned, and I wear make-up every day. I think it's important to look after yourself.'

'Would you say you were vain?' Laura asked, her lips curling up into a slight smile.

'I don't think so. I just like to look good. But I also know there are more important things to worry about.'

'Like what?'

Issy tried to think seriously about her answer but her nerves got the better of her and her mouth starting moving before her brain could stop it.

'Like family. Like friends. Like being happy. What's the point in looking good, putting all this effort in, when you've got no one to enjoy it with and nowhere to go? My family means everything to me.' She laughed nervously. *I sound like such a melt.*

Laura and Harry smiled at each other knowingly.

'Right, well great. OK, so now we're going to throw some questions at you. Don't think about your answer too much – just say the first thing that comes into your head,' Harry said.

This was worse than being back at school. She *really* hadn't prepared for this.

'Favourite colour?'

'Blue.'

'Bit boyish isn't it, darling?' Harry said.

'Bit sexist isn't it, darling?' Issy shot back before she could help herself. He should *not* have told her not to think before she spoke. Thankfully, Harry laughed.

Laura said, 'You did tell her to say the first thing that came into her head.' Issy could have kissed her.

'Favourite animal?'

'Tiger.'

'Drink?' Harry continued.

'Tequila.' Issy fleetingly wondered what the hell any of this had to do with hairdressing.

'Actor?'

'Channing Tatum.'

'Ohhh me too, I love him.' Harry smiled. 'What annoys you?'

'Rich Tea biscuits.' They stared at her as if she was crazy. Maybe she was crazy. 'They're so plain and boring.' *As if that explains it.* 'I'm not crazy about custard creams either.' Why couldn't she stop talking? Why was she acting like some sort of insane biscuit connoisseur? This was all Zach's fault. Him and his stupid Hobnobs.

'What's the most important thing in the world to you?'

Issy didn't miss a beat. 'My family.'

Harry and Laura continued to fire questions at her for what felt like hours. They asked her what sort of people she liked, what sort of people irritated her, what made her laugh, how easily she lost her temper. On and on it went. She felt wrung out. Finally, as they started to wrap things up and they were saying goodbye, Issy had a thought.

'Don't you want to see if I can actually cut hair?' she

asked looking down at the huge bag she'd been lugging around all day. They both looked at her, and then at each other as if this hadn't occurred to them.

'Not really,' Harry said, 'it was lovely to meet you.'

'You too, Hazza!' *Why can't I stop talking?!* she thought as she walked out of the room.

As Issy stepped out onto the street, she spotted Molly and Zach waiting for her.

'What are you doing here?' She pretended to be annoyed, but she was so pleased to see them.

'Taking you for a much-needed drink,' Zach replied, grabbing Issy's monster bag from her while Molly linked her arm. As if Issy would ever refuse a drink.

They walked round the corner and settled themselves into a nearby Wetherspoons and Zach bought the first round. After taking a couple of calming sips of her glass of rosé, Issy launched into telling Molly and Zach everything that had happened in the meeting. The more she talked, the more depressed she started to feel, certain that she'd made the worst kind of impression.

'You actually said Rich Tea biscuits annoyed you?' Zach asked.

'I know, I know,' Issy groaned. 'There's no way they'll pick me now. That was more uncomfortable than my smear test.'

'Issy! Don't say stuff like that in front of me.' Zach twisted his face.

Issy laughed, some of the tension of the afternoon finally leaving her body. 'Sorry!' She sighed and was quiet for a moment before continuing. 'It didn't feel too bad when I was in the room but now . . . I just don't know.'

'That's natural. *Everyone* feels like that when they come out of an interview. If you thought you had it in the bag, you'd be an overconfident wanker. And we,' Molly said with a wicked gleam in her eye, 'wouldn't be friends. Plus, it sounds to me like you came across as a bit of a lunatic. And we know they love crazy people on reality TV. You're a shoo-in!'

'I *think* there's a compliment in there somewhere . . . ' Issy said slowly.

'Course there is. I'm saying that you're the sort of big personality they love for this sort of show,' Molly smiled.

'So when they find out that you're the human equivalent of a Rich Tea biscuit they're going to be *really* disappointed.' Zach looked wildly amused with himself. Issy gave him a playful shove.

'Enough with the biscuits!'

Zach laughed. 'And did they tell you anymore about what the TV show will actually be like?' he continued.

'Not really,' Issy said taking a sip of her wine. 'They asked a thousand questions but when I asked about the show they said they couldn't say anything until they'd picked all the contestants.'

'That's a bit crap.' Zach looked at something over her shoulder. 'Hang on a sec, I've seen someone I know.' Zach stood up and walked off in the direction he'd been looking.

'For God's sake, he can't even have a five minute drink without hunting for birds,' Issy moaned. Molly remained silent as they turned around and watched Zach approach a woman with long red hair.

'She's not his usual type,' Molly said.

'Zach has a type?' Issy said incredulously.

'Good point,' agreed Molly and the girls laughed. They fell into a companionable silence as they finished their drinks.

Issy vowed then and there to forget about the show. There was nothing wrong with her life as it was and, anyway, who else would keep her brother in check if she wasn't around?

'Molly, I'm not unhappy. You know that, right?'

Molly looked at her friend intensely. 'Of course I do, Issy. I just think you're destined for more than Salford and setting perms.' Molly reached over and squeezed her hand.

Chapter Four

'Issy, I'm so excited for you!' Debs gushed. It was evening and Debs and Issy were tidying the salon. It had been cleaned and preened to within an inch of its life and Debs hadn't stopped chatting the entire time. She was beside herself about the TV show.

'I'm so nervous, I don't think I've got the space to be excited as well.' Issy still couldn't believe how quickly everything was happening.

She'd been certain, so certain that she'd blown the interview at the Malmaison and had simply put it out of her mind from then on, until miraculously a couple of days later she'd been called back to a second meeting. Harry and Laura had met her again, but there had been three more execs there, all incredibly intimidating, all interviewing her intensely. It had been another exhausting two hours of incessant questions and probing but spurred on by the fact that they'd invited her back, Issy had felt more confident.

She'd been feistier, more articulate and managed to be intentionally funny – she'd felt more like herself.

But even knowing how well the second meeting had gone hadn't prepared Issy for the phone call that came the next day. She'd had to ask Harry to repeat it when he said she'd been selected. Even after all of her family's support there was no way she'd been expecting to be accepted onto the show just like that.

Ever since then the butterflies in Issy's stomach had been going crazy as if they were having a great big butterfly party. The last time she'd felt this proud of herself was when she'd been accepted into The Hair Academy. It had been a long time since she'd had the fire in her belly but now, along with the butterflies, there it was. It hadn't disappeared after all.

She'd taken her dad to sign the contracts with the production company, Smash Productions, and had finally found out a little more about what she was letting herself in for. The show was called *Can You Cut It?* and it was going to be a hairdressing competition with eight contestants, who would all have to live and work together.

The part that Issy immediately felt unsure about was living with seven strangers. Even when she'd lived in London she'd only had two flatmates and she wasn't sure how she'd cope living with so many other people. She had to keep reminding herself that the producers had also said that people would leave the competition every week – she might be one of the first to go so there was no point in getting ahead of herself. Issy was due to move into the apartment in five days and there was so much to think about and organise. The challenge made her feel alive but there were still so many unknown factors that she had to push to the back of her mind.

The production crew was coming to the salon tomorrow to film her introduction VT, which was why she and her mum were cleaning and tidying so thoroughly, and as she worked away Issy couldn't help but think she was setting herself up for a fall. She'd watched enough reality TV to know that people often made tits of themselves, which made for great TV, but she didn't want that to happen to her.

Her family was being supportive, pushy, proud – everything Issy knew they would be. Zach had told everyone that his kid sister was going to be the next Sam Faiers. Her mum was talking about getting 'Vote Issy' T-shirts printed even though they didn't know if there was any voting involved yet. Her father was simply proud of her for taking the leap he worried she would never take. And Molly had been around every day since Issy had got the call, going through Issy's wardrobe with a determination that would've made Victoria Beckham proud.

Issy watched her mum fondly as she refolded already perfectly folded towels. Issy owed her everything. She'd taught Issy her craft, and she'd shaped her into a woman with the confidence to follow her dreams. Issy had let that confidence slip away over the past few years but now she was being given a second chance. She was ready for it, she wanted to make her mum proud, to make them all proud, but at the same time she was still anxious about leaving her family again.

Deep down Issy knew they would be fine without her. Her dad had recovered and his decision to slow down at work showed that he was taking his health seriously. Her mum might be scatty but she was firmly in control when it came to their family. And Zach had always been content with his life. He'd been a good footballer when he was younger, he'd even had trials but he'd lacked the desire to push for more. He was now a popular man around town, a great mechanic, and the object of many crushes. He was happy. They were all happy.

It was time for Issy to get back out there. It was time for her to show the world what she was made of.

'Right, love, I think the TV people will be happy with the state of the place,' said Debs.

'It looks great, Mum. It always does.'

'Shall we go? Big day tomorrow.'

'God knows how I'm going to sleep.' They made their way to the front door. 'I'm going to miss working here.'

Debs put her arm around her daughter. 'We'll miss you too but you're doing the right thing. Time for you to chase that dream of yours, love.'

As Issy and her mum walked home in contented silence, Issy realised that Molly had been right. There was more to the world than biddies and blue rinses – and Issy was ready to find out exactly what that was.

Chapter Five

Issy couldn't keep still as her mum put the finishing touches to her hair and make-up.

'Issy, stay still or you'll end up blinded by eyeliner.'

'Sorry, Mum,' Issy felt almost drunk on adrenaline. Her mum stepped back, put the top back on the eyeliner and they both looked at her reflection in the mirror. Her long dark hair was glossy, her make-up strong but not overdone. She was wearing her work uniform of fitted black blouse and skirt, but instead of her usual ballet pumps she'd added a pair of four-inch heels she usually reserved for going out. The pain would be worth it her mum had reassured her, although that was easy for her mum to say – she had lived in heels for as long as Issy could remember, which meant that as well as being roughly as tall as a hobbit, she had the feet of one too. The rest of the family joked about Debs' feet but never to her face – she was far too sensitive about her height. At only 5 foot 2 she was the smallest member of the Jones family by far.

The atmosphere in the salon was buzzing with anticipation, and the imminent arrival of the TV crew had sent the place into a spin. Her mum was even more dolled up than usual. Anyone would think *she* was the star of the show. Princess was sitting regally on a new cushion on the waiting room sofa near the front desk. She was usually left to her own devices but today Alice had been charged with keeping an eye on her. The two other stylists, Karen and Brenda, were dolled up to the nines wearing the outfits they normally reserved for bingo at the social club, but they were also nervous about being filmed. Ironically, Issy was the calmest of them all and she was as jumpy as a box of frogs.

It was a Saturday so luckily Molly didn't have to work and could pretend to be Issy's client. Violet had turned up too, even though her last set had been a couple of days before, wearing a purple velvet dress that was probably her Sunday best, blue eyeshadow and bright pink lipstick. Vi had decided she could sit in the waiting area to make the salon look busy. She had said she was doing them a favour, but Issy suspected she couldn't wait for her moment in the spotlight. Between Vi and Princess, Issy felt pretty sorry for Alice.

Thankfully, the other clients hadn't had a problem when Issy had called them up to tell them there would be a TV crew in the salon that day. In fact, they'd been delighted. It wasn't just Vi who wanted their moment in the spotlight, it seemed.

Zach had been desperate to make an appearance but Debs had banned him and Kev because she thought it would look odd. Having Vi and a rat-sized ball of fluff sitting on a velvet cushion was perfectly normal for a salon apparently but not her dad and brother . . . Issy couldn't see her mum's logic so she made a last-ditch attempt to reason with her.

'Zach could have been having his weekly sunbed,' Issy pointed out.

'I'm not having his tanning habits revealed on national TV. It would give your dad another heart attack. And anyway, you know how Vi gets when he's around. One look at her horny little face and they'd probably pack up their cameras and leave thinking we're all a bunch of weirdos.'

'That's true,' Issy laughed. 'Although I'd love to get Vi's horny face on TV.'

'What do you mean Zach's tanning habits?' Molly asked.

'Really?' Issy turned to her friend. 'You think he's that colour naturally?' At that moment, the door opened and a swarm of people descended on the salon as if they owned the place. There were cameras and booms and bags of kit everywhere within seconds. Issy took a deep breath. *Here we go*, she thought.

Pandemonium didn't come close to describing the scene that followed.

'Issy, great to see you again.' Laura shook Issy's hand formally, smiling in that serious way of hers. She was in a hoodie and her long, thin legs were encased in skinny jeans ending in her customary scruffy Converse.

'Hi Laura, how are you?' Issy said, as the nerves began to ripple around her stomach again. She felt sick.

'Good. Now listen, don't be nervous.' Was it that obvious?

Clearly. 'We're going to film you doing your job, and then we'll talk to you.'

Danny appeared at Laura's side at the same moment as Debs joined the group.

'Hi, I'm Deborah, Issy's mum,' Debs introduced herself. Issy's mouth dropped open. *Deborah?* Her mum was talking like the Queen. Well, the Queen's slightly rougher sister from Salford.

'And I'm Violet. Pleased to meet you.' Vi leapt up and pushed her way past Issy, hand outstretched.

'Alice,' Debs shouted, still in her bizarre voice. 'Please take Violet to the waiting area.'

'Nice to meet you, Deborah. I'm Laura, the producer on the show. I'll be looking after your girl.'

'That's good to know, pleasure to meet you.' Debs smiled, and gave Laura an air kiss.

Issy nudged her. As Laura and Danny went back to talk with the rest of the crew, Issy hissed, 'Why are you talking like that? And what's with the Deborah?'

'Like what? I always talk like this. And that's my name!'

'No you don't. And you're called Debs. It's like you're trying to sound as if you're from Cheshire,' Vi shouted from across the salon.

'Oh, who put twenty pence in you?' Debs muttered.

'She's right though, Mum. You sound like a tit.' Before Debs could argue, Issy added, 'Please try to relax, Mum. They picked me for me – because of how you and Dad brought me up. And I can hardly be myself with you going on like you've got a Corgi instead of a Chihuahua, can I?!'

Princess growled from her cushion. Debs smiled at her

44

daughter. 'You're right, love. I'm sorry. I just – I just didn't want to let you down.' She clapped her hands to get the attention of the salon. 'OK, let's show these producers exactly what we're made of.'

Issy hugged her mum but not before seeing Vi pushing Princess off the cushion so she could sit on it herself. Issy shook her head. If she had been one of the TV show people, she'd be wondering what the hell they'd walked into.

Laura reappeared with a tall, slim but muscular man, with tousled blond hair and deep blue eyes.

'This is Ryan, one of our sound men. He'll mic you up. The two camera guys will be filming but please ignore them and focus on me, it'll be easier,' Laura told her.

'Hi, Issy,' Ryan smiled, displaying a mouth of even white teeth. In one of the mirrors Issy could see Molly behind them gawping open-mouthed at him. Issy tried to give Molly a 'stop staring' look, but Molly didn't notice.

'Hi, nice to meet you,' Issy said. He was pretty cute, in that chilled out, surfer kind of way. Not Issy's type though. She preferred men who were more groomed. The just-rolled-out-of-bed look wasn't really her thing.

'I'm Debs, pleasure to meet you.' Debs batted her big eyelashes. She was obviously as impressed as Molly was with the arrival of the sound man.

Perhaps this really was a mistake, after all, Issy thought. Princess was growling, and out of the corner of her eye Issy could see Vi trying to charm the camera man, and now her mum was putting a shift in with the sound guy. All they needed to finish off the image was Zach walking through the salon with nothing but a packet of teabags covering his modesty. What if the producers took one look at her life and decided they couldn't have her on the show? Either that or her mum was going to run off with Ryan the sound man and she'd have to explain that to her dad. At this point Issy wasn't sure which would be worse – or more likely.

The salon had gone too quiet. Issy glanced around. Brenda and Karen were rooted to the spot, staring at everything that was happening. Their clients sat mutely in the chairs. Alice was stood in between Princess and Vi, unsure which one she needed to control the most. No one was cutting any hair.

'Laura asked me to mic both of you up,' Ryan explained, producing two small mics wired to boxes. 'We need them to go under your blouses, and then we can clip these on the back of your skirts.'

'Oh how lovely,' Debs said, as she started to lift her blouse up.

'Bloody hell, Mum!' Issy turned red.

Ryan looked amused. 'Perhaps if you feed it up yourself and then I'll clip it?' he suggested. Issy tried to ignore the disappointed look on her mother's face.

'Sorry about all this,' Issy said to Ryan as he sorted out her mic.

'Don't be. This is the most fun one we've done so far,' he replied, and she noticed how his eyes crinkled when he smiled and instantly she felt more at ease.

Once they were all mic'ed up, Laura directed Issy to work on Molly's hair as normal, chatting to her while they filmed, then when they were at ease in front of the camera Laura left them to it. Another camera was trained on Debs who was sat at the reception desk with Princess clutched to her chest and Laura started asking her questions about Issy. Issy dreaded to think what she was saying, or *how* Her Highness was saying it. She attempted to tune it out and focus on the task at hand. Molly's hair.

'So, Molly, what are we doing today?' Issy asked, trying and failing to sound natural.

'Uh – uh – uh ...' Molly's eyes kept darting to the camera.

'Cut? Colour? Mohawk?' Issy teased.

'What?'

'Molly, what do you want me to do to your hair today?' Issy smiled.

'I – I – I ...' Molly looked upset and Issy wanted to kick herself. Molly's stammer was under control unless she was stressed and, of course, right now she had a TV camera pointed at her and a crew gawping at the screen. It hadn't occurred to Issy that these circumstances might set Molly off and she was annoyed with herself for it. How could she have let something that important slip her mind?

'Sorry, Mol. Shall we do a trim and blow dry today?' Issy hoped no one noticed her friend's discomfort.

'Yes, sounds great.' Molly smiled with relief and Issy gave her shoulder a small squeeze by way of apology.

At around one o'clock Laura suggested taking a break for lunch so the crew could get something to eat. Or rather, so they could tell Danny their order and he could go and fetch everyone's sandwiches. Alice was instructed to put the kettle on and Issy was sure she saw a look of solidarity pass between Alice and Danny. *Those two poor downtrodden youngsters should run off together, get married and have little runner babies together*, Issy thought with a smile.

'What's so funny?' Molly asked.

'I was thinking that Danny and Alice should run off together and leave everyone to get their own sandwiches and make their own bloody tea.'

'But then who would keep Vi in check?' Molly said.

'Not a job I'd want,' Ryan said, joining them.

'What?' Issy wondered how he heard.

'Your mics – I'm the sound man, I hear everything,' he said, sounding amused.

'Shit! I'll have to remember not to slag you off then, won't I?!' Issy retorted, a mischievous glint in her eye.

Ryan laughed. 'Yeah, you best not! It's a perk of my job. It's how I found out your mum thinks you look like a younger version of Angelina Jolie.'

'Oh shit. Tell me she didn't say that on camera?' Issy turned red.

'Yep, she did. And you do look a bit like her if you squint.' He laughed, and so did Molly. Loudly. 'Sorry, I'm only teasing. So how do you think it's going?'

'I don't know. It's all happened so fast. I'm worried I've been picked so that I can be the knob of the show.'

'Don't be silly. You're one of the most natural people we've filmed so far,' Ryan said kindly.

'Nothing natural about me,' Issy joked, flicking her extensions.

'I don't believe that,' Ryan said. 'Seriously though don't be worried. You're coming across great.'

'What are the other contestants like?' Issy hadn't planned to ask that question but curiosity had got the better of her.

'Well, I haven't met them all yet, but there are a couple who might be . . . interesting.' Ryan grinned.

'Tell me more! Please,' Issy demanded. She was suddenly desperate to know who she'd be spending the new few weeks with.

'I can't. More than my job's worth, but it will be a good show. If you want my advice, keep your head straight.'

'That's my plan. My dad would kill me if I did anything stupid,' Issy said, a little disappointed by Ryan's professionalism.

'Well, it is a competition, so be careful. Scissors at dawn and all that.'

'Eh?' Molly asked.

'You know, people want to win so watch your back.'

Before Issy could probe further, Ryan was summoned away by Laura. Issy watched him walk away, his words ringing in her ears. *Be careful.* What the hell had she signed up for?

'Issy, he is so fit,' Molly hissed, interrupting her thoughts.

'He's all right, not my type though,' Issy replied. Neither of them saw Ryan grinning where he stood. They'd already forgotten about the mics.

'Issy, you've been great. You too, Debs. Thank you for letting us disrupt your day,' Laura said.

Issy had spent the last two hours talking about herself, but finally, thankfully, they were finished. Good thing too as she was sick of the sound of her own voice. She'd had to answer questions as though no one had asked them. If she heard them say 'put the question in the answer' one more time she would pull her hair extensions out.

'It's not as easy as you think, talking about yourself,' Issy said.

'No, but you'll get used to it. In the house you'll be on camera the whole time,' Laura told her.

Issy hadn't realised they'd be filmed in the apartment too. She was going to have to start paying more attention. 'All the time? Sounds scary.' Understatement of the century.

'Don't worry. It will become second nature to you pretty quickly. Right, we'd better head off. Issy, I can't wait to see you in the house. You're going to be a real asset to the show.' She shook Issy's hand and started to round up the crew.

'What did she mean by that?' Issy asked Ryan who was standing nearby.

'Issy, relax. She only meant that she likes you and she wants you to do well,' Ryan replied before taking the mics off Issy and Debs, who continued to bat her eyelashes at him. 'Oh, and Issy, I hope there's a guy who is your type in the house,' Ryan said with a wink.

'What?' Issy said in confusion to his departing back.

'Well, that was quite the day.' Debs put her arms around her daughter.

'Hmmm. It feels a bit like a game I don't know the rules to.'

'Just do what feels right and you'll never go wrong. That's what your dad would say anyway.' Debs kissed Issy's cheek.

'True.' Issy looked over her mum's shoulder. 'Now, which one of us is going to wake Vi up?'

'You do the honours. I really hope they didn't get her snoring on camera.'

Chapter Six

As Issy got ready for her girls' night out, her mind was only half on applying her false eyelashes – the other half was still buzzing about the previous day's filming. It had gone pretty well, at least she thought so, excusing Vi's persistent and embarrassing cameo.

So tonight she was hitting Manchester with the girls as a combination leaving do and well done for getting on the show celebration before she had to move into the apartment with the rest of the cast. Issy knew she wouldn't be gone for long but she was going to miss her friends, especially Molly. They spent so much time together Zach often joked they were 'more than friends'. Really hilarious.

Issy stood still for a moment and looked around her bedroom. She'd always loved her room. It was cosy and girly and since she'd come back from London her mum and dad had redecorated it for her so it was a bit more grown up. Gone were the boyband posters and cuddly toys and in their place were framed photos and scatter cushions. There was one wall of red wallpaper but everything else was white, apart from the spot on the floor in front of the mirror where Issy did her make-up and regularly dropped her foundation, much to Debs' horror.

She had been happy in this room for years but it was time to leave and Issy knew that now. Her room, her scatter cushions, her foundation-stained carpet would always be there if she needed them – but it was time to see what else the world had to offer. Starting with Manchester city centre tonight. Feeling excited and positive, Issy went downstairs and walked into the living room where her parents were watching TV.

'Right guys, I'm away out.'

'You might want to put the rest of your outfit on first, love!' her dad said.

'What? You think it needs a necklace or something?' Issy joked back, eyes twinkling. She knew fine well what her dad was getting at.

'I meant some trousers, young lady!'

'Kev, leave her be. She looks lovely. Have fun, darling, and tell Molly we said hello.'

'Will do, Mum. Love you, bye!' Issy ran out of the front door and into her waiting taxi. She could still hear her mum and dad playfully bickering about her outfit choice until she closed the cab door. It was the same every week and every week Issy wore what she wanted – and every week poor Kev was outvoted. It had become more of a daft game than a serious reprimand and it was another one of the things Issy would miss.

Molly's house was just around the corner but Issy never walked it. If the truth be told her heels were too high for walking and her barely-there dress may look great but it didn't provide much respite from the bitter Northern evening air – although she'd never admit either of those things to her dad. Issy pulled up outside Molly's house and Issy could see her best friend's face at the front window. Within minutes, Molly was out of her house and next to Issy in the back of the taxi.

'Hey, wifey.' Molly looked down at Issy's feet. 'I have shoe envy! Are those your new Kurt Geigers?'

'Yep. Painful but beautiful,' said Issy, admiring them. 'So Luce has Whatsapp'd and said she and the others are heading straight to La Cubana.'

'Perfect.' Molly looked over at her. 'You ready for this? Your last night out with us?'

'I'll only be gone for a few weeks, I'm not disappearing for good!' Issy checked her face in her Stila compact. 'But it's as good a reason as any for a night out with my girls.'

Molly linked her arm through Issy's. 'I'm so happy for you. One reminder: tequila is not your friend – especially when there are cameras around.'

'How dare you? I never want to hear you saying anything like that about tequila again!' Issy laughed. 'It's going to be weird, living with strangers.'

'Are you nervous?'

'Yes. And excited. I'm not sure what I'm letting myself in for but I'm ready for this.'

*

La Cubana was a new Latin-themed bar that had opened up in Spinningfields a few months ago. Dimly lit with exposed brick walls and treated wood tables, it served twenty different kinds of tequila and all the barmen looked like Antonio Banderas's sons. Which was funny because Issy lived a couple of doors down from one of them – and she knew he was born and raised in Salford.

The rest of the girls were already there by the time they arrived and even though the bar was heaving it didn't take long to find them. They always attracted plenty of attention and tonight wasn't any different. Issy and Molly grabbed a couple of drinks before joining the group.

After all the hugs and congratulations and a round of tequilas, Issy felt herself relax properly for the first time in days. She hadn't realised how wound up she'd been feeling until now. Once she'd decided to go for it with the show, everything had happened so quickly and now she was finally able to enjoy what was happening to her. She couldn't wait to get started.

Two hours and a few more shots later, Issy felt like it was time to move on so they headed to Evissa, one of their favourite clubs. There was a queue but one of Zach's mates worked the door so he waved them straight in. They nodded to a few people they knew as they entered the club.

'Is Zach out tonight?' Molly asked.

'Nah, he had to work late so said he'll be out tomorrow night instead. The women of Manchester are safe until then. Come on, it's been at least ten minutes since I had a drink,' Issy said as they made their way to the bar.

As ever, it didn't take long to get served and then they snagged one of the corner booths. Lucy was in the middle of telling the girls about the date she'd been on the previous night when a group of lads came over and started chatting to them. One of them, Dean, singled Issy out. He was tall, had dark hair and green eyes. Issy wasn't really in the mood – tonight was all about the girls. But then again, a little flirting never killed anyone and he did have lovely eyes . . .

'Do you fancy a drink?' Dean asked.

'Sure. Gin and tonic, please.'

Dean disappeared with his friend who'd been talking to Molly, and Molly took his seat next to Issy.

'What do you think?' Issy asked.

'His name's Paul. He seems nice enough but he's not really my type.' Dean's friend was shorter than him with curly strawberry-blond hair. Molly liked tall, dark and hand-some.

'He's ginger, Mol!' laughed Issy. 'Nah, babe, I'm kidding. He's not that bad, is he?'

'Solid eights, I'd say,' Molly replied.

They were still talking about them when they reappeared with the drinks.

'So you girls having a good night?' Dean asked.

'Yeah. We've not been out long but I'm already tipsy and I've still got both of my eyelashes on so I'm calling it a suc-cess so far,' Issy joked.

'I bet it's perked up now you've met us,' Dean said.

'Are you having a laugh?' Issy hoped he was joking oth-erwise he was a total knob.

'Don't you know who we are?' Paul said with a frown.

Oh great, thought Issy. *You* are *both total knobs.*

'Er, no. Should we?' Molly sounded as unimpressed as Issy felt.

'Obviously you aren't football fans, then?' Paul said.

'My dad and brother are. They've always got it on the telly at ours, but I still don't recognise you,' Issy said matter-of-factly.

'Well, we really don't like to talk about it,' Paul said trying his best to look humble. He failed.

'Eh? You brought it up!' Molly exclaimed.

Issy couldn't control her giggling. Molly clearly wasn't a fan of this double act either.

'We play for Tranmere Rovers!' Dean ploughed on admirably.

'Tranmere Rovers? Calm it, Becks – if we'd known we would've asked for autographs,' Issy said.

The lads didn't seem to understand what was going on. And they certainly weren't aware that Issy and Molly were taking the mick out of them. Most girls were obviously impressed by Tranmere Rovers.

'So do you fancy getting out of here? We've got an apartment near Deansgate Lock, and a bottle of Disaronno.' Paul looked hopeful.

That was it for Issy and Molly. Neither could keep a straight face any longer and collapsed into fits of giggles. It was time to put these lads out of their misery.

'Sorry, lads. Thanks for the drinks and it was, ahem, lovely to meet you but we're out with the girls tonight.' *Let them down gently*, Issy thought.

'What? So you're not coming back with us?' Dean looked confused and Issy decided this must be his permanent expression.

'It's a no from us, I'm afraid.' Molly tried to look serious while doing her best Simon Cowell expression.

'Didn't you hear about the Disaronno?' Paul was sounding desperate but Issy had had enough.

'Listen, you two. We tried to be nice but you're not getting the message. I don't care if you play for Manchester United and you have a whole brewery in your living room. We said we're out with the girls, so jog on!'

As she finished, the rest of the booth burst into applause and laughter. Unbeknownst to them, their little exchange had attracted a bit of attention. Paul and Dean, the twatful twosome, seemed to finally get the hint but they weren't going to let Issy have the last word.

'Slags!' Dean spluttered in his rush to get away.

'Yeah, yeah. Go back to your Disaronno!' Molly shouted. She turned to Issy. 'I need another shot after those two helmets. Don't you, mate?'

Issy put her arm around her friend and they headed to the bar. As Molly leaned across the bar trying to get the barman's attention, Issy smiled to herself. It was moments and nights like this with her best mates that she would miss while she was filming. She was feeling slightly emotional – though she knew some of that would be down to the tequila. When she was in London, she and Molly had still managed to spend most weekends together but now it could be a couple of months before they got to see each other properly. As her eyes twinkled with a mixture of tequila and tears, she grabbed a surprised Molly and gave her a big bear hug.

A knock on the bedroom door woke Issy with a start. Her head was banging and her eyes didn't want to open. She felt something crawling on her cheek and flicked it off in a panic, then relaxed when she realised it was just one of her eyelashes. She was still wearing one shoe. God, how much had they drunk? Her bedroom smelt vaguely of cheesy chips but predominantly of garlic mayo. She prised her eyes open and looked at the other side of her bed where Molly was still snoring. She was wearing a packet of Monster Munch on her hand like a mitten.

'Molleeeeeeeeeeeeeeee,' Issy croaked out and shook her until Molly sat up, startled.

'Where the hell am I?'

'My bed.'

'Oh, that's a relief.' Molly scratched at her face with her Monster Munch-encased hand. Discovering a lone one in the bottom of the packet, she pulled it out and put it in her mouth.

'Mate. That's disgusting!'

'They're pickled onion. My favourite,' Molly replied indignantly.

'Uggh, Molly, I feel like death. My head is banging and my mouth tastes like arse.'

'Yeah, I hate my life,' Molly concurred.

There was another knock at the door.

'Yeah?' Issy called out.

'It's Zach, are you guys decent?'

'No!' they both screamed at once.

Chapter Seven

The biggest suitcase that the Joneses owned was lying on Issy's parents' bed. Molly and her mum were trying to help Issy pack. Her dad and Zach had disappeared to the pub and Princess had been banished after she kept climbing into the suitcase.

Issy had spent two days shopping in Manchester. She'd raided The Trafford Centre, picking up skater dresses, skinny jeans, printed blouses and various tees. She had treated herself to some House of CB bandage dresses, and had even bought a jumpsuit for nights out. She'd also piled five pairs of stilettos, two pairs of Kurt Geiger platforms, a pair of courts from Topshop, some River Island Chelsea boots and her Converse for casual, although she wasn't expecting to be that casual on camera.

Packing was proving impossible. Issy had no idea what she'd need and so she was taking something for every occasion. She hadn't even started thinking about putting together her make-up and hairdressing kit yet, and she was already stressed to death. She hated packing. The Prosecco was helping, mind. They had got through a bottle and a half in the past two hours.

'I literally have *nothing* to wear,' Issy wailed, carrying an armful of dresses.

'Calm down,' Debs said. 'You have more dresses than The Saturdays. You just need to get organised.'

'What about this?' Issy asked, holding up her favourite midi skirt.

'Definitely,' Molly said. 'Pack that stripy co-ord too. The black and white one.'

'I like you in that tea dress as well,' Debs said. 'The tartan one.'

After an hour, with a bit of organisation and with the rest of the Prosecco, Issy was finally packed. Debs and Issy sat on the suitcase while Molly tried to get it closed, but Debs kept sliding off and Issy couldn't stop laughing.

'Let's wait for Dad and Zach to get back,' Issy said in the end, admitting defeat.

'I'm knackered,' Molly added.

'Let's go downstairs and have some more bubbles then,' Debs suggested. 'I've got some Pringles in the cupboard. I'm starving.'

'It still doesn't feel real,' Issy said once they were settled in the living room. 'This time tomorrow I'll be in a flat I've never seen with a bunch of strangers. And people will know who I am.' Although she had never wanted to be famous, that was now a real possibility. It was starting to dawn on Issy that though the public might love her, they could just as easily hate her. At least she'd have the chance to show off her hairdressing skills but even then, what if she panicked and fucked up – on national TV? Bollocks.

'If I mess up on TV, will you still love me?' Issy grabbed Molly's hand and pretended to cry.

'Nope.' Molly took her hand back and sipped her drink. 'I'll be like Issy who?'

'And I'll change the locks,' Debs said, joining in.

They heard a key in the front door and moments later Kev and Zach walked into the living room.

'Please tell me we missed the packing,' Zach said.

'Yeah but we need you two to get the case closed and Zach you'll have to carry it downstairs.'

'Why me?' Zach asked indignantly.

'Because you're fit,' Molly said, turning red. 'I ma–ma–mean . . . I meant strong!'

'Have you three been drinking?!' said Kev.

Debs pointed her finger at Kev. 'No,' she almost yelled. 'You've been drinking!'

'Oh God,' said Kev. 'Come and give me a hand with the case, son. These three are about as much use as a chocolate teapot.'

'Zach! Before you go upstairs, bring us in the cocktail sausages from the fridge. And see if there are any of those mini scotch eggs.' The Prosecco munchies were kicking in and Issy was keen to make a night of it.

'Molly, are you staying over?' Kev asked as they made their way back into the living room having dragged Issy's bulging case and bags into the hallway.

'Please do, Mol,' Issy implored.

'Sorry Issy, I'd love to but I've got to get back. I've got such an early start tomorrow – I have to set up a new project for the kids before they arrive at school.'

'Oh, of course, hon.' Issy was disappointed but tried to hide it; she didn't feel ready to say bye to Molly yet. 'I'm going to miss you.' Issy felt a wave of emotion at the thought of not being able to see her every day.

'You're going to be fantastic, Issy. Promise you won't forget us.'

'Don't be daft.' They stood up and both stared at the luggage that took up almost the entire hallway, before enveloping each other in a huge hug.

'She's only going to Manchester for a few weeks, not Australia. Women.' Zach shook his head.

'Zach,' Debs said, 'take Molly home will you, it's late.'

'It's only round the corner. I'll be all right,' Molly protested.

'Nah, I'll take you, come on.'

Issy was on the verge of tears as she hugged Molly goodbye again.

'I'm so proud of you,' Molly said into Issy's hair. 'You're the best friend a girl could ask for and a brilliant person, and now everyone gets to see that.'

'I really hope I don't mess this up, Mol.'

'You won't. But if you do, come home and I'll get you so drunk that you'll forget all about it.'

'You are the perfect friend. I love your face.'

'Love yours too. And soon the whole country is going to

get to love it as well.' Molly paused and looked at Issy. 'God, we're pissed.'

The two friends laughed and hugged. As Issy closed the front door behind Molly, she couldn't help but think her whole life was about to change.

Chapter Eight

Issy had been tossing and turning all night. One minute she'd been too excited to sleep, and the next she'd felt sure she was making a mistake. In the cold light of day, she'd given herself a stern talking to. This was the decision she'd made and it was the right one for her and her future, she was sure of it. She still had to fight the urge to bite her nails in a way she hadn't for years but the minute she'd got up, got dressed and slipped on her nude court shoes, she'd immediately felt more confident.

Now, with the car the production company had sent waiting and her family ready to see her off, Issy felt a flutter of excitement in her stomach.

'Love, you'll do us proud,' Debs said, grabbing her for a warm motherly cuddle and kiss.

'You'll get there and you'll love it. Remember to be yourself and if you don't like it then you can always leave,' Kev said, enveloping her in a bear hug. 'We're behind you, no matter what happens.'

'Try to last until at least the third week, yeah? Then I can live off your fame for a bit. Oh, and if there are any fit girls on the show, invite us round.' Zach looked bleary-eyed; seven a.m. was too early for him. Issy gave her brother a kiss on his cheek, and he grabbed her and squeezed her. 'Love you, little sis,' he said quietly.

They herded Issy into the car and the last thing she saw before going round the corner was each one of them grinning and wildly waving her off.

The driver told Issy that there was an information pack for her on the back seat. She picked it up and read through it, grateful for the distraction.

The show was being filmed in a disused office building that had been renovated for *Can You Cut It?*. The salon was state of the art and would be downstairs, and the contestants would live together upstairs in the converted apartment. The revolutionary aspect of *Can You Cut It?* was that it would be aired almost as soon as it was filmed, which meant that editing and production would be working non-stop. They wanted it to be cutting edge – *pun fully intended*, Issy thought – and to stand apart from some of the newer reality shows that weren't aired until the whole series had been filmed.

Issy was a smart girl and she knew that the show needed to get decent ratings for it to be a success. She thought of all the reality TV she watched and loved and wondered if people out there would adore their show in the same way.

Their show, Issy thought. *This is ours*. An unexpected shiver of excitement ran down her spine. This was actually happening.

The driver stopped outside a large building in the centre of Manchester. This was the building where Issy was going to spend the next six weeks – hopefully. The side door opened and Danny emerged. She couldn't believe how happy she was to see a familiar face. She hugged him and he took a step backwards, his face red.

'Hi Issy,' he said, clearly overwhelmed by her warm greeting.

'Hiya, Danny. You all right?' Danny nodded in response, still getting over her enthusiasm, Issy assumed. The door opened again and Laura and Ryan came out.

'Issy, how are you?' Laura asked.

'Excited. Nervous. I have no idea what's happening. Where's Harry?' Issy stopped herself as she could feel she was starting to ramble.

'Harry won't be around on the set, so you won't be seeing so much of him anymore – he stays behind the scenes. You look great, by the way.' Laura gave her hand a squeeze.

'Hey, Issy,' Ryan said, looking as if he had just fallen out of bed again.

'Hey,' she replied. 'Overhear anything good lately?'

Ryan held his hands up. 'As if I'd do anything like that.'

'Ryan will mic you up and then we'll film you arriving in the house and meeting the others,' Laura said, all business. 'Don't worry, they're not all terrifying.' And with that, she left.

'What did she mean by that?' Issy asked, as Ryan helped her fix her mic. It was harder than last time as she was all fingers and thumbs. He put his hands on her shoulders and steadied her.

'Issy, breathe. Laura said that to see how you'll react. Not everyone has arrived yet but the contestants that I have met all seem, well, pretty normal.' Issy raised an eyebrow at him as he continued. 'I'll be here. If you do start to feel a bit shaky, mutter a code word into your mic and I'll come and rescue you.'

'A code word?'

'Yeah, say "badger" or something like that.'

Issy laughed.

'Seriously, Issy,' Ryan continued. 'You're going to be fine.'

'Don't worry, I'll be OK. No "badger" necessary.' Issy smiled up at him. 'But thank you.'

Once Issy was set up with her mic and they'd checked it was working, Laura reappeared with a cameraman in tow.

'OK, Issy. This is it. You ready?'

Issy took a deep breath. 'As I'll ever be.'

Issy pushed open the door and walked into the apartment. It was light and airy and open plan. The living area looked cosy with bright scatter cushions, L-shaped sofas and squishy bean bag chairs. There were wood floors throughout and the walls were exposed brick but Issy loved the neon signs which had clearly been specially commissioned to give random flashes of colour and added a bit of personality to the house.

She didn't have time to take in any more of her surroundings because the next thing she knew she was being greeted by one of the most striking women she'd ever seen. She had short, pale lilac hair, dramatically swept over to one side. *She looks like Agyness Deyn*, thought Issy. She wore thick-framed glasses, a black tunic and heavy black boots. There was a beautiful and elaborate tattoo on her forearm.

'Hi, I'm Lexi.'

'Hiya, I'm Isabelle but you can call me Issy.'

'Good to meet you.' Lexi gestured towards the girl and the boy who were approaching them. 'This is Steph, and that's Tim. Do you fancy a drink? We've cracked open the wine.'

'Oh God, yeah. Thanks.' As Lexi walked off to grab her a glass, Issy turned her attention to the other two contestants. 'Hey,' she said, smiling warmly at them. 'You's OK? What have I missed?'

As Issy sipped her wine and they exchanged stilted greetings and chat about how great the house was she studied her three new housemates. Lexi was effortlessly cool and Issy instantly warmed to her. Tim was shorter than Lexi with messy black hair. He looked nervous and was far quieter than the girls. The third housemate, Steph, was from Edinburgh. She was a bit shorter than Issy, with a longish blonde bob. She looked almost as uncomfortable as Tim.

Issy was a bit surprised. Aside from Lexi, the other two didn't look like hair stylists at all. But she couldn't ponder it for too long because the door swung open again and in walked the next housemate.

Well, hello sailor! Issy thought. *This is definitely more like it.* The guy approaching was tall, fit, with naturally blond hair and a sun-kissed glow. He looked like an Abercrombie & Fitch model.

The beautiful man crossed the room in a couple of strides and before Issy had a chance to regain her composure, he was introducing himself.

'Hi, I'm Jason. I can't believe I'm here, this is mad. Are you all shitting yourselves as much as I am?' He had a thick Liverpudlian accent.

Lexi whispered into Issy's ear, 'He looks like he's carved by angels.' Issy couldn't help but laugh. She wasn't wrong.

'It's all a bit ... well a bit ... ' Tim trailed off. Issy wondered how the hell he'd managed to get on the show. He couldn't even string a sentence together, poor kid. He was going to get eaten alive.

'Hey, everyone. What's happenin'? I'm Aaron Yates,' an enthusiastic voice said, and they turned to see a young-looking lad, very slim, with a pierced lip and eyebrow, short dark hair and very tight jeans standing in front of them. 'Oh my God, this is amazing. I can't believe I'm here!' He flung his arms out and gave a theatrical twirl.

Aaron was a breath of fresh air. His energy was infectious and suddenly the atmosphere lifted. *This is going to be fun*, thought Issy, relieved.

'This is nuts. We've all agreed to be on a show that we know nothing about. How stupid are we?' Aaron continued gleefully.

Issy didn't know whether it was nerves or excitement or the second glass of wine, but she was starting to feel giddy. Her dad would be mortified – she made a mental note never to bring this moment up with him – *Joneses can handle their drink*, she could almost hear him saying and Zach would have her life for being a lightweight if he knew. *Best keep this one to myself*, she thought.

Half an hour later they were all finally getting into the swing of things. Nerves were dissipating, drinks were flowing and the banter was starting to feel more natural. Issy, not for the first time, thanked God for alcohol.

They were all sitting on the sofas and beanbags, chatting and getting to know each other, when Issy heard the door open again. They all turned to see a girl walk through the door. She was tall, blonde, thin, and all limbs. She reminded Issy of a baby giraffe. As she got closer Issy could see she had a slightly horsey face with a long thin nose. She was wearing a short cream dress and jacket, with pearls around her neck and a Chanel handbag hooked over her arm. The bloke next to her was wearing sunglasses, jeans, a plain grey T-shirt, and a big grin. He looked older than the rest of them.

'Wahey! New arrivals!' Aaron yelled.

'Christ, mate, you're hyper,' Jason laughed.

'So c'mon, who do we have here?' Lexi asked.

'Amelia Goodhill-Smythe,' announced the baby giraffe. 'But you can call me Mia.'

'Very kind of you,' Lexi said in her best *Made in Chelsea* voice.

Lexi pulled it off better than Issy's mum but Issy still had to stifle a giggle as people started filtering over to introduce themselves. It was blatantly obvious that Amelia wasn't coming to them. So one by one the group slowly gravitated around her and the other new arrival.

'Hi everyone, I'm Rory. Can someone get us a drink? I'm hungover as fuck.'

'That'll explain the shades, mate. Top bants.' Jason walked over to Rory and they slapped hands in a show of masculine solidarity. A bromance had been born.

Steph walked over and handed Rory a bottle of Corona. 'You might want to watch your language on TV,' she offered, looking genuinely concerned.

'Fuck off!' Rory roared with laughter and the rest of the group followed suit. The ice was well and truly broken.

And with that, their group was complete.

Rory was from Essex and a proper lad. It only took half an hour and he and Jason were getting on like a house on fire, already chatting about football and 'birds'. Issy was drawn to Aaron and Lexi who seemed fun and up for a laugh. But Steph and Tim were trapped – Amelia Goodhill-Smythe was holding court on one of the sofas, talking *at* them. Issy felt a twinge of sympathy and wondered if she should save them from what looked like a pretty shit conversation.

'It's not healthy. I don't eat carbs, dairy, or processed food,' Issy heard Mia explain to Steph and Tim.

'What's that you're talking about?' Issy said, leaving her conversation with Aaron and Lexi and walking over to join them.

'I'm a vegan,' Mia said by way of explanation.

'Are you? I'm a Leo,' Rory called over.

Mia snorted. 'Very funny,' she said disdainfully while the rest of the room laughed. Issy was really starting to like Rory.

As if she could read her mind, Lexi came over to Issy's side and whispered, 'I suggest we put Dairylea in madam's toothpaste. I bet Mrs Vegan Vag won't like that, will she?' Mia had already gone back to lecturing poor Steph and Tim about clean living.

Issy burst out laughing. Aaron joined them.

'You's two better not be bitching without us, mind,' he said.

'It's not me, it's *her*!' Issy laughed. She lowered her voice. 'We're talking about Mia and her *dietary* requirements.'

'Eugh. I can tell I'm not going to be a fan,' said Aaron. 'She's a knob.' And the three of them fell about laughing.

Mia broke off again from her monologue and shot them a suspicious look. 'What are you three giggling about?'

'Spread cheese,' Lexi said.

'Oh,' said Mia and wrinkled her nose. 'Classy.'

'I like Philadelphia,' Tim offered. And that set them off again.

Drawn by the laughter, Jason and Rory joined them and they all settled onto the sofas.

'So where you from, Is? Is that a Manc accent I can hear?' Jason said.

Issy smiled. 'I'm from Salford, babe.'

'Where *is* Salford?' Mia demanded, her blue eyes narrowing. Her nose really was incredibly long. Issy tried to stop herself from staring at it, but it was too much to ignore.

'Just down the road,' Issy replied.

'That explains a lot,' Mia sneered down her long, annoying nose. For a moment, Issy was shocked and then she recovered herself.

'*What* did you say?'

Before anything could escalate, Lexi thankfully jumped in.

'You done any training, Issy?' she asked.

Issy was grateful for the distraction. The last thing she wanted was to start kicking off on her first day, but that Amelia 'call me Mia' was winding her up already.

'Yeah, I was at The Hair Academy in London.'

'Were you?' Lexi said with a smile. 'Go on, girl.' Lexi looked at Mia and smiled, and then shot Issy a sympathetic look.

'I'm here really because my career hasn't gone like I planned,' Lexi said. 'I work in a lovely salon in Maidstone, but I don't really feel like I'm going anywhere. I thought this could shake things up a little bit.'

'The Hair Academy?' Mia snapped, talking over Lexi. 'Personally I don't believe in places like that. You learn by doing. I work under the world famous Florentine Augustus.'

'Really?' Jason said awestruck. 'Florentine is such a ledge!'

Florentine was a successful hairdresser based in London who only did the hair of A-list celebrities, supermodels and certain, more stylish members of the royal family. For the first time, Issy couldn't deny that she was impressed. Mia already worked in one of the top salons in the country. Could she really compete with that?

'She's a close friend of the family. It means I get to meet the royals, people with titles and only the most serious A-listers. Kate and Pippa are always popping in.'

'Oooh, first name terms. You bessies?' Aaron said.

Mia shot Aaron a filthy look.

'Pippa's got a wicked arse,' Rory said, lightening the mood.

'You're not wrong there,' Jason said. 'So Mia, if you're already working under Flo, hobnobbing with the Middletons and the like, what you doing on this show?'

'I want to share my talent with the world,' Mia said, flashing a dazzling smile in Jason's direction. Issy was reminded of those cheesy American pageants where the dim wannabe beauty queens were asked what they wanted more than anything and always answered with 'world peace'.

A couple of the housemates started laughing but it quickly tailed off when it was clear that Mia was serious. After that, they sat in awkward silence for a while. Amelia and her shit craic had killed the mood.

Three bottles of wine and half a crate of Coronas later and Issy had learnt that Jason mainly cut footballers' hair but was cagey about which ones. Rory was a traditional barber from Essex who wouldn't know the difference between a Hollywood A-lister and a *Geordie Shore* cast member. He thought the show would improve his chances with the girls. Issy liked him – he was a proper Jack the Lad. The girls watching the show would love him. Tim worked in a Bristol salon and Steph in a small place in Edinburgh but neither of them said much more than that. Steph's boss had encouraged her to enter the show, thinking it might increase her confidence. Issy wasn't so sure but she was a nice girl. Aaron was similar to Lexi – he worked for a big chain in London but wanted to do something a bit more creative with his career.

Issy was buzzing. It had been so long since she'd been around like-minded people with ambition and drive and stories to tell. She knew she was in the right place and she finally felt truly thankful that her dad had spotted that ad in the local paper.

The sound of the door opening pulled Issy out of her daydream and back into the present. Laura walked into the apartment.

'Hi everyone. Looks like you're settling in and getting to know one another, which is great. But please remember to act like the cameras aren't here.'

A jolt went through Issy as it dawned on her that she *had* completely forgotten about the cameras. She'd been enjoying herself so much, chatting to everyone and listening to their stories, that the cameras had completely slipped her mind. *I bet that half bottle of zinfandel hadn't helped either*, Issy scolded herself.

Laura continued, 'I know we've thrown you in at the deep end, and I'm sure you've already got loads of questions for us, so I'll let you know what is going to happen next. We've cut the cameras for a while to reset and then we're going to bring in the judges.'

A frisson of excitement went through the housemates. Lexi did an excited little clap, Steph went pale and Rory and Jason high-fived each other, muttering something about how they hoped at least one of judges was fit.

'Once we've done the scene with the judges,' Laura carried on, 'you'll be taken off for individual interviews or "vox pops". The VPs can be quite a long process but once everyone's finished, we'll take a step back again and leave you guys in peace. But don't forget that the cameras will still be rolling. Be yourselves. We want you to relax, have fun, get to know each other and enjoy your first night in your new home.'

Before she walked away, Laura addressed the cast in earnest. 'I know you're all excited and probably dying to get smashed. I can see a couple of you are already on your way.'

Is she talking about me? thought Issy. *Shit, I bet my face is bright red. It always goes bright red when I drink.*

'But this is still a competition, you lot, and you're going to be set your first challenge tomorrow. However, no one will be leaving the show until the second episode – we want to give the public a chance to get to know you and see your work before people start getting eliminated from the competition.'

'Well, if no one's leaving this week, surely we can get as pissed as we want?' Rory said.

Laura smiled at Rory. 'I knew you were going to be trouble, Mr Mundy.' Laura paused, making sure she had everyone's full attention. 'There might not be anyone leaving this week, but after that, one person will be leaving each week. No exceptions.' She looked pointedly at Rory, and Issy thought she saw his Adam's apple quiver. 'Now, as well as our two permanent judges, there will be a celebrity guest judge each week and half the vote will be down to the three of them. The other half will be based on public opinion on social media. Try to keep that in mind for as long as you're on the show. But the most exciting part of this entire experience is that the final three will take part in a completely live challenge, which will be the climax of the competition.

Everything from now until then is designed to create momentum towards the live final – that's what you should all be aiming for.' Laura looked at them intensely. There was a still silence in the room as Laura's words sank in. Issy was practically buzzing with excitement and it hit her for the first time that this was really happening.

'We're bringing a whole different concept to reality TV and you're all going to play a huge part in making sure it's a success.' Issy noticed that all the colour had drained from Steph's face. *She looks terrified*, Issy thought sympathetically. 'There are other rules you need to know about but you'll find those in the welcome pack waiting for you on the coffee table. Does anyone have any questions?' They all shook their heads. 'OK, good. In that case, I'm going to disappear. The cameras will roll again, and you'll be introduced to your judges shortly.'

With that, Laura exited the apartment quickly, leaving the cast to speculate who their judges would be.

'Fuck me, that was intense,' Rory said.

'I know, right?' Aaron said. 'I wonder who the judges are.'

'I already know who one of them is going to be,' Mia said.

'How?' snapped Lexi.

'Florentine is good friends with one of the judges,' Mia explained breezily.

'Tell everyone else then,' said Aaron.

Mia tutted like a schoolteacher. 'Patience is a virtue. You'll find out soon enough.'

Issy turned to Lexi and said quietly, 'She really is warming my piss.'

Just then the door opened and in walked one of the most beautiful humans Issy had ever seen in her life.

'Hi, everyone. I'm Eva Whitman,' the famous American supermodel said in her soft southern drawl. She was stunning, with her long wavy golden hair, beautiful green eyes and a figure straight from a Victoria's Secret catwalk. Issy had never been this close to someone so famous, and especially not someone she idolised. Rory whistled appreciatively. Even Tim managed a smile.

In the excitement of Eva's entrance, no one had even noticed the tubby, toadlike figure next to her. He cleared his throat.

'I know I need no introduction, but I'm Alexander Fox, the world famous hairdresser.'

'Who?' Steph whispered to Issy. Issy shook her head discretely. Now wasn't the time.

Issy knew the name even if she didn't know the face. Alexander Fox owned a chain of expensive salons called The Fox's Den, where they served you champagne and fancy coffees with tiny little biscuits – not a Hobnob in sight – while making you overpay for basic haircuts. His client list was more footballers' wives and glamour models than A-listers but he was very well-known in certain circles. The contestants continued clapping although Issy felt it was with far less enthusiasm than they had for Eva. *Is he pouting?* Issy thought. Alexander moved so that he was standing in front of Eva, partially obscuring her. She stepped to the side so she was next to him once more. *Definitely pouting*, Issy thought. *What a wanker.*

'You are all very lucky to be here,' Alexander said.

Loudly. 'I'm one of the top hairdressers in the country and over the next few weeks you'll get the benefit of my expertise. I'm delighted to welcome you on the show and I'm *thrilled* to tell you that the winner of this show will get ... '

Alexander paused for dramatic effect.

'The winner of this show will get to run one of my salons.'

Is that it? Issy thought.

Alexander carried on, 'You will be completely responsible for the running of one of my prestigious salons, which is pretty much every hairdresser's dream.' Issy wondered how she would cope if she won. She wasn't sure she wanted to work for this man. It certainly hadn't been *her* dream.

'And in addition,' Eva said with a warm smile, 'the winner will also get to launch their own line of haircare products in conjunction with me. It will be a fully collaborative process and we'll work closely together on everything from business strategy to marketing to campaign management, but it's important to remember that although I'll be helping you, it will be *your* range.'

OK, Issy thought. *I'm back in the room. Now* that's *a prize.*

'We're also here,' Eva continued, 'to give you your scissors.'

Well I managed to pack them, thought Issy, *it's not like I'm a total idiot.*

But then she looked to where Eva was pointing in the kitchen and saw what they'd been resetting for. On the table were eight boxes which the contestants all rushed over to. Each was labelled and inside was a pair of gold-plated Kasho scissors, engraved with their names. Issy picked hers out of the box and gazed at them. She'd been saving for a pair for ages.

'As you know,' Alexander said as they were all exclaiming over the scissors, 'these are the very best in hairdressing. They're the only brand I allow my stylists to use, but only the winner will be able to keep their scissors – at the end of each show the person who is voted off will have to hand their scissors in.' Alexander looked almost pleased at the prospect.

'So good luck, everyone. Get a good night's sleep tonight because it all starts tomorrow!' Eva said, cutting Alexander off.

'Yes,' Alexander added, looking pouty again. 'I was going to say good luck. May the best scissors win.' He laughed so hard at his own joke that Issy could see his pink stomach wobble through his tight, sheer, white shirt, and she cringed.

Chapter Nine

After the judges left, Laura took them, one by one, into a room where they were asked to talk about their first impressions of one another, the show and the judges. Rory was the quickest, Tim was gone the longest and Issy was somewhere in the middle. She was genuinely looking forward to working with Eva and she hoped that came across on camera. She tried to stay off the subject of Mia. There was being honest and then there was coming across like a moany cow. Issy had decided to hope Mia's stuck-up ways were down to nerves.

Now that the interviews were out of the way and they'd met the judges, Issy was dying to have a proper look around the apartment. They'd been asked to stick to the main living area initially while their suitcases were brought up – Issy figured that hers was probably taking them longer than they'd banked on – and Laura had finally given them free reign to explore. The apartment seemed like a decent size but was it big enough for eight people? Probably not. *We're going to get under each other's feet*, Issy thought. *We might start rowing.* But then all thoughts left her head when she noticed the giant bubblegum machine in the corner by the stairs to the mezzanine-style bedrooms.

'Have you fucking seen this?!' Rory yelled, pointing at the watercooler that they had just realised was filled with Jägermeister. Jason was already lying underneath it and Rory flicked on the tap. 'Oh my God! This place is amazing!'

'Guys,' Lexi called out. 'Come and see the bedrooms.'

They all excitedly ran upstairs to the bedrooms. There were only two. The one on the left looked as though its previous inhabitants had been a family of Care Bears, all pinks and purples and fluffy cushions. *A bit overkill*, Issy thought, *this must be the girls' room. Subtle.* The room across the hall was a stark contrast to the girls' room and clearly intended for the boys. It was all different shades of blue and had one of those novelty washing baskets with the tiny little basketball hoops over the top – Zach had the same at home. The lads' reaction was priceless; they were screaming like schoolgirls and ripping off random socks to see who could get the first slamdunk. Both rooms had two sets of bunks – but not your average bunk beds. These bunk beds had swag. Each bunk had a queen-sized mattress and as well as a ladder, there was a slide.

While the rest of them were exploring their new bedrooms and choosing who they were going to bunk with – it was a no brainer for Issy, it had to be Lexi – Steph walked up the stairs with Tim and Mia holding the welcome pack.

'It says here in the welcome pack that there's one room for boys, and one room for girls,' Steph said.

'No shit, Sherlock,' Aaron shouted from one of the top bunks in the boys' room.

Issy laughed. 'What else does it say, Steph?'

'There's a room that's off limits to us.'

'Now you're talking!' Jason said. 'What's in it?'

'It's the production room, and apparently that's where all the cameras are and there will always be a member of the crew in there if we need anything,' Steph said as she scanned through the welcome pack. 'And there's another room with a "confession cam" in,' she continued with a puzzled expression. She began to read directly from the pack. '"The confession cam will be open to housemates 24/7. Confession cam is the perfect place to go to vent, to get things off your chest or have some banter with the camera, one on one. Please use this room as much as you like."'

'It's like the diary room in *Big Brother*,' Issy said.

'I'm gonna be all over that like a tramp on chips,' Jason said.

Lexi caught Issy's eye. 'Bunk buddies?'

'Do you even have to ask?' Issy said with a smile.

'If they think I am sleeping in a *bunk bed*,' Mia said the word like it had peed in her stilettos, 'they can think again,' and she flounced straight off to the confession cam.

'She's one stuck up princess,' Rory said. 'Probably needs a good shag. I might offer her my services,' he said, laughing at his own joke.

Without really thinking about it, Issy scrambled onto the top bunk, wondering if there was any way of getting into bed elegantly or if her arse would be in the air for the next few weeks, and Lexi flopped onto the bottom one.

Steph hovered near the door, obviously unsure about whether to take the remaining bottom or top bunk for herself.

'Steph, pick a bed, don't worry about her majesty,' Issy said, hoping she didn't sound bitchy because she didn't mean to. It was clear that Mia was a drama queen, and if there was one thing Issy didn't have time for, it was drama queens.

'She'll probably refuse to sleep in here anyway,' Lexi said.

'OK, but, well, if she wants the bottom bunk I can always move,' Steph said as Mia reappeared.

'There *is* another room, which has a double bed. I think they designed it in case any of the contestants want to shag.' Mia pulled a face. 'I have told the producers that I am going to be sleeping in there, and no one can stop me.' With that, she flounced out. Again. She loved a flounce. *I don't think I've ever flounced*, thought Issy. *I'd probably fall over.*

'She's getting on my tits. I hope she's not going to be this annoying the entire time. I'm pleased she's not in our room though. I'd rather go for a colonic than share a room with that pillock,' Lexi said.

Issy howled with laughter and Steph let out a giggle, although she clapped her hand over her mouth immediately afterwards as if to stop any more escaping. *#GiggleFreeZone* thought Issy, which only made her laugh harder.

'Right, enough about her,' Lexi declared. 'Let's talk about the important stuff. Who do you fancy?!'

Issy glanced towards the door to make sure the lads were still pre-occupied before she answered. Tim had drifted off to join them in the boy's room and was sitting uncomfortably on the edge of one of the bottom bunks. 'Jason's pretty fit,' Issy said.

'You think?' Lexi said, screwing up her face. 'He's not really my type. In an ideal world, I'd like a cross between Rory's looks and Aaron's personality. It's a shame Aaron's gay.'

'Is he?' asked Steph, wide-eyed. Issy and Lexi exchanged amused glances.

'I think so,' Issy said kindly. Steph was ridiculously naive ... Once again Issy thought how it was going to be an interesting six weeks. She hoped Steph lasted long enough in the competition to gain some confidence.

A little while later, and they were all chilling in the living area.

Rory opened the fridge. 'Who wants a drink?' he said, pulling out bottles and cans.

'I think I've already had enough,' Tim said, looking uncertain.

'Pusssssssssssaaaaaaaaay,' Rory yelled, waving his arms in the air.

'I'm up for a bevvie,' Jason said, flashing his Colgate-advert-worthy smile.

'I need one too,' Issy agreed, knowing Lexi would join her.

They settled down with their beer and wine and Mia started flicking through the welcome pack and found the list of house rules.

The worst one was at the top: from tomorrow, they were

only going to be allowed their mobile phones twice a day. And even then that was at the production team's discretion. They were told to send any last texts, tweets or Instagram posts, and then label their phones with the stickers in the pack and put them on the table by the door where someone would collect them. Issy texted her parents and Molly to tell them that contact would be limited. Issy didn't like the idea of giving up her phone. It was normally surgically attached to her and she didn't know how she was going to cope without it. It was going to be a struggle.

As Mia continued reading, it soon became clear to Issy that they were now at the mercy of the production team. Whatever they wanted the contestants to do, they had to do it. There were also hints that they would set up any scenes that they felt would make entertaining viewing, and although there would be a few nights out on the town – which would be filmed – they were expected to stay in most evenings.

Every week they would face a different hairdressing challenge, but they wouldn't be told what it was until each challenge was about to start. There was so much to take in and Issy's head swam with a mixture of wine and rules.

Eventually they finished going through everything in the pack and Rory disappeared outside on the balcony for a smoke. The two cameramen were still there, filming their conversation. *We better get used to cameras in our faces all the time*, Issy thought, finally kicking off her shoes.

'What on earth are we supposed to do now?' Mia asked. 'I'm so terribly bored.'

'Have a glass of wine,' Jason suggested.

'I only drink champagne,' Mia said haughtily.

'Why don't you go and ask the confession cam? They might bring you some,' Lexi suggested.

'So, we have to sit around talking, is that it?' Mia shook her head. 'At least I have my own room,' she said with a smirk.

'How the fuck did she get her own room?' Rory asked as he returned.

'It's supposed to be the shag pad,' Issy explained laughing.

'I am *not* sleeping in bunk beds,' Mia said indignantly.

'Course you're not, princess. Right, I Have Never or Beer Pong?' Rory said.

'I really don't think so,' Mia said before stomping off to the confession cam for the second time.

'You realise that being in front of the confession cam means you get more air time, don't you?' Aaron said. 'It'll be *The Mia Show* at this rate, which is exactly what she wants.'

'I thought it was somewhere you went to let off steam,' Jason said frowning.

'Remember what Issy said about *Big Brother*? It's exactly the same. All the divas go in the diary room to get more air time. If any of us had any sense we'd be fighting her to get in there instead of being out here playing fucking drinking games!' Aaron said.

'Oh, sod her. Let her have her camera time. I much prefer the drinking games,' Lexi said.

'Well said,' Issy agreed.

Issy was already getting on with the other housemates

and, even though it was early days, she wasn't looking forward to when they started getting voted off. Unless it was Mia. Issy didn't suffer fools gladly and Mia was already rubbing her up the wrong way. She didn't care where Mia had trained or who her family was friends with. They were all in the same boat and Mia was no better than anyone else. Issy hoped again that Mia's behaviour was only initial nerves and as they settled in, she would calm down. With this in mind, Issy vowed to make more of an effort with her.

'Are you OK, Mia?' Issy asked softly, as she returned.

'I'm perfectly fine. It's just not what I'm used to. I guess I'll have to have a glass of wine, as they won't give me champagne. Tim, be a darling and get me a glass will you.' Tim jumped up immediately. 'You see, I'm not really used to sharing my space with people. I have a rather large flat in Chelsea and I only live with Horatio.'

'Who's Horatio? Is that your fella?' Lexi asked.

'My Pekinese.' Mia paused. 'Horatio, if you're watching, Mummy loves you.' Issy looked at her. She had tears in her eyes. Actual tears. Over her dog. Who she'd been away from for six hours at most. *Bore off*, thought Issy. *Ah, shit. I was meant to be being nicer to her. Take two.*

'Who's looking after him?' Issy asked, forcing herself to continue making an effort.

'Mummy and Daddy. Well, the housekeeper actually, luckily she's good with dogs. I'm doing this for him too, you know. For his future.'

'You are still talking about your dog, aren't you?' Aaron asked, brow knotted in confusion.

'Not any dog. He has quite a pedigree. Oh, darling, I miss

him so already.' She managed to squeeze out a few more tears. No one knew what to do.

'Are you going to be all right?' Issy asked. She wasn't really buying it but she didn't want to appear heartless. The girl was crying, after all.

'I'll, I'll manage. Please don't worry about me. I'll be fine.' Mia took a sip of the wine that Tim had handed her and gave a barely-suppressed grimace.

'Oh for fuck's sake. Is this for real?' Lexi did not pull any punches.

Mia shot Lexi a filthy look. *Here come the fireworks*, Issy thought. She hadn't expected them so early, but it was inevitable with Mia around.

'Right, let's all go to the confession cam,' Aaron suggested, breaking the tension and thankfully the argument as well. The way he bounced up reminded Issy of a small child; his enthusiasm was infectious, which was a good thing because it looked as though Lexi was about to explode.

Having squeezed into the small room, they all piled onto a two-seater sofa facing the wall with a built-in camera.

'This is our first night so we all wanted to come and say hi,' Aaron said, waving his arms around and almost knocking Tim's glasses off.

'Hi Dad, Mum, Zach and Molly,' Issy shouted. She sounded lame but she didn't care.

'We love the apartment,' Lexi said, sitting on Issy's lap. 'Well, most of us do anyway,' she hiccupped.

Jason opened his mouth to say something but was interrupted by Rory running up to the camera, pulling down his pants and flashing his tattooed arse at the camera.

'Mooooooooonie!' he shouted.

'What's that say on your arse?' Aaron yelled over the laughter as Rory turned back, giving them all a flash as well.

'It says your name,' Rory answered, pulling his trousers up.

'What, Aaron?' Aaron's face was a picture of confusion.

'No,' Rory went on. 'It actually says "Your Name". It's for when I'm picking up birds, so no matter what they're called, I can always say to them, "I've got your name tattooed on my arse."'

'That's hilarious, mate,' Jason said, clapping him on the back.

The room echoed with the sound of all their voices raised in laughter, the mood easy and light. All their voices except one.

'Eugh. Let me out of here. That is disgusting. This is clearly not what the confession cam was made for,' Mia stormed.

'Mia, come back,' Rory called after her retreating back. 'Arses can have confessions too!'

And with that, they all collapsed into hysterics.

That night in bed, Issy couldn't sleep. She was restless but she didn't want to wake anyone. Steph was fast asleep, Lexi was snoring gently. Issy quietly climbed down from her bunk and went to the kitchen to get a glass of water. There were no clocks in the house so Issy had no idea what time it was as she crept towards the kitchen. Although she hadn't done anything embarrassing she knew she'd been a bit drunk on camera and now things were quieter she couldn't stop worrying about how she may have come across. As she walked through the living room to the kitchen she saw Rory passed out, fully clothed on the sofa. She grabbed the spare duvet from their room and covered him up with a smile. At least she could count on Rory – no matter what she'd done that night, he'd definitely done worse.

As Issy downed a glass of water she realised that living in this house, with these people, might not be so bad. This show might be exactly what she needed to kick-start her life.

Chapter Ten

At six a.m. the silence in the apartment was pierced by their alarm. Issy tried to prise herself out of bed, but her body wasn't getting the message. It reacted as if she'd been hit by a car. She was shattered – she hadn't got much sleep after she'd gone back to bed. Not the best start to the first day.

By the time Lexi, Issy and Steph managed to crawl out of bed, Mia was already in the girls' bathroom.

'How long are you going to be?' Lexi shouted but all they could hear was running water. Lexi and Issy took turns banging on the door, becoming more and more agitated. Steph looked worried that she was about to find herself in the middle of a fight.

Finally Mia responded.

'Yee-ees?'

'We're all waiting to get in out here,' Lexi shouted.

'The early bird catches the worm,' Mia trilled. 'You'll have to wait your turn.'

Issy had a face like thunder. 'That girl is about as funny

as standing on a plug.' They had to be downstairs by eight and all the girls still needed to shower.

'I'll kill her,' Lexi muttered sounding murderous. 'Selfish tit.'

'Threatening violence is against the rules,' Steph said seriously, and Lexi rolled her eyes.

'What's going on?' Jason wandered upstairs, carrying a mug of steaming coffee. Issy was pleased to see that he was fit when she was sober as well.

'Princess Mia has commandeered the bathroom.' Issy banged on the door again. 'Come on!'

'All the lads have finished showering so you can use our bathroom, if you want,' Jason said.

'Really? Thank fuck for that,' said Lexi.

'I could kiss you,' Issy said before she could stop herself. Jason grinned. 'Well, crack on, girl.'

Issy laughed as she walked back to her room. She *loved* a Scouse accent.

Lexi, Issy and Steph each had a quick shower and when Mia finally emerged from the bathroom, they were almost ready themselves. Mia's hair was neat and her make-up was flawless. She was going for a barely-there, 'I woke up like this' look. But the jig was up because they'd all been banging on the bathroom door for two hours.

'You could've done your hair and make-up in your room,' Lexi pointed out.

'The light is better in the bathroom.' She stalked past them without a care in the world. No single fucks given.

'I don't think I've ever met anyone more frustrating,' Lexi seethed.

'She's not going to be easy to live with,' Issy said as she blended some High Beam into her cheekbones, 'but everyone will see what she's like too.'

'She's not actually breaking any rules,' Steph added helpfully.

Issy and Lexi exchanged a look. At least they had each other.

Chaos of the morning over, Issy was buzzing about seeing the salon for the first time. She walked into the living room with Lexi where almost everyone was assembled and Danny and Ryan were waiting for them. The only person missing was Rory. Finally he joined them, wafting the smell of cigarettes over all of them. Issy definitely preferred any man of hers to smell of cologne.

'Needed a fag to wake me up,' he explained apologetically.

'Right,' Danny cleared his throat, and Ryan started mic'ing everyone up. 'So, this morning, you're all going to see the salon for the first time. We'll film the whole thing so, as ever, Laura wants you to be yourselves, say what you see and generally look around and just do you. Then go and stand by the station that has your name on it. Does all of that sound OK?' he asked. Everyone nodded. Issy couldn't wait to get inside.

They trooped downstairs, all of them buzzing like old fridges, and made their way into the salon on the ground floor.

'Oh my God,' Mia exclaimed as she stopped in the middle of the floor. The black, white and gold salon was a recreation of one of Alexander's salons. Issy would've preferred something more modern – the colour scheme was Alexander through and through. The gold floor almost glittered, the leather furniture was covered in white velvet cushions and the mirrors had heavy, gold frames.

Ryan joined the crew who were already in the salon. There were two cameramen, one was operating a large camera on wheels and the other had a smaller, handheld camera. Issy spotted three other fixed cameras and she guessed there were probably other cameras behind all the mirrors too. It was clear that there weren't going to be any secrets in this salon but that didn't bother Issy. She was here to cut hair and have a laugh. She had nothing to hide.

Rory put his sunglasses on. 'This colour scheme is killing my vibe. It's doing nothing for my hangover.'

'It's regal,' Mia said. 'I like it.'

'The floor is fucking glittery gold,' Rory replied.

'It looks great,' Steph said quietly, looking slightly lost.

'It's definitely . . . ' Issy struggled to find the right word. 'Eye-catching,' she said finally.

'That's one word for it,' Lexi said. 'Right, I'm going to find my work station.'

Each of the eight hairdresser's chairs had one of their names beautifully embroidered on the back of it and their engraved scissors sat in front of the mirror. Issy was relieved to see that her station was next to Lexi's. They weren't very close but at least Mia was on the other side of the salon, next to Jason. Rory, Steph and Tim were in a row at the back and Aaron was the other side of Lexi. She'd really lucked out here. They all stood behind their chairs, not quite sure what to do next.

'Morning,' Laura said, entering the salon. 'I hope you all had a good first night. Firstly, let me introduce the other people in the salon. You've already met Ryan, Dave and Lee the sound guys. Lee is in charge, so see him if there's a problem. There are three fixed cameras, and two moving ones.' Laura gestured to the cameraman controlling the larger camera. 'That's Steve, our senior camera man.'

Steve nodded at the contestants. 'Hey. Don't mind me – I'm only here to point the camera.' Steve was a stocky man and was so big that he dwarfed the camera. Issy detected a Cockney accent and there was a quality about him that reminded her of her dad.

'A couple of tips to make your lives, and ours, easier,' Laura continued. 'Be natural and don't seek the cameras out. We'll let you know when we want you to talk directly into them. All the cameras are positioned so that every inch of the salon is covered. You're being filmed all the time and we'll get the shots we need. Don't you worry about that.

'So, now the fun really starts. Today we want you to spend some time with the judges so that you can get to know them better and they can get to know all of you too. We're going to divide you into two groups – one of the groups will be with Eva, the other with Alexander. Don't read too much into this. We have to do it this way for ease of filming.'

Please let me be with Eva, Issy thought, crossing her fingers behind her back.

'Right, if you stay behind your chairs, I'll tell the judges that you're ready for them.'

Laura disappeared and a few minutes later the doors opened again and Alexander and Eva walked in.

Eva glided across the floor, in her nude peep-toes and royal blue midi dress. She looked like she was on a cat-walk – effortlessly chic. Alexander on the other hand plodded along clumsily, desperately trying to keep up with Eva while trying to retain his composure. Just like the day before, his pink shirt strained over his stomach and Issy wondered why no one had ever told him he looked like a weeble. His hair, a small patch of blond that sat on his head, was the result of a hair transplant, Issy was almost certain. They were such an unlikely pair, it was like watch-ing a giraffe walk alongside a bald baby hippo. Issy smiled as she thought about this, imagining the little angry baby hippo trying to cut hair, but it was wiped off her face when Alexander, who was now in the centre of the room, shot her a filthy look. It was like he'd read her thoughts.

'Right, guys and girls, we are going to split you into two groups for today. I will mentor one group, Eva the other. But this is a hairdressing competition and I am a hairdresser so I don't need to say which group is the luckiest.' Alexander let out a loud laugh. Eva gave a thin smile. *Good*, thought Issy. *Eva thinks he's a helmet as well*.

'But then, I have been voted as having World's Best Hair for five years in a row so I must know something about it,' she replied lightly.

One all, thought Issy.

'Well, you got lucky, didn't you darling?' he said sharply. 'Being *born* with nice hair.'

'Can someone bring Alexander a saucer of milk please?' she laughed, and the crew laughed along with her. Alexander at least had the grace to blush. Steve had focused his camera on them; their little tiff was probably exactly what the producers wanted. *That was smooth,* Issy thought. *I want to be Eva when I grow up.*

'So, my group is . . . ' Alexander paused dramatically, looking at each of the contestants. 'Jason, Mia, Steph and Aaron.' He smiled, displaying his over-whitened teeth. 'Congratulations! Please come and stand next to me.'

'Meaning the rest of you are with me,' Eva said and Issy gave a silent prayer of thanks.

Issy along with Lexi, Tim and Rory followed Eva into a room at the back of the salon. 'This is the green room. You guys will wait here when you're not needed in the salon,' Eva explained. 'Alexander has taken the others into our dressing room but normally you'll all be in here together. We wanted to take a bit of time to get to know you while they get some shots of the studio.'

The room was small and basic. There were a couple of sofas and a large armchair, which Eva was now sat in. There were also tea and coffee making facilities, and a fridge full of water and cans of Diet Coke.

'I want you all to know that I'm here for you, if you need anything. Anything at all,' Eva smiled. 'This is my first TV show in the UK, so I'm in the same boat as you. It's all very new and daunting for me too so don't feel uncomfortable coming to me about any issues you may have. I want to help you as much as I can.'

'Well, Mia hogged the bathroom this morning,' Lexi said. 'We had to use the boys' bathroom, which is fine for one day but we can't do that every morning.'

Eva laughed. 'Lexi, all of you, this is a game. Mia may

already know how to play it so you need a strategy too. I bet she's in front of the confession cam a lot too, right?' They all nodded. 'Remember the public are a judge on the show too. Half of your weekly vote is down to them. The more camera time you get, the better they'll get to know you. Confession cam equals one-on-one camera time. So get in that room. Got it?'

'If we can get Mia out of there,' Issy joked.

'Honey, drag her out if you have to. This is a competition and you all need to bring your A-game one hundred per cent of the time.'

Yes! thought Issy. Eva was the dog's bollocks. But something still wasn't sitting right with Issy.

'Ah, Eva, I'm here to be myself and show my talent, that's all,' Issy said.

Eva looked Issy in the eye. 'Listen, Issy, whether you like it or not, this *is* one big game. And Mia is some player already, but luckily for you I am your coach.'

Issy smiled. She felt safe in Eva's hands.

'Right, let's talk about tomorrow. You're all going to do a simple cut and style on someone. Alexander and I will feed back on your work but no one will be going home and there won't be a guest judge for this first challenge. This episode is when the public start learning about the show and all the different personalities on it. It's your first opportunity to show them who you are.

'In a minute you'll be given your phones back for one hour. After you've reassured your friends and family that we haven't dragged you into a cult, take some time to update your Facebook, Twitter and Instagram. I'm sure you're all pros at social media already, not like me, I'm far too old for all that.' Eva laughed. 'But it's another great way to interact with the public.'

'Can we tweet about Alexander's hair?' Lexi asked. 'Can I create it its own Twitter account? @FoxysShitWig?'

'Oh God, don't talk about his hair. It's his pride and joy.' Eva shook her head, laughing. 'But between me and you, it's horrendous. Tim, are you OK?'

'Umm, yes, sure.' Tim was jiggling his leg up and down nervously and he kept running his hand through his hair making it even messier than normal. *Poor lad*, Issy thought, as she gave him a reassuring rub on his shoulder. *He's not cut out for this. Why on earth did he ever apply for this show?*

Eva ran through a few more things with them and then they were given their phones back. Issy called her dad immediately and told him she was all right and had survived her first night in the house. She Whatsapp'd Molly, Zach and her mum, had a look on Twitter and then jumped over to Instagram. After taking a selfie with Lexi, fiddling for ages with the filters and settings, she finally posted it and spent the rest of the time scrolling through the *Daily Mail* sidebar of shame to see what Kim Kardashian was up to.

After an hour, Danny and Ryan reappeared and while Danny collected their phones, Ryan started switching over their mic batteries. They shuffled along like obedient children; even Rory was doing what he was told.

'Are you guys all right?' Ryan asked.

'Yeah. Thank God we're with Eva today,' Issy said.

'You should've heard Alexander,' Ryan said. 'He was basically telling his group that they have to destroy you. I'll probably get shot for telling you that.' His lips were curled into a smile.

'Your secret's safe with me,' Issy whispered conspiratorially.

Ryan leaned in. 'I knew I could trust you,' he whispered back, his breath close to Issy's face. Issy smiled at him as he walked away.

'If I liked the blond scruffy type, I'd be into him. He's so fit,' Lexi said.

'He's nice, but he's a bit unkempt,' Issy replied. 'He looks like he should be on *Home and Away* or something.' Anyway, she wasn't thinking about men at the moment. Right now, it was all about scissors, not schlong.

Chapter Eleven

A sharp beeping woke Issy from her uneasy slumber. After complaining about yesterday's bathroom struggles, they'd all been given individual alarm clocks. Fighting hard against the urge to go back to sleep, she swung herself out of bed, slid down the slide and made her way to the bathroom. It was only five a.m. *A time that should only be seen on the way home from a night out with the girls*, Issy reflected.

Lexi, Steph and Issy had decided that if they were efficient they could be in and out of the bathroom before the main alarm went off, although Issy was convinced that the early start would kill her. *Who would willingly get up this early?* As Issy stood under the powerful stream of hot water, she could feel her body waking up. Slowly. Very, very slowly.

Issy let her mind wander back to the previous evening. They had all been more subdued than their first night – after a few hours in the salon the reality of their situation had finally hit them, as well as the tiredness. Aaron had been particularly quiet and when Issy had asked him if he was OK, he'd said that he'd wished he'd been put in Eva's group and he didn't think Alexander liked him that much. Mia, on the other hand, was over the moon about being in Alexander's group. She kept banging on about how she felt like they were 'kindred spirits' and that they had so much in common. She kept saying things like, 'Our talent is almost identical. It's like we share one creative mind.' Issy had wanted to tell Mia that she was a knobsack but then she remembered Eva's advice and had kept her mouth shut. That could wait for the confession cam.

Issy returned to the bedroom, and gently shook Steph awake. Lexi woke up at the same time and went to make them all coffee while she waited for her turn. Issy smiled to herself as she blow-dried her hair – it was like a military operation. They'd all united against a common enemy.

An hour later, the three of them were dressed, made up and styled. They sat on the sofa, drinking coffee and eating toast with Nutella, feeling pretty pleased with themselves. When Mia emerged from another hour long session in the bathroom she stopped short, her eyebrows knotted in annoyance.

'Morning, Mia,' Issy said sweetly.

'How on earth . . ?' Mia stomped off to her bedroom in annoyance.

'Eva was right about her,' Lexi said. 'She's totally got a game plan. Did you see how angry she was?'

Issy nodded in agreement. 'Yep. Raging. OK, we've got a few minutes so I'm going to the confession cam,' she said.

Issy still hadn't spent any time in front of the confession

cam, last night she'd felt too drained, despite what Eva had said. She found the idea of talking to an inanimate object weird. It made her think of her Auntie Louise who used to talk to her fruit bowl. God rest her soul. But it was part of the show so Issy needed to suck it up. Knowing that didn't stop her feeling like a pillock though.

'Hiya. This is weird. OK, no, I can do this. So, I'm waiting to go to the salon for the first challenge. I know no one's going home today but we're all still a bit nervous. I know I am. Apart from that, I'm doing OK. I miss my family a bit. And the girls, and my mum's salon. Hi guys. I'm even missing Vi, you daft old bat. It's weird living with strangers. I mean, everyone's sound and Lexi's wicked. I feel like I've known her for ages, but I still miss everyone from back home. The only thorn in my side at the minute is Princess Mia. She's not my cup of tea and to be honest, I think she's a bit of a knob. Actually, I don't think she's a bit of a knob. I *know* she's a knob. A massive knob. She's waiting for her knob prince. She's knob royalty. She's the queen of all knobs! Oh my God. I can't believe I just said knob that many times. On that note, I'm gonna go. Byeeeee!'

'You all right, Is?' Lexi asked as Issy returned to the living room. 'You look like a sack of shite.'

'I hate that room. I only went in to talk about how I'm settling in and how we're all getting along. And the next thing I know I've knighted Mia, Lady Knob.'

'What are you talking about?' Lexi screwed up her face in confusion.

'Mate, I've got no idea.'

104

'Listen, it sounds to me like you were slagging of Her Highness,' Lexi said laughing, 'And I'm completely on board with that.'

'Oh fuck it, it's done now.' Issy stretched and yawned. 'These early starts are going to destroy me!'

'Not a morning person?'

'You won't get any sense out of me until at least lunchtime, babes. Looks like me and Red Bull are about to take our relationship to the next level if I'm going to get through this show.'

All mics were checked before they were led into the salon. Laura, Danny and the rest of the crew were already there. Eva and Alexander hadn't arrived yet.

'Right, guys,' Laura began. 'We're going to set things up and film Eva and Alexander arriving. You should all be standing at your stations when they walk in and then they'll explain today's challenge and what they want to see from you. The challenge will be aired at the end of the first show – the finale of the first episode. This episode will set the tone for the rest of the series and will determine whether people will continue watching or not.' She gave them all a steely look.

Although she hadn't said it, Issy got the message loud and clear: if the first show was shit they were all in trouble.

It took a few minutes for the crew to set up and all of a sudden it was showtime. Eva and Alexander walked in and Issy's stomach fluttered with excitement. Despite the past couple of days of film, this is what she'd been waiting for, and she couldn't wait to get grafting on the first challenge.

Eva greeted Laura and the rest of the crew warmly and Alexander immediately demanded attention.

'Where's my mic?' he snapped as Ryan rushed to sort him out.

'Hi, everyone,' Eva said, as she and Alexander made their way to the centre of the salon. 'Are you all excited about your first challenge?'

'It's hardly a challenge, cutting a bit of hair,' Alexander said. 'Laura, can we get the exposure turned down on those lights? The lighting is positively clinical.'

'Sorry, Alexander, with the majority of the cast being under twenty-five, this lighting is perfect. We can't change it for any one person I'm afraid,' Laura said matter-of-factly.

'If you're worried about those wrinkles, we'd have to turn the lights off for people not to notice them. Anyway, don't be daft, age equals experience,' Eva said.

'It wasn't me I was thinking about, honey,' Alexander shot back. 'It was your brassy highlights that I was worried about. You really must let me pop a toner on them.'

'I forgot how selfless you were, Al. *So* considerate. But let me worry about my hair. Laura, let's get this show on the road, shall we? The lights are fine.'

With that, Alexander had no choice but to shut up as the cameras started rolling.

'Good morning, everyone,' Alexander said. 'Today, you will be taking part in your first challenge – a simple cut and style. Nothing complicated or fancy but something that will show off your strengths. You need to remember two things. One: the idea here is *not* to do a total makeover. The clients don't want anything drastic done to their hair. We don't want them crying into their cappuccinos after you've given them a mullet. Understand?'

The contestants nodded.

'The second thing is to make sure that you're talking with your client. Explain what you're doing and make them feel at ease. Ask them about their holidays!' He laughed, and Issy was almost certain that she saw Eva roll her eyes.

'And three: Behave as though this was your own salon,' Eva said, her American lilt relaxing them all. 'Let's get started.'

The salon doors opened and eight women walked in. Some were blonde, some brunette but they all had mid-length, straight hair. A pretty girl with long blonde hair sat down at Issy's station.

'Hi,' Issy said brightly. 'I'm Issy.'

'I'm Tammy,' the girl said with a smile. Issy noticed her accent.

'Are you local?'

'Manchester born and bred.'

'I'm from Salford. We're going to get on like a house on fire. Right...' Issy started playing with Tammy's hair. 'You've got lovely hair. I'm thinking a few layers to add texture and I'm considering a fringe as it would really suit your face shape. How do you feel about that?'

'I've been thinking about getting a fringe for a while, but I don't want it constantly in my eyes and getting on my nerves.'

'No, babe, agreed. No one has time for that dishevelled I-just-got-out-of-bed-and-my-hair-is-all-over-the-place-but-don't-I-still-look-fit thing anymore! I like girls looking classic and glamorous. If you're happy to go for it I'll make sure it's low maintenance and I'll show you how to clip it back for those days when you don't have time to style it – or are too hungover to be arsed.'

Tammy considered the idea for a moment, twirling one end of her hair, then she smiled excitedly.

'Go on, you've convinced me. Let's do it!'

'The perfect client! Trust me, it's going to look fab, you'll love it.'

Everything fell away when Issy was working – it was just her and her client in the room. Issy was in the middle of a conversation about Tammy's job in PR and really enjoying the fact that this was a cut that didn't involve a blue rinse, when she felt hot breath on her neck. She turned to see Alexander standing inches away.

'Hi Alexander,' she said, wondering why he was standing so close to her. She noticed his forehead glistening and had to resist the urge to take a step back.

'I could give you a bit of critique, but carry on as if I am not here,' he said patronisingly. Issy saw Tammy make a face in the mirror. Issy stifled a giggle and by a miracle of Zeus she managed to smile at him.

'Alexander, would you be a darling and come over here please? I would so love some of your advice.' Mia's voice cut across the salon.

'Absolutely my dear girl, I'm on my way,' he replied, practically skipping across the salon.

'Are you all right, Issy?' Eva asked as she came over to the chair.

'I think so. Tammy has such lovely hair so I'm keeping things simple and adding some layers and a fringe.'

'That'll look great. You have the perfect face shape for a fringe,' Eva said to Tammy.

'That's what I said!' Issy's confidence in the cut lifted, she and Eva really were on the same page.

'Thank you,' Tammy said, looking starstruck.

'Any problem getting in the shower this morning?' Eva asked Issy with a smile.

'None, thanks to you.'

'Glad to hear it. OK, keep up the good work, I'm going to check on Lexi.'

Alexander can jog on, thought Issy. She had Eva in her corner so she wasn't going to let that chubby pompous pillock wind her up.

The bell sounded to tell them their time was up. They downed tools and were told to stand beside their client. Issy fidgeted as the two judges visited each person in turn. It was like good cop–bad cop, and Issy was last which meant she had to listen to all the other critiques before her own turn. Alexander was mean about everyone except Mia and Aaron, whereas Eva tried to offer constructive advice to each contestant. It seemed like hours but finally Eva and Alexander approached her after finishing with Lexi. Lexi had given her model a beautiful bob and she was smiling after receiving positive praise from Eva and lukewarm words from Alexander. Issy felt proud of her new friend.

'Hi, Issy,' Eva said. 'Tammy looks stunning. I love how

the cut you've given her has added volume and texture to her hair, and the fringe really suits her.'

'Thank you,' Issy said.

'Well, the girl would look good whatever you did with her. And yes, it's a decent haircut but, Issy, I've seen much better.' Issy looked at Eva whose eyes were full of sympathy, in comparison to Alexander's look of arrogance and self-importance. Lexi shook her head. And Tammy looked confused in the mirror; she'd loved her new fringe. Issy was furious. She wasn't egotistical but she knew she'd done a good job.

'You've seen much better haircuts?' she asked, feeling her temper flare.

'Yes, Isabelle, I am afraid I have,' he sneered.

'But not when you look in the mirror obviously,' she fired back, unable to help herself. Instantly Issy regretted her decision. *Bollocks! Nice work with the whole 'not letting him wind you up' thing, you tit.* Eva's eyes were wide, Tammy gave a gasp and even Lexi winced. The salon was silent as everyone else stared.

'How *dare* you?' Alexander shouted, his face so red it looked like it would explode. 'I'm a judge and a respected hairdresser. Who do you think you're talking to?' He was shaking, he was so angry. Issy was mortified. *Think before you talk, Issy. Think!* She wasn't sure whether to answer him or apologise or even try to make a joke out of it. But before she could decide, Alexander stormed off. Filming for the first episode had come to an end and she had already made an enemy in Alexander. Brilliant.

Chapter Twelve

Issy and Lexi were hiding out in the green room cracking into the Diet Cokes while the others had gone back to the apartment. The crew was packing up their equipment and Laura was trying to get them to hurry up so they could get on with the edit. No one noticed that they had hung back; Issy was too stressed out to face the others yet.

'He deserved that,' Lexi said, trying to comfort her. 'Although you've got some balls.'

'I know, not the wisest decision I've ever made, but he was winding me up and being so rude to everyone. Why has he got it in for me in particular?' she asked.

'It's not just you, he told me my bob was "dated". He only likes posh knobs who tell him how unreal he is, even though he's a tosser. So, basically, Mia.'

'Still, I let my temper get the better of me. Probably exactly what he wanted. When will I learn, Lex?'

'Everyone thought it was funny though. Steve could barely hold the camera still.'

'Really?' Issy almost smiled.

'And the sound guys. Ryan was almost crying. He looks really fit when he laughs.'

'He's quite fit anyway,' Issy conceded.

'But not your type?'

'Nah not really, but just because Hobnobs are my favourite biscuit doesn't mean I can't appreciate a good jammy dodger.'

'You've lost me.' Lexi looked confused. 'Why are you talking about biscuits? Are you hungry?'

'No,' laughed Issy. 'It's a metaphor . . . I think?'

'Oh. I like bourbons.' They both laughed and Issy felt the last of her bad mood dissipate. Laughter really was the best cure for a self-righteous old ball-bag.

'So, Ryan,' Lexi continued. 'He's fit but a bit too clean-cut for me. But add a few tattoos and piercings and I wouldn't say no.'

Issy laughed. 'He's a nice lad as well, almost 'too nice' for me. You could do a lot worse though, maybe suggest some tattoos to him?!' They sat sipping their Diet Cokes and thinking about men and biscuits for a while. After a few minutes the door opened and Ryan put his head round.

'Girls, you're supposed to be in the apartment. They're giving you your phones in a minute, so I'd get up there if I were you.'

'Shit, sorry. We're going.' Lexi stood up.

'Issy, what you said to Alexander was hilarious.' Ryan grinned.

Issy smiled weakly. 'I wish I hadn't though.'

'C'mon, we all have regrets, but there's no excitement in being nice all of the time, is there?' Ryan said, a smile teasing his lips. 'After all, nice lads never get the girl.' With that, he left the room. Lexi's face turned red with embarrassment as they realised what had happened.

'Fuck!' Issy said. 'When am I ever going to get the hang of these mics?'

'Are you all right, Issy?' Kev asked. Just hearing her dad's voice instantly made her feel calmer.

'I guess. I haven't had the best day, Dad.'

'Bloody hell. You've only just got there. What's happened?'

'I was rude to a judge on camera. He deserved it but still, I should be able to control my mouth by now.'

'When have you ever been able to control your mouth, love? You get that off your mum. She always says exactly what she's thinking, no filter, whether people ask for her opinion or not. Anyway, we said you had to be yourself and it sounds like that's what you're doing,' he laughed.

'Thanks . . . I think! I miss you already,' Issy said.

'And we miss you, but you must be enjoying some of it.'

'I am. Lexi is great and I love working with Eva. Just had a bit of a bad day today, that's all. They're editing the first show now and it'll be out next week. I can hardly believe it – it's going to be airing so quickly.'

'Your mum hasn't shut up about it. That's all she talks about at home and in the salon. I'm going to get some bloody earplugs if she doesn't change the subject soon,' Kev complained. 'So what's next?'

'I don't really know. We don't get told much. We'll probably have to go straight into the next challenge as time is so tight.'

'OK, then. Try to stay out of trouble and call us again when you can.'

'Will do. Give my love to the others. And Dad?'

'Yes, love?'

'Who are you trying to kid? Earplugs won't be able to block out Mum's soulful Salford sounds when she gets going. You'll need reinforced industrial headgear for that.' Issy ended the call with the sound of her dad's good-natured grumbling ringing in her ears and a smile on her face.

'Cuppa?' Lexi asked as Issy joined her in the kitchen.

'Yes please.' Lexi busied herself making drinks and Steph came in to find them.

'Don't know if you heard but Laura is on her way to talk to us,' Steph told them.

'OK we'll be right there. You all right?' Issy asked.

'Yeah, but Mia's been crying because she spoke to Horatio,' Steph said.

'She wasn't crying,' Lexi said, rolling her eyes. 'She was wailing like Gywneth Paltrow accepting an Oscar. I had to come in here otherwise I would've wet myself trying not to laugh.'

'Please tell me she's playing up for the cameras,' Issy said. 'That can't be her normal behaviour?'

'She just wants sympathy,' Steph explained. 'Anyone who

behaves like that over missing their pet after two days can't be right in the head.'

'You're learning, babes,' Lexi said, putting her arm around Steph.

'Is! You had testicles the size of footballs today,' Rory said as they joined everyone else on the sofas.

'It was rude and disrespectful,' Mia cut in. 'If you can't take criticism you shouldn't be on the show.'

'I can take criticism but his was unwarranted and felt unnecessarily mean. It wasn't constructive at all,' Issy defended herself.

'Really? He's a judge with a wealth of experience and you work in a small town hairdressers. I know who I'd listen to,' Mia smirked.

'I'm surprised you could even hear us today, what with your head being so far up his arsehole,' Issy said without thinking. She regretted it immediately. Again.

'I'm going to the confessional,' Mia said indignantly, standing up and stalking off.

'Of course you are,' Issy sighed at Mia's departing back. 'What is wrong with me?' She groaned and covered her face with her hands.

'Issy, you stood up for yourself, that's all. Don't worry about it,' Jason said, leaning over and giving Issy a much-needed hug. She let herself enjoy being in his muscular arms for a moment longer than was strictly necessary.

'You might want to be a bit more careful, though,' Steph said. 'For your own sake. I don't agree with her but Mia has a point. Alexander is a judge and he could make things difficult for you.'

'Eva's a judge too,' Aaron pointed out. 'She's lovely and wants to help us but she knows what's going on. She can definitely deal with Alexander the Arsehole.'

'Yeah, bollocks to him. He's like a weasel, a fat weasel. Can you even get a fat weasel?' Rory added.

'Um, he didn't like my haircut much either,' Tim said quietly.

'What was wrong with it?' Lexi asked.

'It was different lengths.'

'How did that happen?' Lexi said.

'Nerves, I think. My hands kept shaking.'

Issy gave Tim a sympathetic smile. He needed to get a grip otherwise he wouldn't be with them much longer.

Mia came back from the confession cam.

'That was quick,' said Aaron.

'Issy's not the only one who can be direct when she wants to.' Mia looked Issy straight in the eye.

Issy felt her blood boil. Mia was clearly looking for an argument, but she wasn't going to rise to it, and it helped that Jason had put a calming hand on her arm. Thankfully there was a knock at the door. Aaron jumped up and let Laura in.

'Hi, everyone,' she said. 'I wanted to let you know what's going to happen over the next few days. The production team will be working on the edit for the first show but you'll continue to be filmed between now and then. I may not be around as much now that things have kicked off so Danny is going to be your main contact from now on.' She opened the folder she was carrying and pulled out a few sheets of paper, which she passed around. 'Here's a schedule for the

116

next three days, which takes you to Monday when you will face your second challenge.'

'What's the next challenge?' Jason asked.

'Nice try. You'll find out on camera, on Monday. Anyway, guys, you're doing a great job so keep doing what you're doing. We're getting a takeaway in for you tonight and no early start in the morning so have a couple of drinks and unwind – at least some of us can have a lie-in tomorrow.'

Issy quickly scanned her copy of the schedule, distracting herself from Mia's crap attempt at throwing shade. As she looked through she realised they weren't leaving anything to chance – everything was detailed from when they were needed in the salon to what time they could expect to be back in the apartment each evening. It was going to be hectic.

'You'll see that at some point, each of you has an individual interview with Eva and Alexander,' Laura continued. 'We're going to film this as if you're in the final three. I know it sounds strange but we need to get this done now because of the tight schedule. You'll need to talk to them about how thrilled you are to have made the final, what you hope the future holds, that sort of thing. Any questions?'

'So, we have to pretend we're in the final?' Issy could only imagine how mental they were going to sound faking getting to the final before they'd even done one proper challenge.

'Yes,' Laura nodded. 'Things will get more manic once the show starts airing, so we're taking the opportunity to get as much of this sort of thing done now. We've also listed some topics on the sheets that we'd like you to discuss in the house. We're starting to get to know you all a bit now, but there's still more the audience will want to know so bear those in mind when you're talking to the judges. Any more questions?'

'For the next three days I have to stay in the apartment?' Mia asked. 'With them?'

'Mia, you live here, you stay here until you get eliminated,' Laura said patiently but with a stern look. 'The cameras are on in the apartment so you're still being filmed. You'll have to clean the salon and house at some point too. We need to see normal living as well as everything else.' Laura smiled tightly. 'If that's all, I really need to get back to the edit.'

Laura left quickly and Issy absorbed herself in going through the schedule.

The door was flung open and Danny struggled in, laden down with bags. 'Chinese takeaway,' he said as he took the bags of food through to the kitchen.

'Don't you ever go home?' Issy asked him.

'Apparently not when we're filming like this,' he smiled. 'It's exhausting but it's my first job in TV. You've got to pay your dues, Is.'

As they started dishing the food out onto plates, Issy looked at her new 'family'. They were a random group but she was starting to settle in and if she could learn to control her temper she might just make it out the other side in one piece.

'Ah this is better isn't it?' Issy said as she settled down with a glass of wine and plate full of sweet and sour chicken, rice, a couple of spring rolls and a cheeky duck pancake she hadn't been able to resist.

'I'm not sure about this meal, it's so unhealthy.' Mia wrinkled her nose in disgust. She was refusing to drink the wine, and she played with an almost empty plate of food. Issy wondered if it was possible to survive on air and crocodile tears.

'Don't you get hungry?' Issy said.

'I have self-control. My body is a temple. And I don't think we have access to a gym.'

'That's a point, Mia. I'm going to have to work this off somehow.' Issy popped the last of the pancake in her mouth and looked longingly over at the containers still in the kitchen. She loved a cheeky takeaway but if this was to be their fare for the next few weeks she was going to need to get to the gym every day to make sure she didn't turn into a hippo.

'I'm going to call production and ask after dinner,' Mia said.

'Great,' Issy smiled and Mia even smiled back at her. That girl was like Jekyll and Hyde.

'Mia, darlin', have a glass of wine, you might feel better,' Rory suggested.

'I'll try but it's very difficult. I'm not the sort of girl who drinks cheap rubbish.'

And like that, Issy was wound up by her again.

'Mia, when you work for Florentine, do you really get royalty coming in?' Jason asked.

'Only minor royalty really, and lots of titles. I do know the royal family though. Mummy and Daddy and I always go to the Queen's garden party.'

'So, do you have a title?' Rory asked.

'Well, no. Not really.'

'So you're technically a commoner just like us?' Rory pointed out.

'There is absolutely nothing common about me,' Mia replied, offended, before downing the glass of 'rubbish' Rory had handed her. As her nostrils flared at Rory's comment and her face turned a funny shade, Issy was reminded of a horse once again. Did posh people have equine ancestry? She laughed to herself at the thought and as she did she accidentally snorted wine from her nose. They all looked at her.

'You OK?' Lexi asked. Issy shook her head, wiping her nose.

'I'm being daft, babes,' she said giving her a look which said she'd talk to her later. 'Mia, more wine?' she asked graciously, pushing her wicked thoughts away.

Chapter Thirteen

'So, Issy, tell us how you feel about getting to the final?' Alexander asked.

Issy hesitated. It wasn't easy to take this seriously but she was trying.

'Don't worry Issy,' Eva said, sensing her uncertainty. Alexander tutted and Issy tried to ignore him. 'Just take your time. I know this is strange.'

Eva had hugged Issy warmly when she'd first entered the room whereas Alexander had looked at her as if she was a waitress who'd brought him the wrong bottle of wine. Issy hadn't seen him since he flounced – no wonder he and Mia loved each other – out of the filming in the salon. In the interests of professionalism she apologised, which Alexander had pompously waved away with a gesture that could've meant 'not to worry' or 'I don't want to hear from you'. Issy was wearing one of her favourite dresses – an electric blue midi. Eva had complimented her on it, and Alexander had looked at it with disdain. *This is going to be fun*, she'd thought. Steve was on the large camera and Ryan was in charge of sound today so at least Issy had allies in the room. If only Alexander didn't have a face like a smacked arse. Oh, he really wasn't going to forgive her.

'Right, Issy, tell us how you feel about being in the final,' Alexander said again, through gritted teeth.

'I'm amazed,' Issy said. 'I love hairdressing, obviously, but with so many other talented stylists to compete with I really didn't think I'd make it this far.'

'What would be the best thing about winning?' Eva asked. 'The prize, money, fame?'

'I've always wanted to work on my own product line. I had this ambition to develop a range that offered something for everyone. A collection that has good quality products but is also affordable for normal people. I hate those products which cost the earth and promise hair like Rapunzel but are really no different to a supermarket's own brand. So I'm most excited about being able to develop that.' Eva smiled and Alexander scowled.

'What's been the highlight of the show for you?' Alexander asked.

'The guidance from the two of you has been amazing. And meeting the other contestants, I know I've made some lifelong friends. Working on a TV show like this has taught me a lot. It's all been insane!' Issy smiled, hoping she didn't sound like too much of a twat.

'And finally,' Eva asked. 'What will you do if you don't win?'

'I don't want to think about that. I want to enjoy the final without worrying about the outcome. I feel like whatever happens I'm ready for the next step in my career and that's thanks to *Can You Cut It?*'

'Thank you, Issy.' Eva smiled warmly.

'Is that it?' she asked. 'Am I done?'

'You certainly are,' Alexander said.

'Issy, that was great,' Eva said, frowning at Alexander. *So she spotted it too*, Issy thought. Eva gave Issy a hug and then Issy walked out of the room but not before hearing Alexander say, 'What a waste of time. I'll be shocked if she lasts until the third week.'

'I don't think I was meant to hear that,' Issy looked at Ryan, who was waiting for her outside.

'Welcome to my world.' He put his arm around her. 'Don't let him get to you.'

Issy didn't say anything. It was weird having to talk about getting into the final so early on but now that she had, she wanted this more than ever, all reservations gone. She'd show Alexander.

In an unexpected act of apparent kindness, Mia had managed to arrange guest passes to a local gym for anyone who was interested. Because Issy really didn't want to spend any time alone with Mia, she had persuaded Lexi to come with them. Issy threw on her no-nonsense Nike gym kit and a hoodie in the bathroom before going to grab her.

'Are you wearing that?' Issy said when she walked into the girls' bedroom. Lexi was wearing a basketball shirt, some shorts, and skull-covered Vans.

'It's the best I can do, and you're lucky that I agreed to do this at all.' Issy tried not to laugh – Lexi really didn't look pleased.

Mia was waiting for them in the living room, dressed head to toe in Stella McCartney gym gear, but just before they left Jason appeared, wearing his gym kit as well.

'Room for one more?'

As they hit the gym Issy couldn't help but compare her gym buddies. Mia was on the treadmill running so fast, her legs flying everywhere, Issy could only think of horses. Lexi had been slumped on an exercise bike, barely moving, scowling and swearing under her breath, but was now nowhere to be seen. Jason, showing off some rather spectacular muscles, was lifting weights. Issy was hot – and not just from the exercise; Jason was in great nick. As Issy climbed the Stairmaster, her mind wandered from Jason's abs to the show, and the fact that she was glad there were no cameras around them now. It suddenly hit her how pressured it was, being filmed all the time.

'Are you nearly done?' Jason had left his weights and was leaning on the machine. His muscles looked great up close. Issy tried to surreptitiously wipe some of the sweat from her face.

'Yup, I'm knackered.'

'Come on. I'll buy you a smoothie.'

As they walked into the bar they spotted Lexi – she was already sat at a table with a bottle of water and a Dairy Milk in front of her.

'Where's Mia?' Issy asked, sitting down.

'She found a yoga class and pretty much pushed the

instructor out the way and started leading the bloody thing,'
Lexi said, rolling her eyes.

'So exercising didn't help you release any endorphins
then, babes?' Issy laughed.

'Did it shite! Mia's still a helmet. I hope she Nama-stays
out of my way for the rest of the night. In fact I'm going to
go back to the apartment now so I can get a shower before
Mother Earth gets back and hogs it.'

'This list of nicknames we've got keeps growing! OK,
we'll see you back there soon.' Issy said.

'Right what do you want?' Jason asked, as Lexi left.

'Surprise me,' Issy said with a smile.

Jason returned a few minutes later with a green-coloured
liquid that, thankfully, didn't taste as bad as it looked.

'Thanks,' Issy said as she realised that it was the first time
they'd spent any time alone together. Privacy had been
scarce over the past few days, even when they were away
from the cameras.

'You know, I don't think she's all bad,' Jason said.

'Who?' Issy said, frowning.

'Mia. I know she isn't the most friendly, and I've noticed
that she's especially bitchy to you. But sometimes people like
that are . . . well, I just wonder if there's more to it than her
being mean for the sake of it.'

Issy sipped her juice. She was attracted to Jason – she had
eyes – but she hadn't quite figured him out yet. He came
across as quiet, which she hadn't been expecting when
they'd first met. She was used to men as attractive as him
being arrogant but he didn't appear to have an ego at all.
'What do you mean?' she asked, intrigued.

'I was thinking that why, if she's so rich, knows royalty and works for Florentine Augustus, has she come on a show like this?'

'She said she wants to "share her talent", remember?' Issy tried not to sound like she was taking the piss, Jason sounded so earnest.

'I don't think she has it as good as she says,' Jason continued. 'Maybe there's more to her than meets the eye.'

'Maybe,' Issy said. She wasn't convinced but some of what Jason was saying made sense.

Jason looked thoughtful. 'You know how they gave us a list of things to talk about on camera?'

'Yeah, it's a bit weird but I guess we're learning how TV works.' Issy was surprised at how set up the show was turning out to be. They'd each been given a list of topics they were supposed to talk about in the apartment and Laura had said it was essential that they tackled them all.

'The thing is, Issy,' Jason paused. 'You know they've said we should talk about our families?'

'Yeah.' Issy wondered where Jason was going with this. 'That's pretty standard, right?'

'I don't really want to talk about mine on camera,' he said quietly. 'It's complicated.'

Issy felt an instant pang of sympathy for Jason. He looked so sad. 'Just say that then. I'm sure that would be OK.'

'What if someone pushes me to say more?' Whatever Jason was keeping to himself, Issy wanted to help him however she could. She wanted to probe further, but he looked so unhappy that she knew this wasn't the right moment to press him for details.

'Don't worry, I'm sure they won't force you to talk about something that makes you uncomfortable, but if they do, I'll back you up, babe.'

'Thanks, Issy. It helps to know that I've got a friend in the house.' He finally looked up and smiled. Issy smiled back. Jason would tell her what was going on with his family when he was ready. In the meantime, she'd make sure he knew that he could trust her.

Chapter Fourteen

When her alarm went off at five o'clock on Monday morning, Issy wanted to scream. She didn't think she'd ever get used to the early starts. *The only cloud in my otherwise clear sky,* she forced herself to think positively. Over the last couple of days, she'd spent more time with Lexi, laughed so hard with Aaron and Rory she thought she might wet herself, and grown a little closer to Jason. They'd had to clean the salon yesterday and Issy had actually enjoyed it. She usually hated cleaning but they'd had a laugh as they'd polished and cleaned together. Well, everyone apart from Mia who'd cried off on 'medical grounds'. Issy knew that all this 'bonding time' was being forced by the production team but she didn't mind – she was enjoying herself and was genuinely bonding with most of the others.

There had been one tense moment the previous evening when, as encouraged, they had all been talking about their families. Jason had turned pale and clammed up so Issy had covered for him. She wanted to know what was bothering him but was prepared to wait until he felt comfortable enough to confide in her.

'Ugh,' Issy groaned as she stretched in her bunk. 'Here we go again.' Issy started humming the *Mission Impossible* theme tune as she slid out of bed and made her way to the shower. Although Mia hated that they had managed to find a way to get in the bathroom before her, she, thankfully, hadn't been able to do anything about it.

As Issy shampooed her hair with her favourite revitalising shampoo, she thought about the day ahead. They were going to be set their second challenge today, but this one actually counted – their first elimination would follow in the next episode. There was a dedicated social media team who would be posting pictures and updates on Instagram and Twitter all the time the challenge episode was airing and they'd then collate the public's reaction ahead of the elimination episode. They were also going to meet the first guest judge today. Everyone had a theory about who it would be – as much as Issy hoped it would be Channing Tatum, she knew that was wishful thinking.

And then the very first episode was airing that evening.

'Big day,' Issy said to herself, washing the last of the suds out of her hair. 'Big fucking day.'

A few hours later and they were all in the salon. They were mic'ed up and ready, so Danny instructed them to stand by their stations and wait for the judges to arrive. Issy's adrenaline kicked in just as the doors opened and Alexander and

Eva walked in. Issy looked to her left, catching Lexi's eye and they exchanged excited smiles.

'Hi, guys. Welcome to this week's challenge!' Alexander said, clapping his hands.

'This is your second challenge but the first one that will be judged by us and the public. Do your absolute best because someone will be going home at the end of it,' Eva explained.

'You're going to be judged every week from this point on so you need to ensure you up your game every single time you step into this salon,' Alexander told them.

'They understand that. You've told them enough times, honey!' Eva said.

'It doesn't hurt to remind them. I do know what I'm talking about.'

'Of course, Alexander.' There was a gleam in Eva's eyes. 'But then my hair has earned a few million dollars so I guess I might know what I'm talking about too.'

Issy loved that Eva didn't let Alexander and his massive ego walk all over her. Eva had a reputation for being an incredibly successful and shrewd businesswoman but she remained grounded at the same time. She'd married her British bodyguard over a decade ago in a quiet ceremony and had settled in England ever since. They had two beautiful children together and they did their best to keep their personal life out of the public eye. But being nice didn't mean you had to be a pushover too. *She's literally my hero*, Issy thought.

'Right,' Alexander said, shooting Eva a dirty look. 'Today's challenge is a makeover. Your client's hair can be coloured, cut, shaved – whatever you decide. We'll be taking photos before and after, so we can compare the different styles and decide whether your handiwork has made your client look better, as good as before, or – heaven help you – worse.'

'And to help us with the judging we have someone very special joining us,' Eva said.

'Yes,' Alexander cut in. 'Please give a very warm welcome to our first guest judge.'

The salon was silent and after what seemed like an age the door opened and in walked a tiny woman wearing leather trousers and a sheer black vest. *Is she really far away or actually that small?* thought Issy, cheering and applauding along with the others as English pop star Vanessa Wild made her way over to Eva and Alexander.

'Hi guys,' she said, her strong south London accent ringing through the salon. 'I'm so happy to be here today. You've got a lot of work to do and I'm excited about seeing what you all come up with. Creativity in all its forms completely excites me. Just stay away from me with those scissors!' Vanessa laughed. Vanessa's style trademark was her waist-length jet black hair. Rumour had it that she had only ever let one hairdresser near her hair – the same woman who'd given Vanessa her very first haircut in her local salon. Issy had always thought that if the story was true she'd like Vanessa even more.

'Right,' Alexander said, 'it's time for you to meet your models.' All of the judges turned to face the salon doors as they opened again and eight very different looking women walked in. Eva took a step forward towards the contestants.

'We're not going to allocate the models today. Rather

than us deciding who gets which model, you're going to choose yourselves.' Eva paused. 'It's not an open free-for-all though I'm afraid. You're going to pick straws – whoever gets the longest chooses first, the shortest goes last.' Eva held up a fist full of coloured plastic straws.

Jason had picked the longest straw so picked first, choosing the girl everyone wanted. Her hair was long, thick and looked like it could have anything done to it. Issy, having been able to go third, chose Sam, a girl with curly, strawberry blonde hair. She wanted to try some different highlights on her to bring out the brighter reddish tone. *I wonder how she'd look with straight hair?* Issy pondered. She could feel her heart pounding. The potential for transformation was what she loved most about hairdressing.

The contestants got to work and the judges spent some time walking around and chatting to each of them about what they had planned. Issy was finishing applying the highlight colour to Sam's hair when Vanessa approached her station.

'Nice hair,' Vanessa said.

'Mine or the model's?' Issy asked.

'The model's, but yours is lovely too.'

'Thanks,' said Issy. 'But I'd give anything for hair as long as yours.' Her voice sounded normal but inside Issy was buzzing. She couldn't believe she was having a conversation with *the* Vanessa Wild.

'So, you're . . . Issy.' Vanessa read her name on the back of the chair. 'Nice to meet you. So what's your plan for Sam here?' she asked, smiling at the starstuck-looking Sam in the mirror.

'Firstly, some highlights. A lovely warm blonde to complement the redder tones in her hair. Sam's never coloured her hair so we're going to take this slowly.' Issy squeezed her shoulders and smiled at her reassuringly in the mirror as well. 'So how come you're doing the show?' Issy asked Vanessa.

'I've got a new single out soon and the word is that this show is going to smash it. Plus I love Eva and I love hair, so it all made sense. Win–win really.' Vanessa noticed that Issy was staring at Sam's hair intently. 'What are you thinking for the cut, then?'

'I wondered about a long bob and then straightening it. What do you think?'

'I reckon she'll look more sophisticated like that. Let's face it, she's a bit *My Little Pony* at the moment,' Vanessa said before wandering off to talk to Aaron.

Seeing Sam's crestfallen face, Issy said, 'Don't worry, hun. You'll be pure Emma Stone meets Joan from *Mad Men* by the time I'm done with you.'

When Eva came to check on Issy a little while later, Issy was so lost in what she was doing that she barely noticed the supermodel standing by her station.

'Sorry,' Eva said, laughing at Issy's startled expression when she finally noticed Eva. 'Didn't mean to scare you!'

'No, no, it's OK. I'm almost finished.' Issy looked around the salon. 'How's everybody else doing?'

'Well . . . ' Eva took a deep breath and filled Issy in on what had been going on.

Alexander had said something to offend Steph, so she'd

been in tears and had to be coaxed back from the green room as her model sat waiting. Jason had felt the pressure and had sworn – and his model had complained about his language.

'Jason's language?' Issy said in surprise. 'Surely Rory has the monopoly on that one?' *Or me?* she thought honestly.

Eva shook her head. 'Maybe. But Rory's model had a meltdown because she said he made her look like a man to which he replied: "Well that must make me gay 'cos I'd still shag ya!" so he's been a bit busy trying to deal with that error in judgement.'

Issy tried not to laugh too hard but Eva hadn't finished yet. Apparently Tim had inadvertently given his client a perm and Mia kept complaining that her model's hair was 'in terrible condition'. Even Lexi had had a minor wobble when her colour had come out wrong – she *was* dying her client's hair blue though. Issy looked around at the chaos in the salon and wondered how she hadn't noticed.

Eva patted her shoulder. 'But you're doing a great job!' she said before moving on. Sam beamed at Issy.

'Thank God I got you,' she said, perking up.

Chapter Fifteen

'Fuck me, I'm nervous,' Rory announced, pulling off the top of a bottle of Corona.

All of the contestants were sat in the living room, every pair of eyes glued to the huge TV that hung on the wall. They'd all got stuck into the beer and wine on the coffee table, even Mia had taken a glass without complaining, but the cocktail sausages and Percy Pigs had gone untouched. They were all too nervous to eat. The first episode of *Can You Cut It?* was about to air. They had briefly been allowed their phones so they could speak to their families and get on social media, urging people to watch the show but they'd been taken away again before the show aired. Issy looked around and knew that the others were feeling the same as her – excited yet apprehensive.

'Can you believe we're going to be on that screen in a minute?' Lexi said.

Issy sipped her rosé. 'I know, it's mad. There's no

turning back now. I wonder how many people will be watching?'

'They'd better be watching in their millions,' Mia snapped. 'I was promised this show would have huge ratings.'

Issy noticed that Tim was quieter than usual. If that was possible. 'You OK?' she asked him.

Tim gave Issy a small smile and shrugged 'I just don't know after today. That challenge was brutal. I don't think I want to be here.'

'What do you mean?' Steph looked distressed.

'My nerves got the better of me. I know I haven't exactly been the star of the show and my cut the other day was a whole new level of dreadful so they're definitely going to show a lot of that tonight, aren't they? Of course they will. It was too tragic not to be shown, but I really don't want to relive that humiliation again.' He shook his head sadly. Issy felt so bad for him. It was true, his cuts had been awful so far but having to relive them while the rest of the country watched too … *Shit just got real*, Issy thought. *And that's the most I've ever heard Tim say in one go.*

'You'll be all right, mate,' Jason said, passing Tim another bottle of Corona. 'We're all terrified but what's done is done and people are going to start leaving the competition soon so, tonight, let's have a drink and make the most of being here all together, the full squad.'

'Sounds like a belter of a plan to me. Here's to us, the original *Can You Cut It?* crew!' Rory said, slapping Jason on the back and raising his Corona in a toast.

Fuelled by nervous excitement, they all followed suit, clinking their various glasses, cans and bottles together.

Jason caught Issy's eye over the toast and held it. She didn't want to break the stare but then the opening credits for *Can You Cut It?* began and her attention was needed elsewhere.

There was a still silence after the first episode finished. It had been entertaining, slick and full of energy. The format of the competition and having them all live together worked really well on screen. The thing that had taken them all by surprise was the differing amounts of airtime they'd each been given. It hadn't been divided equally and the biggest shock for Issy was that she had had the most. Issy and Lexi exchanged a glance before turning to look at Mia – she was suddenly very glad all the scissors were downstairs in the salon.

Steph looked confused – she'd barely been on screen at all. Tim was reeling from Alexander's final comment about him: 'Stevie Wonder could cut hair straighter than that no-talent imbecile.' Lexi, Jason and Aaron all looked pretty pleased. They'd each had a decent amount of time devoted to them and had come across well. They'd shown Rory drunkenly falling sleeping on the sofa and Issy covering him with the spare blanket.

'Thanks for that, Is,' he'd said. 'I knew you were sound.'

Issy had noticed that whenever one of them would talk about their family, the scene would cut to a close-up of Jason's face, who always remained silent during those conversations. The section about his background had been really basic, avoiding any mention of his home life. His instant bromance with Rory had been hilarious to watch though, and Issy wasn't going to lie – she'd felt a flutter of something every time his handsome face appeared on screen. *Get a grip, you fanny*, she thought to herself. *You're here to cut hair.*

'That was fucking out of this world,' Jason said stretching so that Issy caught a brief glimpse of his lower abs.

'They loved you!' Aaron said, bouncing over to Issy. 'You looked so fit on screen. You could turn a gay man straight! And OMG that bit in your mum's salon was hilarious. Really hope Vi comes to visit some time.'

'It's mad watching yourself on the telly. It doesn't feel real,' Issy said, shaking her head and mentally reviewing the parts she'd been in. She'd loved watching her mum's madcap salon on the screen and her spats with Mia and Alexander had made good viewing, her growing friendship with Lexi had added another layer to the show and she'd been pleased with how good her first haircut had looked. Alexander had said some hurtful things about it, and about her after their argument, but Eva had sung her praises and clearly most of what Mia had said about her was too boring to be shown. All in all, Issy was over the moon.

Lexi put her arm around Issy's shoulders. 'But it is real and you were brilliant. You should be really proud of how you're coming across. How we're all coming across.'

'I wouldn't get too excited,' Mia said, narrowing her eyes. 'It's only the first show. There's plenty of time for the truth to come out.'

'And what truth would that be?' Issy didn't want a fight but that girl could push her buttons. She went from Hannah Montana to Miley Cyrus in seconds.

'Well we all saw the way you were sucking up to Eva for a start.' Mia's eyes were blazing with fury. 'And Eva's vain and stupid enough to be blinded by your fake flattery. Luckily Alexander is wise to your games and knows you're nothing more than average.'

'Take it easy, Mia,' Jason said calmly.

'And what about that scene when you tell Alexander he's your inspiration in "too many ways to count"?' Lexi stormed. 'You've got your head so far up his arse, you can taste his morning croissant and wheatgrass shot.'

'You *would* support her,' Mia spat. 'Don't think I don't know what you're up to. The more time you spend with Issy, the more air time you get. You're so obvious. Your friendship is contrived and fake. Not to mention your desperate flirting with all the boys.'

'Flirting? Fuck off man! It's called interacting, making friends, being nice. These terms are probably all pretty new to you but most people are familiar with them. And by the way you're the one who's obvious,' Issy said incredulously. 'You've had a game plan since day one. Don't take it out on me because it's not working.'

'Fucking hell, girls,' Rory said. For once, he didn't look happy. 'Let's all calm down and have a drink, yeah? You're killing my buzz. Percy Pig, anyone?'

Issy would've laughed if she wasn't so angry. What the fuck was Mia's problem? It's not as if she'd sat in the production room and edited the show herself. It wasn't Issy's fault that even after all of Mia's attempts to be otherwise she was still coming across as a boring princess.

'Let's just leave it. It's not worth it,' Issy said to Lexi, who looked ready to tell Mia every single one of the creative nicknames they'd came up with for her. Issy stood up.

'Where are you going?' Jason asked her.

'To the confession cam.' *I need to calm down*, Issy thought.

'Of course!' Mia laughed bitterly. 'Run off for even more camera time. Who would have thought innocent little Isabelle from Salford had all this up her Primark sleeve!'

'My sleeve might be Primark, babe, but at least I don't walk around acting like a Louboutin when really I'm nothing but a Croc!' And with that Issy flounced from the room with the sound of Lexi, Rory and Aaron whistling and cheering her retort. All Issy could think was, *Oh God, did I just flounce? Am I flouncing right now? Fuck's sake, Mia has actually driven me to flounce! Mental Note: No more flouncing.*

Issy dug her nails into the side of the chair as she talked into the confession cam. She'd been in there for half an hour already.

'That girl is fucking nuts. I thought we might be able to keep things civil but she clearly doesn't have any intention of living with me harmoniously. And you know what? I don't care. It's no surprise that they didn't spend much time focusing on her. She's so dull, paint watched her dry! I'm not going to waste any more time thinking about her.' Issy paused as a little doubt crept in. *What if the public agreed with Mia and thought Issy had planned all this? Thought that she wasn't being herself or that she had some evil little game plan?* She was feeling so confused. She wished she could talk to her dad.

There was a knock on the door and Lexi poked her head round.

'Can I come in? Or do you think checking on you is just another part of my elaborate plan?'

'Come in, you dick,' Issy laughed. 'I'm just letting off some steam.'

'Also known as slagging off Princess Mia?'

'Yeah, pretty much.'

'Look, babe, Mia's pissed because they showed her having tantrum after tantrum, being snide to everyone and licking Alexander the Arsehole's arsehole. And she can't cut hair for shit. You saw her at her salon. Even there all she did was swan around with that dim-witted dog under her arm. Princess Tiger-Lily looks like she'd eat Horatio for breakfast. Mia wanted to be queen bee but she's not.' Lexi grinned at Issy. 'You are.'

'I didn't come here to be queen bee,' Issy said. 'Anyway, your salon looks so edgy. I can't believe your hair is the most normal in there! So much has happened and it's only the first show. It could all change.'

'Of course it could, and after a couple more glasses of wine, that's what Mia's realised too. She's trying to flirt with Rory and Jason.' Lexi shook her head.

Issy stood up. 'This I have to see.'

It was clear that Mia had downed an impressive amount of wine while Issy had been in front of the confession cam. She was wedged in between Rory and Jason, a hand on each of their knees. She was trying to look at them through what Issy assumed were meant to be hooded, sultry eyes but was in actual fact the slow-blink, red-eyed look of the wasted. And it was definitely more than a little bit creepy. Both men kept exchanging amused looks over Mia's head.

'Do you think I'm pretty?' she slurred into Rory's ear, while running her hand up Jason's leg.

'Course I do, princess,' Rory said. 'Pretty fucking smashed.'

Mia pouted. 'Don't be mean. You think I'm pretty, don't you, Jasey?'

Help me, Jason mouthed to Issy. Issy shrugged innocently. She was enjoying watching the show but Jason kept looking at her pleadingly, with those big puppy-dog eyes of his. She couldn't resist for much longer.

'I'm going to get some more wine from the fridge,' she said, standing up. 'Can someone help me?'

Jason leapt up. 'I will.'

'Do you need a second pair of hands?' Rory asked anxiously.

Jason thought about it for a moment and then shook his head. 'Nah, mate, you stay where you are.' Rory looked as though someone had pissed on his chips. *Knob*, he mouthed at Jason as Mia snuggled in closer to her only remaining victim.

Jason followed Issy into the kitchen. She opened the fridge door, which was large enough for them both to hide behind, and they both collapsed into laughter.

'How did she get so drunk?' Issy asked when she'd got her breath back.

'She carried on moaning after you went into the confession cam and downed about three glasses, one after the other. I don't think she drinks that much so it hit her all at once.'

Issy had her back to the inside of the fridge door and there was barely any space between her body and Jason's. The fridge was cold but she was burning up.

'You know,' Issy said slowly, 'I'm not acting up for the cameras. I never expected there to be so much focus on me.'

'I know that. Don't listen to Mia. No one else thinks you're playing games – and the public won't either.' He frowned at her intense gaze. 'What's wrong? You're not that worried about Mia, are you?'

'No, no. I'm not thinking about her at all. I just . . . I want you to know that as soon as you're ready to talk about your family, I'll be here.'

He pushed her hair away from her face and smiled down at her. 'I'm really glad you're here. It helps having a friend in the house.'

'What about Rory?' Issy teased. 'I thought he was your true love, *Jasey*.'

'He's a top lad,' Jason laughed. He looked like he was about to say something else when they were interrupted by a tipsy Tim staggering into them in search of another restorative Corona.

Issy hurriedly grabbed a couple of bottles from the fridge and she and Jason re-joined the others. She didn't have the chance to talk to him alone again but every time she looked up she caught him looking at her and they'd exchange a secret smile. Issy didn't want to get distracted but she liked Jason and the chemistry between them was obvious. *It might come to nothing but it would be fun to find out*, Issy thought and her earlier reminders of keeping her head in the game were completely forgotten as the wine kicked in.

Chapter Sixteen

It was the day the contestants would be filming their first judging panel and Issy was having her make-up professionally done.

'How come we've got make-up artists all of a sudden?' she asked Hannah, the woman working on her.

'Apparently the exec producer decided you all needed your hair and make-up done after seeing the first show.' Hannah stepped back to get a better view of Issy's contoured cheekbones. 'He didn't think everyone was looking their best. That's what I heard anyway. So, how are you finding this whole experience?'

'I'm loving it,' Issy said. 'It's different to anything I've done before but, still, it's great. And I've met some interesting people.' She raised her eyebrows.

Hannah looked at her knowingly. 'I saw the first episode, and interesting isn't the word I'd use to describe all the contestants. Brilliant telly though.'

Issy couldn't help but feel a little proud. The show had received such a terrific reaction in the press since the first episode had aired and she had played a small part in that. She closed her eyes as Hannah worked some eyeshadow onto her lids. It was nice to sit back and let someone else look after her – she could get used to this. If Mia would stop berating her poor make-up artist it would be close to relaxing. Issy could hear her behind her, kicking up a ridiculous fuss.

'I don't want someone I don't know working on my face! What experience do you have? Have you ever done Kate or Pippa's make-up?'

The thing was, Mia thought she was a natural beauty and though Issy had to admit she did her make-up perfectly well, the truth was that Mia had looked pale and insipid on screen. But no one was going to tell her that. So despite being shouted at, the poor make-up artist was soldiering on.

'Hey, Is.' Ryan approached her chair. 'Just doing the sound checks.' Issy opened her eyes to see him smile at her as he fiddled with the little black and silver mic pack. He'd had a shave and Issy couldn't help but think that he looked better with a bit of stubble. It suited him. He looked up and caught her staring.

'Everything OK?'

'Fine,' Issy said. 'I just noticed that you had a shave. I miss the stubble.'

'Don't worry, it'll be back before you know it.' Ryan stood up. He towered over her anyway but as she was sitting down he appeared even bigger. 'How are things since the first episode aired?'

'We had a bit of drama afterwards. Mia started kicking

off. Standard. She was saying I was playing games so I'd get more airtime. We had a bit of a row and now she's ignoring me, which I'm taking as an added bonus.'

Ryan smiled. 'I wouldn't want to get on the wrong side of you, Miss Jones. You strike me as someone who can hold their ground,' Ryan said, helping her down from her chair. 'But take my advice: get a thick skin and don't sweat the small stuff – Mia's not going to be the last person to say bad things about you.'

'I know,' Issy said, checking her reflection in the mirror. She loved what Hannah had done to her. She turned to face Ryan. 'My dad told me to be myself before I moved into the house and that's what I'm trying to do. I don't really know how to be anything else.'

'Clever man, your dad.'

'He is. Not that I'd ever tell him that. Can't have all these men getting carried away with themselves thinking they know it all, can I?'

'Something tells me you don't let the men in your life get away with anything.' Ryan adjusted Issy's wire. His hands grazed the bare skin on her arms and she tried to ignore the shiver that went through her. First Jason and now Ryan? She was becoming a soft touch.

Before she could think any more on it, Laura called Ryan away and they were herded through to the studio.

'Issy, can you talk us through the thinking behind this style?' Eva asked.

They were in the judging room. There were three stools at one end, which Eva, Alexander and Vanessa were sitting on. Eva and Vanessa were poised elegantly but Alexander looked shorter than ever, his legs dangling helplessly from the stool like two fat Richmond sausages.

Before they'd entered the room, Laura had taken them through what was going to happen. The judges would talk to each of the contestants individually about the challenge and discuss the before and after photos from their makeovers. The photos had been posted to social media as soon as the first episode had finished and the public had been posting their opinions online ever since. By the end of today's filming, they would be ready for the first elimination.

'Of course,' Issy smiled. 'I loved her hair but I thought I could do something that would make the most of her bone structure and beautiful green eyes. So I took a colour that was a bit lighter and blonder than her natural colour for the highlights and worked on building in structure and texture. The bob was a drastic change but it's a more elegant look.'

'Your model loved it. She was delighted with what you did,' Eva said.

'The colour is beautiful,' Vanessa added, nodding.

'Thanks,' Issy said, feeling a little embarrassed at the praise.

'Yes, your model was very happy.' Alexander sounded bored. 'But it's not quite what I would have done.'

'What would you have done?' Vanessa asked.

'That's beside the point.' He waved his hand dismissively. 'Issy just might want to consider the less is more philosophy in future.'

'Thanks for the feedback, Alexander,' Issy said as graciously as she could. Seriously, that coming from a man who was sporting what looked like a cockatoo on his head?

'Well I loved it,' Vanessa said. Alexander shot her a look. 'Very modern without being too edgy. Timeless I'd even say.'

Alexander barked, 'Right, that's enough. You can go.'

Not even Alexander's abrupt dismissal could wipe the smile from Issy's face.

Issy walked into the green room. Mia was taking her turn in front of the judges, Lexi and Steph were still in make-up so it was just her and the boys in the room. There was a TV screen where the other contestants could watch their conversations with the judges as they were being filmed.

'Where's Tim?' she asked, looking around.

'Think the poor bastard's in the toilet throwing up,' Rory told her. 'How you feeling?'

'Good. Happy. Vanessa and Eva were lovely. Alexander thought my work was wank and hates me. So no surprises.'

'He only likes Aaron and Jason. And Mia, obvs,' Rory said.

'Don't know why he likes me,' Aaron said, a puzzled look on his face.

'He's got a thing for you,' Rory said.

Aaron pulled a face. 'I wouldn't go near him with yours, darling!'

'Are you making this up?' Issy asked.

'No, I swear on Strongbow, it's true. He thinks Mia and Jason could work for him, but he's got his squinty little eyes on you, mate.' Rory looked at Aaron.

'How do you know all this?' Jason said.

'I shagged that proper fit blonde bird from production when you knobbers were at the gym, didn't I? She told me – when she wasn't screaming my name.'

'Rory, you're kidding?' Issy shook her head. She was continually torn between thinking Rory was a total pig or the funniest person she'd ever met.

After all the judges' interviews had been filmed, they were given their phones for a couple of hours. All of the interviews had gone as expected, although Tim's had been particularly brutal. Even Eva had struggled to find anything positive to say. He hadn't said a word to any of them since he'd left the judges and he'd barely cracked a smile when Rory had offered to show him his "your name" tattoo again.

Issy phoned her dad's mobile. He picked up almost immediately.

'Issy, love, we wondered when we'd hear from you. We watched the first episode and we're so proud. You were great.'

Before she could respond, Issy heard a muffled conversation at the other end and then her brother came on the line.

'Is, you should hear what everyone's saying about you. They're all talking about you. My little sister is going to be a star! Is that Mia really as much of a tit as they're making out?'

There was more muffled talking as her dad took his phone back. Issy smiled, picturing father and son fighting over the phone. She hadn't said a word yet.

149

'Issy, it's Dad again. I can't get a minute of peace when your brother's around.' Issy heard her dad say something to Zach about getting back to work. 'How are you?' he asked eventually.

'I'm having the best time, Dad,' Issy said. 'There are some bad moments but nothing that's a real problem. I love being here. I miss all of you though. I even miss Vi!'

'Vi came over to watch the first episode. I thought it would just be us and Molly but your mum decided to invite half of bloody Salford,' Kev complained grumpily.

Issy laughed. 'I couldn't believe they kept in the part where Mum said I look like Angelina Jolie, total cringe. Bet they're all loving their moment in the spotlight. So you liked the show?'

'We loved it.' Issy could hear the smile in Kev's voice. 'You did us proud. Your haircut was clearly the best as well – by a country mile, love. That Alan, or whatever his name is, the poncy pillock, doesn't know what he's talking about. I like Lexi though. She's got a good head on her shoulders. And Eva, well, she's very ... nice.' He paused before adding, 'Don't tell your mum I said that.'

'Your secret is safe with me. Is Mum around or is she at the salon?'

'She's at the salon, love. Give her a ring – she's been dying to talk to you. She's been chewing my ear off about missing you ever since you last called.'

'OK, I'll do it now. Love you, Dad.'

'We love you too, love. Oh and Issy?'

'Yeah?'

'No matter what happens or how crazy it gets, remember

to keep your head straight and be yourself. After all, every-one else is taken, kid.'

'Got it, Dad.'

When Issy finally finished talking to her mum, her ear was red from the heat off her phone and she feared she may be partially deaf for life after listening to her mother's chatter for twenty minutes. Debs had been beyond excited when she'd called. Vi, who of course was at the salon, had spent the phone call chipping in over Debs with her thoughts on Rory, how she could show him a thing or two and asking Issy to find out if he liked older women. In all honesty, Issy reckoned Rory would probably take Vi up on her offer, and the very idea made her wish she could shampoo her mind.

Once she'd hung up she went on to her Instagram. She had thousands of new followers already and loads of new comments on old selfies she'd posted. She started to scroll through, astonished at the number of people who were now following her every update. She found the pic she'd taken last night of her and Aaron, drinks in hand, and posted it with the message:

Post show drinks with this little scamp @AaronCutIt. We've definitely earned them! Thanks for all your support so far guys. Hope you're enjoying the show as much as we are! xxx

Her Twitter feed had gone just as mad. She'd gained over seven thousand new followers, and she'd been retweeted and favourited so many times she'd had to turn the tones off on her phone. It couldn't keep up with her ever-refreshing feed. But the support she was receiving was so overwhelming. She tweeted about the upcoming vote:

@IssyCutIt: soooo nervous about the first vote! Don't wanna leave! Loving it here #CanYouCutIt #BuzzingLikeAnOldFridge #VoteIssy

They'd all been asked to update their usernames so that people could easily find them and follow them, but it was looking like Issy didn't need that help. Danny came over to retrieve their phones and for the first time since she'd arrived, she wanted to resist handing it over. There was too much activity online to catch up in a snatched hour every so often. She wanted to respond to the support as quickly as possible so that people would stay interested in her. Issy reluctantly handed it over but she couldn't stop a sigh escaping.

Ryan popped up from seemingly nowhere. 'Issy, crack a smile. It's just a phone. You'll get it back soon.'

'Sorry,' Issy said. 'I just didn't expect so much reaction and love on social media. They warned us this might happen but I wasn't prepared for it to blow up so quickly.' She plastered a smile on her face.

Ryan looked at her steadily. 'It's easy to get caught up in the whirlwind. Just remember to keep your feet on the ground – it may not last forever.' He squeezed her shoulder before walking off.

Issy stared after him. Her dad's words echoed in her ears. *Remember to keep your head straight.*

Chapter Seventeen

The eight contestants were stood in a semi-circle facing the judges. It was elimination time.

'Let's get started,' Eva said, clapping her hands. 'You've each had your judges' interview and all the votes have been collated. It's time to find out who will be leaving the competition today.'

'Some of you have done much better than others,' Alexander cut in. 'The judges' vote is based solely on your skills as a hairdresser. The public, however, may be judging on more than that.'

'That's a good point,' Eva said, flashing him a brilliant smile. 'Although a huge volume of the comments have been about their haircuts. Let's take a look at a few.'

There was a large screen between the judges and the contestants, and the tweets started flashing up on it.

@PartyGrl93: Nice Audrey Hepburn cut @RoryCutIt #TeamRory

@EmmaLucyLou: Wow @IssyCutIt dragged her model into 2015. Beeeooootiful #IssyToWin

Jason winked at Issy and she grinned back. She thought she saw a look pass between Mia and Alexander but she wasn't sure.

@StevieBoyLegend: looks like something from Planet of the Apes @TimCutIt #monkeymess #WhatWasHeThinking

'Sorry, Tim.' Eva looked at him apologetically.

@CoolLadyJas: loving @LexiCutIt. She's too cool for school #BlueHairGang #SmurfLife

'There really is no accounting for taste,' Alexander sighed.

@Melz1990: OMG @JasonCutIt is tooooooo fit. He can cut it with me any day #MarryMe

Jason raised his eyebrows at Issy and she had to hold in a laugh. She knew exactly how @Melz1990 felt.

@BBassBoy: daaaaamn @AaronCutIt cute cut, cute boy #niceguns

Rory slapped Aaron on the back so hard he almost sent him flying across the room.

@ElizaBeautie: I think @MiaCutIt needs a personality transplant. Boring haircut too #Snore #MammaMIAThatWasBad

Mia looked thunderous. Issy didn't like the more malicious side of social media but she couldn't help but admire the particularly imaginative hashtag.

@1D4Alwayz: blink and you'll miss @StephCutIt #CanYouCutIt #CYCI

'That's only a small taste of what the public have been saying about you,' Vanessa said gently. 'As the guest judge, I have the honour of announcing who came top in this week's results. Eva and Alexander will then reveal who is in the bottom two. Good luck everyone.'

The three judges were stood together, Alexander in the middle.

'The winner of this week's challenge and the contestant who received the highest combined vote is . . . ' Vanessa looked at them, a big smile on her face, 'Issy!'

'Fuck me,' Issy said. Jason grabbed her by the waist and lifted her off the ground.

'You beaut,' he said into her ear, his voice low.

'Nice one, Is,' Rory said. Lexi grinned at her broadly.

Issy collected the photo of her makeover from Eva, who squeezed her hand and then Issy moved to the opposite side of the room in *America's Next Top Model* style. Alexander avoided eye contact with Issy altogether and seemed keen to put her victory behind him and press on with the rest of the verdicts. Once the excitement had settled down the rest of the cast's names were called and they moved to the other side of the room to stand with Issy until only Rory, Mia, Steph and Tim remained.

'OK,' Alexander said sombrely. 'It's time to announce who is in the bottom two.'

'The makeover photos of the two contestants who received the lowest votes will come up on the screen,' Eva said.

They all turned to look. Even though Issy knew she was safe, her heart was still hammering in her chest. The photos flashed up and there was a gasp in the room.

Tim and Mia were in the bottom two.

Tim looked sad but not that surprised. Mia's mouth hung open in shock. Issy hadn't thought that much of Mia's makeover but she'd thought it was better than Steph's so even she was a bit surprised that Mia was in the bottom two.

'This is preposterous!' Alexander boomed. 'How is Mia in the bottom two?'

Eva ignored him and turned her attention to the contestants. 'It's now time to find out who the first contestant to leave the show is. The hairdresser who received the lowest vote and will be leaving the competition today is . . . ' Eva looked at the screen. One of the photos disappeared and the losing one filled the entire screen. 'Tim.'

Tim lowered his head, looking almost relieved. *This wasn't for him*, Issy thought. *He probably can't wait to get out of here.* Mia was shaking with anger, clearly unable to believe that she'd been so close to leaving after the first vote.

'Tonight's going to be a barrel of laughs,' Issy whispered to Aaron. He looked at Mia and rolled his eyes.

'Housemates, please say your goodbyes to Tim as he is now out of the competition and won't be returning to the apartment with you all. Tim, please hand in your scissors – you evidently can NOT cut it,' said Alexander, completely devoid of emotion.

They'd been warned to expect that catchphrase as it was one of the show's taglines and she'd thought it was ridiculous but coming from Alexander it just sounded so harsh. Issy had known when she met him that the man had no tact, but now she was starting to wonder if he had a heart either.

'Tim, you've been a fantastic contestant and I'm sad to see you go so soon. I hope you take what you learnt in your brief time on *Can You Cut It?* and use it positively,' Eva offered, lightening the mood slightly.

Issy and the rest of the cast ran over to hug Tim and say their goodbyes. Despite knowing it was probably the best for Tim, and the right decision given their first week, Issy was gutted for him. Steph started to cry and even Rory and Jason looked visibly upset. They'd known this was the nature of the competition but it didn't make saying goodbye any easier. Poor Tim was relatively quiet. As always.

One down.

'Issy,' Eva said, coming over to her once filming had finished. 'I wondered if you could stay back for a quick chat.'

'Sure.' Issy racked her brains, but she couldn't think of anything she'd done wrong. Not recently, at least.

Laura gathered them together for a quick debrief. 'Now that the show has started airing we'll be giving you more time with your phones so that you can work on building your social media platforms. You have no idea how powerful your presence on social media is becoming. It's such a driving force for the show.' She looked at her watch. 'You'll be going back up to the apartment now and I'll be coming over at eight. We have an announcement to make, which will be filmed.'

With that, they were dismissed. Tim had been sent out to start packing already while they'd done some pick-ups to the camera, but it had been a long, tiring day and the rest of the contestants started for the door straight away while Issy lingered, waiting for Eva. Jason came over to her.

'You coming?'

'I'll be up in a minute. Eva wants a word.'

'OK, but don't be long,' he said, stroking her arm with his forefinger. 'I'll need you to protect me from Mia if she starts knocking back the sauvignon blanc again.'

Issy was transfixed by the muscles under his shirt. 'I don't think you'll have any trouble defending yourself.'

Jason took a step closer. 'But I like it when you come to my rescue.'

Issy glanced over his shoulder and could see that Eva was waiting for her. 'I better go.' She reluctantly took a step back. 'I'll be there as soon as I can.'

'So, how are you?' Eva asked as soon as they were alone in the green room.

'I've got to be honest, I'm on a high after winning. I never thought I'd come first in any of the votes. The whole thing is crazy but I'm loving it.'

'Good,' Eva said. 'Keep that positive attitude. I saw the argument between you and Mia and I wanted to check that you weren't upset by it. But it looks like you're OK.'

Issy nodded. 'I'm fine. She saw me as a threat even before the first show. She's just one person though. I'm getting on with everyone else.'

'So I see,' Eva said with a smile. 'Enjoy yourself, Issy, and stay focused. When I was a model I came across the worst type of people imaginable. It was awful at times, and it's made worse when you're away from home. But I learnt from it and it toughened me up. You're already a lot tougher than I was.'

'My problem is that I don't want to lose my temper.' Issy thought for a moment. 'And I don't Mia her to know that she can make me that angry again.'

'Use the confession cam,' Eva advised. 'Or ignore her if you can. Just don't stoop to her level.'

'OK. Thanks, Eva. I really appreciate your help.'

'No problem, honey.'

As Eva hugged her, Issy felt a mix of emotions. The day had been intense. She knew now that the public liked her and she'd won the first challenge, so she was on top for now. The only problem was that Mia knew that too and that would only antagonise her further. No doubt Mia would be seething about being in the bottom two. Issy took a deep breath and steeled herself before she walked into the apartment. Who knew what she'd be walking into?

*

The atmosphere in the apartment that night was subdued, to say the least. Mia was eerily silent but that didn't stop her glaring at Issy at every opportunity. Steph looked like she'd been crying and even Rory was quiet. Jason tried to start a few group conversations but no one seemed interested so eventually he and Issy hid out in her bunk, talking about their home towns and their friends. Issy was telling him about the night Molly had got stuck in a club toilet, when they heard the apartment door open and Laura and Danny's voices. Issy and Jason re-joined the others on the sofas as Ryan and Steve emerged from the production room.

'Hi, guys,' Laura said. 'Things must seem horribly real now that the first contestant has left. It's normal to feel low at this point but remember that you're still being filmed while in the apartment and that we need to ensure every episode is entertaining. We're going to reveal your next challenge tonight and then we'll leave you to your pizza and wine. There won't be any filming in the salon tomorrow so if you want to go to the gym, let us know and we'll arrange passes for you – but we will send cameras with you this time.' Laura leafed through her clipboard. 'Once we're set up there will be an announcement on the TV screen. You all need to be sitting on the sofas facing the screen so Steve and the rest of the crew can catch your reactions.'

Ryan cleared his throat. 'I need to change your mic batteries. Carry on as if I'm not here.' He flashed Laura a smile. *Is she blushing?* Issy thought.

Once the crew were ready and the cast members were in place, the TV screen flickered to life. A man, dressed in an expensive-looking suit appeared. Issy looked around but the blank looks on everyone's faces made it clear that nobody else knew who he was either.

'Hello, contestants,' he said in a deep, commanding voice. 'I am Thomas Farrell, your executive producer.' He paused, letting that piece of information sink in. 'I'm extremely pleased with your performance so far and the reaction the first episode received. It's early days but the first show was undoubtedly a success, and the second episode is gearing up to be even more so. So keep up the good work.' He paused again, then narrowed his eyes. 'However, a show like this takes commitment. Now that the first contestant has been eliminated, you'll see that it requires much more than simply showing up and cutting hair. We're looking for a star and every second you're being filmed counts.' He suddenly flashed them a wide smile. 'Now, onto the exciting bit. We're turning things up a notch for your next challenge. This is a huge privilege and honour for each of you, and I'm thrilled to tell you that the day after tomorrow, you'll be travelling to London to work on ...' His pause seemed to last for hours. *Get on with it*, Issy thought. 'London Fashion Week!'

They all burst into excited chatter – even Mia cracked a smile. *I'm going back to London*, Issy thought. *For Fashion Week. This is going to be insane.*

Laura filled in the blanks once the announcement had been made and the crew had stopped filming. They were going to spend a few days in London and would be there when the second episode aired. Their challenge would be working for Henry Wu, a young fashion designer who had been making waves recently, and who had his first major show coming up during Fashion Week. It was the kind of work Issy had dreamed of doing when she'd been at The Hair Academy.

Danny gave them their phones and Issy took hers to her bunk and started scrolling through all the posts and messages when one particular DM caught her eye. It was from Josh Mason from the reality TV show, *The Trustafarians*, a show about ex-public school boys who were now working in the City, but seemed to spend most of their time going to parties, meeting for brunch and bloody marys and shagging models and dim socialites. Josh – or Posh Josh as the tabloids had labelled him – was clearly the star of the show, with his clean-cut looks and floppy hair. Issy loved the show. She and Molly always watched it on a Sunday night with a Dominoes. Out of all the lads on the show, Josh was the one Issy fancied.

Loved the show, Issy. You're totes my favourite. Josh x

She'd never imagined that she'd ever even get to the point that he started following her on Twitter. And now here he was, casually sliding into her DMs like it was no big deal. She tried to remain calm. She failed. *Thanks! I love your show too!* she replied trying to act like she was not buzzing her boobs off. *Molly will die when I tell her about this*, Issy thought. She suddenly realised how little she'd thought of her friend in the past few days. They were usually Whatsapping and calling all the time, but with all the filming Issy had barely had time to miss her. She was about to flick through her contacts and give her a call to discuss the Josh sitch when Lexi jumped up and joined Issy on her bunk.

'There you are,' she said. 'You talking to your family?'

'Sort of. Well, actually no,' Issy said guiltily. 'I just got a DM from that Posh Josh from *Trustafarians*.'

'Who?' Lexi asked.

'*The Trustafarians.* Do you watch it? Josh is so fit. Fitty McFitson.'

'I know who you mean. Looks a bit like a young Hugh Grant but a bit more of a tosser? So what's he saying?'

'Just that he likes the show and that.' Issy checked her phone. 'Wait, he's sent another one.'

You look good on the TV. Are you as fit in person? ;) We should meet up if you're ever in London. J x

Her phone vibrated as another DM came through from Josh, this time containing his phone number. Issy quickly typed out a reply.

Thanks for the number. We don't get much phone time but might be in London soon. Will let you know. I x

'First Jason, now this Josh,' Lexi said, laughing.

'Jason and I are just friends,' Issy protested. 'We've flirted a bit but that's it.'

'I'm not judging, mate,' said Lexi. 'Wish I could get that much action. My DMs are as dry as a nun's vagina. Have you responded to your other messages?'

Issy looked guilty. 'I haven't. And I've run out of time now, haven't I?'

Just before Issy handed her phone back to Danny she flicked through to her Whatsapp with Molly and felt a fleeting stab as she saw there had been a message from her that she hadn't responded to. *Next time*, Issy thought, *I'll make sure I reply next time.*

Chapter Eighteen

The busy streets of London felt like home. Issy looked at the streets, the tube stations and all the landmarks as their car drove them through Central London. She'd missed this place and was thrilled to be back. After the announcement about London Fashion Week, spirits in the house had been high again. Even Mia managed to be civil to everyone. *We're a fickle lot*, thought Vicky, *but it's not like Tim was a massive talker.* She felt her phone vibrate in her bag and fished it out. They'd been given their phones back for the duration of their drive to London. It was a Whatsapp from Josh.

Great to speak to you yesterday cutie. Can't wait to see you in London. Jx

After Lexi going on that she'd be a fool not to, Issy had phoned Josh the previous day, the next time they'd been allowed their phones.

'Hello?' a posh voice had said.

'Hi, it's Issy.' And then she'd rather embarrassingly added: 'From *Can You Cut It?*'

'Ah, Issy. Hello! This is a nice surprise. How are you?'

'I'm good. What you up to? Can you chat for a bit?'

'Absolutely. I'm just in the airport hotel in Paris. Charles De Gaulle.'

'Who?'

'The airport. Charles De Gaulle. I'm waiting for my flight back to London.'

'Oh, right. Actually, I'll be in London from tomorrow. We're doing some filming for the show. It'll be hectic but they've promised us a bit of time off.'

'Perfect. We have a break in filming for a few weeks. Maybe I can take you to dinner one night?' he asked.

'Maybe,' Issy said, with a smile.

'Well text me when you can,' Josh said, 'and we'll arrange something.' They'd both hung up and Issy had smiled for the rest of the night.

Issy typed out a reply to Josh's message.

Lovely to chat with you too Mr. Dinner Saturday if you're still free? We're heading back on Sunday. Will be in touch when I know what our schedule is like. I x

As she hit send, she noticed that there was an unread message from Molly from the previous day.

Hey Is, I know you can't reply to this straight away but had a horrible day today. The recorder lesson with a bunch of tone-deaf five yr olds was the high point. Missing you loads but so proud of you, wifey. Text when you can. M x

Issy felt terrible. She still hadn't replied to Molly after her first message. She'd been so preoccupied talking to Josh last night that she hadn't even had the time to go through the rest of her messages. She started to type a response but then she looked out the window and realised she had run out of time. They'd arrived at the hotel and Danny was holding his hand out to take their phones back. Shit.

They'd had to film their arrival at the hotel, which had taken a while and caused a small traffic jam, but eventually they all made it to the reception desk.

'I am not staying here,' Mia was saying as Issy joined the others.

'Mia, you have to,' Laura said firmly.

'But my flat is nearby. Why can't I stay there?'

'Because you're in the middle of filming,' Laura said. She was trying to remain calm but the fact she kept clenching her jaw gave away her frustration. 'All the cast must stay together. No exceptions.' Laura turned to the rest of them, effectively dismissing Mia's tantrum. 'Rooms have already been allocated. Mia, you're sharing with Steph. Lexi and Issy, you're in the second twin, and the boys are in the triple room.'

Thank fuck I'm with Lexi, Issy thought.

'Right, I'll leave you to it,' Laura said. 'You've got an hour to get settled and then I need you all again for a briefing.' Laura's phone rang, and she turned around to answer it, indicating that they were free to go.

As Lexi and Issy made their way to their room, Issy let her mind wander to Josh. It had been a while since she'd been on a decent date. Maybe he'd take her somewhere fancy. *Nowhere too posh though*, she hoped. The scene from

Pretty Woman popped into Issy's head, the one where Julia Roberts didn't know which fork to use, and Issy cringed. *I hope that doesn't happen to me. I haven't a clue about forks. Oh God. What have I let myself in for?* For the first time since she'd started filming, Issy's head wasn't entirely full of thoughts about cameras, haircuts and scissors. Instead it was filled with thoughts of forking.

Two hours later and they were all standing in the middle of the small meeting room they'd been briefed in. The cameras were on them, catching the stunned expressions on their faces.

'So we have to work on two different looks to go with two different outfits?' Jason said.

'For the same show?' Aaron added.

'That's right,' Alexander said. 'Two looks on two different models for Henry's show. Between you, you'll be styling almost all of his models.'

'It will be a lot of work, and you'll need to be fast yet diligent,' Eva went on. 'This is our chance to separate the weak from the strong,'

Time to get serious, Issy thought. Two looks for London Fashion Week was a big ask, yes, but it was also an opportunity for her to shine. Josh would have to wait.

Chapter Nineteen

Issy was jostled for the millionth time that day and she gritted her teeth. They were waiting for the final rehearsal before tomorrow's fashion show and it was chaos. Everything was being filmed and the extra crew and equipment they brought with them was adding to the madness. The past two days had flown by in a blur of models, hair, cameras, lights, action, and every single cast member was exhausted. Issy was seriously considering using matchsticks to keep her eyes from closing and she was genuinely concerned she may have drunk the world's supply of Red Bull.

The theme of Henry Wu's show was a cross between *Frozen* and *Frankenstein*. When they'd been told this, Issy's first thought had been, *What the fuck?!* But once she'd met her models and seen the outfits they would be wearing, that familiar feeling of anticipation and excitement had started up again. They had the tiniest gap in the schedule so she found the quietest spot she could and started flicking through her sketchbook. It was filled with ideas but she knew the two she wanted to use – a beautiful head of blonde curls, full of coloured Swarovski crystals on one; and a sleek blue-tipped jet-black crown, finished off with an intricate design of pearls and feathers for the other.

'Issy,' Danny said breathlessly. 'You need to come into our main dressing room, where the cameras are. You can't hide away from them.'

'I'm not hiding,' Issy protested, standing. 'I was just trying to find a quiet five minutes to memorise my plans.'

'Don't worry about that.' Danny grabbed her hand and quickly led her through the crowds to their temporary green room. 'Let's go!'

The logistics of filming at London Fashion Week weren't exactly straightforward. How they'd got permission in the first place was beyond Issy. All of the designers were so passionate and secretive she couldn't believe they were allowing their art to be shown on lowly reality TV. *I guess any publicity really is good publicity*, Issy thought. There were hidden cameras in their hotel rooms but they weren't allowed at the show itself, so it was roving mini-cameras the whole way. There was only so much freedom the crew were allowed at the show, however, so the contestants would be doing most of their styling in a separate room, which Danny flung the door open to, having gripped Issy's arm the whole time he was dragging her there.

'I found her!' Danny almost shouted it to the whole room, and everyone swivelled to look at Issy. *When did it get so difficult to have a moment to myself?* she thought.

'Sorry, sorry,' she said, flustered. 'I just wanted some quiet to go over my ideas one final time.'

Mia eyed her sketchbook. 'May I see?' She held out her hand and though her smile appeared genuine, Issy could see Steve training the largest camera onto their exchange and she knew better than to trust her.

'It will be more entertaining if everyone's styles are a surprise, don't you think?' Issy said casually.

Mia's smile faltered for a fraction of a second before it was back in place. 'So you won't show me your sketches?' There was an edge to her voice now.

Issy looked Mia in the eye. 'I feel nervous showing people my sketches.' Issy's voice was steady. 'It can really throw me off before I start work.' It didn't, not in the least, but it would be a cold day in hell before Issy would show Mia her ideas.

'Oh, right,' Mia stuttered, caught off guard. 'I didn't realise. Never mind.' She started busying herself, tidying her station.

Laura appeared, and started speaking quickly. 'Your models are ready for you,' she said. 'You know the drill by now. Try to ignore the cameras and focus on the task at hand. Any questions, ask Danny please.' She left as quickly as she'd appeared.

'How are you?' Issy asked Ryan, as he checked her mic. 'I haven't seen you for days.'

'I've been here,' he replied with less enthusiasm than usual. 'Keeping my ear to the ground, listening to everything.'

'Everything?'

'Everything. Looking forward to your date?'

'How did you know about that?' Issy said in surprise.

'You rang that guy when you were still mic'ed up,' Ryan explained. His expression was unreadable.

'So you heard everything? Isn't that a bit of an invasion of privacy?' Issy said with mock disgust.

'I can't believe you still haven't got the hang of these mics, Issy,' Ryan said shaking his head, looking genuinely sad. 'Anyway I only heard your side,' he said. 'You sounded happy. Excited, even.'

'First dates are always exciting,' she said. She was getting the impression that Ryan was mad at her but she didn't know why.

'I guess.' Ryan finished doing whatever he needed to the battery mic. 'I better get on. Good luck.' And he was gone.

What just happened? Issy thought. Ryan was usually so cheery. But she didn't have time to think about it any further because there was a sudden flurry of activity as the cameras started rolling and the first round of models entered the room.

Issy cleared her mind of everything except the huge task ahead of her. It was time to get to work.

Henry Wu was inspecting the models' hair. Each contestant was standing in between their two models as he slowly made his way around. He was a short man and barely uttered a word as he paused at each station. He approached Issy and she was sure she heard him say something but she was so tired she didn't know if she could trust her own mind. The last few hours had been the most stressful and the most exhilarating of her life. She thrived on adrenaline but they didn't have as much space as in the salon so it had been more claustrophobic than they were used to and the Red

Bull was beginning to wear off. Still, Issy was pleased with how her models looked. She could only hope that Henry and the other judges felt the same.

Finally, all the models had been approved. The cast members were able to watch the show from the sidelines and Issy couldn't believe the kick she got seeing her models, the hair she'd styled, step out onto the catwalk. One of Lexi's models walked onto stage and there was an audible gasp from the audience. Lexi had constructed her hair into an elaborate birdcage and it looked spectacular. *Amazing*, Issy mouthed to Lexi. *My girl is going to win this week*, Issy thought, pride swelling up inside her – surprised a little about how selfless she felt about it. *This isn't only a competition, these are real friends.*

The show finished just after five but still their day wasn't done. Issy was impatient to get back to her phone so she could text Josh, but they each had to film individual VTs, talking about what they'd thought of the day and of London Fashion Week. Issy had been so anxious to get away and get ready for her date that she hadn't hit all the points she'd been asked to and she had to re-do it. When she'd finally got back to the hotel room and managed to check her phone she had a message from Josh:

Wonderful. Zuma in Kensington at 7.30? Hope you like sushi – I'll book us a table. Jx

Issy checked the time and almost passed out. She had less than hour to get ready.

'Issy!' Lexi exclaimed ten minutes later, having watched Issy clip her ear with the straighteners for the third time. 'Give me those before you don't have an ear left. Sit. Let me do it for you.'

'Thanks, Lex. I'm all fingers and thumbs. What are you doing tonight?'

Issy relaxed slightly as she passed Lexi the straighteners and she got started on her hair, mercifully avoiding any contact with her ears.

'I'm shattered so I'm going to get an early night. A bit of telly, maybe a takeaway Nandos and sleep.'

Issy momentarily envied Lexi and her early night, but she'd got her second wind now. And Josh was waiting. 'Do you know what the others are doing?'

'Mia's already snuck back to her flat to see Horatio, the boys are heading out, and I guess Steph is staying in?' Lexi shrugged her shoulders.

'Poor love,' Issy said. 'Nice girl but not really meant for TV. Her skills aren't bad but she doesn't have any flair.' Issy caught Lexi's eye in the mirror. 'Unlike you. That birdcage was A-MAZ-ING!'

Lexi blushed. 'I just got in the zone and it all seemed to work out.'

'Babe, that was hairstyle goals today! You slayed and your models owned that catwalk. This week is yours.'

'Thanks, Is. Maybe after all this we can open a salon together,' Lexi suggested with a wink.

Issy hailed a cab from outside the hotel.

'Zuma, please,' she said to the driver who nodded. She settled back in her seat and watched the streets whizz by. A whole evening without cameras, mics and pointed comments from Mia. Bliss. Issy wasn't a huge fan of sushi, but she hadn't wanted to appear difficult or unsophisticated so had said that was fine. *At least this eliminated the fork conundrum* she thought. *Now I've got chopsticks to contend with. Balls.*

She checked her phone and saw two missed calls – one from Molly, and one from Zach.

Shit, Issy thought. *I* still *haven't replied to Mol's message from the other day.* She couldn't believe how quickly all of her routines of back home had been forgotten in the whirlwind that had been the past week or so. And there was so much to tell Molly. She scrolled through her contacts and was about to dial her number when the cab pulled to a stop outside the restaurant. Issy stuffed her phone back in her clutch, paid the driver and climbed out of the cab, promising herself that she'd hide in the loo and call Molly once they'd got into the restaurant. She could see Josh standing outside the restaurant and butterflies filled not just her stomach but her entire body, and like that all thoughts about anything else drifted away.

'Hi, babe,' she said as she approached him.

'Issy Jones!' Josh held her by her arms and bent down to kiss her on both cheeks. She got a waft of his aftershave. *Was that Creed? Nice.* His dark hair gleamed and he was wearing a tailored coat over jeans and a smart shirt. He was groomed in a different way to the lads back home. He was smoother, more expensive-looking. She doubted he had any tattoos.

He took in her knee-length, figure-hugging bodycon dress and raised an eyebrow. 'You don't disappoint, Miss. You are even better in the flesh.'

'So your smooth-talking persona isn't just for the cameras, then?' Issy said. 'I'd better watch myself tonight. Come on, let's go inside. I'm starving. It's been such a long day,' Issy said with a confidence she didn't really feel. It felt so strange to be in front of someone whose face she knew so well, but who she'd actually never met before. *Fake it til you make it, honey*, she told herself.

'I can't wait to hear about it,' Josh said, placing a hand on the small of her back and leading her through the heavy glass doors of the restaurant.

Issy tucked into her tuna sashimi – she quite liked it, thankfully it was nothing like the tins of John West that her mum bought for her dad and Zach's sandwiches – took a sip of champagne and smiled at Josh as she tried to concentrate on what he was saying. He had beautiful dark brown eyes, like pools of liquid Dairy Milk, and between being distracted by them and concentrating on not spilling food all down herself it was hard to pay attention to the conversation.

'Where are you Christmassing this year?' he asked.

'What?' Issy asked, her fork – it had replaced the chopsticks immediately after her first bite almost ended up in her lap – stilled, halfway to her mouth. *Was Christmassing a word? Are we using it as a verb now?*

'You know, darling, where are you spending Christmas?' He paused briefly but before she could respond he went on. 'We're going to St Lucia. It's in the Caribbean. We have a little place there. The entire family likes to spend Christmas in the sun.'

'We're going to St Helen's,' she replied with a teasing smile.

His eyebrows arched. 'Oh really? Where's that?'

'Wigan,' she said, deadpan. Josh choked on his champagne. 'It's where my dad's side of the family is from.' Josh was temporarily lost for words and for the first time that evening Issy felt unsure. Did he not understand she was trying to have a laugh? Anyone could see they were worlds apart but Issy's attitude had always been that the elephant in the room only got bigger unless you embraced it, tusks and all, so she laughed it off.

She took a deep breath and ploughed on with her tuna sashimi. There seemed to be endless courses going on here, so she might as well sit back, enjoy, and try to get some banter in where she could.

'So, c'mon, where's the best place to go out in London these days?' Issy broke the silence that had started to become uncomfortable. *Surely this has to be safe ground?* she thought. *And at least I can find out what clubs have changed in the past three years.*

After that, Issy let Josh guide her through the menu, helping her to order. He seemed to enjoy getting her to try new things. She didn't like everything but most of it was edible at least, and, awkward start aside, Josh turned out to be great company. He was so self-assured when telling her about his experiences filming his TV show and he showered her with advice about how to deal with all the sudden attention.

'You'll get used to being famous and recognisable more quickly than you'd expect,' Josh said.

'I don't really see myself as famous,' she said, shaking her head.

'The thing is, Issy, you kind of are. The show is a hit

already and you're one of the favourites. When we started our show, we were the same. We had no idea it would attract so much attention so quickly either, and it's been quite the learning curve.' He smiled kindly. 'So any time you need someone to talk to who understands what you're going through, you know where I am.'

'Thanks, that's very sweet.' Issy took a sip of her third glass of champagne. *I could get used to being wined and dined,* she thought. *I can't wait to tell Molly.* There was a momentary pang of guilt as she remembered in a rush the unanswered messages and missed calls. She'd been so wrapped up in their conversation that she hadn't so much as sent a text, but Issy pushed that to the back of her mind. *Tomorrow,* she vowed, *I'll get back to Molly tomorrow.*

'I've got a surprise for you,' Josh said as he paid the bill. He hadn't thought twice before pulling his bank card out when the bill had arrived. Issy glimpsed the total as the waitress keyed it in and almost dropped her champagne. She could've bought half of Topshop for that amount of money – and all for some fancy fish? She felt like telling him you could get cod and large chips from her local chippy for four quid eighty but she thought that would be rubbing salt – and vine-gar – in the wound.

'And what's that?' Issy asked, feeling light-headed. How had the champagne gone to her head already? She was so glad the cameras weren't around as Zach would have never let her forget it if she started getting lairy.

'You'll see,' he said cryptically, taking her hand.

He hailed a cab when they were outside the restaurant

and he talked quietly to the driver so Issy couldn't hear what he was saying. *London's beautiful at night,* Issy mused, remembering how much she'd loved living here. She and Josh chatted easily as they rushed through the streets and Issy rested her head on his shoulder. She felt so . . . comfortable with him.

When the cab stopped, Issy looked out of the window and saw that they were on Westminster Bridge near the South Bank. *Thank God it's not chucking it down,* thought Issy. Josh paid for the cab and they started to walk along the river, away from Big Ben.

There were a few people about, but it was a lovely evening and the lights of the London Eye were attracting a queue of tourists still. 'I've never been on the Eye,' Issy mused as they made to wander past.

'That's good news.' Josh stopped and smiled down at her. 'Because I've arranged a special trip for us, in our own private pod.'

'What?' asked Issy, stunned. She'd thought the surprise would be a walk along the river, maybe a cheeky glass of rosé and a snog if things were still going well. The London Eye was seriously romantic.

'Come on,' he said, grabbing her hand. 'We're in the priority queue so we won't have to wait.'

Bypassing the queue, Josh got out the tickets and pulled her along to wait for the next pod. Issy marvelled again at how confident he was. And sneakily checked out his bum. *Top marks all round,* she thought.

As the door to the pod opened, Josh blocked her view a little and said, 'And of course no evening would be complete without champagne – and because we didn't get dessert ... chocolates.'

He moved to one side to reveal an ice bucket with a bottle of champagne chilling in it, and some delicious-looking truffles. Before she could stop herself, Issy threw her arms around Josh. Then after a second, she pulled quickly away, laughing and slightly embarrassed. They were inside the pod now and the doors closed as it slowly started to move.

'You really do know the way to a girl's heart, don't you, Mr Mason? Chocolate is my Achilles heel. Now if you'd said chocolate Hobnobs, my clothes would have probably fallen off ... ' Issy joked, trying to regain some composure, but she'd never been so thoroughly spoiled on a first date.

'I'll remember that!' Josh joined in Issy's laughter.

'Sorry if I'm being over the top, it's just, this is so nice. I've always wanted to go on the Eye but never got round to it when I was living here. Thank you.' She kissed his cheek.

Their capsule continued to slowly move and the view of London began to spread out before them as. Glasses of champagne in hand, they gazed out down at the city.

'It's beautiful.' Issy was awestruck.

Josh turned Issy so that she was facing him and tipped her chin upwards. He kissed her softly on the lips. 'I think you're beautiful.'

Issy kissed him back, thrilled with the rush of the evening, with the fizz of excitement and champagne. And as Josh wrapped his arms around her waist and kissed her long and intensely, every thought apart from his lips on hers left Issy's head and for the first time in weeks she let herself get entirely lost in the moment.

'You ok, babe?' Josh said as they walked down the steps of the Eye. 'It's getting late. Do you want to come back to mine and we'll watch a DVD?'

'I don't know.' Issy hesitated. She knew what watching a DVD meant. *Everyone* knew what 'watching a DVD' meant. And it was getting late. 'I should go back to the hotel, I have to be up early.'

Sensing her hesitation, Josh pulled her in for a hug. 'I do really mean that we can watch a DVD, nothing else if you don't want to. It's just that we don't know when we'll see each other again, and I'm not ready for tonight to end. We can relax and you can unwind after today's filming. I'll even sit through a rom-com if that's what you want.'

Issy smiled. 'OK, you twisted my arm.' Not that she needed much arm-twisting, it was more like gentle arm bending. The truth was, she didn't want the night to end either.

Josh's flat was exactly as it looked on TV. Big, modern, plenty of cream furniture, and wall hangings that probably cost more than Issy's mum spent on biscuits in a decade. Issy was curled up on the sofa, enjoying a steaming cup of hot chocolate.

'I'll put the film on. Is *The Notebook* OK?'

Issy was startled. What kind of man owned a copy of *The Notebook*?

'You have *The Notebook*?' she exclaimed. 'Do you also have a vagina?'

Josh burst out laughing. 'OK, OK, Mrs 'I'm too tough for *The Notebook*'. What are we watching instead then? My DVDs are all over there.' He gestured to an entertainment centre with dark wood cupboards surrounding it. Issy made her way over, opened the cupboards and started mooching through his collection.

'You're on. You know, you can tell an awful lot about a person by their DVD collection. You're very brave letting me sift through them like this.'

'I've got nothing to hide. Be my guest,' Josh replied smoothly.

'I suppose you've already dropped *The Notebook* bombshell on me . . . Surely it can't get much worse than that?'

'Cheeky. I'm comfortable with my sensitive side. You can't embarrass me. Now hurry up and pick a film so you can get back on this sofa.' He patted the empty space she'd left behind and made pretend puppy-dog eyes at her.

Issy laughed. She liked this guy – despite his girly taste in films. She grabbed his copy of *Gangster Squad* and popped it into the DVD player before settling down next to him. He immediately pulled her in to rest her head on his chest, her eyes drooping.

'Don't let me fall asleep,' she said, yawning.

'I won't.' He kissed her forehead.

And that was the last thing Issy remembered before promptly falling into a deep sleep.

*

Issy woke up with a start, head pounding and with a serious case of dry-mouth. She opened her eyes, disorientated. Where was she? She sat up and took in her surroundings. Josh's flat. Of course, it all came flooding back. She was alone, fully clothed, and had a soft blanket covering her. She pulled her phone out of her clutch but it was dead. Slowly, Issy stood up and went to look for the bathroom. How much champagne had she had? She splashed some water on her face and looked in the mirror. She looked like hell and her mouth tasted like arse. She left the bathroom and softly padded into Josh's room. He was still fast asleep. Issy gently shook him awake.

'Josh?'

Josh stirred. 'Issy? What time is it?'

'I don't know my phone's dead.'

Josh reached for his Gucci watch on the bedside table. 'It's only seven,' he groaned.

'I'm sorry for waking you. I didn't mean to fall asleep here.'

'Was the sofa OK for you?' Josh stroked the side of Issy's face. 'You looked so cute, curled up under that blanket. I didn't want to wake you.'

'It was fine. I really need to get going though. We're heading back to Manchester today and I don't think I'm allowed to stay out all night. I'll probably get in so much trouble if they find out, babe.' Beer fear kicked in and Issy's hungover brain started to wildly speculate about the most horrendous outcomes to this situation. What if they kicked her off the show? What if Eva shouted at her? What if Lexi disowned her for making her sleep in the room on her own and became best friends with Mia? *Issy. Get a grip*, she silently reprimanded herself.

'Of course.' Josh stretched and sat up in bed. Only then did Issy realise he was topless. 'I'll find you a cab.'

'Don't worry, I can get my own cab.' Issy was now distracted by his naked torso and was wondering how much he was wearing under the duvet.

'OK, well, give me five minutes, and I'll see you out.'

When Josh finally emerged, he was wearing a bathrobe which was a bit too short. One gust of wind and 'Josh Junior' would be on show to all of London.

'I'll walk you down,' he said.

'Dressed like that?' Issy said. 'You'll freeze.'

'You're worth it,' he replied.

Issy couldn't shake the feeling that something wasn't right, but she consoled herself that it was probably just the hangover and anxiety about staying out all night. She'd had a lovely, romantic evening with Josh and it wasn't a crime to fall asleep on a guy's sofa. Still, she couldn't stop wondering if she would she get into trouble with the producers. Things were going so well. She didn't want to ruin them for herself now.

Josh opened the door to the street and before Issy had a chance to do anything, he grabbed her and kissed her passionately. *Whoa, son! That's a bit much for seven a.m., isn't it?!* Issy thought, painfully aware of Josh's short bathrobe and the fact that she hadn't had a chance to steal his toothbrush. Over-amorous bastard.

'See you soon,' he said when he eventually let her go and looking at her intensely.

'I hope so. Er ... thanks for a lovely night.' Issy wasn't quite sure what was going on but she knew she wanted out of broad daylight, out of last night's dress, and for this walk of shame to be over ASAP.

As she climbed into the first black cab that came past and they drove away, she was too busy waving at Josh through the back window to notice the photographer lurking in a doorway on the other side of the street.

Chapter Twenty

Issy managed to get back to their hotel and sneak into her room without being caught doing the walk of shame – or 'the stride of pride' as Lexi had called it when Issy had woken her up and told her all about her night with Josh.

She jumped in the shower, hangover dissipating in the hot water along with the rest of her make-up from last night. As she showered, the last of the fear that something dreadful was going to happen left her. She couldn't believe her luck that she'd seemingly got away with it without being spotted. The last thing she needed was to give Alexander another reason to pick on her. And from now on she was going to be a model contestant. So she decided to keep the details to herself – apart, of course, from telling Lexi – until she knew what, if anything, was happening between her and the enigmatic Mr Mason.

*

They were back in Manchester and the contestants were gathering in the green room. Filming for the next results show was about to begin.

'I don't *believe* this! But then again *nothing* surprises me when it comes to you!' Mia stormed in and slammed a newspaper down on the table.

Issy nearly jumped out of her skin. 'What?'

'You weren't happy stealing all the limelight on the show, were you?! Had to get your dirty little paws all over Josh as well?'

'Josh? You know him?'

'Yes, I know him! Our parents are old friends.'

'Good for you, babe,' Issy replied sarcastically. She had no clue what was going on. 'How do you know about me and Josh?'

'The entire country knows about your sordid little sleep-over!'

Mia threw the newspaper she'd hit the table with at Issy and the front page headline screamed out at her.

DID SHE CUT IT? POSH JOSH AND A BIT OF ROUGH!

Issy felt sick to the stomach as she looked at the grainy tabloid shot of Josh in his wisp of a robe, kissing her on his doorstep. She looked horrendous, wearing the previous night's clothing and next to no make-up. If you looked closely enough you could see that her eyelashes were hanging off. Classy. Issy closed her eyes and steeled herself before reading the article. Her heart was thumping hard in her chest, a mixture of apprehension and rage washed over her as phrases kept jumping out.

Wearing a dress that left little to the imagination ...
'She was all over me,' Josh told a close friend ...
Wild night of passion ...
'She's not my usual type.'

Issy covered her face with her hands and fought back the tears. 'That's not what happened at all,' she whispered feeling deflated and sick to her stomach. 'It's all lies.'

Lexi took the paper from Issy and started reading. 'He's saying you shagged him all night! Tosser,' Lexi stormed.

'Josh Mason is *not* a liar.' Mia was seething.

'He's either a liar or a scumbag who can't keep his mouth shut about his conquests. Which would you prefer?' Lexi snarled. 'What a gentleman.'

The paper was slowly being passed round the other contestants and Issy couldn't bring herself to look Jason in the eye as he finished reading. His silence on the matter told her everything she needed to know.

'I did go back to his place,' Issy admitted reluctantly. 'But we were just going to watch a film and then I was going to get a cab back. Only I was shattered from the show and all the filming. I fell asleep before the film even started. Next thing I know, I'm waking up on his sofa, *alone*, I might add, and fully clothed. Nothing happened.' Issy felt a sudden shock of anger. 'He suggested we watch *The* bloody *Notebook*, for God's sake! If that's not a cock block, I don't know what is!'

'Do you really expect us to believe that?' Mia said, hands on hips.

'I don't *care* what you believe,' Issy said, trying to keep the wobble from her voice. 'I couldn't care less what you think about anything. You made up your mind about me before that story was even printed.'

'Mate.' Rory put his arm around Issy in an unexpected flash of empathy. 'It sounds like you've been set up.'

The colour drained from Issy's face. She'd read enough gossip mags to know that plenty of celebs claimed that what they'd been accused of wasn't true. She'd always assumed that if a celeb denied something it was because they'd been caught in a sticky situation and didn't want to lose face. She'd never given much thought to whether those things had actually happened the way they'd been reported, or if there was a more malicious side to it. She had certainly never considered how the people involved might feel reading about the intimate details of their so-called lives reported on by others. But here she was, experiencing it first-hand . . . And it was shit.

'Rory's right, Is,' Aaron said. 'The bastard set you up. I mean, look at what he's wearing – it's obscene! Whereas you quite clearly weren't aware what was going on. No offence, babe, but you look a bag of piss there.'

Harsh but totally fair, conceded Issy.

'Josh isn't like that!' Mia stormed. 'He's my, my . . . friend. I've known him for years and he'd never do anything like that!'

Mia's hesitation didn't go unnoticed.

'He's your "friend"?' Lexi raised an eyebrow sceptically. 'Sounds to me as though you'd like to be a little bit more. Is that why you're taking this so personally?'

'No.' Mia practically spat the word out. 'We're just friends, and I certainly won't be entertaining the notion of

188

anything else now Issy has been there. The idea that I'd be considered second best to her is laughable.'

'Who do you think you're talking to? Listen, if you want him, he's yours.' Issy felt her resolve strengthen. The idea that the whole of last night – the champagne, the chocolates, the London Eye – had all been a ploy for some sordid little story made Issy feel empty. Suddenly the whole night had gone from being potentially the beginning of something, to a hollow, cheap affair. But Issy forced herself to put all of that embarrassment and disappointment in a box for later.

She stood up to look Mia straight in the eye. 'But let me say this. This story is all lies. And look.' She opened the paper to the full story and the photo of them getting onto their capsule at the London Eye. 'He didn't even tell me where we were going, I had no clue. So where did this picture come from if he hadn't tipped someone off? This is all him. He's a desperate and fame-hungry little boy. You're welcome to him if that's your type.'

Before Mia could respond, Danny was whisking them all into the judging room. Issy wanted nothing more than to spend five minutes on her own crying, calming down, or both, but she wasn't going to give Mia the satisfaction of seeing her upset.

The judging passed by in a blur. Issy couldn't focus. Thoughts of Josh and how he'd mugged her off filled her head. She was usually such a good judge of character, could spot a dickhead a mile away, but she hadn't seen this one coming. The excitement, the romance, maybe even drinking the champagne all night, had clouded her judgement. She'd got carried away. She'd wanted to believe the fairytale was true. Had the signs been there all along but she'd chosen to ignore them? It wasn't the first time she'd been played but this was so ... public. And cruel. And deliberate. *What are Mum and Dad going to think?* Issy gave herself a mental shake. She was missing the judging. She didn't need to look like a gormless twat on TV along with everything else.

Henry Wu was the guest judge and it was down to him to announce the winner.

'So, Henry, who's this week's winner?' Eva asked.

Henry grunted something inaudible and pointed at Lexi.

'Lexi?' Alexander asked, shocked. 'Are you sure?'

Henry nodded mutely.

The other cast members congratulated Lexi, even Mia cracked a smile. Issy was genuinely pleased for Lexi – she deserved the win – but it was a real effort to behave normally for the cameras. Aaron was called up to collect his photo, safely through to the next challenge, and then Issy was called. She was finishing third in the challenge, a podium place if it had been the Olympics. She should've been relieved, proud, anything, at still being in the competition but her legs felt like lead as she walked up to the judges and the smile on her face felt fake.

Steph and Rory were in the bottom two, and the judges started on their more involved critique of their work. Alexander's voice droned on and on – and on – about how Steph had no creative flair, and that Rory needed to stop giving his models a short back and sides. Issy zoned in and out until she noticed the larger camera was pointing in her direction. She tried to plaster a shocked yet interested look on her face as Alexander took great delight in showing Steph the public's indifferent reaction to her presence on the show.

'It's now time to find out who will be leaving the show,' Alexander said. 'The hairdresser who received the lowest vote and will be leaving the competition today is . . . ' Their eyes were all fixed on the screen. 'Steph.'

'Housemates, please say your goodbyes to Steph as she is now out of the competition and won't be returning to the apartment with you all. Steph, please hand in your scissors – you evidently can NOT cut it,' Alexander continued. He liked doing that bit far too much. *Evil toad*, thought Issy.

Steph handed over her scissors, and the cast members said a tearful goodbye and just before the camera stopped filming, Alexander called out in clear, crisp tones, 'Maybe if you focus more on the challenges, Issy, and less on snaring yourself a rich boyfriend you'll do better in this competition, my dear.'

Issy went very still. Alexander smirked at her before sweeping out of the room. There was a beat of silence. Nobody knew what to say.

Suddenly, Eva was at her side. 'Issy, come with me please.' She grabbed her arm and propelled her out of the room and into her dressing room.

Eva sat down next to Issy on her sofa. 'Are you ok?' she asked kindly.

Issy shrugged. 'I don't know. Did Alexander really say that on camera?'

'Yes, he did. But he's a bitter little man, so don't take a

blind bit of notice. I actually wanted to know if you're OK about the article.'

'It's complete bullshit, Eva. It's all lies, not one bit is true! Except maybe my name.'

Eva looked intensely at Issy. 'I believe you, Issy. But how did you let this happen?'

'I got over excited,' Issy admitted, relieved that Eva had believed her straight away. Maybe others would as well. 'Josh DM'd me and it went from there. He seemed nice. Sweet, a gentleman, even. And I liked him. I suppose I was a bit starstruck. I never expected him to like me and I definitely didn't expect it to be all over the papers. I wasn't prepared, and none of it's true!' Tears of frustration welled in Issy's eyes. 'And now I look like a total bellend.'

Eva put her arm around Issy. 'I'm so sorry this happened to you, honey. I don't think the show has prepared any of you properly for the media attention you're going to receive.'

'Do you think Josh had this planned from the beginning?' Issy asked quietly.

Eva hesitated for a moment before answering. 'It's possible. The ratings for *The Trustafarians* have been declining for some time and there have been rumours that the production company are thinking about bringing in a whole new cast. You come along, from seemingly nowhere, and are immediately loved by the public. Josh may have seen that as an opportunity to raise his own profile with the TV execs. I'm sorry, Issy. It definitely looks to me like you've been played.'

That didn't sit well with Issy at all.

'It didn't even occur to me that anyone could be so

manipulative. I'm so annoyed at myself.' Issy wiped away her tears angrily.

'Just be more careful about who you choose to trust. You know, he might have done you a favour.'

'How?'

'The first time you get bad press is always the worst. But it's happened now, it's out of the way, and you'll know to be more aware of who might be using you in the future. You're naive and too trusting, Issy. It's incredibly endearing but it will end up being your downfall in this business if you aren't more careful.'

'But what do I do now? Should I issue a statement or something?' Issy was completely out of her depth and she hated it.

'No, definitely don't issue a statement. Carry on being you and use the cameras, the show, the confession cam, to get your side of the story across. My advice would be to not go after Josh. Take the moral high ground and make it clear that you didn't spend the night how the papers reported it. You can turn this round by being honest and open. Don't be afraid to show your vulnerable side. I know you hate it but the public need to see that you have one. Alexander and Mia will be trying to paint you as some sort of gold-digger now to turn the voters against you.' Eva slowed down, taking in Issy's mortified expression. 'You're going to be fine, and you'll get through this. But it will get worse before it gets better. What is it you Brits say? "Today's news is tomorrow's chip wrappers?"'

'Yeah, I suppose. I know you're right but God, what a mess. I need to speak to my parents, Eva. I need them to know that none of it is true.'

'You'll be getting your phones back tonight. Call them. Explain to them what happened. If I know you well enough to know you're telling the truth, they certainly will.'

Issy made her way back up to the apartment. She felt marginally better after her conversation with Eva but the knot of dread in her stomach remained. Things would be better once she'd spoken to her parents, once they'd reassured her that they didn't believe a word of what had been written about her. A little voice piped up from somewhere inside. *But what if they* do *believe it?*

Chapter Twenty-one

Issy collected her phone as soon as she got back to the apartment and went straight to the girls' bedroom. Thankfully, Lexi, sensing she needed some time alone, stayed on the sofa with the others and let her have some privacy. *Mia's probably off bitching about me to the confession cam,* Issy thought bleakly.

There were dozens of missed calls from her parents, Zach and Molly. Others had sent Whatsapps, asking if she was OK, if it was true, if Josh had been a decent shag and if the rumours about the size of his penis were true. *He could be hung like a wasp for all I know,* Issy thought desperately. *I've got no bloody clue!* It upset Issy to see that people who knew her were jumping to the wrong conclusions immediately.

But all that was nothing compared to the abuse she was receiving on Twitter. Strangers, people who didn't know her from Adam, were calling her a slag and easy. Young girls were expressing their disappointment in her actions and, teenage boys were asking if they could have a 'go'. Some of the tweets were quite creative, despite being graphic and lewd, and under different circumstances Issy might have even laughed:

@badlad91: @IssyCutIt I wonder if Issy is still dizzy from giving posh josh a good nosh?!

But some were horrific:

@misstraceyps: So @IssyCutIt has dropped her knickers at the first chance of shagging a Z lister jst to get sum publicity?! #SHOCK #LOOSE

@CityFan89: @JoshTrustafarians What's @IssyCutIt like in the sack then mate? Would you mind if I went next?! #worthago #slag

But the ones that killed her the most were the ones that said she'd let them down:

@princessbex95: @IssyCutIt you were my fave on @CanYouCutItTV but I can't believe you'd sleep with that creep! #lostrespect

Issy was beginning to realise the kind of influence she and the rest of the contestants had already started to have on impressionable minds and what type of scrutiny they were under. It was a responsibility she hadn't expected, and she wasn't sure if it was something she wanted. No one had talked to or prepared them for this and it was too much.

Issy took a deep breath, pushed the comments of the haters to one side, and phoned home, half-willing her parents to answer as quickly as possible, half-hoping they wouldn't answer at all. She just hoped they would let her explain her side of things before giving her an earful.

'Mum!' Issy felt such relief at hearing her mother answer.

'Issy, love.' Debs sounded subdued. 'Are you OK?'

Before Issy could answer, Kev came onto the other extension.

'Explain yourself.' Kev's voice was firm and low. Issy knew she was in trouble. 'And I mean from the beginning, Isabelle. How did you get yourself into this mess?'

Issy heard the familiar echo as she was switched to speakerphone. She took a shaky breath and explained everything that had happened, from that first DM, to how special Josh had made her feel on their date. She told her parents about how happy she'd been until she'd seen the paper and now things were falling apart. Her voice cracked when she got to the part about some of the more aggressive and abusive tweets she'd received. By the time she had finished, she felt utterly drained.

'So that posh pillock set the whole thing up?' Kev growled and in the background she heard Princess Tiger-Lily also growl, and for once her dad didn't even tell her to shut up.

'I think so,' Issy said miserably. 'The photographer and the quotes to the paper are definitely him. But it's how he behaved on the date that I can't get my head around. He seemed so genuine.' And for the first time since reading the article she allowed herself to say what she'd been thinking and what, if she was honest, was really making her feel most stupid about the whole thing. 'I actually thought he liked me.'

'Oh, love,' Debs said. 'You're not the first girl to have her head turned by a handsome face and a fancy dinner. Maybe this was too much to ask of you. You should forget about that pig, come home and put this whole thing behind you.'

'I'm not quitting, Mum.' Of that, Issy was certain. Things were bad, yes, but she wanted to get through this, get back on track with the show and the competition. She might have allowed a man to get under her skin but she certainly wasn't going to give him the satisfaction of seeing her quit the show over him. No chance.

'No daughter of mine is falling at the first hurdle,' Kev said. 'We get it, Is. We knew there would be press attention, but we weren't prepared for it to affect us too. But, love, we really thought you had your head screwed on. I'm starting to regret ever putting you up to all this. I've got to take some of the blame too, I guess.'

'Dad, please.' Issy couldn't bear it if her parents were disappointed in her, and felt stung that they would think she would even put this on them. 'I feel bad enough as it is. *Please* stop making me feel worse. I didn't know any of this would happen. I didn't *mean* for any of this to happen.'

Kev sighed. 'I know, I know. It's just been a tough day on all of us.'

'What do you mean?'

'It doesn't matter,' Kev said.

'Kev,' Debs cut in. 'What did you say that for?'

'What's happened?' Issy's heart was hammering in her chest.

'Nothing, Is. Your mum's right – it's nothing we can't handle.'

'Since when does this family keep secrets from each other? Can you please just tell me what's going on?' Issy asked.

Kev sighed. 'It's your brother. He had a bit of trouble with one of the mechanics at the garage.'

'What kind of trouble?' Suddenly her dad's earlier comment about it affecting them became clear.

'Nothing major, don't worry. Just a couple of the younger lads were saying things.' Kev paused. 'About you. I was in the office so didn't hear any of it but Zach was right in the thick of it and . . . well, he lost his temper, didn't he? Ended up going for one of them, gave the lad a black eye and a broken nose, we think.'

'Oh God.' Issy couldn't believe it. Zach was protective, of course, but he wouldn't hurt a fly. He'd never been violent with anyone. Zach was too laid-back to mug himself off with fighting and arguing – it wasn't him. Issy was the one with the temper. 'Is Zach OK? Where is he? He didn't get locked up, did he? Oh God. I'm so sorry. I need to speak to him.'

'Calm down, Issy. He's fine. Of course he didn't get locked up. The lads all agreed they were out of order and it had got out of hand,' Kev reassured Issy and her body sagged with relief.

'Zach went out with Molly about an hour ago,' Debs said. 'She was round ours, wanting to know if we'd spoken to you yet, when Zach came back. He was wound up, the angriest I've ever seen him, so I sent him off for a walk with

Molly to calm down. No one can be angry around that girl.'

Issy was relieved that Zach was with Molly. Her mum was right about the effect she had on people. But she wished she could be there, that she could be the one to calm her brother down. Especially since this was all her fault.

'Mum, Zach knows that I'm not like that. I've never slept with anyone on the first date, and I never would. He knows that stuff in the paper is bollocks, doesn't he?'

'Of course he does.' Debs sounded tired. 'We all know you. It's just seeing you on the front page like that, and hearing people saying nasty things about you. It was a shock for all of us.'

'Speak to your brother,' Kev said. 'You'll have to call Molly to get to him. Zach's phone is at home. He's been getting messages off some lads from town, which was winding him up even more so your mum made him leave it here.'

How many people were going to be affected by Posh Josh, the royal knob? Fame-hungry dick, Issy thought angrily.

'I'll call him right now. And I am sorry,' Issy went on. 'Really I am.'

'Don't be sorry,' Kev said. 'Just be careful. We're here for you, love, and want to help you, but we don't know the rules to this game and there are some dirty players. So make sure you watch yourself from now on.'

'Zach!' Issy yelled when he answered Molly's phone. 'Zach, listen. It's not true, what he said. I didn't sleep with him, I swear. I—'

'Is,' Zach interrupted wearily. 'I know, OK? I know.'

'But how? I've only just got off the phone with Mum and Dad. They told me what happened.'

'Because I know you. But the rest of country doesn't and when that pubeless, spotty little kid started . . . I lost it. I'm sorry but I snapped.'

'No, I'm sorry.' Issy felt a fresh wave of tears rise up. 'I went on date with a lad I liked. That's all. I had no idea it would cause this much drama. But now it's been turned into this massive great big thing and it's a total mess. Mum and Dad are bickering, and not just in the way they usually do, and you're punching teenagers in the face. Has Molly been getting grief as well? Is she there?'

'We're in the King's Head. She's gone to get us some drinks. And I don't think she's getting too much hassle.' Zach hesitated.

'What is it?' Issy asked. Her stomach was already in knots. She didn't know if she could take much more.

'It's just, er . . . OK. So I think she's had to do a bit of damage control with some of your friends.'

'What do you mean?'

'Bollocks, I don't think she wanted me to say anything. Er . . . Look, I can see Molly on her way back from the bar. She can tell you.'

There were some muffled sounds at the other end and Issy was sure she heard Molly whisper to Zach, *What did you say that for?* before coming onto the line.

It seemed as though everyone was trying to protect her, which just made Issy feel worse.

'Is,' Molly began. 'Look, about what Zach said—'

'What have the girls been saying?' Issy interrupted.

'It's not all of them,' Molly said slowly, choosing her words carefully. 'But a couple needed some convincing that the story in the paper wasn't true.'

Issy's stomach dropped. Didn't her friends know her better than that? She had no words left, so she sat there, letting the tears fall.

'Babes, don't cry!' Molly said.

'I'm not,' Issy said, her voice thick with tears.

'Liar. Issy, don't do this to yourself. You find out who your real friends are in situations like this.'

'I s'pose.' A thought occurred to Issy. 'How did you know the story wasn't true?'

'Because I know my wifey would never cheat on me.' Molly laughed, and despite herself, so did Issy. 'Now, tell me what actually happened. I want the *real* gossip! It feels like we haven't spoken in ages. Don't leave anything out.'

And for what felt like the hundredth time that day, Issy recounted every single detail of that night and the following morning.

'Arsehole,' Molly hissed when Issy had finished. 'I'm never watching that show again. Twat!'

'I feel so stupid, Mols. I thought he liked me. And the stuff people are saying about me on Twitter . . . ' Issy trailed off.

'Come on, Is,' Molly said. 'You know better than to take any notice of anyone on Twitter. They're keyboard warriors with no life. Man up!'

'OK, Taylor. I'll do that,' said Issy.

'I mean it,' Molly insisted. 'It's shit and that Josh is a bastard but you need to put it behind you. Don't take any notice of Twitter or the papers. Try not to even read either of them. They'll be talking about something else tomorrow. With any luck some twat will flash their fanny getting out of a taxi tonight and you and Posh Josh will be long forgotten.'

Issy laughed again. God, she had missed Molly.

'Please though, babe,' Molly continued, 'don't let me see you moping around like a wet dishrag on the show, feeling sorry for yourself. You've got a real chance at winning, so get your focus back and get your side of the story out there.'

'That's kind of what Eva suggested too.'

'It's hard to be this beautiful and this smart at the same time. It's such a burden. It's good to know that there's someone out there sharing my pain,' Molly joked.

Issy laughed again and let go of the last of the tension in her body. 'Mols, I wish you were here right now.'

'I know. But we're still rooting for you so keep your head up. Just, no more dates with twatful knobs, OK?'

'Don't worry,' Issy said more fiercely than she intended. 'I'm never falling for any of that shit again, mate.'

It was only after Issy had hung up that she realised she hadn't asked Molly how she was.

Chapter Twenty-two

Jason was the only person on the sofas when Issy walked into the living area.

'Where is everyone?' she asked, flopping down next to him.

'Lexi and Aaron are in the confession cam, Mia's shut herself in her room and Rory is God knows where. We've only lost two people but it feels so much quieter already, doesn't it?'

'It's weird. It's only been a couple of weeks but so much has happened already.'

'It's not like I'd thought it would be,' Jason mused.

'Jase, I want you to know that the story in the papers—'

'Is, you don't have to explain anything to me.'

'But I want to. You were so quiet in the green room earlier. I thought maybe you were angry with me.'

'I'm not angry with you, Is. A bit jealous and a bit pissed off maybe.'

204

Now that threw Issy for six. She hadn't expected Jason to be so honest. It was endearing but it also made her feel like such a callous bitch, on top of everything else.

'Wow ... Er, thank you.' *Thank you?! What the fuck are you saying, Issy?*

'Thank you? Issy, you're shit at this, aren't you? This is why I know you didn't sleep with Josh. You couldn't pull a muscle,' Jason laughed.

'I'm not usually that bad at all this. I just didn't know where I stood with you. I thought maybe we were just mates who flirted a bit?' Issy was confused. 'I still don't understand to be honest.' She knew she had a bit of chemistry with Jason but hadn't thought it would lead to anything. And after everything she'd been through today she wasn't thinking clearly enough to deal with this right now. 'Jase, listen—'

'No need to say anything, Is,' Jason interrupted, with a smile. 'I know you've had a long day and some huge heart-to-heart with me is probably the last thing you need on top of it all. Let's just leave it. I'm good at bad timing.' He smiled and shrugged. 'Have you spoken to your family?' he asked, swiftly changing the subject.

Issy nodded, relieved to be on safer ground. 'It was intense, but I feel better now.'

'Good. You're lucky, you know,' Jason told her.

'I am? I don't feel that lucky.'

'I mean because you have a family that care about you. They wouldn't go mad or lose it if they weren't bothered.' Jason closed his eyes, head resting on the back of the sofa. He was quiet for so long, Issy thought he'd fallen asleep.

'Jason? You OK?' she asked eventually.

Jason opened his eyes and stared at the ceiling. 'I was just thinking about my parents.'

'Why don't you want to talk about them?' Issy asked softly.

'It's hard,' Jason said, turning to face her. 'I want to. I want to remember them, but it's painful and I'm not looking for sympathy in here. I don't want you or anyone else to get the wrong idea about me.'

Issy shuffled closer. 'I'm never going to get the wrong idea. What's the story with your parents?'

'I don't have one. There's nothing to tell . . . ' he trailed off. 'It's been years but I still miss them.'

Years? Were Jason's parents . . . ? Issy hadn't wanted to say it out loud but had suspected it was something like this. Even so, the pain in Jason's eyes and tremble in his voice as he spoke was hard for Issy to process. She wrapped her arms around him. 'I don't know what to say.'

'It's fine – no one ever does. That's why I try not to bring it up. It makes everyone feel so awkward.' Jason paused and Issy gave him a look that told him to continue – she wasn't going anywhere. 'I was six when . . . I was shunted from one foster family to the next. It wasn't bad but it wasn't great either. As soon as I was old enough and could afford it, I moved out on my own.' Jason smiled sadly at Issy. 'Maybe that's why I like it here so much. Instant family, no more coming back to an empty flat.'

Issy tried to think of a world without her mum and dad, and just the thought of it brought tears to her eyes.

'I can't begin to imagine what it was like for you,' Issy said. 'And I'll never be able to understand what you went through but if you ever want to talk about anything, I'm here.' She hugged him again. 'You're not on your own anymore.'

Later that evening, the remaining contestants were gathered on the sofas. The atmosphere was awkward. Especially as Mia kept throwing Issy dirty looks, which she tried to ignore. She had no more emotion left to give today, she was pooched, so Mia could enjoy her evils for one night. Sad cow. Issy had stuck close to Jason who'd been quiet since their conversation earlier and between trying to avoid another row with Mia and covering for Jason's somber mood, Issy couldn't wait to hit the hay. The door to the apartment opened and Laura walked in. She looked exhausted.

'Hi everyone. Hope you're all OK,' Laura said.

'You OK?' Aaron asked.

'I've been in the editing suite all day with the production crew. I'm completely exhausted.'

It never stops, Issy thought.

'Issy,' Laura continued, 'about today's newspaper story, we know that it's false and we're sorry that you're going through this. Eva talked to the producers about the conversation you had earlier and we agree with her that you should just use the cameras and social media to get your side of the story across. Try to take the high road but it's best to get your voice out there. It's then up to the public to decide who they believe.' Mia let out a derisive snort. Laura shot her a look and continued. 'There will be some backlash but experience tells us that it won't be long before the public lose interest in the story.'

'OK. Thanks for the advice, Laura,' Issy said.

'Or you could just say he's shit in bed and has a tiny little todger?' Rory offered. Even Issy laughed along with everyone else – everyone except Laura and Mia of course.

Laura shook her head and turned her attention to the rest of the contestants. 'So, tomorrow, you'll be taking part in a masterclass with the judges. Alexander will talk about designing and executing hair styles, Eva will talk about haircare products, marketing and that side of the business. We have a lot to get through, so you'll be flat out for the entire day and most of the evening, I'm afraid.' Everyone groaned. 'I know, I know. It's intense and we're all on our last legs. Trust me, I understand. But get through tomorrow and then you'll have forty-eight hours out of the salon before we have to start filming the next challenge. We'll need bits and pieces from you and you'll still be filmed in the apartment, but you won't have the pressure of the challenge so that should give you a little time to recharge. Right, unless there's anything else, I should get back to that fucking editing suite . . . Sorry about that . . . Christ on a cracker, I'm knackered.'

The cast all laughed a little at seeing the normally so professional and reserved Laura crack. *It's getting to everyone*, Issy thought.

'Actually,' Jason said. 'Can I have a quick word in private?'

'Sure.' Laura nodded.

'Wonder what that's about,' Lexi said as the two of them disappeared into the boys' room.

Issy shrugged. She guessed it had something to do with

what they were talking about earlier – but she wasn't about to spill Jason's secrets, not after he'd trusted her.

Issy had her phone back for half an hour. There was a Whatsapp from Zach.

Call me when you can. Me and Molly have had an idea! Z

'Hey,' she said when her brother answered. 'I got your message. What's up?'

'Me and Molly decided you could do with cheering up after we spoke to you earlier. You sounded about as much fun as a poke in the eye. Do you think you'll be able to get away tomorrow night? We want to take you for dinner and drinks ... Mostly drinks ... Drinks with nibbles ... All right, probably loads of drinks and a few crisps.' Zach laughed.

Issy thought about it. 'I'd love to but I don't know if I'll be allowed out of the apartment. They're being so understanding about all the agg I've caused so far I really don't want to push my luck anymore.'

'Just ask them. The worst that can happen is they say no, Is,' Zach said. 'We just think it will be good for you to spend some time with your family. It might help you put this whole Josh thing behind you and get you back on top form for the show. Surely you can tell the producers that you need this?'

'OK, I'll try. Thanks, Zach. You're right though. This would be just what I need right now.' Spending time with Molly and Zach always put Issy in a good mood. It had only been a couple of weeks since she'd seen them but it felt like a lifetime ago. 'Let me see if I can speak to Laura and I'll text you before they take our phones away again.'

Issy all but ran to the production room and knocked on the door. A bleary-eyed Laura opened the door.

'What is it, Issy? Is everything OK?'

'I'm really sorry to disturb you, I know you're busy, but I just needed to ask you something.'

'Go for it.' Laura stretched and yawned.

'I know we have a busy day tomorrow but if we get done filming in time, do you think I could leave the apartment to have dinner with my brother and best mate?' Issy asked hopefully.

'I don't know.' Laura looked doubtful. 'Tomorrow's going to be intense and you shouldn't really be doing anything away from the cameras right now.'

'Please.' Issy was suddenly desperate to see them. 'This thing with Josh has thrown me and I think my performance on the show will suffer because of it. Spending time with my family will help me get my head on straight.'

'OK, OK.' Laura held her hands up, clearly too tired to argue the toss. 'Filming will take as long as it takes but if we get done early and there's time, then yes, you can spend the evening with your brother and friend.'

Issy threw her arms around Laura before realising that Laura wasn't exactly the hugging kind. She pulled away, embarrassed, but couldn't keep the smile from her face.

'Thanks, Laura. Really. It'll mean so much to me.'

Issy quickly typed out a message to Zach.

Crazy day of filming tomorrow but if done in time, I can have dinner with you and Molly! I x

Her phone buzzed with a reply almost immediately.

Sweet! We'll come into Manchester. See you then, sis. Z

That night, Issy went to sleep with a smile on her face. It had been a truly dreadful day, but just the possibility of seeing Zach and Molly the next day made her heart that little bit lighter.

Chapter Twenty-three

'I don't understand.' Issy narrowed her eyes at Laura. 'Last night you said that if we finished filming then I could go out for dinner. You said yourself that we've been racing through and should be done in a couple of hours. So why are you now saying no?'

Laura sighed. She didn't have time for this. 'Look, this was supposed to be a surprise. Nothing was definite and I honestly didn't know which way it was going to go or if Harry would want to include it, but after you and I spoke last night this all got confirmed and this is the first chance I've had to speak to you all day.'

'What surprise?'

'Jason asked me last night if he could take you out on a surprise dinner tonight to cheer you up after the whole Josh thing. Harry loves it – he thought it was a great idea. They want a bit of variety on the show so he liked the fact that this wouldn't be in the apartment or the salon.'

'Wait.' Issy shook her head. 'So this dinner with Jason, it's going to be filmed?'

'Yes.'

Issy felt conflicted. It was sweet of Jason to try to cheer her up but she'd been so looking forward to seeing Zach and Molly. 'Why didn't Jason say anything to me?' she asked.

'That is kind of the point of a surprise. You not knowing,' Laura pointed out dryly. 'It also means that when he tells you later, you still have to act as though you don't know anything about this. Or Harry will know I've ruined it and his tiny bald head will explode.'

'Do I *have* to go?' Issy made one last attempt to change Laura's mind.

'Yes.' Laura nodded. 'It's all set up. The restaurant's booked, and there's a small crew ready to go with you tonight.'

Laura's voice was firm. Issy knew she couldn't get out of this.

'Then can I have my phone for five minutes? I need to tell my brother I can't make it after all.'

'I thought you said you were just filming in the salon today?' Zach did not sound pleased. 'Now you're saying you're going out to dinner with someone else?'

'Zach, what am I supposed to do?' Issy had to make him understand. 'I just found out about it a few minutes ago. I didn't plan this. The producers did. I have to go and anyway, you were only offering crisps.' Issy was trying to lighten the mood.

'So they're filming you?'

'Yes.'

'This sounds as set up as what Josh did. You're going to be filmed going out with another lad.'

'It's not like that. Jason and I are friends and he wanted to do something nice for me.'

'Me and Molly wanted to do something nice for you too. But I suppose it doesn't count as we can't guarantee a film crew.'

'What? Listen Zach, it's in my contract. I can't say no.' Even to her ears it sounded like a weak excuse, but it was the truth. Issy was trapped. 'You know I really wanted to spend time with you two tonight.'

'But not enough to say no to the show.'

'Zach, please don't be like this. The show is my life at the moment. I have to give it my all, plus I really can't afford to push it any more than I already have.'

'All right, Is. I get it. It doesn't matter. It's just that Molly was really looking forward to it. She's really missing you, you know.'

'And I'm missing her. Listen, you two can still go. You're already in Manchester. You may as well.'

'I suppose we can. But it was you we came here to see.'

'Zach, I really am sorry.'

'I know, mate.' Zach sounded resigned. 'Look, try to have a good time tonight and maybe we can do something else another time.'

'OK. You two have fun tonight.'

'You too. Bye.'

Issy rang off and stared at her phone for a moment. When had things become so hard?

*

214

Issy walked into the green room. Lexi, Rory and Aaron were lounging on the sofas. They were almost done filming their masterclass with Alexander.

'Right.' Aaron stood up. 'I've been summoned to go see Alexander. Wish me luck!'

'You need more than luck with that bitter old twat,' Issy said. Aaron shuddered and left.

'I'm so bored,' Rory declared. 'We need to do something to shake this place up.'

'Not enough store-cupboard action?' Lexi asked.

'The bird got found out, didn't she? She got fired and Laura had a stern word with me. She's fit when she's mad actually. Anyway, apparently if I want to shag anyone it has to be one of you.'

'Don't look at me,' Lexi said. 'I'm not having blondie's sloppy seconds. Besides, I think Mia's the one for you,'

'Challenge accepted,' Rory said. 'Mia!' he yelled. She appeared in the doorway.

'Yes?' she asked.

'I wondered if you fancied coming out with me tonight for a curry and a pint.' Issy wasn't sure if Rory was being serious or not.

Mia's eyebrows shot up in surprise. 'A curry?'

'Yeah,' Rory said. 'And a pint. Have you never had a curry before?'

'Of course I have. I spent a week eating authentic Thai curries while holidaying in Pattaya last year.'

'I have no idea what you just said. But I'm talking about Indian. We can split a jalfrezi. It's gonna change your life. What do you say?'

'Will it be filmed?' Mia asked.

'Dunno.' Rory shrugged his shoulders.

'You could request that it's filmed,' Lexi suggested, an evil grin on her face.

'I will ... Then it might make it worth my time.' Mia looked pleased. 'I'll call Laura.'

'Is that a yes?' Rory asked.

'Yes, why not?' Mia disappeared to find Laura without giving Rory a second glance.

'Do you think Mia wants a showmance?' Lexi asked.

'She's not that popular, so probably,' Rory replied.

'That doesn't bother you?' Issy asked.

'I don't care. As long as I get a curry and maybe a fumble with HRH Princess Prissy Knickers, I'm sound.'

Issy laughed. Rory came close to crossing the line a lot of the time, but if he was a bastard at least he was a hilarious one.

'You all right, Issy?' Lexi asked. They were done filming for the day and had hidden away in their bedroom on their bunks.

'Sort of. My brother and Molly wanted to take me out to dinner tonight. Laura said I could go but then at the last minute said no. Turns out Jason's organised a surprise for me, which they want to film.'

'What kind of surprise?'

'He asked if he could take me out to dinner to cheer me up. He wanted to surprise me with it tonight apparently, so Laura had to tell me when I started kicking off about not seeing Zach and Molly.'

'Ah, I see.' Lexi climbed up to join Issy on the top bunk. 'At least it's for a good reason. The show comes first right now, and Jason's being really sweet.'

'I know but I feel like I've let Zach and Molly down. Again.'

'You haven't. There's nothing you can do about it. What the producers want, the producers get. That's the deal we signed,' Lexi pointed out.

'You're right but I sounded so pathetic when I was explaining that to Zach. I'm so lucky to be here but I'm whinging all the time and acting ungrateful. I'm starting to sound like a broken record, aren't I, babe? I need to buck my ideas up. It's not like Jason doesn't have enough to think about.'

'Like what?' Lexi asked.

Awwww shit, Issy. What did you say that for?

'Well just with the competition and everything going on ... He should be looking out for himself and not worrying about me.' *Well saved, Issy, well saved.*

'I suppose, but he's probably asked because he likes you,' Lexi said.

'Maybe, mate, but I don't need romance right now. In fact the last thing I need is more man drama. Tonight will just be about two friends having a nice time.'

'Totally, honey. A nice, private dinner for you and Jason ... And the production crew ... With the entire nation watching.' Lexi grinned. 'So intimate, so cosy!'

'I keep forgetting about the cameras. It's going to be weird. Oh, and you have to act surprised when Jason reveals the surprise later. I'm not supposed to know about it.'

'Now they're expecting us to act too?' Lexi shook her head. 'The term reality TV is being redefined.'

All the contestants had been told to assemble on the sofas. Issy suspected Jason's 'surprise' was about to be revealed. She was touched that Jason wanted to do this for her, but it was starting to feel contrived. Her life was becoming one long set-up. Jason cleared his throat.

'Issy, I know you've been upset about what that twat did to you so I wanted to organise something special to cheer you up. So would you come out to dinner with me tonight?' *He sounds nervous*, Issy thought.

'Dinner? Really?' Issy's tone was too bright, she could tell. She could only hope it rang true on camera and she didn't just look like a cheesy idiot.

'Yes,' Jason said. 'I've booked a table at Rosso's. Thought we could dress smart, have some drinks, nice food and get away from the madness for a while. What do you think?'

'Aw, Jase, that's well nice of you. And you've been such a great mate to me through all this. I'd love to. It sounds like just what I need.' Issy tried not to look at Lexi, who she knew would be struggling to keep a straight face, and concentrated on Jason instead.

'Ah, Jase,' Rory said, slapping him on the back. 'If only I'd known, we could have had a double date.'

'I'd rather eat glass,' Mia said, rolling her eyes.

Issy may not have been sure about tonight's filming but she was very sure that she'd never seen anyone look more handsome than Jason did. He was wearing a gorgeous dark navy suit that fitted around the curve of his muscles perfectly, complete with white shirt, and a grey tie and pocket square. *Wow*, thought Issy, *he's gone to town. This ensemble is clearly not from Burton's Menswear.* Issy was in her favourite black jumpsuit from AQ/AQ and had matched her favourite MAC red lipstick and nails with her bag and shoes.

They were settled at a secluded table in Rosso's, an upmarket Italian restaurant in Manchester city centre. Issy sipped her wine and tried to relax. She was doing her best to enjoy the evening but she was acutely aware of the conspicuous amount of cameras pointed at their table, and of Ryan and the rest of the crew in the background.

'I'm really sorry,' Jason said, his blue eyes wide and sincere.

'What for?'

'I didn't want them filming this, but they insisted, so I thought, well, I thought at least we'd get some time together away from the house and salon.'

'Don't be daft. It's fine. I understand and it's still a really sweet thought. It's just that it would've been nice to have one night out without everyone watching, where we could properly relax.' She sighed.

'That's what I wanted for you when I asked Laura about tonight. I'm sorry it's backfired.' He looked a little upset and Issy hated herself for not being able to at least pretend she was having a good time. It wasn't Jason's fault the cameras were there. *Get over it*, she said to herself. *Start making an effort with the poor lad.*

'I'm the one who should apologise. I'm sorry for being such a miserable cow. Right, let's order, forget about the cameras and get drunk, eh? After the week I've had I think we deserve it.'

'So, how are you feeling after everything that happened yesterday?' Jason asked as they tucked into their mains.

'I don't know really. I knew that we'd have things written about us but I wasn't prepared for so much so soon, I suppose. Especially when it's so wildly incorrect. Bad stuff about me coming out that's true, I suppose I'd have to take on the chin, but barefaced lies that I can't control? It's so frustrating. I still feel used by Josh and I'm angry at myself for getting taken in and mugged off.' Issy smiled at Jason across the table. She was aware she'd got caught up in the moment and was ranting and was desperate to tone it down quickly. *Let's not let him know you're a total pyscho right away, babes, OK?!*

'But I'll get over it,' she tried to add casually.

'Have you heard from Josh since it happened?'

Issy shook her head. 'Nothing. And I'm not planning on getting in touch with him either. He can jog on.'

'You shouldn't be so hard on yourself,' Jason said. 'We all make mistakes. We all fall, it's how we pick ourselves up that defines us.'

'My dad said something like that too.'

'Great minds think alike,' Jason answered with a smile and once again Issy caught herself thinking how fit he was. *Stop it, slag tits, he's your mate.*

'I know what you're saying. The thing I'll really have to

get used to is that I'm not just making daft mistakes that me and the girls laugh and cringe about the next day. I'm making them with the whole country watching,' Issy said ruefully. 'We all are,' she added pensively.

Jason laughed. 'Oh babe, stop it! You're so serious. This was meant to be a nice night out to take your mind *off* all of this. You've got to roll with the punches and come back out on top. True, I'm sure that most of us on the show are going to come up against this at some point but, Is, if anyone could handle going through it first ... it's you. You're strong. I haven't known you for long but I know you're a good person. Everyone else will see that too.'

'I hope so. I'm just going to be more careful about choosing who to trust in the future.'

Jason stared at his plate, lost in thought. 'I've spent most of my life not trusting people: pushing them away because I was too scared to get close to anyone in case I lost them. It hurts too much.' He looked up into Issy's eyes. 'I love that you aren't like that, Issy. Don't change. You're making me rethink all of that.'

'You must think I'm so self-centred, spending all this time talking about my stupid, schoolgirl problems. They're nothing compared to what you've been through.'

'It's OK,' Jason said with a smile. 'We're all allowed our bad days. I didn't confide in you so you'd see me differently or treat me like a victim. I did it because I want to trust you.' He picked up his glass in a toast. 'Here's to making tomorrow a good day.'

It was a bit cheesy and Issy thought she'd look like a right knob on TV, clinking glasses with him, but she went along with it.

'I'll drink to that.'

Issy yawned. 'I'm stuffed,' she said.

'Me too,' Jason groaned. 'But it was worth it.'

Once she'd relaxed, Issy had ended up having a good time. She and Jason had chatted about things other than the show and the Josh drama, and even though she thought she'd seen Ryan shaking his head when Jason had been talking about how many footballers had been on his previous client list, she hadn't let that bother her. Issy got the sense that Jason was trying to impress her and it was a nice feeling to be worth impressing.

They walked out of the restaurant but had to go back inside because one of the cameras had been pointed at the wrong angle. Issy felt like a right pillock going back in, only to have to 'leave' again – especially with all the other diners watching but eventually they got the shots they needed and Issy and Jason were in the back of the car the production company had provided. Ryan was up front, in the passenger seat.

'You guys have a nice time?' Ryan called back to them.

'Yeah,' Jason said. Issy waited for him to elaborate and when he didn't she piped up instead.

'The food was delicious. Did you see the size of my seabass, Ryan?' Issy added, frowning slightly at Jason.

'I bet you say that to all the boys,' Ryan laughed.

'Shut up! But it was lovely, thanks.'

Jason looked pissed off and as she looked away from

his thunderous expression, Ryan caught Issy's eye in the rearview mirror. He raised his eyebrows and she shook her head slightly. She had no idea why Jason was being so rude.

They let themselves into the apartment a short while later and quietly walked towards the bedrooms. Everyone else had gone to bed.

'Hey,' Issy whispered. 'What was that about in the car?'

'What do you mean?' Jason asked.

'With Ryan. You barely said anything when he asked us about our night.'

'Oh, it was nothing. I just don't like him that much, that's all.'

'Really?' Issy was surprised. Ryan was so nice and laidback, she'd have thought it was impossible *not* to like him.

'He's too full of himself. Tries to be everyone's friend but he's a grass, I reckon, and a nosey prick.'

'Wow. Strong. Why don't you tell me how you really feel?' Issy wished she hadn't asked. She didn't want to argue with Jason but she couldn't understand anyone having a bad word to say about Ryan. 'I don't think he's like that,' Issy said.

'Doesn't matter. Let's not end the night talking about him,' Jason said, taking a step closer to Issy. 'I had a really nice time, Miss Jones.'

'I did too. Thank you for taking me out. It really did take my mind off things.'

'I'm glad.' Jason bent his head and for a moment Issy thought he would kiss her mouth but he kissed her cheek instead. 'Goodnight, pretty lady.'

''Night.'

That night, Issy fell into a deep and peaceful sleep dreaming about what hers and Jason's kids would look like. Damn her overzealous subconscious!

Chapter Twenty-four

The following morning, Issy was heading to the kitchen when she heard Jason and Mia's voices. She paused before she walked through the door. It wasn't in her nature to eavesdrop or be sneaky but there was something about Mia that she didn't trust and she wanted to know if her instincts were right.

'So they filmed you having dinner with Issy?' Issy heard Mia ask Jason.

'Yeah, they did. Did they film your date with Rory?'

'Of course. And it wasn't a date! As if I'd go anywhere near him in real life.'

'Should make for interesting viewing,' Jason said.

'Yours too.' Issy could hear the sneer in Mia's voice. She'd had enough of this girl.

'Morning,' Issy said brightly, walking into the kitchen.

'Hey, babe,' Jason said easily.

Mia scowled at Issy and flounced off without a word.

'I see Mia had her weetabitch this morning,' Issy said drily. 'Have you already made coffee, J?'

'Coming right up.'

A few minutes later Issy and Jason joined the others on the sofas.

'How was last night?' Lexi asked.

'Good. Fun,' Issy replied, smiling at Jason. 'The restaurant was lovely, the food was delicious, and the company wasn't half bad either.'

'Oi you! I was boss company. She's just trying to act cool,' Jason teased and grabbed Issy in a playful headlock, tousling her hair.

'Geeeerrrruuuuuufffff!' Issy laughed and pathetically tried to fight him off.

'Pile oooon!' shouted Lexi before diving onto the giggling couple.

'We had a marvellous time didn't we, Rory?' Mia cut through the laughter.

'Er, yeah. I guess so.' Rory was pulled away from the fun by Mia's shrill tones. He looked hungover. Issy assumed he'd had to drink his way through his 'date' and Mia's self-obsessed diatribe.

'So, while Aaron and I were hanging around the house last night, like a couple of undateables, and you's were all off doing God knows what – I don't want the details by the way you scruffy bastards – we decided we needed to have a house night out,' Lexi said, climbing off Issy's lap.

'Oh God! Why would we want to do that?' Mia protested quickly.

'To have a bit of a laugh, you melt. Anyway, I've already

spoken to Laura,' Lexi said, dismissing Mia's protests as quickly as she'd made them, 'and she thinks it's a wicked idea. So we're off out tonight. There won't be any filming but she wants us to bond a bit more. She was saying that they need more from us as a group, now that we're almost halfway through the show.'

'Are we nearly halfway through already?' Aaron said. He looked paler than usual, and tired. They were all exhausted but there was something particularly unsettling about his expression today.

'I guess we are. What is it, three more eliminations? And then it's the live final,' Jason said.

'I wonder who's going home next?' Issy knew who she wanted to go.

'Well, it won't be me. I'm not going anywhere,' Mia declared, standing up. 'If we're out tonight, then I'm going to start getting ready now. And where's Laura? I simply will not go out without a manicure first.'

Rory perked up at that and grinned. 'Thank God she's gone.'

'So I won't be needing a hat for the wedding then?' Lexi laughed.

'Not unless they legalise bestiality and that daft cow marries Horatio. She's nuttier than squirrel shit. Hands down, worst date of my life.'

'So is that you and Mia done then?' Issy asked.

'I'd still shag her, like!'

'That's my boy!' Jason slapped Rory on the back. If only Mia didn't have to come out with them tonight.

*

227

Laura had been to see them as they were getting ready for their night out. She'd told them that they would be heading to a club called Luxe and that the cars would be picking them up in an hour.

'You need to spend more time together as a group,' she'd said. 'The biggest piece of feedback we've been getting is that you don't seem to be gelling enough. People have to believe there are some real friendships and relationships being formed here and at the moment things all seem a bit superficial and stilted between some of you. Take this time away from the cameras to have fun and get to know each other better. If you can do that, it will come across on the show and do us all a favour.'

Issy reflected over Laura's words as she was carefully applying her fake eyelashes. They were constantly being told what to do and tonight, which had started off as fun and exciting, was becoming increasingly monitored. There was no getting away from it – the show, the attention, the incessant refreshing of her Twitter feed whenever she had five minutes with her phone. It was constant. Even tonight – a supposed 'night off' – had an ulterior agenda. Nonetheless Issy was determined to let her hair down and enjoy her few hours away from the house and all its hidden cameras. It was exactly what the doctor ordered.

'You look great!' Lexi exclaimed, walking into the bedroom. Issy was wearing a black crop top and white midi skirt from ASOS with red court shoes and her favourite Mulberry Clemmie clutch. Lexi sat down on the chair next to the bunk. 'Did you speak to Molly today?'

'No, I tried to call but she didn't pick up. I Whatsapp'd

her and she replied saying she was fine, and that she and Zach had a nice time last night. I wish I'd managed to speak to her though.' Issy took a step back and looked at herself critically in the mirror. That would do. 'Lex, I wanted to ask earlier but I couldn't get you on your own – is Aaron OK?'

'So it's not just me who thinks he's acting weird?'

'Nah, babe. I've definitely noticed a change in him. He's so much more subdued, he looks stressed to death. What do you think is up with him? You reckon the competition is getting too much?'

Lexi frowned. 'I'm not sure. He was quiet last night and when I asked him what was wrong, he said it was nothing. But he's definitely hiding something.'

'Let's chat to him tonight, try and get it out of him after a couple of drinks. My dad always says "a drunken person's words are a sober person's thoughts".'

'Mr Jones sounds like a wise man.'

'Yeah, he's a regular font of knowledge – if you want to know about alcohol or Man United.'

Rory popped his head round the door. 'C'mon ladies. Move yourselves. We've got drinks in the living room.'

Issy surveyed her five cast mates. They were stood around the kitchen counter, waiting for Rory to refill their shot glasses with tequila for the second time. *We are one odd bunch*, Issy thought to herself. Rory was wearing a retro Ellesse T-shirt with the collar turned up. He resembled Danny Dyer in *The Business*. Aaron was rocking ripped jeans, a long grey jumper and a black leather jacket. *He wouldn't look out of place on stage with One Direction*, thought Issy. In contrast to the other lads, Jason had opted to go smart in a shirt, black fitted jeans, blazer and pocket square – he looked as great as he had the night before to Issy. Lexi was in a beautiful emerald green jumpsuit with gold accessories, and Mia was head to toe designer – of course. Issy was sure her dress was a Victoria Beckham number. Whatever she thought about Mia as a person, she had to admit that she had good style. All in all, and despite their differences, they looked great and Issy was pleased to see everyone had made an effort. She had a good feeling about tonight.

'Here's to a night of fun,' Lexi said, necking her tequila.

'And to putting that knob Josh behind me.' Issy raised her own shot.

'I'll second that,' Jason concurred.

'Oh for God's sake. Can we all stop making such a fuss over poor little Issy?' Mia said, exasperated. 'You couldn't wait to go out with him and if the pictures are anything to go by you weren't complaining on the date either.'

'Oh my God, Mia. I only kissed him! The stuff about me sleeping with him is utter bollocks!' Issy tried to keep her cool and tossed back her tequila, hoping it would cut Mia off.

'Whatever. You were all over him like a cheap suit,' Mia wrinkled her nose, 'so spare me your protestations. A picture speaks a thousand words.'

'I don't care what you think, Mia. Just you keep talking and keep showing your true colours. You're mugging your-self off here, not me, and I won't play into your hands,' Issy said, all the while reminding herself not to throw her glass of wine in Mia's face.

'Yes, you do. You care what *everyone* thinks of you. But you're not the star of the show anymore now, are you?'

'C'mon girls,' Rory said, pouring out some more tequila. 'Let's have another drink, yeah? Make love not war!'

Mia ignored him and ploughed on. 'You should've known better than to think someone like Josh would ever look twice at someone like you, without there being something in it for him.'

'What's that supposed to mean?' Issy said. She knew *exactly* what Mia meant but she wanted her to say the words.

'Josh will end up with someone with class, with style, and with grace. He'd never seriously date some working class imbecile whose idea of fine dining is Nandos!'

'I like Nandos,' chimed in Rory still desperately trying to diffuse the increasingly awkward atmosphere.

But Issy wasn't listening – she saw red.

'Listen to me, Mia. You have no idea about me or what I'm like. Eating in Nandos doesn't make me classless just as eating in Nobu doesn't make you classy. It's about how you conduct yourself and how you treat others. You treat no one in this house, or any of the crew, with any respect and we all see through your shit-stirring and game playing. This isn't going the way you planned, you're bitter and that's why you're attacking me. End of.'

Mia laughed bitterly. 'Oh ... And there they are, ladies and gentleman. Issy's true colours.' Mia started a sarcastic slow clap and it dawned on Issy that despite all her best intentions she'd played straight into her hands. *Now who's the twat?* thought Issy.

'OK, that's enough,' Jason said, stepping in between the

two of them. He put his hands on Issy's shoulders. 'Calm down, babes. Leave it now.'

Before Issy could respond, there was a knock at the door. Their cars were here.

It was midnight and they were settled into their private booth, a magnum of Grey Goose vodka on the table. They'd been recognised as soon as they'd walked in and had spent the first hour after their arrival taking selfies with fans on their walk through the club to their cordoned-off area. There was a lot of support for Issy and it had helped her calm down after her fight with Mia. She had avoided speaking, touching, even looking at Mia since they'd left the apartment. She wasn't going to let her ruin the night, that was for certain.

'Come with me,' Jason said, grabbing her hand and pulling her to her feet.

'Where we going?' Issy asked as he led her to the other side of the club.

They found a quieter table towards the back of the club. Issy stood with her back against the table and Jason leaned into her, his hand resting on the wall beside her head.

'I wanted to talk to you in private,' Jason said into her ear. 'Are you OK after what happened earlier?'

Issy nodded. 'She makes me so fucking angry but what winds me up the most is that I allow her to get under my skin. I just need to be the bigger person and ignore her from now on.'

'She's jealous of you, that's clear to anyone, babe. I tried to give her the benefit of the doubt when the show started but I shouldn't have bothered – not after what I saw tonight. She's a major game player and all about the drama – that's not what I'm here for.'

'You were trying to see the best in her,' Issy said. Jason was leaning in so close, they were almost touching. It was hard to focus when there was almost no space between them.

Jason turned his head and his lips brushed Issy's cheek. She knew that she should stop what was inevitably coming next – it was too soon after what had happened with Josh. But Jason wasn't Josh. He'd been her friend from day one and there had always been a spark between them, a real one. Issy didn't know if it was the tequila, the vodka, or the fact that she was fed up of analysing every decision she made, but when Jason's lips found hers she didn't resist. She wrapped her arms around his neck, pulled him in closer and kissed him deeper.

When they eventually broke apart Jason smiled down at her.

'That was worth waiting for,' he said. He looked around to see if anyone was watching before going in for a kiss on her neck.

Issy pushed him away, laughing. 'Behave! We should really get back to our booth,' she said.

'Fuck that, Issy. Do you know how long I've been waiting to kiss you?' He laughed. 'Since I first met you. I want to stay here and kiss you all night, not run back to the rest of the group and all the bitching and drama.'

Issy was both taken aback by Jason's confession and made up by it at the same time. She would have liked to do the same if she was honest but they were starting to attract some attention and she didn't want some overzealous selfie-taker catching them at it and then posting it all over Instagram.

'Tonight's about us bonding as a cast, J – and we aren't doing a very good job so far, skulking in darkened corners necking on with each other.' She was pleased it was dark and he couldn't see her blushing. 'Come on,' she said, leading Jason back across the club.

Issy slid in next to Lexi, who grinned at her. 'Where have you two been?'

'Just talking,' Issy said innocently.

'Yeah right,' Lexi said. 'And you and Mia are BFFs. Don't try and kid a kidder, Jones.'

Issy laughed with Lexi. As she looked across the table at Aaron, who was pouring himself a very generous measure of vodka she remembered their plan. She nudged Lexi. 'We should talk to Aaron. You see those measures he's pouring himself? You'd think he's on *Geordie Shore* not *Can You Cut It?*. If we leave it much longer he won't be able to speak, let alone cut hair.'

Lexi nodded, a concerned look on her face. 'Hey, Aaron,' she called across the table. 'Come for a smoke?'

Issy, Lexi and Aaron were sat on some posh garden furniture in the smoking area.

'What's going on with you?' Lexi jumped straight in. 'You've been in a weird mood all day, and now you're getting completely smashed on your own?'

'Nothing's the matter,' Aaron slurred. His eyes were red and Issy wasn't sure if that was from the booze or tears.

'You can talk to us.' Issy put an arm around his shoulders. 'There aren't any cameras around now and you know you can trust me and Lex. We're worried about you, Aaron.'

'Do you promise not to say anything?' Aaron asked.

'Yes, of course,' Lexi said. 'Tell us what's wrong. We might even be able to help, kid.'

Aaron stared at his hands for a few minutes. Issy and Lexi exchanged a glance. What was going on?

'It's Alexander,' Aaron said eventually, and then stopped.

'We all hate Alexander, mate. I'm right with you on that one.' Lexi took a frustrated drag of her cigarette.

'What about Alexander?' Issy said gently. She sensed there was more to this than Alexander just being his usual knobby self.

'You know there's always been a bit of bants about how he fancies me?' The girls nodded and Aaron continued. 'Well it's true and it's not LOLZ at all. He's been putting a shift in with me massively.'

'What do you mean?' Lexi asked, frowning.

'Small things at first. An inappropriate comment here and there, a hand that stayed on my back for too long. That kind of thing. I just assumed he was a dirty old man and didn't think too much of it.'

'But it's been getting worse?' Issy asked.

Aaron nodded. 'He started saying things like "stick with me and you'll go far" and then he's rubbed up against me a couple of times. In the salon, when the cameras aren't on us.'

'What? Fucking dirty old prick!' Lexi exploded. Issy felt sick.

'And then yesterday, remember that he asked to see me in

235

private? He came onto me, properly. Nothing subtle about it. He tried to kiss me and when I pushed him away and told him I wasn't interested he kicked off.'

'What did he say?' Issy wasn't sure she wanted to hear the next bit.

'He said that I needed to grow up and realise that this was how it worked within the industry. That clichéd old line about me scratching his back and him scratching mine. Although I know "his back" is the last thing on his mind. He didn't actually say it out loud but he was basically saying that if I didn't do what he wanted then he'd find a way to get me kicked off the show.' Aaron burst into tears. 'What am I supposed to do?'

'You *have* to tell Laura or Eva,' Lexi said, a determined look on her face. 'Laura will listen. Tell her what's happened and I bet she'll help you.'

'I can't. They're not going to believe me – it's only my word against his.'

'Aaron, come on.' Issy pulled him into a hug. 'You have to tell them. He's sick, using his position of power like that. It's disgusting and he shouldn't get away with it.'

'But he's the big judge with the big prize. If he walks, that will ruin the show and they're not going to let that happen.' Aaron sniffed into Issy's shoulder. 'I don't want to leave the show but the thought of Alexander touching me . . . it makes me sick.'

'You're not actually thinking about going through with it?' Lexi said, astonished.

Aaron just looked at them with wide, scared eyes and it was painfully clear to Issy just how young he was.

'We'll figure something out,' Issy said. 'Together.'

'Yeah,' Lexi went on. 'And in the meantime, we'll make sure he doesn't get you alone again. Consider us your personal bodyguards. Kevin Costner, eat your heart out.'

'Thanks,' Aaron sniffed. 'But I can't see an easy way out of this one.'

Chapter Twenty-five

Challenge day. So much had happened since London Fashion Week, it was actually a relief to be back in the salon, cutting hair. This challenge was about getting their models ready for the red carpet of an awards ceremony. Their guest judge was the soap star, Summer Trainor. She'd been voted sexiest female soap star for three years in a row and was the face of the country's best-selling shampoo. She was a goddess and Zach worshipped her – he even had her calendar hanging in the garage.

After Aaron's revelations, their night out had come to a swift end. Neither she nor Lexi had been in the mood to party, and Aaron had been too upset to argue. By the time they got back to the booth Rory had disappeared with some girl. Jason had started asking where they'd been but Issy couldn't muster more than a quick peck on the lips as a reply. She and Lexi had promised Aaron they wouldn't say anything about Alexander until he'd decided what he was going to do, but Issy didn't like keeping it from Jason. He'd been nothing but honest with her from the start and she felt like she was deceiving him. But a promise was a promise.

That morning, they'd all been subdued as they made their way to the salon, each one lost in their own thoughts. Apart from Rory. Rory was just hungover as balls. So much for their night of bonding. Laura was not going to be pleased. If anything, morale was worse than before their aborted night on the tiles.

Issy was chatting to her model, when Summer came over to her station.

'Ooooh, it looks lovely so far,' Summer cooed.

Summer by name, summer by nature, Issy thought. 'Thanks hun. My brother is obsessed with you by the way – he'd be so jealous if he knew you were here,' admitted Issy.

'Bless him!' Summer leaned into Issy conspiratorially. 'Well, if he's fit babes, hook me up! I wanted to talk to you anyway – all that business in the press? Don't give it a second thought. It's happened to me more times than I can count, but I'm still here,' she said cheerily, doing a little twirl before walking off.

Issy laughed and then spotted Alexander at Aaron's station. Aaron had been a mess all morning – unfocused and distracted – and his work was suffering as a result. Alexander put his hand on Aaron's shoulder and leaned in to say something in his ear. Issy saw Aaron stiffen. The cameras were on and to anyone else it would look as though Alexander was offering Aaron words of encouragement, but Issy knew better and her skin crawled. The worst part was that Alexander would never implicate himself on camera. The slimy creep was too aware for that.

'Issy,' a voice interrupted her thoughts. It was Eva.

'Hiya, Eva,' Issy said, smiling.

'How are you?' she asked, her head tilted in concern.

'I'm good. Better. It's been a mad couple of days but it's good to be back in the salon, gives me something productive to focus on.'

'I'm glad to hear that,' Eva said.

'Yeah,' Issy went on. 'I'm over the business with that knobber.'

'A charming turn of phrase, Issy.' A smile curled at Eva's lips. 'But totally appropriate in this case. What brought on this change?'

'Oh, nothing really,' Issy said breezily, glancing in Jason's direction.

'Right, nothing,' Eva said, following Issy's gaze. 'Well, nothing looks pretty good to me.'

A couple of hours later, the challenge was finished and the judges had done their rounds. The 'after' photos were taken and then each contestant was shunted through their vox pop about their hairstyle and what had been going on since the last challenges. It was nearly nine o'clock before Issy got back upstairs to the apartment that night. She was shattered.

'Hey you,' she said, wandering into the boys' room and finding Jason alone. 'Where is everyone?'

'Lexi and Aaron are having some kind of deep and meaningful on the balcony, Rory's not back from filming yet and Mia's in the confession cam,' Issy rolled her eyes. *Where else would Mia be?*

'Come here.' Jason reached out to Issy. She let him pull her onto the bed and they lay like that for a few minutes.

'Is,' Jason began. 'Are we OK?'

'Yeah, of course. Why?'

'Last night, after you came back from speaking with Lexi and Aaron, you were so distant. Did you tell them about me and you? Do you regret it?'

Issy sat up and looked down at Jason's face. 'No, no I didn't say anything and I certainly don't regret it at all. I got caught up in something else, nothing to do with you, you've got nothing to worry about.'

Jason pulled her back down and Issy rested her head on his chest. 'Good, because I like you, Issy Jones.'

Issy smiled. 'I like you too.'

'Issy, I can hear Aaron being sick in the bathroom,' Lexi said. It was judging day and Issy was pulling up the zip on her skirt.

'Oh God. What can we do?' Issy asked.

'Nothing, that's the problem.' Lexi looked like she was about to say something else and then stopped herself. 'Stupid fucking cameras,' she muttered.

Issy understood how she felt. Whenever she and Lexi started to talk about Aaron they had to shut it down before they said too much on camera. Nothing was secret in the apartment.

'It's probably just nerves about the judging today.' Issy gave Lexi a pointed look.

'You're right. Thinking about Alexander's face makes me want to throw up too.' Lexi's voice was full of venom.

'Come on,' Issy said, grabbing hold of Lexi's hand. 'Let's go support our lad.'

Later that morning they were gathered in the green room, getting their mics checked before going through to the judging. Slowly everyone else filtered out until Issy was the only one left and she found herself alone with Ryan.

'So, how's things?' Ryan asked.

'They're starting to calm down. You know, since the Josh thing.' Issy thought about saying more but then remembered what Jason had said about Ryan. Was the nice guy routine just an act?

'And Jason,' Ryan probed. 'Seems like the two of you are getting on.'

Issy nodded. She didn't want to be rude – Ryan had been one of the first crew members she'd met and he'd always been kind to her. 'We're spending some time together, taking things slowly. I don't want to make the same mistake I did with Josh.'

'I get that,' Ryan said. 'It's good to be careful when you're getting to know new people.'

'Right.'

There was an awkward silence. Finally Ryan finished doing his checks and Issy was practically running to the door when he called out to her.

'Hey, Is. Just be careful, OK?'

Issy nodded. It wasn't until she was in the judging room that she remembered her dad had said exactly the same thing to her.

*

'As usual, some of you shone and some of you were disappointing,' Alexander said.

'I wouldn't say that,' Summer cut in, in her South London accent. 'I thought most of them did a good job.'

'They did,' Eva agreed, ignoring Alexander's pout. 'There's still room for improvement though so don't get too comfortable.'

'OK,' Summer said. 'The judges have voted and we've combined those with the public vote. This week's winner is . . . Issy Jones!'

'Congratulations, Issy,' Eva said warmly. 'I loved what you did with your model, and so did the public.'

'I can't believe it,' Issy said, as she collected her photo from Alexander, who looked like he was sucking on a lemon.

'And to mark the halfway point, we're also giving the winner a prize,' Summer said.

'Your brother Zach and best friend Molly will visit the apartment this afternoon,' Alexander said quickly and without ceremony. But even his dry delivery didn't dampen Issy's spirits.

'That's amazing! Thank you so, so much!' Finally, after all that messing them around the other night, she would get to see Zach and Molly.

The judging continued, with Lexi the second one through. Aaron, Jason, Mia and Rory all stood together, waiting for the photos of the bottom two to appear on the screen.

Alexander opened his mouth to speak but Aaron got there first.

'I can't do this.'

'I'm sorry, Aaron,' Eva said. 'What was that?'

'I said I can't do this,' Aaron said, more clearly the second time.

Issy and Lexi looked at each other. They had a horrible feeling they knew what was coming.

'Let's get to the end of judging, shall we?' Alexander said, looking nervous. 'And then we can talk about whatever the problem is.'

'No,' Aaron said firmly – it was clear he'd made his decision and he wasn't afraid anymore. 'And I certainly don't want to talk to you about anything.'

Summer wasn't looking quite so cheery anymore. 'What's going on? What's this about?'

'Aaron,' Eva said kindly. 'Is there something you'd like to talk about?'

Aaron curled his hands into fists and stared at Alexander who was starting to squirm. 'Do you want to tell them or shall I?'

'What the fuck is going on?' Rory said.

'I don't want to be part of this show,' Aaron said clearly. 'And I refuse work with him anymore.' Aaron pointed at Alexander.

'How dare you?' Alexander blustered. 'Of all the—'

'You're a creep,' Aaron cut in, really finding his stride. 'And I never want to see your dirty, old, botched-botoxed face ever again.'

Eva looked panicked. 'One of you tell me what this is about. I'm sure we can fix this.'

'Let him walk,' Alexander said. 'He has no talent anyway.'

'No talent? Don't make me laugh. The only thing I don't have is the stupidity to play your game. No prize is worth this,' Aaron said. 'I want to leave. I *am* leaving.' Alexander looked incandescent with rage but didn't say another word.

'I don't think, I'm not sure. Aaron . . . ' Eva trailed off.

Aaron walked unsteadily over to Issy and Lexi and hugged them both.

'I'm sorry,' he whispered. 'I didn't plan that, it just happened.'

Issy hugged Aaron again, tears in her eyes. 'You've got nothing to apologise for.'

He looked at them both directly. 'Don't you bad bitches *dare* think of walking out because I have. Especially you, Issy. Lexi and I both think you're here to win this. I'm going because I have to, but one of you crazy ladies has to win this for me. They say the best revenge is living well. I say, the best revenge right here is winning. You're going to slay this for me.'

And with that, Aaron walked out of the room without looking back.

There was a beat before chaos erupted. None of the cast members knew what to do but the crew started running around, talking fast, clearly in crisis management mode. Laura ran out of the room like a bat out of hell, Danny close on her heels.

'What on earth was all that about?' Jason asked. Issy opened her mouth to speak, but one look from Lexi, and she closed it again.

'We need to *do* something,' Issy hissed to her.

'I know but we can't just start shouting the odds,' Lexi whispered. 'Let's see what Laura says when she comes back.'

'Look at him,' Issy said, nodding towards Alexander. 'With Aaron walking out he thinks he's got away with it.'

It was almost an hour before a very worried-looking Laura reappeared.

'Aaron won't tell us exactly what's going on but he's refusing to come back,' Laura told them. 'He's packing his stuff and is getting ready to leave.'

'I want a private meeting with the producers. Now,' Alexander demanded. 'That fame-hungry nobody clearly has it in for me and is all set to drag me through the dirt just to get his fifteen minutes. I refuse to allow this to happen!'

'He's not fame-hungry,' Lexi shouted. 'That's not what this is about!'

'I will not discuss this in front of you people,' Alexander yelled. 'Don't forget your position here.'

Laura took control of the situation. 'Alexander, go to your dressing room. I'll call the executive director and we'll sort something out. Everybody else, go and wait in the green room. I'll be in to talk to you soon.'

Every head turned when Laura entered the green room.

'I'm sorry to say that Aaron has walked away from the show. A car picked him up a few moments ago and he won't be returning to the apartment.' Laura paused, running her hands through her hair. 'I've spoken to the exec producer and we feel that we have enough footage of that judging to make that episode work. We are going to edit it to show Aaron walking out because he didn't think the show was worth it.'

'So you're not going to show that it was because of Alexander?' Lexi said angrily.

'Look. We can't show one-sided, unsubstantiated accusations like that and Aaron doesn't actually go into any details. There would be huge legal implications if we chose to air something that is nothing more than half-truths and Chinese whispers. We wish Aaron the best but we have to protect the show.'

'This is bullshit!' Lexi shouted.

Laura looked at each of them steadily. 'Your signed contracts are very clear about this kind of thing. You agreed that the show's producers reserve the right to edit the footage in whatever way they feel most benefits the show. And you also agreed to support that editing in public.' They all exchanged glances; they hadn't seen this steely side of Laura before. 'Doing it like this really is in everyone's best interests. We all still have jobs to do and there's still more filming to be done today, so let's get on with it. Issy, your brother and Molly will be here in an hour. They'll arrive at the apartment and will stay for two hours before leaving. Make sure you introduce them to everyone, show them round, talk about—'

'Wait,' Issy interrupted. 'They're still coming this evening?' She couldn't believe it. Surely they weren't expected to act as though nothing had happened?

Laura nodded. 'Of course. And then tonight, we've arranged for you and Jason to have a romantic picnic in the salon after dark. Steve and Ryan will be sorting out the setup so we need you to get upstairs as soon as we're done in here.'

'What? A picnic in the salon? That's ridiculous,' Issy said.

'I agree, Laura. You're making me look like I've got no swag – who has a picnic in a salon? Don't picnics have to be outdoors for a start?' Even Jason, usually so chilled and compliant, was struggling to make sense of this.

'It will be romantic OK? And more to the point, you will enjoy it. Also it's meant to look as though Jason has planned it as another surprise. So again, you will look surprised, OK? Am I making myself clear?'

Issy looked at Jason who shrugged his shoulders.

'I'm not really feeling that romantic,' Issy said. 'And why do we have to do it at all?'

'So she gets to see her family, and then have a private date with Jason?' Mia was fuming. 'What are the rest of us meant to do while Issy's off hogging the limelight? Shine her shoes?'

'That's entirely up to you, Mia, although personally I could think of better ways to spend my time. The fact is Twitter has been going crazy over Issy and Jason – the viewer are loving the two of them together – so we want to move things along faster. The rest of you will spend the evening together in the living area. We want you to talk about your night out and today's events. Talk about Aaron leaving, how it feels without him, but *do not* talk about his reasons for going. Is that understood?'

'Fine,' Jason said, playing peacekeeper. 'We'll do what's best for the show.'

'Firing Alexander is what's best for the show,' Lexi muttered.

Laura shot her a look. 'Get back to the apartment, all of you. There's work to be done.'

'This is fucking shit,' Lexi said, after Laura had left the room.

'This is TV,' Rory replied.

Chapter Twenty-six

'I hate this.' Lexi punched her pillow in frustration. 'I've sent Aaron a message saying we're behind him but it doesn't feel like enough.'

'I know,' Issy said, sitting down next to her friend. 'But there's nothing we can do from here. Laura's made that quite clear. I didn't realise she had that in her locker – I was actually quite scared of her. But as soon as we're both out of the show, we should go and see him – make sure he knows that we'll always be mates. While we're in here the best we can do is to rep his corner as much as we can.'

'I just wish I could do something more than that.' There was a look in Lexi's eye that Issy didn't like.

'Lex ... what are you thinking?'

'I know what Aaron said, and I know he's right. We can only take Alexander down from the inside. Maybe there is something we can do from here.'

'Like what?'

'I don't know yet but Alexander can't get away with this. Aaron would've made the final. It's not fucking fair.'

'Be careful, babes.' Issy had lowered her voice even though there was no point. Their mics would still pick up every word. 'You saw what Laura was like earlier. The top dogs have clearly made their decision. We just have to deal with it.'

'Why? Why do we just have to deal with it?'

'Because that's the deal we made when we signed the contracts. I don't like it either. I don't know about you but I know that most of us were just so pleased to be chosen for the show we would have signed on the dotted line regardless of what they said. And now we're discovering the hard way the full ramifications of what that means. Like Rory said, this is TV, I guess.' Issy fell silent and Lexi nudged her.

'Hey. C'mon. We can't spend the rest of the time with faces like slapped arses, however we feel. When are Molly and Zach getting here?'

'Any minute now. I just wish it was at a better time.'

'You'll feel differently once they're here.'

'I hope so,' Issy said. 'Not sure about this surprise picnic tonight, though.'

'At least you'll be spending the night with someone you like,' Lexi said, raising an eyebrow. 'I don't think the Mia-Rory romance has really taken off.'

'Yeah I thought things had gone a bit quiet after the other night. What happened?'

'I heard a couple of the soundmen talking. Their date didn't go down so well – they don't think anyone's going to buy it. People like Rory but not Mia, so if anything they reckon it's going to backfire for her,' Lexi explained.

'Couldn't happen to a nicer girl,' Issy said drily.

Issy launched herself at Zach and Molly as soon as Danny brought them to the apartment. Lexi had been right – after the day's events, seeing her brother and best friend was just what Issy needed. Ryan followed them in, smiling at Issy's reaction but the harassed look in his eyes was obvious. *The crew must be all over the place after Aaron's exit*, Issy thought. *What a day.*

'Sorry to break this up,' he said, 'but I need to mic you guys. As soon as I have I'll let you get back to your hug fest.'

'No problem, mate,' Zach said. 'Hey, are you the sound man that came to my mum's salon?'

Ryan nodded as he helped Zach with his mic box. 'Yeah, that one was fun. Your mum was lovely – very ... erm ... welcoming.'

'That's one word for it,' Issy said, remembering her mum's not-so-subtle flirting. 'Mum was bad enough but Vi was even worse.'

'Ah, Vi,' Ryan said, putting his hand over his heart. 'My one true love.'

'Hands off, mate. Vi's mine,' Zach said good-naturedly.

'I'll fight you to the death, for that one,' Ryan said, laughing. 'I love a feisty woman.'

'Don't we all,' Zach said approvingly. 'Don't we all.'

Issy and Molly exchanged a look. Men. But she was glad that her brother had been able to offer Ryan a bit of relief from his chaotic day.

'OK,' Danny said once Ryan had finished arranging the mics. 'You've got a couple of hours together. Issy, we need you to introduce Zach and Molly to the rest of the contestants and then show them round the apartment.'

'Sure thing, no problem,' Issy said.

Molly leaned into Issy and lowered her voice. 'Do they always tell you what to do like that?'

'Yep,' Issy whispered back. 'Takes some getting used to.'

'I need to head off. Laura's waiting,' Ryan said. 'Nice to meet you, Zach, and it was lovely to see you again, Molly.' He headed for the door and Issy followed him.

'Hey,' she said, catching his sleeve to stop him. 'You OK?'

'I'm fine.' Ryan rubbed his eyes tiredly and Issy had a sudden urge to hug him. 'It's all a bit crazy since Aaron walked out. I have no idea what time I'll get home tonight. How about you guys?'

'Angry, upset, frustrated.' Issy gave a small laugh. 'You know, the usual.'

Ryan reached for Issy and for a moment she thought he might hug *her* but he seemed to change his mind at the last second, and squeezed her arm instead. 'Go spend time with your family. I can see why you and your brother are so close – he's a good judge of character.' And with that he left.

What did he mean by that? Issy thought.

A few moments later and they were gathered in the living area with the rest of the housemates. Issy went through the motions of introducing everyone and was amused at Mia's reaction. Even Miss Prissy Knickers wasn't immune to Zach's charms.

253

'So you're Issy's brother? I guess we know who got the looks in your family,' she trilled.

Zach stared at her for a moment. 'Careful, Mia. Almost sounds as though you're flirting with someone from the lower orders – don't want to give people the wrong impression, do you?' In that moment, Issy had never loved her brother more. Even Molly was looking at Zach in admiration.

Mia at least had the decency to blush. 'I'm, well . . . er, I don't know what you mean,' she said weakly.

'Of course not, sweetheart,' Zach said, raising his eyebrows. 'Guess it must be the way they edit the show.'

'Must be!' Mia quickly stood up. 'Lovely to meet you anyway. I'll leave you and Issy to catch up.' And she was gone.

'Sorry about Princess,' Lexi said, shaking her head. 'Just ignore her. We do.'

'Good plan.' Molly smiled at Lexi. 'It's so nice to meet you. I feel like I know you already, I've watched every episode. Is that weird?'

'A little,' Lexi admitted. 'But that's what we signed up for!'

We seem to be saying that a lot lately, Issy thought.

'Thanks for backing Issy up,' Zach said. 'Not that she needs it, but either way it's good to know she's got a friend in here.'

'Two friends,' Jason said pointedly. 'I've got her back too.'

'Sure,' Zach said bluntly.

'So, Zach,' Jason asked when an awkward silence fell, 'you into footie?'

254

'Yeah, course.' Zach nodded, reaching for a biscuit. Issy had dug out the Hobnobs.

'Who do you support?'

'United. You?'

'Liverpool.'

'That's a shame,' Zach said. Jason laughed. Zach did not.

'Some of Jason's old clients are footballers,' Issy said, trying to lighten the mood. It wasn't like Zach to blatantly make so little effort.

'Like who?' Molly asked.

'Just a team near me,' Jason said dismissively.

'Well, go on,' Zach pushed, 'tell us which team.'

'Tranmere Rovers.'

Tranmere fucking Rovers. Issy was mortified. Zach burst out laughing.

'They're really up and coming,' Jason persisted. Lexi laughed but quickly stopped when she saw the look on Issy's face.

'I'm sure they are,' Zach said. 'So, nice tan, Jason. Sunbed?'

Issy rolled her eyes. There was no stopping her brother when he was like this.

'No, I usually go for a spray tan,' Jason replied. Issy died a bit inside. Jason was killing her here. *At least have the decency to sound a little bit embarrassed, mate.*

'Seriously?' Zach looked incredulous.

'Yes,' Jason said indignantly. 'It's the best way to get an even spread.'

'Don't be soft,' Zach said. 'A sunbed gives you a better colour.'

'I disagree.' Jason shook his head. 'Spray tans are deeper.'

'Faker maybe. Sunbeds bring out your natural colour. Everyone knows that real men use sunbeds. Spray tans are for lasses,' Zach finished.

Issy and Molly leapt up at the same time, always in sync.

'Show us your room, Is,' Molly said at the same time as Issy half-shouted, 'Come see my room!'

'I just don't like him,' Zach said. He, Issy and Molly were alone in the girls' bedroom.

'Why not?' Issy asked. She trusted her brother but he hadn't even given Jason a chance.

'It's a vibe,' Zach said. 'He's too full of himself. Tranmere Rovers and spray tans ain't exactly much to boast about. I bet he waxes his chest.'

'That's not fair,' Issy said. 'There's more to him than that. You need to spend some time with him.'

'He's fit,' Molly said. Zach shot her a look and she threw her hands up in the air. 'He is!'

'Yeah, if you like blokes who look like birds,' Zach said.

'Look, he's been really good to me,' Issy said, ignoring the fact that Zach wasn't even making any sense any more. Jason's muscles were all man. 'It hasn't been easy in here and he's helped me get through some tough days. He's protective, just like you.'

'I dunno, Is,' Zach said doubtfully. 'My gut's never been wrong, and my gut tells me that something isn't right.'

Molly placed a hand on Zach's arm to stop him from saying anything more. 'Is, be careful,' she said. 'After what happened with Josh, it might not be a good idea to rush into anything.'

Since when did Molly take Zach's side? 'So, you agree with Zach?' Issy said.

'No ... Maybe ... I don't really know.' Molly looked at Zach. 'I think he's doing the over-protective big brother bit and I know that always annoys you. But his heart is in the right place. So maybe just slow down, take a bit of time to get to know Jason before things get serious.'

'That's what I'm doing!' Issy said, frustrated. 'Can we change the subject please?'

'Yes,' Molly said gratefully. 'So, there's this kid in my class—'

'So is there *anything* you liked about him?' Issy interrupted. She couldn't let this go.

'Is,' Zach said, his face serious. 'Let's not talk about this anymore, OK? Mol, what was that you were saying?'

Issy tried to pay attention to Molly's story but she wasn't really listening, too consumed by her own thoughts. She'd never dated anyone her brother hadn't liked before. What would happen if things got serious between her and Jason?

The mood had lightened once they'd got back to talking normally, about the salon, about Princess Tiger-Lily and Molly's job and the latest come-on that Vi had given to Zach. He'd turned her down. Again. Issy sadly saw Zach and Molly out, but as she shut the door behind them, she realised she felt more grounded somehow. Whatever happened with the show, she'd be going home to her family at the end of it and that thought would keep her going, whatever *Can You Cut It?* threw at her.

And that included getting through this stupid 'surprise' romantic picnic.

To be fair, it looked amazing. There was a picnic blanket spread on the floor, surrounded by tea lights. A large hamper sat to one side, filled to the brim with everything from gourmet sandwiches and cocktail sausages to strawberries and Hobnobs. Two bottles of champagne were chilling in ice buckets, along with a couple of sparkling champagne flutes. If this had been a genuine surprise, Issy would've been touched and thrilled that someone would go to this much effort for her. But it wasn't a surprise, it was all fake. A whole team had put this together and that thought depressed her.

Right, let's get this over with, Issy thought.

'Oh my God.' Issy put her hands to face and looked at Jason. 'This looks amazing! You did this for me?' And the Oscar goes to . . .

'Do you like it?' Jason said, pulling her close.

'I do,' Issy said. 'It looks incredible. Let's crack open that champagne.' Drinking her way through this charade was the only way she'd be able to get to the end of the evening.

They settled themselves on the blanket. Jason opened one of the champagne bottles with a loud 'pop' and poured them a glass each. Issy took a sip, remembering that the last time she'd had champagne she'd been with Josh. She pushed the thought away. Jason wasn't Josh. The picnic might have not been his idea, but what Jason was saying to her now and how he was treating her was all him – this was genuine – and she needed to hold onto that. So what if the show had set the whole thing up? She could still enjoy herself.

Issy leaned forward and planted a light kiss on Jason's mouth. 'Thank you,' she said, their faces still inches apart. 'You didn't have to do this.'

'You deserve to be spoilt,' Jason said in a low voice. 'I like you, Issy. You know that, right?'

'I do,' Issy replied. 'And I like you too.'

Jason pulled Issy to him and kissed her deeply. The picnic might be fake but their moment was completely real.

Chapter Twenty-seven

'Agggghhhhhh!' A scream pierced the silent morning.

Mia ran from the bathroom and into the living room, where Issy and Lexi were sitting. Lexi spat out a mouthful of coffee and Issy gasped. Mia's face was boot-polish brown.

'Which one of you did this?' Mia screamed at them.

'What's happened to your face?' Lexi asked.

'As if you don't know,' Mia screeched. 'I put my night cream on last night and this morning I look like this! Why would any of you do this?'

'We didn't do anything!' Issy said. She was trying her best not to laugh, knowing that would only aggravate the situation, but it wasn't easy. Mia looked ridiculous.

'Don't lie to me!' There was no calming Mia down. She was out for blood.

'We're not lying,' Lexi said as calmly as she could manage. 'We didn't do anything to your face cream, I swear.' She was struggling to stifle her laughter.

'I'm going to *kill* whoever did this!' Mia shouted before running off to her bedroom. The sound of the door slamming reverberated throughout the house.

Rory stumbled out of the boys' bedroom, looking dreadful. He'd been drinking even more than usual since Aaron had left.

'What's all the noise about?' he groaned, flopping down on the sofa.

'Mia,' Issy said. 'Her face is . . . well, it's turned an attractive shade of . . . er, shit.'

Rory smiled weakly. 'About bloody time.'

'Eh?' Lexi said. 'What do you mean?'

'I swapped her face cream for some of your fake tan after that shit date we went on,' he said, stretching. 'It's taken ages to work.'

'What did you do that for?' Issy hissed. 'Mia thinks it was us.'

'Ah, sorry, babe,' Rory said apologetically. 'I was bored, and she's a bellend so I thought it would be funny.'

'It was funny,' Issy admitted. 'But you need to come clean.'

'OK, OK. Let me sober up first. I can't . . . Oh God.' Rory bolted upright. 'I think I'm going to be sick,' he declared, before doing his best impression of Usain Bolt and running to the bathroom.

Mia reappeared a moment later with an Alexander McQueen scarf wrapped round her head.

'I'm waiting for an apology,' she demanded.

Issy sighed. 'Mia, we already told you that it wasn't us.'

'I'm not a fool,' Mia declared. *You certainly look like one*, Issy thought. 'You've had it in for me from the start, but I didn't think even *you* would stoop so low.'

'Mia,' Issy said through gritted teeth. 'Get a grip. And listen to what we're saying. We. Didn't. Do. It.'

'If you didn't do it, who did?'

'Me,' Rory said, returning to the sofa a couple of pounds lighter and a couple of shades greener. 'It was meant to be a joke. Sorry.' As far as apologies went, Issy had heard better but she was grateful that he'd 'fessed up.

'Did they put you up to this?' Mia said, pointing at Lexi and Issy.

Jesus Christ. She doesn't give up, Issy thought.

'Nah, man,' Rory said, shaking his head. 'It was all me. By the way, you look like Dot Cotton right now.'

'You pig. How dare you? And to think I even let you think I would entertain the possibility of dating you!' Mia cried. 'This is bullying!' She ran past a surprised-looking Jason and off to the confession cam. Of course.

'What was that about?' he asked, sitting down next to Issy. They quickly filled him in. He slapped Rory on the back who looked like he might throw up again. 'Top bants, mate.' Jason turned to Issy, smiled and kissed her straight on the lips. 'And good morning to you.'

'Fucking hell,' Rory said. 'I've already thrown up once. You two are going to make me go for round two.'

'Sorry, mate,' Jason said putting his arm around Issy. 'I can't keep away from this one.'

Issy hid her embarrassment with a laugh. She wasn't entirely comfortable with such public displays of affection. Especially when they were so cheesy.

'So what's next for Mia?' Rory said.

'What? You don't think she's had enough?' Lexi said.

'You wouldn't be saying that if you'd heard what she was saying about you's on our "date" Lex . . . Anyway, why not?' Rory shrugged. 'We need some entertainment after all that stuff with Aaron. Everyone needs to lighten up.'

'The face cream thing was funny,' Jason said frowning. 'I admit that. But it's probably not a good idea to keep picking on her. It's not that nice.'

'Since when are you worried about being nice to Mia?' Issy asked in surprise.

'It's not about Mia, really,' Jason said to her. 'I'm just thinking of how it'll look on camera.'

'It'll look funny!' Rory said. 'Listen, she was saying all kinds of crap last night about Aaron. Calling him a liar, really laying into him, she needs taking down a peg or two.'

'She was?' Lexi said. 'Then whatever you have planned for her, I'm in.'

'Me too,' Issy agreed.

'Hang on,' Jason said to Issy. 'I'm not sure that's a good idea. We should stay out of it.'

'Should "we"?' Issy said, raising an eyebrow. 'This isn't about "we", it's about "me". OK? I can think for myself.'

'Hey, I didn't mean it like that,' Jason said gently. 'I'm just looking out for you, that's all. I don't want you getting into trouble.'

'It sounded a lot like you were telling me what to do.' Issy felt herself stiffen against Jason's arm.

Lexi and Rory exchanged a look. Issy knew that being

witness to a lovers' tiff was always mega awks, but it wasn't like they got any privacy in the apartment anyway.

'You're overreacting, babe,' Jason said, grazing her temple with a kiss. 'That's not what I meant at all. Let's not fight.'

Issy turned to look at him. Was she overreacting? *Wouldn't be the first time*, she thought to herself.

'I don't want to fight either,' she said eventually. 'I just hate being told what to do.'

'And I really wasn't trying to do that,' Jason said firmly. 'For the record, I think it's a bad idea but you do what you want to do.'

'I will,' Issy said stubbornly. She turned to Lexi and Rory. 'So what's the plan?'

'Let's set Steph's old alarm to go off at, like, four a.m. or something,' Lexi suggested, 'and hide it in her room.'

'Nice one.' Rory nodded approvingly. 'I'll do the hiding. I'm already in trouble with her so may as well go for gold.'

They continued chatting for a while but Issy couldn't shake the feeling of unease. Had she overreacted with Jason? He'd only been trying to help her. Maybe she shouldn't have been so quick to assume the worst. Zach's reaction to Jason was still playing on her mind and that was probably affecting her behaviour. She snuggled back into his arm, hoping that he'd see that as a sign of apology.

'You may not know this,' Alexander said, 'but when I opened my first salon, my specialism was colouring. It's not just a skill, it's an art form, and this art form will be an important part of your next challenge.'

All of the contestants, apart from Mia, were in the salon taking part in another masterclass with Alexander. The show's make-up artist had tried their best to fix Mia's face but the tan was so dark against the rest of Mia's milky skin she just looked ludicrous. So she'd been given permission to sit the class out. Alexander was walking around like a prancing peacock, chest puffed out and an air of self-importance more usually associated with Kanye West. *Because he thinks he got away it*, Issy thought angrily. *Now Aaron's gone, he thinks he's won.* She glanced at Lexi who'd barely said a word since they'd entered the salon. Her face was set like stone and completely unreadable.

'For the rest of the class,' Alexander went on, 'I'm going to talk you through some ideas about advanced colouring while giving you a demonstration of certain techniques.'

They watched the demonstration in silence. Issy was fascinated by what she was watching but she was still angry about what had happened with Aaron and how easily the show's producers had shut the whole thing down. Her level of concentration was severely suffering.

Eventually the class came to an end and they were allowed to go back to the house. Issy was standing with Lexi, when Jason joined them.

'C'mon, Is, let's go back upstairs.' He took her hand.

'Actually, hang on a sec,' Lexi interrupted. 'Can I have a quick word, Is? Just five minutes in the green room.'

'Sure.' Issy looked at Jason. 'I'll just see you up there, OK?'

Jason hesitated before nodding. 'OK. See you in a bit.'

*

'I don't know if I can do this,' Lexi said, once they were alone. 'I can't stop thinking about what that man did to Aaron. How are we supposed to act like nothing's wrong?'

Issy put her arms around her. 'I don't know, Lex. I'm struggling too. One minute, everything's fine, the next I'm angry all over again. It's his face, man . . . Just pisses me off so much!'

'We must be able to *do* something!' Tears of frustration welled in Lexi's eyes. Issy was taken aback. She hadn't thought Lexi was a big crier.

'It's challenge day tomorrow. Let's get through that and then we can think clearly, without any distractions. It won't help Aaron if we just give up. We need to think about this properly but we can't do that and focus on the challenge too.'

'You're right. I know you're right, but that pig tried to molest Aaron. I keep seeing Aaron's face when he left and all I can think about is how heartbroken I am for him.'

'Aaron wouldn't want us to get cut from the show because of him. One of us needs to win this for him.'

'We can't let bloody Mia win, can we?' Lexi said with a thin smile. She wiped her tears away and stood up. 'Let's get back before lover boy thinks you've left him.'

'I've only been gone five minutes,' Issy laughed. 'We're not joined at the hip.'

'You might want to tell Jason that,' Lexi said as they wandered up the stairs. 'He's been following you around like a lost puppy.'

Issy looked at her in surprise. 'Really? I hadn't even noticed.'

'I suppose we've all got loads on our minds and it's not a bad thing.' Lexi shrugged. 'Some girls like that.'

'Yeah. I'm not normally one of those girls though,' Issy said. 'Maybe I should back off a bit?'

'Do what feels right, babes,' Lexi said, opening the door to the apartment. 'But I can't see Laura liking you two cooling it.'

And for the first time, Issy realised, there were at least three people in her relationship with Jason and she wasn't sure she was the one in control.

Chapter Twenty-eight

A couple of days later and Mia's tan had faded to a nice just-off-the-ski-slopes colour, which Issy thought made her look better but Mia still wouldn't stop complaining, though she deigned to be back on camera again. The cast members were waiting in the green room for the judging to begin. Issy and Lexi had both excelled at the colour challenge, each of them determined not to lose focus after their conversation the other day. But for Rory, things had gone spectacularly wrong.

'I'm off today, I'd put money on it,' Rory said cheerfully.

'You should be OK, mate,' Jason said. 'It's not all down to the judges, remember.'

Rory laughed. 'You've got a point but I don't think even the public can save me this time.'

'He did turn his model's hair green,' Mia pointed out helpfully.

'That'll happen when the hairdresser is still drunk from the night before,' Rory said, his smile wide.

'You don't seem that upset about it . . . ' Issy said.

'He wasn't going to win,' Mia said quickly. 'Why should he care?'

Mia had been woken by the hidden alarm clock for two nights in a row now and she was fuming with all of them. If she'd been infuriating before, she was downright spiteful now. Lack of sleep certainly did not agree with her. They had only meant to hide the alarm for one night but Rory had been drunk when he'd stashed it away and couldn't remember the spot he'd chosen. It was lost for good as far as Rory was concerned. Issy had felt bad about it for, oh, all of two seconds and then Mia had opened her mouth and Issy's guilt had disappeared.

'There's still time for a quickie, Mia,' Rory said suggestively. 'I know a lovely little store cupboard where we won't get disturbed.'

Just as Mia opened her mouth to respond, Danny walked in. 'We're ready for you now.'

The guest judges were a four-piece boyband called Dalston. Issy couldn't tell any of them apart. They had been voted off in the early stages of a TV talent show and released a couple of generic-sounding pop songs since, without any great fanfare. It had been clear during yesterday's challenge that they had very little interest in hair. Instead, they had burst into *a capella* renditions of their forthcoming single whenever they could. It had driven Issy mad.

'Before we start,' Eva said, 'we've got a treat for the remaining four contestants after today's judging. Tonight, Alexander and I will each take two of you out for dinner.'

'You'll get to spend some quality time with one of us and ask us any questions you may have about the finale.' Alexander paused. 'Which is just one challenge and two judgings away for three of you.'

'Right,' Eva said. 'Let's take a look at a few of the tweets that have come in this week.'

@MissyLKK: I want to be @LexiCutIt when I grow up #warrior #shero #CYCI

@RomeoLad98: ah @IssyCutIt is wasted on that TANTASTIC Twat Jason #loveissy #bemywife #bae

@Mystery_Damsel3: @JasonCutIt is too damn #cute. Love his hair! #ishegay?

@Bexxy1993: Rory for prime minister! #legend #CYCI

@EvaWFanGirl: @MiaCutIt is on screen, time to make a cuppa #snore #boreoff

'So, yeah,' the boyband member with the floppiest hair began, 'that's what the public have been saying about you. Now we get to announce the winner, I think. Er, the winner of the colour challenge is . . . ' The four members looked at each other and then said in unison, 'Lexi.'

Issy applauded her friend's triumph and Lexi managed to collect her photograph from Alexander without punching him in the face. *Good job all round*, Issy thought.

'And the person who's come second this week is . . . Jason,' the one who always sang the solos continued on alone, rattling through as if he were bored.

For a moment Issy felt slightly worried about her own place, but then she remembered how tearful Rory's model had been.

'It's time to find out which hairdressers are in the bottom two,' Eva said, lightly steering them back on course.

Everyone turned to look as two photos flashed up on the screen and even though she had been sure she was OK, Issy still felt a sense of relief.

Rory and Mia.

'It's now time to find out who will be leaving. The hairdresser who received the lowest vote and will be leaving the competition today is . . . ' The losing photo filled the screen. 'Rory.'

Rory looked at his housemates in mock horror and Issy smiled sadly. After his performance in the challenge, it wasn't a huge surprise that Rory had been eliminated, but he'd been one of the biggest characters in the house. Things were going to be less fun without him around.

'Housemates, please say your goodbyes to Rory as he is now out of the competition and he won't be returning to the apartment with you all. Rory, please hand in your scissors – you evidently can NOT cut it,' said Alexander.

Why does he enjoy that bit so much? Issy thought. *Bet he wrote that stupid line himself or something.*

They all said their goodbyes to Rory and even though he appeared to be all right with what had happened, the atmosphere was muted.

Issy, Lexi, Jason and Mia were the final four. Which of them would make the final *three*?

Issy was waiting for Eva and Lexi in the green room. Lexi had wanted some time in front of the confession cam and then they'd be going for dinner with Eva. Jason and Mia had already left with Alexander. Issy had wondered for a moment if the producers would make her and Lexi go with Alexander, but someone somewhere had had the good sense to keep them apart.

Ryan appeared to change the batteries in her mic. When he'd disconnected the wires he said, 'OK, your mic is off so no one can hear us. Not that you usually remember anyway. How are you?'

'Sad that Rory's gone,' Issy said. 'It's going to be quiet without him.'

'I meant about Aaron. When you were in here the other day your mics were still on and I heard what you said about Alexander.' He was frowning and Issy realised that she'd never seen him look unhappy before. Tired, yes, but never unhappy.

'Are we in trouble?' Issy asked.

Ryan shook his head. 'No. No one will hear it that isn't supposed to and you've all signed contracts that contain a privacy clause so the producers won't be worried. But is it true, what you said? Did Alexander really try it on with Aaron?'

'Yeah,' Issy said. 'It's the real reason he walked out.'

'I can't believe it.' Ryan paused. 'Actually I *can* believe it . . . Look, I can't say much, I could lose my job, but make sure you stick close to Lexi, OK? Don't trust anyone else.'

'I've been hearing that a lot recently,' Issy said. 'To be careful, to watch my back. It's exhausting.'

'It's necessary. Issy, I'm not trying to scare you. I'm trying to help. I like you, I want you to do well.'

'I'm grateful for that,' Issy said. 'I'd just like to switch my brain off for a while, get some peace and quiet.'

Ryan took a step towards her and pulled her into a hug. Issy should've been surprised but she wasn't, not really. It felt like the most normal thing in the world, to stand there together like that for a few moments, Ryan's chin resting on the top of her head. All of a sudden, Jason's face popped into her head and Issy reluctantly pulled away. It was just a hug between friends but she wouldn't like it if Jason was standing around hugging some other girl.

'Thanks for that,' Issy said, trying to lighten the mood. 'There's nothing that a good hug can't fix.'

Ryan looked at her seriously. 'Remember what I said, OK? Stick with Lexi and be careful of everyone else.'

'I will.' Issy nodded. 'I promise.'

'Right then, let's get your mic switched back on before anyone notices.'

'I struck lucky getting to take you guys out,' Eva said. They were in the car, on the way to Neighbourhood where they were going to have cocktails before heading to Australasia for dinner.

'We definitely got the better end of the deal,' Lexi agreed. 'And we really won't be filmed for the whole night?'

'No.' Eva shook her head. 'Just an hour at the start and then the crew will leave and it will be just us. No mics, no cameras.'

'I like the sound of that,' Lexi said, clearly thinking about everything she wanted to get off her chest without an audience.

The hour that they'd been filmed had been excruciating and Issy wasn't sure why. She was used to the cameras by now, but having to sit there and pretend everything was totally fine ... It just hadn't felt right. It was only once the crew had left and it was just her, Lexi and Eva, that she'd finally relaxed.

'So,' Eva said, taking a sip from her champagne flute, 'tell me what's really been going on?'

Issy glanced at Lexi who was staring at her plate. 'Er ... things have changed,' Issy said slowly. 'It's not as much fun anymore if I'm honest – there aren't as many of us and it's much more intense.'

'I know,' Eva said. 'I'm feeling the change too. But we don't have long to go now so keep your heads up. You're so close to making the final, both of you.'

'Do you know what you might do after this?' Issy asked.

'I'm not sure. I've had some offers for a few things, more than I expected, but this show has taken up a lot of my time. I might just take a little while and spend time with my family before doing anything else. I miss my husband and my kids.'

Issy thought about her own family for a moment. 'You'd really turn down opportunities to stay at home with your family?'

Eva nodded, smiling. 'I've lived the high life, have had a great career so far, and I'm very grateful for that. But I've reached a point now where I'm able to slow down a little and be more picky about the projects I choose.'

'I don't know what will happen after the show ends,' Issy said, 'but if I want this to continue, I feel as though I can't turn anything down right now.'

Eva looked at Issy steadily. 'You can say no to whatever you want,' she said seriously. 'Don't ever feel as though you have to do something, just for a little bit of fame. You don't.'

'This whole process has been an eye-opener,' Lexi said suddenly. 'Not just how the show is filmed and how much of it is set up. The thing I'm most shocked about is seeing what people are capable of. And I'm not sure this world is for me.'

'Lexi,' Eva said gently. 'What's going on?'

Lexi paused, collecting her thoughts. Issy knew she was struggling to decide how much to say. 'I'm not sure I can say,' Lexi said eventually. 'But what I will say is that I don't think I'm cut out for TV. Too much goes on behind the scenes that I don't like. It's sneaky. What should be said is left unsaid, and the good guys don't always come out on top. This isn't the life for me.'

Issy gave Lexi's hand a squeeze under the table.

'Lexi, you have strength and talent, and people have seen that now,' Eva said. 'Whatever you decide to do after this, you'll always have that. So you'd definitely say no to another reality TV show?'

Lexi nodded, determinedly. 'Absolutely.'

'I don't know if I would,' Issy admitted. 'I do find it hard, and I miss my family. Lately I seem to have less and less time to contact them, but I'd be lying if I said I didn't like being a bit famous.'

'And adored by the public?' Eva asked with a smile.

'Who doesn't want to be adored?' Issy responded.

'True, a lot of young girls do want that. But think about what you want to do after the show. I've heard that Aaron has had lots of job offers. Things might seem bad but you never know what's around the corner.'

Issy thought back to her first audition and remembered how doubtful she'd been about everything. Everyone had kept telling her that it would change her life, and it had. Now she was in the middle of a love story that the public were invested in and she knew she was no longer simply Issy from Salford. She was now Issy from *Can You Cut It?* and her life would never be the same again.

Much later, Issy and Lexi arrived back at the apartment. They had just kicked their shoes off when the door opened and Mia and Jason walked in. Mia flounced past them without a word and Issy noticed that Jason looked tired. She had been planning to go straight to bed but she hung back as Lexi disappeared into their bedroom.

'You OK?' she asked Jason.

He shrugged. 'Can I have a hug?' he asked.

'Sure.' She leant in and put her arms around him. He kissed the top of her head.

Their moment of peace was disturbed by a blood-curdling scream. It had come from Mia's room. Lexi came out of the bedroom and they all ran to see what was wrong. As they stood in Mia's doorway, they fell about laughing.

'It is so not funny,' Mia fumed.

'No, you're right,' Lexi said. 'It's fucking hilarious.'

Rory had left Mia a leaving present – everything she owned was wrapped in tin foil. He'd even tried to wrap her bed. Issy wiped tears of laughter from her cheeks. The sheer effort Rory must have gone to in order to pull this off was incredibly impressive. *More effort than he's put into cutting hair all series*, Issy laughed to herself.

'You better help me with this, or I will scream all night.' Mia actually stamped her foot. Issy didn't think anyone over the age of five could get away with stamping their feet, but Mia was clearly the exception that proved the rule.

'I'm really going to miss Rory,' Lexi said.

'Me too,' Issy agreed as they all got to work with unwrapping the foil.

It was late and Issy was exhausted. She had just climbed into bed, when Lexi sat down at the end of her bunk.

'Do you think we should have told Eva about Alexander?' Issy asked. 'I felt as if we should have said something but then I wasn't sure.'

'I know what you mean,' Lexi said. 'I was all set to, but when we were there it just didn't feel right. Not sure why.'

'I don't think she would've defended him,' Issy said sleepily.

'She probably knew something was up. It was a great evening but there was definitely an elephant in the room.'

'An Alexander-shaped elephant in a shit wig,' Issy said yawning.

'Get some sleep,' Lexi said sliding down. 'You'll need the energy because we have to deal with that elephant again tomorrow.'

Chapter Twenty-nine

'Lexi, if I ask you to straighten someone's hair, then you need to straighten their hair. Don't ever ignore me.' Alexander's face was red.

'Why not?' Lexi looked equally as angry. 'So far today you've just given me all the menial tasks and it's ridiculous. Your favouritism is out of control.'

'Do I need to remind you who's the judge and who's the contestant here?'

'You're the judge?' Lexi rolled her eyes. 'You hadn't mentioned it.'

'I really don't think your attitude is Fox salon material.'

'Perhaps you'd prefer it if I groped the clients,' Lexi said through gritted teeth.

'I'm warning you.' Alexander's eyes were bulging.

Issy stopped what she was doing and wondered if she should intervene. This challenge was about replicating a day in the life of an Alexander Fox salon. Or at least half a day. They'd started at seven a.m., and Alexander had wasted no time in showering his favourites, Mia and Jason, with all of the interesting jobs. Mia hadn't made any attempt to keep the smug look off her face. Issy had been given a couple of simple styling jobs, but Alexander had been using Lexi as nothing more than a glorified assistant, and she wasn't happy. The guest judge, favourite daytime TV presenter, Scott Savannah, was trying to pretend that it was all 'fantastic', as he went about interviewing everyone with his customary sunny disposition. On top of that, their clients this time around were all volunteers who were desperate to be on television, and that extra factor was making things all the more challenging. Eva was doing her best to try to maintain a sense of calm, but even her level-headedness and calm demeanour couldn't stem the growing aggravation between Lexi and Alexander. This was turning out to be one of the most difficult days of the competition so far.

Scott approached Issy's station. He and Alexander were good friends apparently, which probably explained why someone with not one single hair on his shiny bald head was a guest judge in a *hairdressing* competition.

'Lovely hair,' he said to Issy. 'What's the inspiration behind it?'

'My client asked to look like Katy Perry,' Issy replied, although her client looked nothing like the pop star.

'Wonderful. What a good job!' And with that, he rushed off to speak to Jason. He flew among them like a pinball, bouncing off each of them and on to the next within a few seconds. Issy felt exhausted just watching him, but he never stopped smiling and even if he was mates with Alexander, he offered some light relief at least.

Lexi and Alexander were still arguing. Issy told her client she would be right back and went to find Laura.

'Where do you think you're going?' Alexander called after her.

'Toilet. I assumed that's allowed?' Issy said to him in the hope his face would turn even redder. It worked.

'Well ... don't be long.' He puffed out his chest. 'Right, people, this hair isn't going to do itself. Chop chop.' He was the only one who laughed at his pathetic joke.

As soon as she found Laura, Issy begged her to do something about Alexander.

'I don't care about him playing favourites, but I know Lexi and she's close to losing it.'

'Look, Issy, think about it. This works in your favour. Viewers will see how he's behaving towards you and you'll get their sympathy. So just ignore it and get on with the show.' Laura's tone wasn't exactly warm. As the show went on she was becoming more and more abrupt with them. Issy tried again.

'*I* can ignore it, but I don't think Lexi can. Seriously, I think you should do something before she kicks off and sets the whole salon on fire or something.'

'Issy, calm down. Everything's going to be fine. Now, get back to work please.'

Issy wandered back to the salon, feeling deflated. Laura's eyes betrayed the pressure she was under. But it was getting so intense, they were all feeling the pressure. She knew that for her own sanity she needed to spend more time phoning home and keeping in touch with Molly, but by the time she'd responded to her fans' messages of support, she had usually run out of time. The public had kept her in the show for this long, so she had to let them all know what their support meant to her in return. They were so close to the end and if Issy wanted to stay in the game, it was a sacrifice she knew she had to make.

Eva approached her as soon as she was back at her station.

'No luck with Laura?' she asked quietly. Issy shook her head. 'I tried to speak to Alexander before we started, told him to give everyone a fair go, but he wouldn't listen. He's got it in for you two.'

'That's been clear from the beginning and I can just about cope,' Issy whispered, 'but I think he's pushed Lexi too far.'

It was two p.m. and Issy's feet were killing her. They were wrapping up for the day and all she wanted to do was collapse on the sofa but the show had other ideas.

'I am not going shopping with them!' Mia stormed. For once, Issy didn't even have the energy to be annoyed at Mia's overdramatic, diva-ish ways.

Laura had just told them that Issy, Lexi and Mia would be filmed on a 'girly' shopping trip to the Trafford Centre. It wasn't Issy's idea of a good time either, but what the producers wanted, the producers got.

'Yes you are,' Laura told her Mia. 'The car will pick you up in half an hour. I suggest that you go and get changed and make the most of it.'

'But—' Lexi started.

'No buts.' Laura held up her hands. 'Mia, you spend your evenings ignoring everyone in the house. The footage we have for the next episode isn't great and we have to ensure that we do better than last week. We're building up to the live final and we can't allow viewing numbers to fall. If you actually made the effort when you were in the house, we wouldn't have to force this kind of thing on you. Now, go.'

The three of them made their way upstairs in silence. Issy couldn't believe she and Lexi were being punished for Mia being as boring as a stale custard cream.

'Maybe a bit of shopping will cheer us up,' Issy said to Lexi when they were in their room.

'Setting Alexander's hideous toupee on fire is about the only thing that would cheer me up right now.'

Hmm, thought Issy, *so I had been right earlier. Arson is on her mind.*

'Lex.' Issy put her arm around her friend. 'I'm worried about you. You seem like a woman on the edge.'

'I'm sorry.' Lexi's eyes swam with tears and she angrily brushed them away. 'I'm still thinking about what happened with Aaron. And the more I do, the angrier I get. I just can't calm down.'

'Come on, babe.' Issy squeezed Lexi tighter. 'An afternoon out with old sourface is just what we need to get a smile back on your face.'

'This is going to be hell, isn't it?'

'Yep. A complete shower of shite. #soznotsoz.'

*

Once in the back of the car, the tension between Issy, Lexi and Mia was palpable.

'This is going to be fun.' Issy tried to lighten the mood but she was failing miserably.

'Yeah, about as much fun as earache,' Lexi said.

'I just don't understand how they expect us to shop together,' Mia said. 'I'm pretty sure we don't shop in the same places.'

'How about you take us to your favourite shops and show us how you manage to look so fabulous all the time,' Lexi suggested sarcastically, but if Mia could detect the sarcasm she didn't show it.

'I'm happy to show you but you'd never be able to pull off that kind of style.'

'You never know,' Issy said. 'I think I'd look quite good in a twinset and pearls.'

Mia shot her a filthy look and the rest of the drive was spent in blissful silence.

'Issy! Lexi!'

They had been in the shopping centre for about five minutes before they were surrounded by young girls asking for their autographs, and photographs. Issy was enjoying herself and she could see that the smile on Lexi's face was genuine – the first real smile she'd seen from her in days. Mia, however, had a face like thunder – no one was that interested in her.

'Of course I didn't expect any Northerners to like me,' she spat. A few of the girls in the crowd turned to look at her.

'You're just a posh bore,' one of them sneered. Mia looked like she was about to slap her.

'From someone like you I'll take that as a compliment,' was all she said instead.

'The only reason you're still here is because Aaron walked,' another girl shouted.

Issy glanced around and became aware that the mood was shifting. Despite herself, she felt sorry for Mia. Being so publically hated couldn't be nice, even for someone with skin as thick as Mia's. It was time to wrap this up.

'All right, girls,' Issy said brightly. 'We've got some filming we need to get on with so we better go now. But it was so lovely meeting you all, and keep watching the show!'

Eventually, they managed to get to a store although they were stared at by nearly everyone they passed.

'We spend so much time in the house and salon,' Lexi said, 'that it's only just hitting me now that the show is being watched by a lot of people.'

'Everyone knows who we are,' Mia said quietly.

'We are, for the moment anyway, famous,' Issy said, unable to contain her excitement. *This, this was why I came on the show. Wasn't it?*

Chapter Thirty

Issy, Lexi and Mia returned to the apartment in the early evening and were greeted by Laura and Danny.

'What's going on?' Issy asked, heart sinking. She was buzzing like an old fridge after the shopping trip but that didn't stop her wanting nothing more than the sofa and a glass of wine.

'We've organised surprises for you,' Laura said. She turned to Lexi. 'Lexi, your friend Becka has come to see you and you get to spend a camera-free evening with her.'

Lexi's face lit up with a huge grin.

'That's amazing! Thank you so much,' Lexi said, her earlier bad mood disappearing.

'And Mia,' Laura continued, 'your brother, Tarquin, has come to see you – and your evening will be camera-free as well.'

'Oh my.' For once, Mia was lost for words. 'I don't know what to say. Thank you.' *Shit*, Issy thought, *she sounds sincere. Maybe she has a heart after all.*

'There's a car waiting for both of you,' Danny said. 'You need to leave now.'

There was a flurry of activity as Lexi and Mia quickly dumped their shopping bags and practically ran out of the front door.

'What about me?' Issy asked once they were gone. Jason wandered up and took hold of one of her hands.

'I've cooked us dinner,' he said, smiling down at her. 'And they've agreed we can enjoy the evening without mics. No filming either. It'll just be the two of us.'

'Seriously?' Issy couldn't believe it. A romantic dinner for two and no filming sounded perfect. Jason was a genius. 'How did you persuade them to do that?'

'It wasn't ideal for us. Viewers can't get enough of your relationship so this isn't exactly what we want, but we understand you all need some downtime and Jason can be persuasive,' Laura said. 'The only condition is that tomorrow I expect you all to get your acts together and focus on making the show as good as it can possibly be.'

'If you think about it,' Issy said, cutting into her fillet steak, 'this is really our first date. And this food is amazing. I can't believe you can cook. Why didn't you tell me? My specialty is cereal,' giggled Issy.

'I have many hidden talents,' Jason said. He went on, 'I know what you mean though. On one hand it feels like our first official date but at the same time it feels like we've been together for ages.'

'It's this house,' Issy said. 'When I used to watch reality TV, I thought people were so stupid, getting so emotional, arguing or bickering and even falling for each other so quickly. But now I'm here, it actually all makes sense.'

Jason nodded and then flashed his Hollywood-white smile. 'I fancied you the minute I first saw you, and then the more I got to know you, the more I liked you.' His smile wavered for a second. 'I wanted to tell you how I felt but then the whole thing with Josh happened and that put a bit of a spanner in the works.'

'I really wish I could just go back and ignore his DM.' Issy sighed. 'I was such a naive twat.'

'Don't be so hard on yourself,' Jason said. 'Lads like him know exactly what they're doing. They've got it down to a fine art. You never stood a chance with that knob. Is, you know that I really care about you, right?'

Issy nodded.

'Good,' he said. 'Because I really want to keep seeing you once the show is over.'

'I think we can arrange that.' Issy leant across the table and kissed him on the lips. She felt so liberated without the cameras watching her every move.

'I'm finding it so hard to keep my hands to myself.' Jason planted a row of kisses along her neck. Issy had wanted to wait, to take things slowly, but it was really ... difficult.

'The cameras aren't on,' Issy said slowly.

'Are you saying what I think you're saying, Miss Jones?'

So there could be no confusion about what she was suggesting, Issy kissed Jason deeply. They eventually broke apart, both of them breathing hard.

'Your bunk or mine?' Jason said, a cheeky glint in his eye.

*

Issy ran her fingers over Jason's smooth chest.

'That's the first time I've ever done that in a bunk bed,' she laughed.

'Me too.' Jason propped himself up on his elbow and looked down at her. 'You OK?'

'I am,' Issy said. And she really was. She'd never felt this connected to someone.

'I'm a very lucky man. You are amazing, Issy Jones.'

'You're not so bad yourself.' Issy pulled him down for a kiss. 'Once the show is over, we can do this all the time. No cameras to worry about. Just imagine it.'

'I am,' Jason said. 'It's what gets me through most days.'

'Not long to go. It'll be the live final before we know it.'

'Have you noticed how tense Laura's become?'

Issy nodded. 'Tell me about it! She's starting to feel the pressure. That's the impression I get, anyway.'

'Has she said something to you?'

'Nah, but Ryan's mentioned something a couple of times and it's clear from the way she's behaving.'

'Ryan. I should've known.' A cloud passed over Jason's face. 'That bloke hangs around you like a lovesick puppy. It's so sad.'

'What are you talking about? He's the sound man. It's his job to be around all of us all the time. It's not just me. Don't be daft.'

'I know, I know. Sorry, it's just . . . I get so jealous when I see you with anyone else.'

'Well that has to stop, Jase. You need to trust me.' Issy was excited about her future with Jason but she couldn't bear any kind of possessiveness.

'I'm sorry, Issy. I know I can trust you. It's just that I've never been with anyone as beautiful as you before.'

'Don't be such a soft cock!' Issy said, hiding her embarrassment with a laugh.

'I'm serious,' Jason said. 'I don't want to fuck this up.'

'Good, because I like you. And no one else.' She kissed him and then reluctantly got out of bed and started getting dressed.

'Do you have to go?' Jason asked.

'I do. Sorry, babes, but the cameras will be coming back on soon and I don't want anyone seeing this part of us.'

'I get that,' Jason said. 'It's just you and me. No one else.'

'Exactly.' Issy leant down and kissed him goodbye before padding across the apartment to her room.

Their night of freedom was over but Issy would always have the memory of it – and it had been amazing.

Chapter Thirty-one

'Are you on something, Lex?' Issy asked, amused. Lexi was humming her way round the room as they got ready the next morning.

'What do you mean?' laughed Lexi.

'You're buzzing like an old fridge, girl. I've never seen you this happy.'

'I just think after everything that's been going on recently and all this shit with Alexander the Arsehole, having a break from the show was just what I needed. And seeing Becka was the icing on the cake.' Lexi caught Issy's eye in the mirror. 'How was your night then, missy?'

By the time Lexi had returned last night, Issy had been sound asleep. Her bedroom antics had wiped her out.

'It was nice,' Issy said innocently, a smile creeping into the corners of her lips.

'Just nice?' Lexi pressed.

'Erm . . . Maybe a bit better than nice.'

Lexi raised an eyebrow and Issy just grinned back. It was crystal clear what Issy and Jason had got up to.

'I have to call Molly today,' Issy said, changing the subject. 'She'll disown me if I neglect her anymore.'

'It's the hardest thing, isn't it? I was telling Becka how much I wanted to talk to her but with our schedule, lack of phone time and trying to reply to every social media message, it's just insane. I can't keep up.'

'The trouble is that we understand because we're living this, but I don't know if you can explain it properly to someone who's not experiencing it all. I'm worried Molly's just going to think I'm a being an ignorant knob.'

'She won't. When I spoke to Becka about it she was sound. Life hasn't changed for them at home but for us, it's completely different. She understood.'

'I know you're right,' Issy said, 'but I still need my family, and I know I've not been paying them or Molly enough attention lately so I *have* to call her today, no matter what.'

They were making their way down to the salon. It was elimination time, the last judging before the final. Her talent had got her this far – Issy just hoped it was enough to make it to the final. In her heart of hearts, she was convinced that Mia would be going home today, which meant the final would be her, Lexi and Jason. If that was the case, no matter who won, Issy would be happy. There had been highs and there had been lows, and Issy had certainly felt the pressure more than once but she wouldn't change this experience for anything. She'd made a great friend in Lexi and she couldn't wait to see how things turned out with Jase. No, life wasn't too bad at all. In fact, she was ballin'!

They had half an hour before filming started so they were given their phones back for a few moments. It was time to reconnect with the other important people in her life.

Issy switched on her phone and felt that familiar feeling of panic when she thought about what to respond to first – her social media notifications were vast, her voicemail was full, and she had multiple Whatsapps and texts. She scrolled through Whatsapp – the messages were mostly from Molly, Zach and her parents. She quickly typed out a group message to her mum, dad and Zach, apologising for being MIA for so long and telling them that she'd call them when she could. With that sent, she phoned Molly, praying she would catch her before school started.

'Issy! I thought you'd forgotten me!' Issy could hear the smile in her friend's voice.

'No, babes, never. I've just been so busy. It's non-stop here. I'm so sorry.'

'I can imagine and don't be daft – I understand,' Molly said.

She doesn't sound mad, Issy thought. *Maybe I haven't been that neglectful after all. Maybe I've just been paranoid.*

'It's weird,' Issy went on. 'We don't have time to read the mags or the papers, and we don't really watch that much TV so I feel so disconnected from reality. The only glimpse I get really is when I get my phone back and have a quick stalk on the *Daily Mail Online*. Even then, I only get minutes. I've got no clue what's going on in the "real world". It's like living in a bubble.'

'It must be a head fuck but honestly, you're doing wicked.

And you're nearly there. The end is in sight. Oh my God, by the way, did you see the pictures of you at the Trafford Centre?' Molly asked. 'They're hilare. You and Lexi surrounded by fans and Mia stood off to the side on her own looking ready to kill someone.'

'No way?' laughed Issy. 'We haven't seen them yet, but that's too funny. Princess Mia will not be happy. I almost felt sorry for her, to be fair – it was a bit much. Anyway, Mol, enough about me. How are you?'

'I'm good, babes. Missing you obviously but everything is good.' Molly broke off to talk to someone in the background. Issy couldn't make out the words but she was almost certain the other voice was male.

'Who's that?' Issy was intrigued.

'What?' Molly sounded flustered. 'It's no one … Just a mate. Anyway, listen, I'll have to go in a minute but you remember it's my birthday next week, right?'

'Of course I do, wifey! I've been at your birthday every year since we were five.'

'Good. I was thinking dinner at Sakana, drinks in Spinningfields, and dancing wherever will grant us entry in the states we'll inevitably be in by that point. Can you make it?'

'Are you doing it on your actual birthday?'

'Yes, the Friday.'

'We don't have our schedule yet but Fridays tend to be pretty quiet, so I'll tell Laura today. It should be fine. They're usually OK if you give them plenty of notice.'

'And bring Jason, if you like. It would be nice to get to know him better.'

'Will Zach be there?'

'Er, yeah, I think he said he was coming. Why?'

'Because last time Zach and Jason were together it went down like a sack of shite. Zach has to promise to be nice.'

'No worries, Is, I'll tell Zach to behave himself. Look, I better go. Good luck today – not that you need it. The final has got your name written all over it. Smash it, babes.'

'Cheers, mate. Fingers crossed. See you next week, Mol. So good to speak to you. Love ya.'

'Love you too. Bye.'

Issy had only managed to get through a small cross section of her Twitter notifications and have a cheeky scroll through Insta when they were called into the judging room. She caught up with Lexi at the door.

'Wish me luck,' Lexi said.

'You don't need luck, you're a definite for the final,' Issy replied. Lexi gave her a funny look, and Issy's heart started beating a little faster. 'That's not what you mean, is it?'

Lexi shrugged and smiled knowingly. Issy knew something was up and instinct told her it wouldn't be good. She just hoped Lexi wasn't about to do something stupid.

Eventually the contestants were lined up and the cameras were rolling. Eva walked in wearing a gorgeous but under-stated outfit of black, tailored cigarette trousers and matching black blazer, with simple gold strappy Jimmy Choos and her hair swept up into a sleek ponytail. Alexander followed looking less elegant and more like a Toffee Quality Street in his shiny gold suit. *Twat.* Scott Savannah came next, a huge smile on his face. Issy had never met anyone so bloody chipper in her life. *#boreoff,* thought Issy.

'Welcome to our last elimination before the live final,' Eva said with a smile.

'You've all done well to get this far but for one of you, this is the end of the line,' Alexander said seriously.

'Thank you so much for inviting me on to this wonderful show,' Scott gushed. 'You're all very talented and I was very impressed with each and every one of you.' *#seriouslyboreoff* Issy thought again.

'Before we get onto the results,' Eva said, 'let's talk about yesterday's challenge. We wanted you to recreate a day in the life of an Alexander Fox salon. You all had to look after a couple of clients, as well as working for the legend himself.'

How Eva managed to say that without laughing, rolling her eyes, or sounding sarcastic was beyond Issy. *She should sack off presenting and go into acting.*

'Some of you did better than others,' Alexander pointed out.

'Come on, mate,' Scott said good-naturedly. 'I thought they were all amazing.'

'Well no, not from a hairdressing point of view I'm afraid, my friend. As a boss I would have had a problem with some of you, particularly Lexi.'

Issy glanced at Lexi. At first her face was unreadable, but then she smiled.

'As a member of staff, I had a problem with *you*,' Lexi said loudly and confidently.

'Lexi,' Eva said warningly.

Lexi ignored her. 'The thing is, throughout this entire competition I've been told over and over again to stay true to myself. And I'm not the sort of person who will happily work for a pervert just because there might be some great opportunity at the end of it.'

'How dare you?' Alexander shouted, looking around for someone to save him. No one did.

'Who's a pervert?' Scott asked, looking worried.

'He is,' Lexi replied. 'Alexander Fox, sex-pest extraordinaire and general dickhead.'

Alexander's face had turned a particularly lurid shade of red. 'You can't talk to me like that!'

'Can't I?' On the outside, Lexi appeared cool, calm, composed. Every word that came out of her mouth was spoken quietly. It was as if she was just having a conversation with her mates down the pub and her casual tone had alarm bells going off in Issy's head. 'We all know the real reason Aaron walked out. You. You and your creepy come-ons. You might think you're amazing, that you're Billy Big Potatoes, but really you're just a fat old tosser with a shit wig. You're not that talented, you just got lucky at some point or sucked up to someone influential. Your "status" doesn't give you the right to force yourself on someone who is clearly out of your league.'

There was a deathly silence in the room. The cameras were still rolling but everyone had forgotten about them. Eventually, Mia piped up.

'You're lying! Just because you know you lost the challenge!' Lexi didn't even bother replying to her.

'I won't stand here and be insulted by you,' Alexander

stated, trying to keep his voice calm, despite being clearly riled. 'Shall we get on with the judging? Not that we need to do it. It's clear who the loser is this week and it's obvious that she's already angry about the decision.'

'You know perfectly well that if it was down to the public and talent, I wouldn't be leaving. But it doesn't matter anymore because I'm so angry with myself for not standing up for Aaron when I should have. I kept quiet when I should've been shouting from the rooftops. Whatever happened tonight, whatever comes out of your mouth next, I was walking anyway.'

'That's enough!' Alexander shouted.

'That's the first sensible thing you've said since the show started, but I've already said everything I had to say.' Lexi smiled. 'Don't bother with the judging. I'm leaving.' And suddenly she was hugging Issy goodbye. Issy was stunned. What had just happened?

'Good riddance to you!' Alexander yelled, his cool well and truly lost.

'Aw fuck you, Bazza,' Lexi said.

'Who's Bazza?' Scott asked, confused.

Lexi pointed straight at Alexander. 'Him. His real name is Barry Griggs. Didn't you know?'

And with that, Lexi walked out of the room, leaving everyone staring after her, open-mouthed.

Laura ran onto set. 'OK, everyone, let's take a few minutes and then we need to reset.'

'You should have stopped that,' Alexander screamed at her.

'The exec producer told me not to. Take it up with him,' she shot back. 'Issy, can you come with me please?' Laura didn't wait for Issy to respond; she just grabbed her hand and ushered her into the green room.

Lexi was sat on one of the sofas, shaking. Issy went straight to her.

'Babes, are you all right?' Issy said.

'I feel fucking fantastic,' Lexi said, laughing. 'I feel so much . . . lighter. Liberated.'

'Are you drunk?' Issy asked.

'No, I haven't touched a drop. But that felt so good. I should have done it ages ago.'

'How did you know his name was Barry?' Issy asked.

'Becka! She did some serious online stalking and stumbled across that little nugget of gold.' Lexi couldn't get the smile off her face.

'Issy, can you try to talk some sense into her please?' Laura pleaded.

Issy took one look at Lexi's face and knew she'd be wasting her breath. 'Sorry, Laura,' Issy said, shaking her head. 'It's too late. Lexi's made up her mind and if I'm totally honest with you, I'm proud of her. I wish I'd done it.' With that, Issy high-fived her mate and pulled her into a hug.

'No, this can't happen.' Laura looked desperate. 'Look, we can reshoot the ending, with you staying. Mia was leaving today anyway – she's not getting the public vote.'

'Give it up, Laura. It doesn't matter, I was over it,' Lexi said, standing up. 'I meant what I said. And there's not a Solero's chance in hell I'm working with that twat ever again.'

'You don't need to take the job if you win but we want you on the show, Lexi. The executive producer has told me to do whatever it takes to get you back.'

'Fire Alexander,' Lexi replied instantly.

Laura's face fell. 'What? You know we can't do that. But I can make him be nice to you.'

'No. You might be happy to turn a blind eye to sexual harassment but I won't do it anymore. I'm leaving while I've still got the morals I came here with. I don't want to end up desensitised, like you lot, and only thinking about what's good for the show.'

'Lexi, Aaron didn't want to make a formal complaint,' Laura said.

'That was his choice, and this is mine.' Lexi rubbed her face. For all her fire and bluster, she looked done in. 'I need to leave, Laura. I can't be here anymore. This shit isn't for me. Is, you understand, don't you?'

'I do,' Issy said, hugging her again. 'I get why you're doing this, but I'm going to miss you so much.'

Laura looked defeated. There was no way anyone was changing Lexi's mind.

'They'll have my fucking head for this,' Laura muttered as she walked out.

Issy was curled up against Jason on one of the sofas in the living area. It had been a long ass day. Once it was clear that Lexi wasn't coming back, Alexander had locked himself in his dressing room and the contestants had been told to wait in the green room until further notice. They hadn't been given their phones so they'd sat there for what felt like hours,

Mia and Issy sniping at each other, and Jason trying to play referee. Eventually Laura had told them they were calling it a day – Alexander couldn't be coaxed out of his dressing room. The final bit of filming would be finished off tomorrow, and the judges would confirm Issy, Jason and Mia as the final three. There was nothing climactic or triumphant about it.

The apartment felt too big with just the three of them. It was too quiet. Issy had got used to the noise and banter. She didn't like the atmosphere now – it was disconcerting. And it didn't help that Mia was sitting at the other end of the sofa, pulling faces at her and Jason.

'I'm going to bed,' Mia snapped finally. 'I can't sit with you two.'

'We aren't doing anything,' Issy pointed out.

'You think you're Romeo and Juliet but you're nothing but a bargain basement Jordan and Peter,' Mia said, flouncing off to her room.

'I'm surprised she even knows who Jordan is,' Issy remarked.

When they were finally alone, Jason kissed her full on the mouth.

'How are you?'

'Not sure,' Issy admitted. 'The apartment feels strange. It's too quiet. Plus I miss Lexi. She should be here, she should be in the final three.'

'You should be on cloud nine, Is. Come on, you need to enjoy this, babe,' Jason said. 'You've made the final. That needs celebrating. I'm so proud of us!'

'Maybe.' Just then, Issy remembered her earlier phone

call with Molly. 'Bollocks. I wanted to ask Laura about next Friday, but with all the drama I completely forgot.'

'What's next Friday?' Jason asked.

'It's Molly's birthday. She's going out. It's before the final so I was hoping we could both go.'

'Sounds good to me. I'd like to get to know her a bit more.'

'It'll be a laugh and God knows we need some fun right now.' Issy hesitated. 'Zach will be there.'

Jason raised an eyebrow. 'I should probably get to know him better too. I think we may have gotten off on the wrong foot,' he said wryly.

'I'd appreciate that.'

'Is, I'm sorry about Lexi. I know you two were close. Is there anything I can do?'

Issy smiled up at him. 'You're doing it. Just talking to me and asking how I am. That's enough.'

'Do you want to stay in my room tonight? And I meant to sleep, nothing else,' he added, when he saw the look on Issy's face.

'Just sleep?'

'Maybe a bit of talking, and I might tickle the back of your neck if you're lucky but yes, just sleep.'

'You know the way to my heart, don't you?' laughed Issy. 'OK, I'm in. I don't feel like being alone right now anyway.'

'Come on, then.' Jason pulled Issy to her feet and wrapped her up in a big bear hug. 'I'll take care of you, Is, I promise.'

Chapter Thirty-Two

If Issy found filming exhausting, she found posing for photos even more so. The closest she'd been to a photoshoot before *Can You Cut It?* was an epic selfie session in the girls' toilets on a night out with Molly when they thought their outfits were particularly on point. Needless to say that experience had not prepared her for this one.

'How did you manage to make a career out of this?' she asked Eva. They were posing together – Eva was in the hairdresser's chair and Issy was pretending to use a curling tong on her. It would've been fun if Issy wasn't posing with a fucking supermodel! She felt like a short, fat, ugly, possibly homeless man compared to Eva and it wasn't getting any better as time went on. In fact, it was getting worse. The first hour had been OK, but they were in hour three now and Issy was starting to lose the will. She needed a Kit Kat Chunky and a bottle of blue WKD.

Issy's mind wandered to yesterday's filming. They'd shot the scene in which they were told they were the final three, but the whole thing had felt flat. Jason had won the challenge but even his victory couldn't lift their spirits. All she could think about was Lexi and how brave she'd been. And how no one would ever see the truth.

Shake it off, Jones! The show must go on, Issy thought. They were in photoshoots all day, they had a full press day coming up, and the countdown to the finale had begun. It was officially a hundred miles an hour from this point on. Issy hoped that at some stage, adrenaline would kick in and the excitement would ramp up because right now, she felt as flat as a witch's tit. Until then though, she'd just make sure there was a smile on her face whenever a camera was pointed in her direction.

Laura wouldn't tell them exactly how much of Lexi's walk-out was being shown, but the episode was airing that night and they were planning on watching it. Issy hoped that they'd done the right thing by Lexi and hadn't brushed everything about Alexander the Arsehole under the carpet.

'Right, Issy and Eva, you're done. Issy, go and wait in the green room. Jason, I need you with Eva,' the photographer barked. With a smile for Eva, Issy gladly left with a new-found respect for models everywhere.

The green room was empty. Issy slumped on the sofa, opened a can of diet coke and tried to relax. The door soon opened and Ryan walked in.

'Hiya, hun,' Issy said. 'How are you?'

'Fine. Almost redundant but fine,' laughed Ryan, his eyes crinkling at the corners in a very cute way, Issy noticed. 'Now that we're nearing the end, I need to start thinking about what happens next.'

'Don't we all?' Issy said. 'You must have offers coming out of your ears though. Geddit? Your ears? Because you're a sound man?' *Smooth, Issy. Really smooth, you knob.*

'Stick to the day job, Is,' Ryan said, smiling. 'Anyway, it's not quite like that, but I'm sure I can rustle something up. Anyway, enough about that. How are you feeling about Lexi leaving?'

Issy sighed. 'Conflicted, I suppose. I miss her and the house is too quiet without her. But I'm proud of her for standing up to Alexander. I wish I'd had the balls.'

'It wouldn't have helped anyone for both you and Lexi to have left.'

'I just keep thinking maybe if we'd both walked out, the producers would have fired him or something.'

'I don't think so. It's too far down the line to replace him. Also, no formal allegations were made so he could have sued the show.'

'He didn't say anything incriminating?'

'No, and trust me, we'd know if he did. Especially me. Remember that I hear everything, it's both my gift and my curse.' Ryan did his best tortured superhero impression, and then sat down next to Issy and stretched his long legs out in front of him. The sat together in companionable silence for a while.

'I'm so up and down,' Issy said finally. 'It's never consistent. It's a total rollercoaster. One minute I'm loving it, and the next I've had enough. Is this normal or am I being dramatic?'

'What does Jason say?'

'About what?'

'What you've just told me,' Ryan said.

'I haven't told him.' Issy shrugged. 'Don't know why.'

'Well, you can talk to me anytime.'

'Thanks, mate.' Issy gave Ryan a playful shove. 'I don't see you around much these days though. So this is nice.'

'It's all about the live final now,' Ryan said. 'We're all rushed off our feet and under loads of pressure but if you ever need to talk make sure you come and find me.'

'God, the live final. I never thought I'd get this far.' Issy turned to look at Ryan, a mischievous glint in her eye. 'My family will be there – including my mum.'

'Oh great,' Ryan said, eyes all wide and innocent. 'It'll be nice to see your mum again.'

'I bet,' Issy laughed. 'She put such a shift in with you last time. She thought you were gorgeous.'

'Did she? Well, it's nice to know one Jones thinks that.' And with that, Ryan patted Issy's knee and walked out of the room.

Issy had just kicked off her shoes and was settling down on the sofa, when Mia joined her. Jason was still downstairs in the salon.

Play nice, Issy thought. *There's not long left, no point spending the whole time at loggerheads.*

'That was one of the longest days of my life,' Issy said.

'Issy, don't try being nice to me now that all of your little friends have gone. You're so transparent.'

Why do I bother? Issy thought.

'Jason's still here,' Issy pointed out.

'Of course, and he loves you,' Mia sneered.

'Mia, you know it's just the live final to go now? You've

made it. You're here. Shouldn't you cheer up a bit? Maybe crack a smile?'

'You know what, Issy? As long as I'm in your company I think I'll struggle to "crack a smile". I just detest people like you.'

'Why?' Issy wasn't hurt by the comment, she couldn't care less about what Mia thought of her, but she was genuinely interested in her answer.

'You really want to know?'

'Yep.'

'Fine. I don't like people who try to be one thing when they're clearly something else. Like you thinking you're gorgeous when you're tacky. I mean, honestly, did you really think Josh would be interested in you? You must be mad. Jason's either stupid or faking it too.'

Issy looked long and hard at Mia. Yes, she'd asked the question and Mia and given her an honest answer, but had the girl never heard of tact? A weaker woman would've been in tears by now.

'Mia, listen to me carefully. I do not care what you think about me. You want to know why?' Despite herself, Mia nodded. 'Because a lion doesn't concern herself with the opinion of sheep. You get what I'm saying? So why don't you go and pour us both a glass of that wine you hate so much and we can drink to the fact that we aren't ever going to be best mates, we both think the other is a dickhead but after next week we will *never* have to see each other again?'

Mia looked as if she was going to say something nasty but then to Issy's surprise, she smiled and said, 'Why not?'

*

306

'What's going on?' Jason asked. It was an hour later and he'd returned from the salon to find Issy and Mia sat together on the sofa, drinking wine, and not tearing each other's hair out.

'Don't worry, we still hate each other but there was no one else for us to drink with,' Issy explained.

'I better get a beer, then.'

When Jason returned with his drink, Issy was surprised when he chose to sit on the other sofa rather than next to her.

'I am so looking forward to getting out of this apartment and drinking champagne again,' Mia said.

'Do you really miss your old life?' Issy said.

'Yes. I hate having to mix with the likes of you.'

'Of course you do, princess,' Issy said.

'Is your family coming to the live final?' Jason asked.

'Well, Mummy and Daddy don't do TV but they're making an exception for me. My brother will be there too. And hopefully Horatio.'

'I'm trying to get some friends to come but it isn't easy.' Jason sounded sad.

'You can share my family. There's enough of them to go around,' Issy offered.

Jason didn't reply. He just smiled and fiddled with the label on his beer bottle. Issy wondered what was wrong, he didn't seem himself.

'Mia,' Issy couldn't believe what she was about to say, 'we're off out on Friday night for my mate's birthday. Would you—'

'Ah, about that,' Jason interrupted.

'What?' Issy asked.

'That's why I was late in the salon. The show's producers have organised for me to do a PA.'

'What's a PA?' Mia asked.

'A personal appearance. I'm going to be paid to go to a club in Manchester.'

'That's great,' Issy said enthusiastically.

'It is, but it's on Friday night,' Jason said.

'Oh.' Issy bit back her disappointment. 'Well, never mind. You'll smash that, babe. I can still go to Molly's birthday and maybe when you're finished you can meet us after?'

'Actually, Is, Laura wants you to come with me. And so do I.'

Issy shook her head. 'No way, Jase. I've never missed Molly's birthday and I'm not about to start now.'

'But I need you,' Jason pleaded. 'I can't do it without you.'

'Jason, I'm sorry but no. You'll either have to turn it down if you can't do it on your own or man up and fly solo for the night. It's only going to a nightclub. You'll be fine.' Nothing was straightforward any more.

'Is, please.' Jason threw a look in Mia's direction.

'Don't mind me,' she said, standing up. 'As riveting as your little relationship drama is, I need my beauty sleep.' With that, she left them to it.

Jason got up and sat next to Issy. He took her hand. 'I have to do this PA. I need the money.'

'What do you mean?'

'I'm skint,' he said quietly. 'I had to give up a good job to do the show. I know I'm in the final but I haven't had money coming in for ages and I could really do with the coin. I have debts.' Jason put his head in his hands. Issy didn't know

308

what to do. She could see that Jason was upset but how could she let Molly down?

'J, you can still do the PA. You don't need me there.'

'But I do,' Jason implored. 'I need you by my side. Everything is so much easier when you're there.'

'Do you know what you're asking of me? Molly's my best friend.'

'I know, but there will be other birthdays. This is my first ever paid gig and if I turn it down word might spread that I'm unreliable and then I won't get anymore. I can't do it without you.'

'I don't understand where this lack of confidence has come from. *Of course* you can do it by yourself.'

'The thought of being up there on stage, alone, everyone staring at me . . . ' Jason's hands were shaking. 'I can talk the talk, but when the spotlight is on me, I freeze up. I can't handle the pressure and I don't want to look like a knob on my own.'

'But you've been filmed this entire time!' Issy shook her head.

'That's different, I can't handle big crowds. I don't know how many more times I can say this – I need you. Please.'

'Babes.' Issy sighed wearily. 'I just don't know. Look, I'm going to bed. Let's talk about this again tomorrow.'

'You're going to your room?' he asked, sounding surprised.

'Yeah, I'm knackered and I think tonight it's for the best. I'm confused and don't want to argue. Please can we just talk in the morning?'

'If that's what you want.' Jason turned away when she went to kiss him goodnight.

Chapter Thirty-three

Issy was sat alone in the green room, rubbing her temples in an attempt to get rid of her headache. Things had been even more manic since the last show had aired – they had shown Lexi calling Alexander a pervert but they'd edited it in such a way that Aaron's name hadn't been mentioned and it looked like Lexi and Alexander were just shouting at each other and disagreeing over the challenge. *The power of television*, Issy thought ruefully. Even so, Alexander was swinging between saying he would sue the show, to threatening to walk out, to announcing he was lining up countless interviews in which he'd be claiming he was the victim of two ambitiously ruthless liars. Laura had instructed them to carry on as normal. *No fucking chance*, Issy thought. The only blessing was that all the drama meant Alexander was keeping out of their way, so Issy had barely seen him.

Issy, Jason and Mia had done countless interviews with the press and they were draining the energy out of her.

Weekly gossip mags, tabloid newspapers, some of the monthly glossies – they had been interviewed by them all and they'd all asked the same questions. She'd had to talk about Posh Josh ('No, there was no sex but I don't need to give him any more publicity by talking about it.'), her relationship with Mia ('I don't think it's a secret that we're not best friends. She think I'm classless and I think she's a tit.'), how she felt about Alexander ('I'm not allowed to talk about that but I wish Lexi and Aaron the best.'), and Jason ('He's amazing. I'm looking forward to seeing how our relationship develops after the show is over.'). Issy was exhausted – she had no more words left, and she was sick of the sound of her own voice. Yet despite this, there was still a part of Issy that was buzzing. She had been interviewed by magazines that she read and loved. And they were going to feature her. This was a whole other world and she was loving it. Fame gave her such an adrenaline rush.

Because Issy had started the interviews first, she'd finished first and was now fiddling nervously with her phone. She'd killed some time posting tweets and had even downloaded that new Periscope app but she knew she couldn't put it off any longer. With a heavy heart, she'd texted Molly to say that she couldn't go to her birthday. She'd had a talk with Jason that morning and she could see how important it was to him. She hadn't realised how much he'd been through. He'd spoken to her about his low self-esteem, and she knew she couldn't turn away from him now that he'd asked for her help. He was on his own after all – she was essentially his family now and she needed to be there for him. It hadn't been an easy decision but Issy hoped Molly would understand.

She knew it was cowardly to send Molly a text but she'd bottled out of a phone conversation. She just couldn't face it. She'd sent the text first thing that morning and she still hadn't heard back. She sighed. She couldn't bear it if Molly was angry with her. She was just mustering up the courage to call her, when her phone beeped. Molly.

Ah, Is. Really? That's such a shame but we can celebrate after the show. Mx

Issy replied immediately saying she would buy her the best present ever and that she loved her. Then she sat back and relaxed. *She deserves a unicorn or One Direction as a birthday present for putting up with me as a best mate,* thought Issy.

A knock on the door interrupted her thoughts. Danny poked his head round.

'Hiya, Danny,' she smiled.

'Issy, Zach is here. Laura said he can come in. Is that alright?'

'Yes! Show him in.' Issy beamed as her brother appeared. She threw her arms around him but he didn't return the hug. She pulled back and looked at his face. It was grim, unsmiling.

'What's wrong? Is it Dad?'

'No, Issy, Mum and Dad are fine. It's you.'

'Me?'

'Why aren't you coming to Molly's birthday?'

'You know about that? The thing is, the show have organised me a PA and I have to do it. I can't get out of it.' A small lie was worth it to spare everyone's feelings, right?

'I don't believe you. You said you asked Laura and that she said you could come. What's changed?'

'Yeah that's true but then this was booked afterwards. They want Jason and me to go. We weren't given much of a choice.' Issy started fiddling with her hair and felt the blood rushing to her face.

'Issy, I'm your brother, I know when you're lying. I can see it in your face.'

'I'm not lying. They need us to do a final push for publicity. That's all there is to it.'

'Really? Because it looks to me as though you're putting some bloke you've known for five minutes ahead of your best friend.'

'Zach, it's not like that, I'd never do that.' Even to her ears, she sounded pathetic.

'Nah, it's exactly like that. And the worst thing is that Molly's being so understanding. She's hurt and upset but she's still not calling you up on the fact that you're being a shit mate. She won't listen to a word said against you. And I bet it took you all of five seconds to decide to pie her off for that creep.'

'Don't call Jason names, Zach. I don't know who you think you are storming in here like this and kicking off but you should know better than anyone that I'd never hurt Molly. She's my best friend.'

'Wake up, Issy! You're treating her like shit. Don't you see? Or are you too busy with your new crowd to realise or even care how you're treating the rest of us?'

Issy couldn't remember the last time she'd seen Zach so furious. And he was genuinely angry. With her. And that made her feel sick.

'Zach, you have to try to understand what it's like. My life isn't my own right now. When the show says jump, we say how high. I want to be there for Molly but I can't be in two places at once. Why don't you get that?'

'All I get is that Molly's barely heard from you since you've been here.' Zach held up his hands. 'I know, I know. You don't have your phones all the time, whatever. And yet you found the time to DM that twat Josh, and tweet and Instagram about how great everything is. But you've got no time for Molly or us? What's happened to you?'

Issy knew she had to answer for ditching Molly's birthday, but where was the rest of the attack coming from? She wasn't having this. 'You don't know anything,' Issy said, her voice rising. 'I've tried to explain but you're not hearing me. And Jason isn't just "some bloke". He's important to me and you have no idea what he's been through. He's not like you and me, he doesn't have a family. He needs me. Molly will have plenty more birthdays and I'll be at all of them, but Jason and I have one shot at this.'

Zach stared at his sister like she was a stranger. Issy didn't like it one bit. 'That's no argument.' Zach shook his head. 'You could tell them no. I don't believe that you don't have a choice. Everyone has a choice. But it's not really about that, is it? You love the fame, don't you? You love it so much, that you've started to neglect everyone who really matters.'

'What? That's not fair! You wanted me to do this show, you all did. You practically forced me into it. And now you're saying all of this to me?' Issy voice was thick with tears. She and Zach never argued like this.

'I just want to know where my sister's gone. Where's the girl who insisted on staying at home when Dad was ill?

Where's the girl who said she never wanted to leave her family? You text us, Is, but when did you last speak to any of us? Properly, I mean. You're on social media all the time – we see it. How do you think we feel, knowing that we're second best to your 'followers' who you don't even know?'

They were going round in circles. What the hell was Zach doing here anyway? And why was he attacking her like this? Why was the fact she wasn't going to Molly's birthday so important to him? Her temper flared and she became defensive.

'Why did you decide to come here now?' Issy shouted. 'What does Molly's birthday have to do with you anyway?'

'It's got a lot to do with me.' Zach's voice was getting louder too. 'Everything, in fact.'

'What the hell are you talking about?'

'Me and Molly are together,' Zach yelled. 'That's why I'm so fucking concerned. Because she's my girlfriend and you've hurt her!'

Issy was stunned into silence. *What?*

'What the actual fuck? How? When?' Issy had no idea what was going on.

Zach sighed and rubbed his hand over his eyes. 'Remember when me and Molly wanted to take you out for dinner after that Posh Josh stuff? You cancelled on us then as well, didn't you?'

Issy remained silent and Zach carried on.

'You told us to carry on without you so we did. We were just drinking and chatting and having a laugh. I saw her in a different light that night, I suppose. It was the first time we'd spent time together like that and I fancied her – so I told her. Then she admitted that she'd fancied me for ages. And it went from there.' Zach fixed Issy with an icy stare. 'And if you hadn't been so wrapped up in your own world, you might have noticed what was going on.'

'I had no idea she liked you.' Issy shook her head. Molly and Zach? The thought had never occurred to her. And this had all been happening behind her back? Issy didn't know how she felt about them being together but she did know that she felt betrayed that they'd kept it from her. 'You lied to me. You were sneaking around behind my back—'

'Behind your back?' Zach said incredulously. 'Listen to yourself, Issy. Once again, you've managed to make this all about you. You haven't heard a word I've said. We tried to tell you but you were too wrapped up in yourself and your new found "fame". You need to sort your head out.'

Issy watched her brother storm out of the room. It wasn't until he'd slammed the door that she let the tears fall.

Issy was still sobbing when she heard the door open. She looked up, hoping it was Zach returning to make amends. But it wasn't her brother. It was Ryan.

'Issy?' Ryan's voice was gentle. 'What's wrong?' He sat down next to her and pulled her towards him.

'My brother was just here. We had a fight. A huge one and we've never argued like that.' Issy sniffed and tried to wipe away her tears with her sleeve. 'I don't want to talk about it.'

'Are you sure?' he asked, stroking her hair soothingly. 'Talking might help.'

'I don't know what I want anymore.' She looked at Ryan,

her vision blurry through her tears. 'Am I a terrible person? Am I a complete bellend?'

'What? No, of course not. This show has been tough, Issy. It's been tough just to work on it behind the scenes, let alone be one of the contributors. I don't know how you've done it at times.'

'Too much has happened,' Issy said sadly. 'And now my brother hates me and I just can't bear the thought of that.'

'He doesn't hate you,' Ryan said. 'He loves you. I don't know what you were fighting about, but he cared enough to come down here and have it out with you in person. If he didn't care, he wouldn't have bothered. Things seem bad now because it's all fresh but give it time. He'll calm down and everything will get better.'

Issy dropped her head in her hands. 'I feel so lost.' Her voice was small. 'Every time I think I'm doing the right thing, someone gets upset. I don't know what to do to make people happy anymore.'

'How about starting with yourself? Make yourself happy and the rest will fall into place.'

'The thing is, Ryan, I'm not sure I know what makes me happy anymore.'

To her surprise, Ryan kissed the side of her head. It was nice, comforting. And completely inappropriate. But she didn't pull away. Ryan's presence was solid, grounding, and it made her feel better.

'The final is around the corner,' he said quietly. 'Get through that and then you can fix things. Your family makes you happy, so that's where you need to start.'

'How do you know my family makes me happy?'

'It was clear the second I walked into your mum's salon that first day. All that chatter and banter. That's your home; it's where your heart is.'

Issy nodded. 'You're spot on. I just wish Zach wasn't so angry with me.'

'Was it really that bad?'

'Yeah, it's Molly's birthday on Friday and I said I'd go. But now Jason has this PA and he needs me to go with him. The show arranged it for him and he needs this for a lot of reasons so I have to go with him. But my brother doesn't understand and now he's seeing my best friend behind my back . . . ' Issy could feel a fresh wave of tears coming.

'What's that about Jason?' Ryan looked at her.

'He's got a PA arranged and he has to go. It's compulsory.'

'Right.' Ryan looked confused but Issy didn't register it.

'And now because I can't make Molly's birthday, Zach turned up and started having a go at me about it. Then he ended up confessing he's with Molly, which made me mad and then he stormed off.'

Issy started crying again. Ryan pulled her in for a tighter hug and she sniffled into his shoulder.

'What the fuck is going on here?'

Issy and Ryan looked up. Jason was standing in the doorway, staring at them. He had a face like thunder.

'All right, mate,' Ryan said, standing up. 'Issy was upset. I was just trying to make her feel better.'

'I could see that for myself. Do you make a habit of going round groping other people's girlfriends? Just do one, will you?'

'Jason, stop,' Issy said. 'Ryan was just trying to be a friend.'

'That's what he wants you to think.' Jason glared at Ryan. 'But I know what you're up to, you snake.'

'I'm not up to anything,' Ryan said. 'But a word of advice. I'd worry less about me and more about why your girlfriend is upset. I notice you haven't even asked her.'

'That's enough,' Issy said, trying to defuse the situation. 'Please just stop.'

'If he stops trying to put a sly shift in with my bird, I fucking will!' Jason shouted.

'I don't have time for this. You need to grow up, Jason.' Ryan looked at Issy for a second before stalking out of the room.

'He was just being nice,' Issy said to Jason when Ryan had gone.

'You're so naive. He wants to get into your knickers.' Jason practically spat the words out.

'Jason, it's been a shit day. I can't be bothered. Please let's not do this.'

'I see. You'll talk to that twat but you won't confide in your actual boyfriend? That's great. What a punch in the dick. Thanks, Issy.'

'Why are you being like this?'

'Because I don't like seeing my girlfriend draped all over another man like a cheap suit.'

'You're being ridiculous! I wasn't doing that! You're being totally unreasonable.'

Jason threw up his hands. 'I can't even look at you right now.'

As Issy watched the third man walk out on her that day, what a hat trick, she buried her head in her hands. She felt utterly alone. How had it come to this?

Chapter Thirty-four

Issy walked quietly to her room. She didn't want anyone to hear her – she wanted to be left alone. After Jason had left her, Issy had gone to see Laura and explained how close to the edge she was so Laura had agreed that she could go back to Salford to see Molly for a few hours. Issy had texted Molly and they'd arranged to meet at Molly's house. Issy wasn't ready to see Zach, but she needed to have it out with Molly face to face.

'Hey.' Jason wandered into her room.

'Ever heard of knocking?' Issy shot at him.

'Sorry, but I didn't think I needed to.'

'After the way you talked to me earlier, you definitely do.'

'You're right, I owe you an apology.' Jason tried to put his arms around Issy but she shrugged him off. 'I just got so jealous seeing Ryan with his arms around you like that.'

'We've talked about this before,' Issy said. 'I can't handle a boyfriend who gets jealous and flies off the handle over silly little things. It's so childish.'

'I know, I know. And I'm really trying, but I don't want to lose you.'

'Well that's a guaranteed way to push me away. Look, I'm off to see Molly now so I can't talk about this right now. I've got other things on my mind, which you'd know if you actually talked to me and didn't just jump to conclusions and shout at me.'

'I really am sorry, babes. It won't happen again. You're the best thing that's ever happened to me.'

'Then don't throw it away by being a twat, J.'

The car that the production company had arranged was going to wait for Issy while she spoke to Molly. Laura had said they weren't going to let any of them out their sight until the show was over and she wasn't kidding.

For the first time in her life, Issy felt nervous ringing Molly's doorbell.

'Hey,' Molly said, as she opened the door. She looked nervous too. She stepped aside and let Issy come in. They walked through to the kitchen in silence.

'Tea or something stronger?' Molly offered.

'What have you got?'

'Wine.'

'Sure.' They sounded like strangers. Issy and Molly had ever been this distant with each other. Molly's hand was shaking as she poured their drinks. She handed a wine glass to Issy and then sat down opposite her.

'So,' Issy said. 'You and Zach.'

'Yeah, me and Zach.' Molly took a big gulp of her wine. 'He said he'd told you.'

'There are so many things I need to say, I don't know where to start.'

'How about at the beginning?' Molly said, not-so-helpfully.

'Fine. Why didn't you ever tell me you fancied my brother?'

'Come on, Is. I've had a crush on him since I was about seven and it's always been pretty obvious. I always thought you knew but you were just too nice to bring it up or waiting for me to tell you or something. Anyway I didn't think I'd ever have to tell you because I never thought he'd be interested in me.'

'So he's never shown any interest in you before now?'

'No. But that night in Manchester, something shifted. Maybe it was the drink, I don't know. It just happened. He says he's ready to settle down, to stop sleeping around and all that.'

'Right,' Issy said slowly. 'Our Zach is now perfect husband material?'

'Is, he doesn't want to date around anymore. He wants to be with one person; he wants to be with me.'

'Fine. But why didn't you tell me straight away? Why did you go behind my back?'

'I wanted to tell you as soon as it started, the minute anything happened, but I could never get hold of you and you weren't the best at getting back to me either. And it was too important to do over Whatsapp. I was planning to talk to you on my birthday, but then you said you couldn't make it.

I got upset, so Zach got upset. I didn't want him to have it out with you, but he wouldn't listen. We weren't trying to hurt you, Issy. We were trying to think of the best way to tell you. We were trying to be considerate.'

'But not considerate enough not to go there?'

'This isn't just some fling. I like him. A lot. And I have for a long time.'

'At least now I know how important I am to you.' Issy's voice was pure ice. Molly stiffened.

'For fuck's sake. It's not all about you. I've barely heard from you since you went on the show, but I've still supported you, tried to be understanding about the pressure you're under. But right now, I'm getting nothing back from you. This friendship is becoming one-sided and you're just oblivious to it. You didn't come to dinner with us that night because of Jason and the show and now you're not coming to my birthday either – because of Jason.'

'That can't be helped. I have no choice.' Issy sounded like a broken record. She was starting to bore herself.

'Of course you have a choice, Issy. You always have a choice.' Molly looked at her and Issy had to look away. It was true, she did have a choice. And she'd chosen Jason – but for the right reasons. She felt guilty, confused and angry – it was a myriad of emotions that made little sense.

'Everyone keeps telling me I have a choice, but no one else has to live through this. You all wanted me to do the show, and now you're saying I don't have to do as the producers say. You can't have it both ways. You've got no idea what it's like for me.'

'That's right. This is all our fault because we wanted the

323

best for you. But we never expected to get lower and lower down your list of priorities. I never said anything before now because I knew the pressure you were under, I *knew*. But one phone call a week, Is. It's not too much to ask.'

'It's been so busy and stressful. There isn't time for everything.'

'We aren't "everything"! We love you, we're your family, and if you'd given us the chance we would have helped you but instead you shut us out and pushed us away.'

'Family? What, you're going to be my sister-in-law now? As if Zach would marry you.' As soon as the words were out of her mouth, Issy regretted them. This wasn't her. She recognised the sound of her voice but these words couldn't be hers. Surely not? What was she doing?

'Is – Is – Is . . . ' Molly burst in to tears. 'I just . . . you – you – you . . . ' Molly put her head in her hands.

Issy stopped and looked at her friend. Molly never stuttered when it was just the two of them. Never. Issy's eyes widened, realising what she'd done. Things had gone too far and now they were in a place they'd never been before. And Issy didn't think she knew the way back.

'Molly . . . ' Issy reached for her friend, but Molly turned her back.

'Just g – g – g – go.'

Issy wasn't a girl who cried a lot but over the last twenty-four hours she felt as if she'd shed her body weight in tears. And more came during the drive back to the apartment. Everything was a mess. She'd fucked it all up. She wanted to speak to her dad but she was too afraid. She'd lost Zach and Molly – what if her dad was angry with her too? She angrily brushed her face clear of tears and pulled some of her make-up from her handbag. She attempted to fix her face as best she could before she pulled up at the apartment, but there was only so much a bit of well-placed concealer could hide. The pain she felt was etched across her entire face.

Jason was waiting for her when she got back inside.

'Hey,' she said, falling into his arms. She was still mad at him but was too drained to pretend that she didn't need the hug. 'Where's Mia?'

'Gone to bed. I take it things didn't go well with Molly?' he asked, his eyes searching her face. She shook her head. 'Let me get you a drink and then you can tell me what happened.'

As Jason poured her a glass of wine and grabbed a beer from the fridge for himself, Issy filled him in on her conversation with Molly.

'It sounds pretty full on,' Jason said when she'd finished.

'It was. I've never had a fight like that with Molly. Ever. Or Zach for that matter.'

'Molly is meant to be your friend. Your *best* friend. She should have told you she was seeing your brother as soon as something happened. It sounds like she lashed out because she felt guilty.'

'Do you really think so?' Issy desperately wanted to believe that this entire mess wasn't all her fault.

Jason nodded. 'I reckon they're just jealous. You're doing amazingly. You're in all the mags, you're smashing the show, the nation loves you and we're really happy.

They're just fucked off your life doesn't revolve around them anymore.'

'I don't know, Jase . . . Molly and my family have always been so supportive of me. They're not like that.'

'Think about it. Molly's a teaching assistant. Hardly the most glamorous job, is it? I bet she's well jel of your exciting new life and she's foaming that you're leaving her behind with nothing but all those snotty little kids. She couldn't begin to understand all the stress and pressure you're under. That we're under.'

'Maybe there's some truth in that, but I don't think I've handled the whole thing very well.'

'That's why everyone loves you, babes. Because you're too nice and you're trying to blame yourself for something that isn't your fault.'

'Do you really think that?'

'Yes.' Jason paused and then said, 'And that's why I love you.'

'What did you just say?'

'I said I love you.' Jason held her gaze.

Issy didn't know what to say. Did she love him too? They hadn't known each other for that long, but everything had been so intense from day one. It was like she'd known him forever. He had a tendency to get jealous, and they still had to deal with that, but he was there for her, in her corner, always on her side. And when everyone who she thought loved her was falling away, she needed someone on her side more than ever.

'I love you too.' And she meant it.

'Things are shit with Zach and Molly right now and

maybe it will never get fixed, but you've got me. I'm not going anywhere.'

Issy pulled Jason to her and kissed him fiercely. He lifted her up and she wrapped her legs around his waist.

'The cameras aren't filming anymore,' he said into her mouth. 'So, my room?'

Issy nodded. 'Yes. Your room. Now.'

Chapter Thirty-five

'What should I wear?' Issy asked Jason. He rifled through her wardrobe before pulling something out.

'Why don't you wear this?' He handed her a white and black midi dress from Rare London. 'Monochrome is classic and sophisticated. You can't go wrong.'

'Bloody hell. Take it easy, Trinny and Susannah.' Issy smiled. 'I love having a boyfriend who knows about fashion.'

'There's nothing wrong with wanting to look good all the time. Except when those knobby Twitter trolls keep saying I'm gay.'

'You're definitely not gay,' Issy said as her thoughts drifted to the previous night and everything she and Jason had got up to. There was no way that man was gay.

'Maybe you could tweet that for me then,' Jason said playfully.

'Fine. I'll say that I can confirm Jason Anderson is *Can You Cut It?*'s resident *straight* heartthrob.'

'It's a start. Come on, finish getting ready so we can meet our public.'

'You mean your public. This is your job remember,' Issy replied.

'What's mine is yours.'

Jason held the car door open for Issy as she stepped onto the pavement. She'd decided to wear the dress Jason had picked out with her black peep-toes. Flashbulbs were going off everywhere. Jason put his arm around her and they posed for pictures. Issy couldn't help but beam as the photographers called her name.

The club, Bijou, was heaving. The manager and a couple of huge bouncers led them through to the VIP area at the back. The crowd parted as they walked through the club, people calling their names and whistling at them. The atmosphere was electric. They were seated at their table, and the manager, Matt, joined them for a drink.

'Is this your first PA?' he asked. Jason nodded. 'It's simple. In about half an hour you'll go up on stage, stand next to the DJ, and say a few words. Just get the crowd going, get the party started – that kind of thing. Afterwards, if you could spend some time signing autographs, posing for photos, then that would be great.'

'Sounds easy enough,' Jason grinned.

'Issy?' Matt asked.

'This is Jason's thing, I'm here for moral—'

'Issy's just a bit shy,' Jason interrupted. 'She'll be fine.'

'OK, great.' Matt looked confused. 'I need to check on a few things before you go on stage so I'll come and get you in a bit.'

'What was that about?' Issy asked when Matt had gone. 'This is your PA. It's nothing to do with me.'

'They must've added you to the bill when I told the crew you were coming with me.'

'I'm going to ask Matt,' Issy said as she started to stand up. Jason put a hand on her arm to stop her.

'Don't do that. It'll look unprofessional. Let's just go with it for now.'

'OK but this is weird. And what am I supposed to say? What do they want me to do?'

'Don't worry. You'll be fine. I'll be by your side, holding your hand and whatever else you need.' He leant over and kissed her and it went a little way in easing her anxiety.

'Hello, Bijou!' Issy shouted into the mic. She was greeted by a cacophony of cheers and whistles. 'I'm Issy Jones from *Can You Cut It?* and this is Jason Anderson.' She handed him the mic.

'Hope you're all having a fuckin' boss time,' he shouted. His reception was a little lukewarm compared to Issy's. 'Come on, everyone. Let's get fucking steamin'!' he shouted. Issy was taken aback. Jason didn't sound like himself. But the crowd was responding to it, which was the whole point.

'OK, everyone,' she continued when Jason handed her the mic. Once she was up on stage, she'd found talking in front of a crowd easier than she'd thought. 'You've been an amazing crowd!' She paused and held the mic toward the audience to catch their cheers. 'If you want photos or autographs with us then we'll be here for a bit. So let's all get smashed!'

The crowd went wild.

*

'My feet are killing me,' she shouted above the noise to Jason. He smiled and nodded as someone else approached for a photo.

It had been two hours since they'd started signing autographs and having their photos taken. People kept coming up to them, which was flattering, if exhausting. Issy's face was starting to ache from all the smiling.

'Issy, we fucking love you,' two girls said in unison as they approached.

'What are your names?' Issy asked as she arranged her lips into a smile again. This was a small price to pay for being made to feel so good about yourself. She leant over and kissed Jason when the two girls had rushed back to their crowd of mates.

'Thanks for bringing me here. It's insane but the most amazing feeling ever!' she said.

'You're welcome, beautiful,' he replied.

Fame really is like a drug, she thought as she left the club, hand-in-hand with her handsome boyfriend. Things at home were a mess and she knew at some point she was going to have to deal with that, but she had Jason standing next to her and people out there who liked her enough to wait two hours just for the chance to say hello to her. Who knew what the future held? But what she did know was that it was full of possibilities. She had to make the most of this amazing opportunity and smash it while she still had the chance. And she wasn't going to let anyone ruin this for her.

Chapter Thirty-six

It was pandemonium. It was the day before the live final and they had one final salon challenge to film. Issy, Mia and Jason had been gathered in the salon for what was likely to be their final briefing and the nervous energy in the air was obvious.

'This is it.' Laura paused dramatically. 'In a moment the judges will enter and take their places. They'll be followed by your models and then your final challenge will begin. The judges will explain what the challenge entails, and after that you'll have three hours to complete it.'

'Here we go,' Issy said under her breath. They'd been here before, done this so many times, but today felt different.

'Remember to stay focused. The challenge will be aired tomorrow night, ahead of the live final the following night. We need a good show, so let's all pull it out of the bag. This is your last chance to give it everything you've got. OK, that's it. Good luck, everyone.'

Everyone took their places and the cameras started rolling. The doors opened and Eva and Alexander walked in, taking their places in the middle of the salon.

'Hi, and welcome to the final challenge,' Eva began.

'I'd like to introduce our guest judge,' Alexander announced. 'As you know, one of the prizes is to manage one of my salons and the other is to develop a product line for the Eva Whitman brand, in conjunction with Vitality Hair Care. So we are delighted to introduce the Managing Director of Vitality Hair, Melody Curtis.' The final three contestants clapped as Melody entered the room. She ran one of the biggest hair product companies in the UK and she had the ability to open a lot of doors for anyone she thought was talented enough. She had a reputation for being smart, fair and creative and suddenly Issy wanted nothing more than to work with her and Eva. Despite the personal lows she was facing, Issy felt a swell of determination go through her. This was her time. She didn't come here to be average. She wanted to win.

'Hello, everyone.' Melody smiled broadly. 'I'm so happy to be back in Manny, my hometown. I've been watching the show and I've loved every minute of it. Now, your final challenge is going to be a simple one but it will allow us to gauge your skills and see how far you've come. All of today's models look relatively similar but we want you to make them look as different to each other as possible. Imagine yourselves as artists and them as blank canvases, OK? We want you to show us your signature style. Cut, colour, finish – do whatever you wish. Just show us *you*. The only condition is that you're only allowed to use Vitality Hair Products of course!'

'It's about showing us your personality,' Alexander chipped in. *Helmet.*

'OK, contestants. Let's begin,' Eva said.

'May the best scissors win!' Alexander shouted for what felt like the hundredth time.

Issy studied her model from all angles. She had chestnut brown hair, which was kept long and straight. It really was like working with a blank canvas. Issy decided to attack the colour first. She wanted to create an ombré look with the hair, or a balayage, just to make sure she was at the forefront of what was cutting edge in the hair world at that moment. Today she was going to stand out for all the right reasons and she felt so alive and ready to smash this task. Once she had the colour right, she'd move on to the cut.

The memory of what had happened with Zach and Molly filled her head but she pushed those thoughts away. She needed to focus. If she let herself get distracted now, then all of this would've been for nothing.

Even so, she still couldn't get her head around the fact her brother and her best friend were together. Two of the most important people in her life had formed a unit of which she'd never be a part of. She felt excluded. She'd spoken with her dad briefly this morning. The conversation had been short and to the point, and Kev had reassured her that they would all be at the live final tomorrow. Issy was relieved that Zach and Molly were still going to be there for her, but she didn't know how she'd react seeing them side by side for the first time. Issy shook her head. She needed to focus.

She had a few minutes while the colour took hold so Issy

took the opportunity to slip away to the green room and grab a coffee.

Ryan popped his head round the door.

'Hi, I was hoping you'd be here,' he said.

'Ryan, hey. I wanted to see you too. After the other day—'

'Yeah, sorry about that. I didn't mean to just walk away but I thought that might be for the best.'

'He just got jealous for a second. I explained that you and I are just friends.' Issy smiled. 'Good friends.'

'Yeah, friends.' Ryan paused. 'Did you sort things out with your brother?'

Issy shook her head. 'I had a big row with Molly instead. They're coming tomorrow but things aren't great. At least I have Jason on my side.'

'Issy . . . ' Ryan's voice trailed off. He looked upset.

'What is it?'

Ryan took a deep breath. 'I need to talk to you about Jason.' The words came out in a rush.

What now? 'Go on,' Issy said slowly.

'I shouldn't really be telling you this, I could get fired, but I think you deserve to know the truth.'

'Tell me.' Issy looked at her watch. 'I've only got a few minutes before I have to go back out there.'

'The thing is, I overheard Jason talking to Mia. Just before filming started. They were both mic'ed up and didn't realise we could hear them.'

Issy remained silent. She didn't like where this was headed.

'Mia was being her usual delightful self and calling Jason

335

a fool for chasing after you like some lovesick puppy. That girl is poison by the way.'

Issy rolled her eyes. 'Tell me something I don't know. That sounds just like Mia.'

'Yeah, I know. No change there. But it's what Jason said that bothered me.'

'What did he say?'

'He said that he knew what he was doing.'

Issy tried to laugh it off. 'Is that it?'

'No.' Ryan ran his hands through his hair, struggling with what he had to say next. 'He told Mia that he was only with you for two reasons. The first was to put you off your game because you're a threat to him in this competition. And the second was because the British public love a love story. You were, you *are*, the nation's favourite so he thought being with you would increase his popularity.'

Issy stared at Ryan in disbelief. 'No.'

'Issy—'

'No . . . Jason wouldn't say that.' Issy was firmer this time.

'It's the truth, Is,' Ryan said softly. He hated to see Issy hurt but he couldn't keep this to himself.

'He said he loved me.'

'Issy, I swear to you I'm not lying. Jason said those things to Mia. And he went on to tell Mia that he was going places, he had bigger fish to fry, and if she was interested she could come along for the ride.'

'Mia and Jason?' Issy shook her head. 'There is no way Jason would be interested in *her*. Now I know you're lying!' She looked at Ryan and narrowed her eyes. 'Maybe Jason was right.'

'What do you mean?'

'Jason said you'd try to come between us, because you like me. He was jealous of you because you can't be trusted. I see that now.'

'I do like you and I'm telling you this because I care about you. That's all.'

'Well, I don't believe you,' Issy repeated. This wasn't true. It just wasn't. She couldn't comprehend it.

Ryan took a step towards her. 'Jason's not wrong – I do like you. A lot. How could I not? You're fun, beautiful, genuine and kind. But this isn't about that. I didn't want to tell you like this. I promised your family I would look out for you and I meant that. This is me living up to my word.'

Issy couldn't find the words to reply. There was too much noise in her head.

'Is, I'm not lying to you, I swear. Jason is a twat and you're too good for him. There are so many people out there who want to hurt you, to use you, and you're too trusting. But that's a beautiful quality so listen to me when I'm trying to help you. Jason is a scumbag and he doesn't care about you.'

'Stop it. Just stop talking, Ryan. I can't listen to you anymore,' she shouted. Laura chose that moment to appear in the doorway.

'What the hell is going on?'

'Ask him!' Issy pointed at Ryan.

'Issy, get your make-up touched up now. You look a mess,' Laura said angrily.

'I'm going,' Issy said. She ran out of the room and didn't look back.

*

Issy walked unsteadily back into the salon. She saw Jason and Mia laughing together. Were they laughing at her? Alexander threw her his customary nasty look. *Oh fuck off, Bazza. This is not a good time.* She bit back tears and tried to plaster on a smile as she made her way to her model. This was not how things were supposed to be. Nothing was as it was supposed to be. How had everything started to unravel so fast?

Issy, Jason and Mia were sat on the sofa in the apartment. The producers had provided champagne and snacks to celebrate finishing the final challenge, but Issy was not in the mood for fun. They only had two nights left and then Issy would be going home. Home. It felt so far away – she didn't know if she even belonged there anymore. And then she had to deal with what had happened on her return to the salon . . .

'I screwed up big time,' Issy groaned.

'Babes, I'm not gonna lie to you,' Jason said. 'Your model didn't look great.'

Issy looked at him sharply. *Where was the support?* Fine, she had been too distracted to pay much attention to what she was doing and had messed up the cut. The model had looked horrified when she'd seen herself in the mirror. Issy had somehow made her look like a cross between a prepubescent Justin Bieber and Worzel Gummidge. How she managed that, she'd never truly know. She had just lost all concentration. She felt terrible for the poor girl. Even Eva had struggled to say something nice about her. Even so, a little comfort from her boyfriend wouldn't go amiss.

'She looked awful,' Mia declared without ceremony or a touch of remorse.

'Thanks,' Issy said. 'That's exactly what I needed to hear right now.'

'Try to see the funny side.' Jason attempted a smile but Issy wasn't having any of it.

'There's nothing funny about it. I was so distracted by everything that's happened, I couldn't concentrate and my hands wouldn't stop shaking.'

'I'm trying to be supportive, Is, but it's not easy. The final is important to me as well,' Jason said. 'You can't let what's going on with Zach and Molly get in the way right now.'

And what's going on with Ryan, Issy thought to herself. 'That's easier said than done.'

'Does it always have to be about you?' Mia snapped.

Issy glared at Mia, ready to fight back. And then all the fight just left her body. 'You're right,' she said wearily. Mia looked surprised. She hadn't expected Issy to give in so easily. 'Ryan said something to me in the middle of the challenge. Something . . . hurtful. That's all I could think about when I was cutting that model's hair and that's why I fucked up.'

'What did he say?' Jason said, his eyes narrowing.

Issy hesitated. She was angry with Ryan but she didn't want to get him into trouble. He wasn't supposed to talk about what he overheard. And yet, she needed her doubts put to rest. 'He said he overheard the two of you talking. About me.'

Issy watched their faces closely. Was that a twitch in Jason's jaw? Had Mia turned a paler shade than normal?

'And what were we saying?' Mia asked innocently.

Issy took a deep breath. 'That Jason was using me to get ahead in the competition. Trying to distract me to throw me off my game.'

There was a moment of silence before Jason spoke.

'And you believed him?'

'No, of course not.'

'Then why did you mess up?' Jason pushed.

'Because I was upset with Ryan for saying it in the first place. But why would he lie?'

'Because he's after you, Is. I've said it before and you didn't listen to me,' Jason said. 'Even now I've been proved right, I'm still the one getting it in the ear.'

'What are you talking about?' Issy asked, frowning.

'You just don't stop moaning. It's draining, Issy. All you can talk about is Molly and Zach. And now Ryan. Have you even thought about how I'm feeling right now?'

'I—' Issy began.

Mia interrupted her. 'You shouldn't even have repeated what Ryan said,' Mia sneered. 'It's insulting to your boyfriend. You have no respect.'

Issy ignored Mia and turned to Jason. 'J, I said I didn't believe him. I just wanted to explain why I was distracted. I hate not doing my best and I just wanted you to know why I wasn't my usual self. I didn't mean anything by it.'

Jason sighed. 'You know what, Is? I'm actually wondering if you're the one playing a game here? It's like you're determined to hurt me.' Jason looked away and Issy was stunned into silence.

*

Later that evening, Issy climbed into bed. Alone. She wanted Lexi, with her wise words and sharp wit. She wanted a hug from her mum and dad. She wanted Molly and Zach not to be mad at her. She wanted Jason to slip into bed next to her. And she wanted to turn back the clock and re-do that model's hair. She wanted a lot of things to be different, but she knew that merely wishing wouldn't change anything. She'd lost everyone and really fucked up this time and she had no idea how to fix it.

Chapter Thirty-seven

Issy woke up feeling squashed, with her back pressed against the bedroom wall. She rubbed her eyes and smiled at Jason's sleeping form. After she'd got into bed the previous evening, Jason had come into the bedroom and they'd talked and talked and talked. She hadn't realised her behaviour had been having such a negative effect on him. She'd been so wrapped up in her own dramas and problems she hadn't considered how he might be feeling as the final approached and thoughts of his absent family consumed him. Jason had made her see how selfish she was being and he'd accepted her apology in the end. As soon as he had, Issy felt instantly lighter and had vowed to put him first from now on.

Jason had convinced her to come back into the living area so they could watch the last episode together. Issy had been reluctant because she knew how badly she'd done but she hadn't wanted to appear self-involved so she'd sat in between Jason and Mia and cringed through the entire episode. It had been excruciating. Her cut was atrocious and she had looked like shite. *But at least it's over,* Issy thought as she tickled Jason's nose. *Just one more thing to get through.*

'Wake up, Sleeping Beauty,' she whispered into Jason's ear. He opened his eyes slowly.

'Hello, beautiful,' he said, his voice thick with morning.

'Today's the day,' Issy smiled. She had no chance of winning after yesterday's performance – she'd come to terms with that – so she was trying to see the positives in the situation; she'd be getting out of here and going back to her family.

And then she could start mending what had become broken. The show had taken its toll on her and she had nothing left in her locker. Well, almost nothing. Issy could get through the live final and then that was it. She was done. Despite everything, however, she was grateful for the one good thing that had come out of the show; Jason. She wasn't going to think about all the shit that had also happened.

'Coffee?' she asked him.

'Not yet. It's our last morning here. Let's make the most of it,' he replied and leant over to kiss her.

As Issy struggled to get her suitcase closed, she couldn't help but think back to that day in her bedroom when she, her mum and Molly had struggled with the same thing. A pang of sadness went through her. It was a physical pain; thinking about Molly hurt. So much had happened since then and Issy almost laughed out loud when she thought about how naive she'd been. Would she have done things differently if she'd been better prepared? There was no way to tell but whatever happened next, Issy would go into it with her eyes wide open and she'd be much more careful about who she chose to trust. And she'd make things right with Molly and Zach.

Somehow.

A few minutes later and Issy, Jason and Mia were seated in the living room, ready for make-up and hair styling. The stylists would be helping them get ready in the apartment because the downstairs area had been transformed for the live final.

'I am so not going to miss this apartment,' Mia said, wrinkling her nose and looking around.

'I might miss it a bit.' Jason winked at Issy, and she smiled back and tried to ignore the butterflies in her stomach.

The final would last for an hour and a half. As well as completing their final challenge, there would be the usual highlights shown throughout the show that viewers would expect. Issy knew she wasn't going to win but the nerves were still there. *This is live, FFS!* Issy thought. And she was going to see her parents, Zach and Molly . . .

'Are you nervous?' Hannah asked as she started pencilling in Issy's eyebrows.

'A little,' Issy said. 'Mostly just because this is live. I know after yesterday's fuck up there's no chance of me winning and anyway, there's no way I can work for Bazza after everything that's happened.'

'He's such a dick,' Hannah said, rolling her eyes. 'You should hear him when he's in the make-up chair. Total diva.'

'I'm not surprised. I just wish he'd got what was coming to him after what he did to Aaron, and Lexi.'

'Maybe he has.' Hannah started applying primer to Issy's face. 'He's a joke in the press. I can't imagine that he's going to be inundated with offers for work after all this. He's a total laughing stock.'

Issy and Hannah chatted easily while Hannah finished Issy's make-up. Eventually she dusted some setting powder over Issy's face and announced that Issy was ready.

'Thanks, Han,' Issy said, jumping down from her seat. 'And thanks for making me look halfway decent every day.'

'Don't be daft, you. You're one of the easiest ones to get ready,' Hannah said, laughing. 'And, Is? The show isn't over yet. You never know how things are going to turn out, so don't accept defeat just yet. Also not winning the show doesn't mean you've lost. One Direction didn't win *The X Factor* and they don't seem too arsed.'

Issy thought about Hannah's words as she walked to her bedroom to get changed into her dress. Was she still in with a chance to win this thing? And did it really matter if she didn't?

There was a knock on the door, and Danny walked in.

'It's showtime, Is,' he said, smiling. 'You ready?'

Issy looked around the room for the last time. Her packed suitcase stood in the middle of the floor. The sheets had been removed from each bunk bed. There were no more clothes strewn about, no more make-up bottles scattered on the shelves, no more discarded fake lashes waiting to get stuck on someone's feet. Everything was gone.

'I'm ready,' Issy said.

*

'OK, guys,' Laura said. 'This is it. When you walk into the salon, the cameras won't be rolling as the producers thought you'd all appreciate a bit of private time with your friends and family. Get the support you need, and then we'll call you back just before we start the live feed so that you can make your grand entrance. So go!'

Issy hadn't seen Laura this energetic for a while and her enthusiasm was infectious. The whole crew could see that the end was in sight and they were all charged with energy. When Mia pushed past Issy and Jason without a backward glance, Issy was too buzzing to be irritated with her. Jason kissed Issy's cheek and then quickly made his way into the salon on his own. Issy was surprised – she'd expected them to walk in hand-in-hand. Never mind. He probably just wanted to see his friends.

The first person Issy saw when she walked into the salon was her dad.

'Dad!' She threw her arms around his neck and squeezed him hard. 'Is Mum here? And Zach and Molly?'

'Issy, get off, will you?!' Kev said, laughing. 'Yeah, everyone's here, we were a bit late so they're still being briefed on the whole thing, but I've skipped that as I wanted to see you now.' Eventually he was able to prise his daughter's arms from around his neck and when he looked down at her face, his expression was serious. 'Love, what's been going on? What are you and Zach playing at? You never fight.'

'I don't know what happened, Dad. Zach just turned up and started shouting his mouth off—'

'Issy Jones,' Kev interrupted. 'Don't you dare take me for

a fool. I'm not half as stupid as I look. Don't try to pin this all on Zach.'

'I'm not.' Issy shook her head. 'I know some of this is my fault as well. But when Zach showed up here, he just kicked off out of nowhere and then he dropped the bombshell about him and Molly, and I didn't know what to think. I was blindsided. They should have told me as soon as—'

Kev held his hands up, interrupting again. 'And when were they supposed to tell you? You haven't exactly been very available to us mere mortals recently, have you? I know, I know, the show kept you busy. But you can't be mad at them for not telling you when there wasn't ever the chance to.'

Issy had nothing to say to that. As always, her dad was right.

'Love, you and your brother are the same – both stubborn. I should bash your heads together.' Kev scratched his head as if he was actually contemplating doing that. 'Zach shouldn't have turned up here just to have a go at you, and me and your mum have told him that. But surely two of the people you love the most being happy together is a good thing?'

'I suppose,' Issy said slowly. She hadn't really thought about it like that. Why hadn't she thought about it like that? What the fuck was wrong with her?

'You need to make this up to them.'

'I know. I will. I promise.'

'Why did you cancel on Molly's birthday?' Kev looked Issy in the eye, his expression stern. *No way I can bullshit my way out of this one*, Issy thought.

'Jason begged me to do the PA with him,' Issy admitted. 'He said he couldn't do it by himself. I felt like he needed me more than Molly did.'

Kev's face hardened. 'Molly has been your best friend almost your entire life. You've known this Jason for five minutes. What do you really know about him? And more importantly, what do you owe him?'

'I know enough,' Issy said, her resolve returning. 'I love him and he loves me. He makes me happy. And as for what I owe him, the answer is a lot! He's been there for me so much in here and I'm sick of people trying to get in between us and split us up.'

'I'm not doing that,' Kev said, softening a little. 'We all want you to be happy. We just want you to be happy with someone who deserves you and doesn't try to take you away from us.'

Issy's eyebrows shot up in surprise. Where had that come from? 'He'd never try to take me away from you! Family means everything to him, and he knows what it means to me too.'

'Maybe that's the problem.'

'What's that supposed to mean?'

Kev paused, seeming unsure about whether to continue. His eyes flicked around the room, filled with cameras and production staff running everywhere.

'It doesn't matter, love,' Kev said gruffly. 'Think all those lights have gone to me head. We'll talk more when this is all over.'

Issy looked at her dad in confusion. 'Dad, if there's something you want to say, then just say it.'

'Don't worry.' Kev kissed Issy's forehead. 'You've got all

this live filming to focus on. You just concentrate on that for now.'

'But—'

'For God's sake, Issy, would you just listen to your dad for once in your life?' Kev said, exasperated.

Issy was taken aback for a second and then her face broke into a big smile. 'See? I haven't changed that much.'

'No, kiddo, you haven't. You're still you underneath it all.' He let the words hang in the air for a moment and then said, 'Your mum's brought that bloody dog with her.'

Issy wasn't that surprised. 'Next you'll be telling me Vi is here too.'

'She wanted to come,' Kev said. 'But she decided to host a party instead. Invited everyone from the salon to watch the final at her house.'

'Really?' Issy was touched. 'Everyone is still watching the show, even after everything?'

Kev looked at Issy as if she'd just said the most stupid thing in the world. Which she had.

'We've watched every single episode. All of us, together. None of us have missed any of it.'

'Oh.'

Right then, at that moment, Issy couldn't work out if that was a good thing or a bad thing.

Issy, Jason and Mia were standing behind the salon doors again. The live final had started, and they could hear the voiceover announcing each of their names. Laura stood just to the left of them, counting down so that they knew exactly when to walk through the doors.

'Go!'

The final three pushed open the doors and walked into the salon. It was something they'd done dozens of times before but this time was different, because this time there was an audience cheering for them. This time they could hear their names being called. This time their families were there. This time Issy felt as though her palms had shower heads on them, the amount she was sweating. *#nervousmuch?* Issy looked up into the audience and spotted her biggest fans quickly.

They were all there – even Zach was clapping. She caught Molly's eye and gave her a small smile. Issy's stomach turned as she thought about their last conversation, and how much she'd upset Molly. And yet here she was, still on Issy's side, still her best friend. *I don't deserve her*, thought Issy. She recalled what her dad had said – she really did have a lot of making up to do.

Mia was waving at her family. It looked as though her parents were there, and Issy guessed the third person was Mia's brother – he looked like a male version of Mia. Mia looked genuinely pleased to see them. Mia happy was a fucking weird sight. *Disconcerting*, thought Issy.

Issy glanced over at Jason, ready to give him a reassuring smile in case he looked upset. He was looking up into the audience and Issy followed his gaze to see a nice-looking grey-haired couple and a pretty girl in her mid-twenties. The girl looked familiar to Issy but she couldn't place her face. Before Issy could think about it anymore, she was at her station and the judges were being announced.

Eva, Alexander and Melody Curtis, walked in to rapturous applause. They waved and smiled as they made their way to the desk that had been installed in the salon. Alexander took the middle chair (*of course*, Issy thought, *you podium-placing pillock*) and Eva and Melody sat on either side of him.

'Welcome finalists!' Eva called into her desk microphone. 'You made it!'

There was more cheering and applause. Alexander was saying something but Issy couldn't hear most of it because the noise from the audience all but drowned him out. When they had finally quieted, he tried again.

'Congratulations to all three of you. You've got one more challenge to get through but before we get to that, let's have a quick word with each of you.' Alexander looked at Issy. 'So Issy, you've had quite a journey on the show. Do you think it's changed you?'

Issy nodded. 'Yeah, I suppose it has. I haven't been perfect and I've made mistakes but I've learnt from them and hopefully it's made me a bit wiser.'

'And after the horror of your last challenge, why do you think you deserve to win?' Alexander went on.

There was some booing from the audience, and Issy couldn't help but feel a little pleased that Alexander clearly wasn't going down well with viewers after everything he'd put her friends through.

'Maybe I win, maybe I don't,' Issy said. 'But I love hairdressing and that will never change. And winning isn't everything. Just ask One Direction.' Issy's eyes found Hannah's off stage and she winked at her. The crowd cheered and laughed – and no one louder than her family.

Alexander looked furious at her answer, but Melody cut in before he could retort.

'You're not wrong, Issy. Thank you,' she said, before looking straight down the camera. 'Stay tuned because after the break we'll hear from Mia and Jason.'

Issy was standing off to the side with Hannah, having her make-up retouched, when she noticed that Jason was talking to the grey-haired couple and the girl she'd seen him looking at in the audience. They were laughing at something Jason was saying and when he slung his arm around the girl, Issy suddenly realised why she recognised her – she looked just like Jason.

'Hey, Danny,' Issy said, calling him over. 'Who's Jason's talking to?'

Danny looked to where Jason was standing. 'Oh, those are his parents and his twin sister.'

'His what?' All the blood rushed to her head. 'You mean his foster family?'

'Foster family?' Danny screwed his face up in confusion. 'What are you talking about? That's his mum and dad, and twin, Amanda. They all live in Liverpool.'

Issy just stared at Danny. 'Is this some kind of sick joke?'

'Seriously, I have no idea what you're talking about. What's going on?'

Issy's head was reeling. She couldn't concentrate. What the hell was going on? Then all of a sudden she thought of what Ryan had told her. She needed to speak to him.

'Where's Ryan?' she asked.

Danny and Hannah exchanged a look.

'Er, he's not here,' Danny said lamely.

Issy narrowed her eyes. 'Danny,' she said slowly. 'Tell me where Ryan is.'

'It's not his fault,' Hannah jumped in. 'We were told not to tell you.'

'Tell me what?' Issy said. She had a horrible feeling about this.

'He was fired,' Danny sighed. 'The producers found out that he told you what he overheard Jason and Mia talking about. It's against the terms of his contract—'

'He's been fired?' Issy's voice was rising and people were starting to stare but she didn't care. 'So he was telling the truth?'

Danny nodded. 'I'm sorry, Issy.'

'I'll fucking kill him!' Issy yelled.

Jason glanced over and a panicked look crossed his face. He started talking to his family quickly and flapping his arms, trying to lead them away but Issy stormed over before he could get them out of the way.

'Hi, Jason,' she said through gritted teeth. 'Aren't you going to introduce me?'

'Um, yes, well . . .'

The older woman, Jason's mother, threw him an exasperated look. 'Honestly, love,' she said. 'Where are your manners? I'm Jason's mum.'

'His mum?' Issy widened her eyes in mock surprise. 'Well this *is* a surprise.' Issy couldn't believe what she was hearing. It felt like she was in a dream, or maybe she was finally waking up from one and everything was starting to become clear.

'Issy.' Jason, sensing that Issy was about to kick off, tried to take hold of her arm but she pushed him away. 'We're going back on air in a minute. Let's talk about this later.'

'No,' Issy said. She was trying her best to keep her voice even but it was hard when all she wanted to do was punch him in the face. 'We're talking about this now. You told me you had no family.'

'What's she talking about, son?' Jason's dad said.

Laura came running over. 'We're back on air in about ten seconds, guys. You need to get back to your stations. Now.'

Issy saw that the judges were sitting back at the desk, and Mia was standing by her station. Whatever happened next would happen on camera. Issy could go and stand next to her station, let them finish the show and then confront Jason about his lies. But the truth was she didn't want to do that. She'd had enough. In that split second, she realised she was done. This show had already taken enough from her. *Fuck it*, Issy thought, *this is happening now*.

'Jason told me that he didn't have any family,' Issy said, loud and clear. 'He said that he was alone.' She was about to add that he'd said they were dead, but at the last second Issy stopped herself. The words were too harsh. She couldn't say them in front of Jason's family. They hadn't done anything wrong.

'She's lying!' Jason said desperately. 'I'd never say anything like that.'

'But you did,' Issy said. 'And then you fed me more bullshit about how you didn't want to talk about it in front of the cameras because you didn't want sympathy votes. What kind of sick, twisted twat lies about something like that?'

'Issy, I never actually said the words, "My parents are dead".'

'Are you fucking kidding me?' Issy said, her voice rising. 'That's your defence? That you *implied* it rather than stating it?'

'Issy.' It was her dad's voice. She turned and saw her parents, Zach and Molly standing behind her. She hadn't even noticed them coming down from the audience. Issy's eyes filled with tears as she remembered everything that had happened over the past few days. It was too much.

'Dad, don't tell me to stop. I need to do this now.'

'I wasn't going to tell you to stop,' Kev said, folding his arms and fixing Jason with an angry glare of his own. 'I was just going to tell you to watch your language. Vi's got your nan at hers and she won't want to hear you going on like that. Even though he deserves it.'

The entire salon was silent. Even Alexander was lost for words. Issy spun round to face Jason again. She felt stronger just knowing her family was standing next to her.

'Are you pleased with yourself? You've lied to me, used me and tried to manipulate me, all to get ahead in some poxy reality TV show.' For a second, Issy thought she might have gone too far when she saw the look of hurt on Jason's family's faces, but she wasn't in the wrong here – not one bit. It was time everyone knew the truth about him. 'Ryan tried to warn me about you, and I didn't believe him. You even twisted that around to make me feel bad and he was right all along. He was telling me the truth. What the hell is wrong with you?'

'Oh for God's sake,' Mia interrupted, walking over. 'Issy,

your stupidity astounds me more and more every day. Why would Jason ever really be interested in you, when he could have me?'

Whoa, déjà vu, thought Issy. *This girl needs to change the fucking record.* 'So you were in this together? Is that what you're telling me? But why? What did I ever do to either of you?'

Jason had clearly come to the conclusion that his game was up and there was no point in trying to hide it any longer. He wore such a look of disdain as he looked at Issy, she wondered how she'd ever thought he was attractive. The man standing in front of her was a total stranger. And a total dick.

'For fuck's sake, Issy. Wake up, will you?' he sneered. 'This show is a game! I thought you might figure it out sooner than this but I was giving you too much credit.'

'Was this just about keeping me distracted from the show?' Issy said, remembering what Ryan had told her.

'What else? Issy, you made it too easy, babe.' He gave her a pitying look. 'It was like shooting fish in a barrel. After what Josh did, all you wanted was a shoulder to cry on. I simply told you what you wanted to hear. Don't go playing the victim now just because you jumped into bed with me and got played.'

And then *smack*!

One second Jason was standing in front of Issy, the next he was spread-eagled on the ground clutching his bloody nose, howling in pain. Zach stood over him, his hands clenched into fists, shaking with rage. Jason hadn't seen Zach's punch coming.

'You,' he said to Jason, his voice low and angry, 'never

356

speak to my sister like that again, you scumbag. You're lucky I hit you and not Issy, she's the hard one. But I saved her the trouble because I couldn't pass up the opportunity to do that. I've always thought you were a wanker. And Tranmere Rovers are shit by the way.' Zach looked at Issy. 'Never trust a man with a spray tan.'

'Babe,' Molly said, reaching for Zach's bruised hand. She stroked it gently and he winced in pain. 'You're going to need to put some ice on that.'

Zach smiled down at Molly. 'It's OK. I've got another one.'

Even though Issy was hurt, angry and confused she couldn't ignore the look that passed between her brother and her friend. They really did like each other, and she'd been nothing but a selfish cow about it.

'I'm sorry,' Issy said to them. 'For everything. You were right. I did put Jason before you and I shouldn't have. I know saying that I'm sorry isn't enough to make up for everything, but I mean it.'

'It's a start,' Molly said, 'and that's enough for now.'

'Yeah,' Zach said. 'But the next time I tell you not to trust someone, just listen to me, OK?'

'OK.' Issy looked down at Jason. He was still curled up in a pathetic twisted heap, like a human pretzel. Mia was crouched next to him, simpering away like the melt she was while his parents and sister stood to the side, their expressions full of confusion and hurt. 'I'm sorry to you as well,' she said to them. 'You shouldn't have had to find out like that.'

They just stood there, looking between Jason and Issy.

Eventually Jason's sister, Amanda, spoke. 'And I'm sorry that my brother is such a twat.'

Eva walked towards them and beckoned to Issy.

'Well that wasn't ideal, was it? How much trouble am I in?' Issy said, looking at the cameras. Yep, they were still rolling.

'You're not in trouble,' Eva said kindly. 'But we do have a show that we need to get on with. Can you pull it together to get through the final?'

Issy thought for a moment. Yes, she probably could pull it together if she wanted to – but did she actually want this anymore? Had any of this been worth it? And she still had one person she needed to apologise to.

'No.' Issy almost whispered it.

'What?' Eva looked confused.

'I can't. Sorry, Eva, but I have to go,' Issy said. 'There's somewhere else I need to be.'

'Ryan?' Eva asked with a knowing smile.

'For fuck's sake! Did everyone know what was going on but me?' asked Issy half-exasperated, half-amused. 'But, yeah, he tried to warn me and I didn't listen. And he got fired for just trying to be a good friend. I need to see him.'

'Then go,' Eva said with a smile.

'What?' Alexander screeched. 'We're in the middle of a live show! You can't just leave.'

'Watch me, Bazza,' Issy threw at him. She turned to her dad. 'Can you drive me to Ryan's?'

'Ryan?' Zach said. 'Is that the sound guy we met when we visited you?'

'Yeah,' Issy said. 'I owe him an apology as well.'

358

'I liked him,' Zach said approvingly. 'Top bants.' Typical Zach.

'Where does he live, love?' Kev asked.

Issy's face fell. She had no idea.

'Here,' Danny said, running up and thrusting a piece of paper into Issy's hand. 'Here's his address.'

'Won't you get into trouble for this?' Issy said.

Danny shrugged. 'Probably. But some things are more important.'

Issy hugged him. 'Thank you. For everything.'

Issy threw one last look in Jason's direction. He had hurt her, publically humiliated her and betrayed her trust in so many ways. And yet, with him looking so pathetic and weak, with Mia pawing at him, Issy knew she'd had a lucky escape. She didn't even feel angry with him – just embarrassed for him. She just hoped she'd found out the truth in time.

'Let's get of here,' she said to her family. 'I'm done.'

'Someone stop that silly little girl!' Alexander shouted.

'Don't you dare,' Debs said calmly. 'And if anyone does try to stop her, they'll have me to deal with. The Jones men might seem scary but it's the Jones women who are the real force to be reckoned with, you baldy little toad. Now get out of our way.'

Chapter Thirty-eight

Issy tapped her seatbelt buckle impatiently.

'Love, pack it in,' Kev said. 'You're making me nervous.'

'Sorry.' Issy sat on her hands. 'How far are we?'

'I'm driving as fast as I can, woman. Just a few minutes away now,' Kev said. 'We'll be there soon.'

'What are you going to say to Ryan?' Molly said.

'I have no idea. I'll figure it out when I get there.' Issy turned around to look at Molly who was squished between Zach and Debs in the back seat. 'Mol, when I think about what happened the last time I saw you, I feel ashamed. I'm so ashamed of myself.'

'I'd be lying if I said it didn't hurt,' Molly said, 'but you weren't yourself. I can see what you had to deal with now.'

'Don't. Don't be nice to me like that. I don't deserve it. That house, that show . . . It's no excuse. I promise to never speak to you like that again.' Issy spotted Zach giving

Molly's hand a squeeze, and she smiled. 'Molly is a good look on you, Zach.'

'Tell me about it,' he said with a grin.

'How's the hand?' Issy asked.

Zach flexed his fingers. 'Sore. But it was worth it.'

'Issy, are you OK?' her mum asked. 'About Jason?'

'No, not really,' Issy said. 'He hurt me and I'm angry at him. But mostly I'm angry at myself for letting myself be fooled. I thought I was a better judge of character than that.'

'He had everyone fooled, love,' Debs said.

Zach coughed.

'Except Zach,' Debs said, patting her son's knee.

'And Ryan,' Issy said quietly.

'This Ryan,' Kev said. 'He was good to you on the show?'

Issy nodded. 'He was. He was just always around. We'd have a laugh most of the time but he was also there if I just needed a hug or someone to talk to. He was kind to me and I was a shit friend to him in return. What the fuck have I been playing at?'

'Language, Issy,' Debs said.

'Sorry, Mum,' Issy said. She started tapping her buckle again. 'I just need to see him again and then this will all be better.'

'I can't wait to see him either,' Debs said, fluffing up her hair.

'I'm going in on my own,' Issy said, throwing her mum a look. 'This is one conversation that doesn't need any audience participation.'

*

361

Issy pressed the buzzer and waited.

'Hello?'

It was him.

'Ryan?' Issy said. 'It's me, it's Issy. Can I come up?'

There was a beat of silence before he said, 'I'm on the first floor,' and the door to the building clicked open.

Ryan was already holding the door open for her when she reached his flat. His feet were bare, and his jeans and T-shirt were as simple as they could be. He looked the same but Issy felt different now when she saw him.

'Hey,' she said.

'Hey,' he said. 'Come in.'

Ryan's flat was just like him – no fuss, nothing fancy, but warm and inviting. He led her into the living room and Issy gestured towards the TV.

'Were you watching?' she asked.

'I was,' he said, a ghost of a smile on his lips. 'Are you OK?'

'Sort of,' Issy said. 'Upset, angry, embarrassed. Not really the day I was expecting but then again I don't know how I didn't realise it all sooner.'

'Don't beat yourself up about it. At least you've realised now.' Ryan took a step towards her, closing the gap between them. 'And now you're here.'

'I'm sorry, Ryan,' Issy said. 'I'm sorry I pushed you away when all you were trying to do was help. I'm sorry I was such a twat. I'm sorry for everything.'

'You've been apologising a lot lately.'

'I've got a lot of making up to do,' she said wryly. 'I've been a total gimp. I lost myself in all the hype and drama. It just took me a while to see it.'

'Not a *total* gimp,' Ryan said, an amused glint in his eyes. 'Just a bit of one.' His expression turned serious. 'But I'd never lie to you, Issy. I care about you too much to do that. And I didn't like seeing Jason treat you like that on TV. If your brother hadn't punched him, I'd have come down to the studio and done it myself.'

'Stop being so kind to me,' Issy said, tears welling in her eyes. 'Everyone is being too nice to me and I don't deserve it. You got fired because of me.'

Ryan gently wiped away the tear that was rolling down Issy's cheek. 'I knew what I was doing when I told you what I heard. I got fired because of me, not you.'

'But—'

Ryan put his fingers to Issy's lips. 'Has anyone ever told you that you talk too much?' He put his arms around her and Issy rested her head on his chest. They stayed like that for a while and Issy was reminded of the hug they'd shared in the green room all those weeks ago. They hadn't said anything to each other then either. They'd just stood in each other's arms, taking whatever comfort they each needed from the other. *He's been there for me since day one*, Issy thought. *It's always been him.*

'I feel like such a fool,' Issy said, into his T-shirt. 'I thought Jason liked me. No, I thought he loved me.' A fresh wave of tears came and Ryan stroked her back as she cried. She'd been so angry and shocked that she hadn't had the chance to fully take stock of what had happened. Now, here in Ryan's home with his arms around her, her mind was settled for the first time in days and she was able to feel everything and she allowed her pain to engulf her. Eventually, though, the tears dried up and she pulled away from him. Ryan looked at her with such a kind expression that she had the sudden urge to kiss him. *What the hell?* Issy thought.

Ryan sensed the change in mood and pulled her towards him again. 'What now?' he said quietly.

'I don't know,' Issy said.

'Can I make a suggestion?'

'Sure.'

'Why don't we spend some time together? No pressure, let's just get to know each other without cameras and mics and you getting called away every five minutes.'

'I can do that,' Issy said. 'But no pressure?'

'No pressure at all,' Ryan said. 'I know you're hurting right now so let me help you. If all that happens is we end up becoming better friends, that's OK.'

'You're sure you want to be in my life?' Issy asked. 'After everything? After the way I behaved on the show? The whole nation is going to think I'm a complete knob. Everything's such a mess at the moment. It might take me a while to figure things out.'

'I can help. It'll take less time with the two of us.'

The two of us. Issy liked the sound of that.

'That sounds like a plan to me,' Issy said.

'Then that's settled. We're pressure-free friends who might get naked with each other one day.'

Issy burst out laughing. 'Too soon, mate. Too soon.'

Ryan laughed and hugged Issy again. 'Thought I'd try my luck. #soznotsoz.'

They both looked at each other and laughed.

Epilogue

NINE MONTHS LATER

'I feel like a proper grown-up,' Issy said as she laid the small dining table in Ryan's flat.

'Because you're setting a table?' Ryan asked, amused.

'No, because we're having people over for dinner and I'm playing house.'

'Have you moved in without telling me?' Ryan raised an eyebrow.

'You're not that lucky, my friend,' Issy said, straightening one of the napkins.

Ryan put his arms around Issy's waist and kissed the back of her neck. 'I don't know, I feel pretty lucky right now.'

They had taken it slowly, and it hadn't always been easy. What had happened with Jason had made Issy question every decision she made for a long time after the end of the show but Ryan had handled that storm with gentleness and kindness. Issy had fallen for him slowly but surely, and what they'd ended up with was a solid foundation based on trust, friendship and a mutual love of his six-pack. It had been three months before they'd had their first kiss, and another three months after that before they'd had sex for the first time. But since then, they'd barely spent a night apart. They had slotted into each other's lives seamlessly, and Issy felt something she hadn't felt in a long time – content.

After the show had finished, she'd been paid to do interview after interview, and the requests were still coming in. She'd even done a couple of guest TV presenting jobs. She didn't know what she wanted to do in the long-term but the work she was getting paid well and it bought her some time while she figured out her next move. She wasn't expecting her fame – if that's what it could be called – to last forever and she knew she wanted her next project to be something she believed in, something substantial. She just wasn't sure what that was.

She'd struggled with all of the press attention at first but Ryan, Molly and her family had kept her steady and she'd got through the worst of it. It had also helped that, for the most part, the public had been on her side after she'd walked out of the live final. There was no way that Jason could win after the way things had gone so Mia had won through default. Issy had rolled her eyes when she'd read about the result in the paper the next day and then hadn't given it a second thought.

Mia and Jason had taken their 'romance' public after the show had ended but they were universally unpopular and one cheap tabloid interview, complete with photos of them both in their underwear, was all the attention they'd managed to get. They'd both fallen back into obscurity and that suited Issy just fine. Pair of twats. She hadn't seen or spoken to either of them since she'd left Jason squirming on the salon floor with a bloody nose, and she liked it that way.

Lexi and Aaron had both stayed out of the spotlight but they all kept in touch and Issy was happy that they were both doing so well – especially as the two of them were doing it together. They'd decided to go into business together and their first London-based salon would be opening next month. Issy and Ryan were going to head down for the launch and make a weekend of it.

Rory, on the other hand, had embraced his five minutes of fame with both hands and was regularly photographed falling out of one club or another, usually with a different lads mag favourite on his arm. Issy got the occasional 4 a.m. phone call from him, trying to convince her to leave her warm bed and Ryan's arms and join him at whatever party he was at. Issy always declined but she did it with a smile on her face. She hoped Rory never changed.

The buzzer sounded and Ryan kissed her quickly before going to the door to let Zach and Molly in. Issy launched herself at them as soon as they walked in.

'Hey, wifey,' Molly said, returning the hug.

'I'm still not sure how I feel about my girlfriend calling my sister "wifey",' Zach grumbled. He entered the flat, carrying his customary offering of a packet of Hobnobs.

'And I'm still not sure how I feel about my boyfriend being *Heat*'s Torso of the Week, but we all have our crosses to bear,' Molly said sarcastically.

'She's got you there, mate,' Ryan said, handing Zach a bottle of Corona.

Zach smiled at Molly. 'She loves that her boyfriend is the fittest man around really.'

One of the most surprising things to happen after the live final was that Zach had turned into a bit of a celebrity himself. Women all over the UK had fallen for him after he'd defended his sister's honour. The fact that he was a loyal boyfriend and was clearly head over heels for Molly, only served to boost his popularity even more. Molly was coping with the female attention her boyfriend was getting pretty well, but that didn't mean she wouldn't give him a bit of grief about it every now and again.

'So have you seen it?' Zach asked Issy.

'I have,' Issy said. 'It's not really the kind of thing a sister needs to see but you look good.'

Ryan sucked in his non-existent gut. 'You make the rest of us look bad, mate.'

'I strongly disagree with that,' Issy said, kissing him.

Zach groaned. 'And that's not the kind of thing a brother needs to see.'

'Leave them alone,' Molly said, playfully hitting Zach's arm.

'Come on,' Issy said, laughing. 'Let's eat. I'm starving!'

They were about halfway through their roast lamb when Issy's phone rang. She would've ignored it but when she saw Eva's name flash up she excused herself and answered the call.

'Hey, Eva,' Issy said, happy to hear from her mentor. They had kept in touch after the show and met up regularly. Eva was a good sounding board for Issy and she was always willing to offer help whenever Issy asked for it. Alexander, however, was not in Issy's life. He'd emerged from *Can You Cut It?* as one of the most hated people to ever come from a reality TV show, and the last Issy had heard he'd checked himself into a 'facility' to help him overcome depression.

'Hi, Issy,' Eva said, her voice warm. 'How are you?'

'Good,' Issy said. 'Zach and Molly are here, we're just having dinner.'

'Oh God, sorry to interrupt,' Eva said hurriedly. 'I won't keep you long then, but I just wanted to see if you're free for lunch on Tuesday?'

'I think so,' Issy said, mentally running through her calendar for the next few days. 'Is something wrong?'

'No, nothing's wrong. I've just had an email and I wanted to discuss it with you. I think this might be the opportunity you've been looking for since the show finished.'

'What is it?' Issy was intrigued. 'Don't make me wait until Tuesday! Tell me now. Please, please, please!'

'OK, OK,' Eva said, laughing. 'There are a lot of details so we can go over everything properly at lunch, but I've been talking with Melody. You remember, the MD of Vitality Haircare? Anyway, they're thinking about developing a new line of products, aimed at teenagers, and Melody wants to discuss the idea with you. It's a bit vague about exactly what she wants, but I think that's part of what she wants to talk to you about.'

'Really?' Issy felt that familiar spark of excitement go through her. This could be what she'd been waiting for. 'Well, whatever it is, I'm definitely interested in finding out more.'

'Great, I'm glad that's your reaction,' Eva said. 'Right, I'll text you the restaurant details for Tuesday. Go and enjoy the rest of your evening.'

'Will do. Thanks, Eva.'

'No problem, honey. Bye.'

'Bye.'

'So what are you hoping Vitality will offer you?' Ryan asked. It was much later that evening. Molly and Zach had just left and Issy and Ryan were cleaning up.

'Right now I'm just open to hearing what they have to say,' Issy said. 'If all they want is for me to put my face to a product line that I have no say in, then that's not for me. But if they want me to be involved in the development of it . . . well, then that's something I could live with.'

'Do you think this is what you've been waiting for?'

'Maybe.' Issy started loading plates into the dishwasher. 'Maybe not. I'm not going to get my hopes up, but I trust Eva and she wouldn't want to talk to me about this if it wasn't something with potential.'

'I agree,' Ryan said. 'It is exciting though, right?'

'It is,' Issy said, smiling. 'If this doesn't work out, who knows what's around the corner? The world's my oyster.'

'Ah, there she is.' Ryan grabbed Issy by the waist and turned her around to face him.

'There who is?'

'There's my girl, the one I met in her mum's salon almost a year ago. The one with the world at her feet, and the self-belief to do anything she puts her mind too.'

Issy wrapped her arms around Ryan's neck. 'Oh, *that* girl. Have you missed her?'

'Terribly.' Ryan ran his tongue along her collarbone. 'I knew she'd come back to me.'

'She's not the same though,' Issy said, trying to keep her thoughts straight as Ryan's hands lifted her up onto the counter and started undoing the buttons on her top.

'No,' he said into her hair. 'She's not the same, but she's still the best person I know.'

His mouth found hers and all other thoughts apart from what his hands were doing to her, left Issy's head.

Issy's life had been irrevocably changed by *Can You Cut It?*. For better or worse, it had altered her, and while the journey to this moment hadn't been an easy one, she would always be grateful for the doors it had opened for her. But it had almost destroyed her and her family. Almost – but not quite. The Joneses were made of stronger stuff. She was still Issy Jones from Salford, but now she was also Issy Jones off the telly. Who knew which Issy Jones she'd be in a year from now? What she did know, though, was that as long as she had her family, Molly and this perfect man beside her, there was no stopping her. *Watch out, world. Issy Jones is coming for you.*

Acknowledgements

Please bear with me here as I have a lot of people to thank so this is going to resemble an over the top Oscars speech! I would like to thank everyone at Little, Brown who has worked on the book, and everyone who has made me feel welcome there. I truly love visiting you all at the office but I enjoy our nights out even more! I now consider some of you fabulous people friends and I feel very lucky. Special thanks to David Shelley (my quiz partner), Jo Wickham (new but on her way to becoming a firm favourite), Rhiannon Smith (patient assistant editor and general star) and Hannah Boursnell (not directly involved but always supportive and amazing!). And of course thanks to my wonderful editor Manpreet Grewal – you have kept me sane and calm at times when I felt overwhelmed by this project and have been a pleasure to work with.

Big thanks to my wonderful new agents Gemma and Nadia who have helped me find time to fit this process into my unrelenting schedule and for putting up with my whinging. I love you!

As always I would like to thank my incredible family. Their unwavering support has already got me through so much and I couldn't do anything without them. Mam, Dad and Laura . . . I don't deserve you.

I want to mention my *Judge Geordie* cast and crew. Juggling both this and my filming commitments at the same time has been a strain to say the least and it's safe to say that these guys have seen me at my lowest ebb and always been there for me. Thank you so much for keeping me positive and strong and having faith in me.

Finally, I would like to thank everyone who has supported me, bought a book, turned up to a signing or just had faith in me. Your belief in me keeps me going!

THE NEW NOVEL FROM
Vicky Pattison

AUTUMN 2015
IN HARDBACK

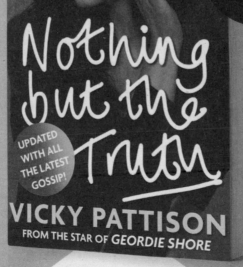